Evil in Carnations

"Collins isn't losing steam in her eighth foray into the world of florist and part-time accidental detective Abby Knight. The fun, family, and romance are still fresh, and the mystery is tidily wrapped up, with just enough suspense to keep readers flipping pages."
— *Romantic Times*

"Ms. Collins's writing remains above par with quality and consistency: fun and breezy, intriguing and suspenseful, excitement and sizzle." — Once Upon a Romance

Shoots to Kill

"Colorful characters, a sharp and funny heroine, and a sexy hunk boyfriend."
— Maggie Sefton, author of the Knitting Mysteries

"Once again Kate Collins delivers an entertaining, amusing, and deliciously suspenseful mystery."
— Cleo Coyle, author of the Coffeehouse Mysteries

A Rose from the Dead

"The latest Flower Shop mystery is an amusing graveyard amateur sleuth that will have the audience laughing." — The Best Reviews

Acts of Violets

"A delightful lighthearted cozy." — The Best Reviews

Snipped in the Bud

"Lighthearted and fast-paced, Collins's new book is an entertaining read." — *Romantic Times*

Dearly Depotted

"Abby is truly a hilarious heroine. . . . Don't miss this fresh-as-a-daisy read." — *Rendezvous*

"Ms. Collins's writing style is crisp, her characters fun . . . and her stories are well thought-out and engaging."
— Fresh Fiction

Other Flower Shop Mysteries

Mum's the Word
Slay It with Flowers
Dearly Depotted
Snipped in the Bud
Acts of Violets
A Rose from the Dead
Shoots to Kill
Evil in Carnations
Sleeping with Anemone
Dirty Rotten Tendrils
Night of the Living Dandelion
To Catch a Leaf

Nightshade on Elm Street

A Flower Shop Mystery

Kate Collins

AN OBSIDIAN MYSTERY

OBSIDIAN
Published by New American Library, a division of
Penguin Group (USA) Inc., 375 Hudson Street,
New York, New York 10014, USA
Penguin Group (Canada), 90 Eglinton Avenue East, Suite 700, Toronto,
Ontario M4P 2Y3, Canada (a division of Pearson Penguin Canada Inc.)
Penguin Books Ltd., 80 Strand, London WC2R 0RL, England
Penguin Ireland, 25 St. Stephen's Green, Dublin 2,
Ireland (a division of Penguin Books Ltd.)
Penguin Group (Australia), 250 Camberwell Road, Camberwell, Victoria 3124,
Australia (a division of Pearson Australia Group Pty. Ltd.)
Penguin Books India Pvt. Ltd., 11 Community Centre, Panchsheel Park,
New Delhi - 110 017, India
Penguin Group (NZ), 67 Apollo Drive, Rosedale, Auckland 0632,
New Zealand (a division of Pearson New Zealand Ltd.)
Penguin Books (South Africa) (Pty.) Ltd., 24 Sturdee Avenue,
Rosebank, Johannesburg 2196, South Africa

Penguin Books Ltd., Registered Offices:
80 Strand, London WC2R 0RL, England

First published by Obsidian, an imprint of New American Library,
a division of Penguin Group (USA) Inc.

First Printing, November 2012
10 9 8 7 6 5 4 3 2

ALWAYS LEARNING   **PEARSON**

To my late husband, Jim, for all the wonderful, golden years we had together

ACKNOWLEDGMENTS

I'd like to thank my family and friends; my editor, Ellen Edwards; and my agent, Karen Solem, for their continued support. I'd also like to thank Donna Phelps, owner of Seasons on the Square (women's boutique), for assisting me with Abby's shower outfit; Keith Gurley, owner of Bon Femme Restaurant, for his delicious signature martini mix called the Bon-tini; and two officers on the local police force, Lieutenant Brian McDonald and Patrol Officer Michelle Kodicek, for their helpful information. A special hug for Julie and Jason for their loving devotion.

CHAPTER ONE

Monday, August 1

Dear Euphorbia,

Half an hour until the flower shop opens, so I'm grabbing a minute to update you. Sorry to have been MIA, but, hey, life is never dull here at Bloomers, even after the chaos of the wealthy dowager's murder died down. So far today, things have been quiet. We started off with Lottie's traditional Monday-morning scrambled egg and toast breakfast, and Grace's gourmet coffee and fresh blueberry scones, so how bad can the rest of the day be?

Wait. What am I saying? Today is Monday—the day Mom always brings in her latest art project for us to sell. Last time it was a whole box of sea glass sunglasses, with frames studded so thickly with sea glass chips that they became instruments of torture. Still, I'm going to remain optimistic because I really want to have a pleasant day, so I'll imagine myself loving whatever debacle Mom bequeaths us. It'll be my new challenge, and you know how I love a challenge.

On the good-news front, I've taken back my bridal shower! Euphorbia, you've been listening to me complain since I began this journal three months ago, so you know what would have happened if I'd allowed Mom, with her outrageous ideas, and Marco's mom, with her take-no-prisoners approach to any kind of event, to pull it off. And heaven help me had my cousin Jillian been allowed to choose my shower outfit from one of the haute couture boutiques she frequents.

Being five feet two, with red hair, way too many freckles, and what my mom refers to as an ample bosom, I don't fit into the kind of garb Jillian's ultra-chic customers do, but she never seems to get that. Well, actually, no surprise there. For a Harvard grad, Jillian doesn't get much. Luckily, Marco, my groom-to-be, the malest of all males, the man who causes women of all ages to drool with desire, likes the way I look, freckles and all. So why should I spend megabucks on an outfit that would only make me look like an upscale fireplug?

A voice interrupted my train of thought. My assistant Lottie swept back the purple curtain that separated the flower shop from my workroom and handed me a slip of pink paper, which, coincidentally, coordinated with her cherry blouse, white denims, primrose Keds, and the rose-colored barrettes in her short, brassy curls. It took courage for a tall, big-boned, middle-aged woman to pull off all that pink.

"Sorry to interrupt, sweetie, but I thought you'd want to know about this phone call."

I read the message—twice. "*Pryce* called here? For me?"

"Disgusting, isn't it? He claimed it was extremely important that he talk to you right away."

Determined not to let anything or any*one* ruin my day, I dropped the paper in the wastebasket beneath my desk.

"Everything Pryce does is extremely important, Lottie, because Pryce is extremely important. Just ask him."

Not that I harbored any lingering ill will toward the heel who had jilted me two months before I was supposed to march down the aisle with him. Now that I looked back, I'd dodged a bullet—make that a hail of bullets—although at the time Pryce Osborne II had seemed like the answer to my prayers. Indeed, according to Pryce, it was a privilege to be joining one of the dynasties of New Chapel, Indiana. *His* family tree had branches that reached back to the founding fathers of our country.

I had nothing to bring to that table. All my family tree had were nuts.

Still, I'd been living at home with my parents, struggling to get through my first year of law school, and Pryce had purchased his own condo, was about to take the bar exam, and had a high-salaried job all lined up. What logical-minded woman wouldn't go for that? Plus he had a plan for us: After I got my law degree, we would rule the justice system.

Only one problem. I flunked out.

With swift vengeance, Pryce's parents stepped in and decreed me an Untouchable for doing the unthinkable. Pryce, who never *ever* crossed his parents, quietly asked for his ring back. My pain was unimaginable.

But as my other assistant, Grace Bingham, liked to say, when God closed a door, he opened a window somewhere. And that window had been humongous, because if Pryce hadn't dumped me, I wouldn't have become the poor but happy owner of Bloomers Flower Shop. Nor would I have met Marco Salvare, the bravest, most sincere, most loving, and, frankly, hottest guy in town. So *merci beaucoup*, Osbornes, for not ruining my life.

"Why don't you let me call Pryce for you?" Lottie asked, rubbing her hands together as though anticipating the chance to tell him off. "I'll let him know you've got more important things to do."

"Perfect." I fished the message from the waste can and gave it back to her. "Thanks."

But . . . on second thought, maybe I *should* return Pryce's call. It would be a great opportunity to let him know I was getting married in a month and a half. Plus, I was nosy. Erase that. I was *curious* as to what was so important that Pryce would be forced to phone *me*. Was he writing a book on how to crush a woman's self-esteem?

"Wait, Lottie. I think I'll return that call after all."

Lottie shook her head as she handed me the pink slip. Her view of Pryce was that he was lower than a snake's belly. It was one of those sayings she'd learned growing up in the rolling hills of Kentucky.

I reached for the receiver, then changed my mind and put the message aside. I didn't want Pryce to think I was eager to talk to him. Picking up my pen, I wrote:

Euphorbia, I will have to tell you about my phone conversation with Pryce later, but only if it's worth memorializing. Otherwise, where was I? Oh, right, preparing for the shower.

Okay, in keeping with my carnival theme, I've purchased plastic cups, paper napkins, and coated plates with a colorful pinwheel design on them. I've ordered carnival masks, flower pinwheels, flower lei garlands, and hibiscus toothpicks. I want this shower to be an afternoon of flowers and fun, not the boring cake, punch, and present-opening event everyone else does.

Marco agreed to attend only if I promised that there wouldn't be any games whatsoever, so I still have to come up with another form of entertainment. I'm thinking of a flower-arranging contest. Or maybe a juggling act. Jugglers who juggle flower-pots? I'll have to investigate this further.

I also have plastic utensils, paper tablecloths in bright yellow—my favorite color, as you know—and I've ordered a chocolate sheet cake that will have candy flowers in the shape of a pinwheel on top. Let's see, what have I forgotten?

"Abby," Lottie said, peering in, "Pryce is on the phone again. Now he's saying it's exceedingly urgent." She snickered. "Maybe his manicurist moved away."

I held up my short, unpolished nails. "I wouldn't be much help there, but thanks, Lottie."

I set my journal aside, then inhaled and exhaled a few times before picking up the phone. I didn't want to sound angry when, in fact, I should want to hug him.

"Hello, Pryce," I said in a cool yet not unfriendly voice.

"Abigail, I need a favor."

No preamble, no warmth, and he'd called me by my proper name, knowing that I'd always preferred Abby. So I didn't respond.

As though he hadn't even noticed, he continued. "One of my friends is missing. I wouldn't bother you except she's been gone for twenty hours now, and I'm starting to fret."

Osbornes never worried. They fretted. It was the superior emotion. "Missing from where?"

"Our lake cottage. I've checked her condo and her shop repeatedly, but there's no sign of her. I'm at my wit's end. She could be in a hospital somewhere or she might possibly have been abducted. She does have a rather large stock portfolio."

"If you think something serious happened to her, Pryce, I'd recommend calling the cops."

He let out an impatient sigh. "You know Mother and Father would never allow me to involve the police unless I'm one hundred percent sure it's a life-or-death situation."

"How do you know it's not?"

"Because of circumstances that I'd rather not divulge over the phone. I have to keep this matter hush-hush, Abigail. Mother and Father are vacationing in Europe and I dare not let them catch wind of it. That's why I need to hire Marco. Would you contact him for me?"

"Yes, but just so you'll know, it would be Marco and *me* taking the case, Pryce. We work as a team." *Rub it in, Abby. That a girl.*

"That's fine," he said dismissively. "I just want Melissa found."

"So her name is Melissa?"

"Yes, Melissa Hazelton. She owns Pisces, the interior decorating shop on West Lincoln. You know her. I introduced you to her at one of our country-club functions back when you and I were, well, you know."

About to make the biggest mistake of our lives?

"I vaguely remember a Melissa. Tall blonde with legs like a weight lifter? Interior decorator more noted for her enthusiasm than her talent?"

"Did you know I'd planned to marry Melissa?"

Oops. Foot-in-mouth moment. Why hadn't he mentioned that at the outset? "So I guess congratulations are in order?"

"Yes, well . . ." He let it hang there and went on. "I'd like to have Marco—and you, I suppose—come out to the cottage as soon as possible while my houseguests are still here."

"Do you think one of your guests may have had something to do with Melissa's disappearance?"

"I have no thoughts on the matter. I merely intuited

that you would need everyone who was here this week-end to be present so you can interview them. Isn't that how it's usually handled?"

He was showing off. "I'll call Marco to see if he's interested in the case."

"Let him know I'm prepared to pay half again as much as his usual fee, and I'm positive he will be."

Ah! The Osborne philosophy: You can make anything happen if you throw enough money at it. "I'll fill him in and get back to you with our decision."

"Grand. I'll be expecting your call, say, within the quarter hour?"

"All I can do is pass along the message." I wasn't giving an inch. Let the worm squirm.

"You're being awfully stilted, Abigail."

"Am I?"

"I hope you're not harboring any ill will toward me."

In as innocent a tone as I could muster, I asked, "For what?"

There was a moment of silence, after which he said, "I'll await your phone call, then. Good-b— Hold on a moment. Jillian is signaling—I believe she's waving hello to you."

My cousin was there? Great. Now I had even less desire to get involved. Not only was Jillian married to Pryce's younger brother, Claymore, but also, whenever she was around, things got crazy.

"Pardon me," Pryce said. "My error. She's signaling for you to come quickly."

The line went dead. I hadn't even had an opportunity to slip in a mention of *my* engagement.

Oh, well. I could do that when I called to tell him that there was no way we'd take his case.

CHAPTER TWO

*Euphorbia, I still can't believe Pryce had the nerve
to call here asking for help, but I'm sure Marco will
understand that we have to say no. Believe me, it's
more than a matter of Pryce having humiliated me
in front of the whole town. Way more. Still, you can
understand how embarrassing it was returning the
wedding band I'd bought for Pryce and had en-
graved with our initials joined in a heart.*

*I have my hands full running Bloomers, not to
mention the gargantuan task of preparing for my
wedding and for my bridal shower, which will take
place in five short days, while keeping our families
at bay. I could go on, but you know my hectic schedule. I simply don't need the added aggravation of
dealing with Pryce.*

*So why am I worried that Marco will think I'm
being churlish?*

I glanced at my watch, saw that it was nine o'clock, and
stowed my journal in the bottom drawer of my desk.
Then, pausing to inhale the perfume of fresh, fragrant

flowers, which always calmed me, I stepped through the curtain into our lovely floral garden setting.

Bloomers is the second shop from the corner on Franklin Street, one of four blocks surrounding the majestic limestone courthouse, which, like the other buildings on the square, was built around the turn of the twentieth century. Bloomers is in a redbrick building three stories tall, with two big bay windows on either side of a yellow frame door with a beveled glass center. The wooden floors and door are original, as are the tin ceilings and brick walls. There's a cashier counter on the left side of the shop at the front, and a bay window that's stocked with floral decorations both fresh and silk.

A glass display case against the back wall holds buckets of daisies, roses, alstroemeria, spider mums, and a wide range of floral arrangements, with a white wicker settee beneath a tall dieffenbachia in the corner beside it. Ceramic figurines, crystal candlesticks, and silk flower arrangements fill an antique armoire on one side of the long room; wreaths and mirrors decorate two brick walls, and potted green houseplants line a curving path that leads to the front door.

Through the wide doorway on the right is our coffee and tea parlor, which also has a bay window. A coffee counter runs across the back, and white wrought iron ice-cream tables and chairs fill the room. This is where customers sip tea or coffee served in china teacups and saucers in a lovely rose pattern, nibble on scones slathered with clotted cream, and watch the activity on the square.

I picked up a fresh cup of coffee from the back counter, where Grace was preparing her machines for the day, walked to the front door, and turned the sign to OPEN. Then I stood at the bay window sipping coffee and watching our regulars cut across the courthouse lawn to get their morning java jolt.

I glanced to the right and saw Marco Salvare, my groom-to-be, striding up the sidewalk, drawing admiring looks from every female who saw him, not that I could blame them. Marco has that sexy Mediterranean look—dark hair and eyes, five-o'clock shadow, and a lean body sculpted from the rigorous training of the Army Rangers. He exudes confidence from every pore, which in itself is extremely appealing. When he adds a smile to the mix—that slight upturn of his mouth—I hang on to the nearest solid object to keep from throwing myself at him.

Today Marco was wearing black boots, slim-fitting dark blue jeans, and a khaki-colored *Down the Hatch* T-shirt. His wavy dark hair looked glossy and thick, with a single lock falling over one eyebrow, giving him a devilishly dangerous look. Just outside the shop, women pulled out their compacts to check their appearances, then stood at the door until he opened it for them, giggling like schoolgirls and fanning their faces when he flashed his enigmatic grin.

The women were still giggling as they trooped into the parlor, not even noticing me standing next to the window. Marco, however, spotted me immediately. Whenever he entered a room, he always scanned it, a habit he'd picked up during his military years. If there was danger around, he'd find it.

Marco had gone into the army upon graduating from college, later moving into the Rangers Special Forces division. After serving with them for two years, he'd joined the New Chapel police force. Unlike my dad, who was a career cop, Marco stayed on only a year. Too many rules and much too political for my man.

Now he owns Down the Hatch Bar and Grill, two

doors north of Bloomers. He'd taken over the bar shortly before I'd assumed the mortgage for Bloomers, and we'd met when my refurbished 1960 yellow Corvette was the victim of a hit-and-run right in front of my shop. He'd volunteered to help me find the driver of the big black SUV, not knowing it would suck both of us into a murder case—and a romance.

"Who's this gorgeous little redhead hiding behind the door?" he asked in a low growl, pulling me close.

Marco was the only person who could call me little and get away with it. I slipped my arms around his waist and lifted my mouth for a kiss, then noticed that several women seated in the parlor were craning their necks to watch. I took Marco's hand and led him into the work-room.

"Still want to marry me?" I asked, leaning back in his arms to gaze into his soulful brown eyes.

"More each minute."

"Despite everything?"

"Despite everything."

He kissed me again, long and luxuriously, until I thought about his answer. "Despite what?"

Marco shrugged, his mind still fogged over from the steamy kiss. "I don't know. What you said. Everything."

"Could you be more specific?"

"Now?"

"Yes. What kinds of things do you love me despite?"

"Okay, I should have said anything, not everything. No, make that nothing. I love you despite nothing." He glanced at his watch. "Do you want to waste any more time on this subject?"

"Not really." I wound my arms around his neck. "I love you despite everything, too."

"Good. So before—"

"You don't want a list of things?"

"I know the list, Sunshine. It starts with my mom and ends with my youngest brother. So before anyone interrupts us . . ."

And then Marco was kissing me the way every woman should be kissed — deeply, passionately, lovingly, and, yes, quite stirringly. Had we been alone — well, never mind going there, because it came to an abrupt stop.

"Pryce called you?" he asked.

I blinked up at Marco, trying to get my brain cells to fire up and my hormones to power down. "How did you know that?"

He reached around me and plucked the message off my desk. "This."

"How did you see that if your eyes were closed?"

"They were closed . . . at first."

"Marco, you don't need to open your eyes while we're kissing. There's nothing dangerous lurking in my workroom."

"Sorry, Sunshine. It's a habit."

I backed up a step. "Please tell me you don't always keep your eyes open or I'll be too self-conscious to ever kiss you again."

"Really?"

"Well, no."

His mouth curved up at one corner. "I'll try to suppress the urge anyway. What did Pryce want?"

"He wants us to find his fiancée. She was among a group of people staying at the Osborne beach house this past weekend and now she's missing. He's been checking her apartment and shop, but hasn't had any luck. I don't have the particulars, but I'm thinking she came to her senses about marrying Pryce and ran as far away as she could."

"You're still angry with him, aren't you?"

I uttered a carefree laugh. A titter, actually. "*Pffft.* No."

Marco said nothing, which usually meant he didn't agree but felt it wasn't worth arguing about. Smart man.

"Oh, and get this, Marco. Pryce says he'll pay half again as much as your normal fee because he needs to keep this matter quiet." I faked a cough. "The Osbornes won't tolerate embarrassment, you know."

"Oh, yeah, you're still angry."

"Am not."

"You don't have to deny it, Sunshine, but you do need to put it behind you."

"It's way behind me, Marco. I'm grateful that things worked out the way they did. Sure, getting the boot from New Chapel law school left a few scars. And then, after just being dealt the worst blow of my life, Pryce and his parents came in with their machetes and finished the job. Do you know how it feels to find out you mean nothing to the person you were ready to spend the rest of your life with?"

"No, and I hope I never do. But let me ask you this. Were you in love with Pryce back then?"

"No."

"That was a quick response."

"I've had a lot of time to think about it. It took me a few months, but I realized finally that I was in love with the idea of marriage to Pryce. The reality of being his wife would have sucked air." I put my hands on Marco's chest. "You're the one for me, Salvare, and I would love you whether we ever got married or not."

He smiled into my eyes. "Know what I think?"

"What?"

"We should take the case."

That was *not* what I expected him to say. *I love you so much I have to marry you in order to live my life fully* was along the lines of what I expected. "Are you serious? You want me to *work* for Pryce?"

He tugged my chin. "You're talking through clenched teeth."

"Am not," I managed to squeeze out.

"Abby, I want our honeymoon to be something special, and this fee will help pay for it. So if you're bothered that much, I'll work the case alone. You don't need to see Pryce ever again."

"I appreciate the offer—it's just that I didn't think you'd want to work for him either. He *hurt* me, Marco!"

"I get that, sweetheart, but what happened is in the past. This is the present, and the case means another paycheck. We don't need to make it personal."

I knew what he was saying—and he was right—but letting go of that old pain was tough. I wasn't even sure I wanted to let it go. It was a reminder to judge a person for who he was inside. With that said, I had to admit Marco's outside was just as attractive as his inside.

Marco searched my eyes. "Do you want me to say no?"

"Kind of."

"Then you've got it, babe. We won't take the case. It's not like another job won't come up."

I heaved a sigh of relief and wrapped my arms around his waist, resting my head against his solid chest. "Thank you for understanding. I love you so much."

He rested his chin on the top of my head and folded his arms around me. "I want you to be happy, Abby."

I heard voices near the curtain, and a moment later the velvet parted and my cousin Jillian stepped into the workroom, followed by Lottie, who mouthed, *I tried to stop her.*

"Still nothing dangerous in your workroom?" Marco muttered in my ear.

"Thank God you're both here!" my tall, willowy cousin exclaimed, sweeping back her long, silky, copper-colored hair. In a bright blue and green sundress, with a green patent leather belt and matching ballet flats, and carrying a white straw hat and bright blue tote, Jillian looked like she'd just stepped out of a Nordstrom catalog. But that was nothing new.

Jillian studied fashion design after college and now ran a wardrobe consulting business, Chez Jillian, out of her apartment, combining two of her favorite hobbies — shopping and spending money.

"You're supposed to stay up at the beach house until an investigator gets there," I said.

She waved it away. "Everyone thinks I'm in our room taking a nap. And let's remember that it's a *cottage*, Abs. The Osbornes don't like the term beach house. It denotes ordinariality."

Jillian's other favorite hobby was making up words. "Ordinariness," I said.

"That, too," she replied.

I glanced at Marco and saw him pressing his fingers against his lips to hide a smile.

Jillian clamped her hands on my shoulders. "Please, Abs, I'm begging you and Marco to help us find Melissa."

"Sorry, Jillian. Pryce will have to find someone else."

"Someone else?" she cried, as though saying, *Dengue fever?*

She lurched toward my desk chair and sank down in it, waving her hand in front of her face, looking suddenly flushed beneath her golden tan. "Would someone get me a glass of water, please? I'm feeling overheated."

"I'll get it," Marco said, and strode off toward the kitchen in the back.

Jillian caught my hands and pulled me down so I was directly in front of her. "Abby, you and Marco *must* take this case."

"No way, Jill. You know how I feel about Pryce."

"So let Marco do it."

"We work as a team."

"Then you'll just have to put your personal feelings aside, because we don't trust anyone else to handle this situation."

"Jillian, read my lips. Unless you or Claymore did away with Melissa, nothing you can say will change my mind. *Nothing*." I thought about what I'd just said. "You didn't do away with Melissa, did you?"

She scowled at me. "Don't be absurd. I didn't care for her personality, fashion sense, or decorating skills, but that's no reason to . . . whatever. Anyway, we don't know that she's come to a bad end. After the blowup she and Pryce had, she may be lying low to torture him."

"They had a blowup?" Now I was interested.

"Yes, but I'll tell you about it only if you take the case."

"Forget it. I don't want to know about their blowup."

"Liar."

"If you're not a fan of Melissa's, Jillian, why do you care so much about finding her?"

She shrugged one shoulder, frowning down at her hands folded in her lap.

I tilted her chin up. "What's going on?"

She searched my eyes, as though trying to decide whether to let me in on something. Then she used a long, manicured fingertip to tuck a strand of hair behind her ear. "I wasn't going to say anything for a few months" — she glanced over both shoulders as though about to reveal a state secret — "and no one else knows yet, so you'll have to swear not to tell a single person until I give you the green light."

"I don't have to swear. I know how to keep a secret."

"Swear, Abby."

Jillian had always been a drama queen, so her request

wasn't all that unusual. Even so, I felt silly. "We're not kids, Jill. Either you trust me or you don't."

"Your choice." She studied the polish on her fingernails. She knew I'd cave eventually.

"Fine. I swear I won't tell what you're about to reveal."

"And if you're lying, you'll stick a needle in your eye."

"Not going to happen."

Jillian leaned toward me. "If something bad *has* befallen Melissa, it will be a huge scandal." She squeezed my hands, tears filling her pretty eyes. "The Osborne name will be tainted forever. We'll be pariahs in our own city. Outcasts. I can't let that happen, Abs."

That made more sense. My self-absorbed cousin had become a true Osborne, more concerned with the family name than with another person's life. "Then you're not even remotely worried about Melissa's well-being?"

"Of course I'm worried about her—remotely—but it's more about someone else's well-being."

"Oh, right. Yours."

"No, but I can understand why you might think so."

"Claymore's?"

"Keep guessing."

"I don't want to play anymore, Jillian. Just tell me."

"Your niece's."

"Tara's at the beach house, too?" Tara was my brother Jordan's thirteen-year-old daughter.

"Oops. I meant to say your first cousin"—she paused to ponder—"once removed."

I had to stop for a moment to figure out what that meant. "I don't have a first cousin once removed."

"In seven months you will."

CHAPTER THREE

I toppled backward, landing on my derriere. "You are *not* pregnant! You're just saying that to get your way."

"Sh-h-h!" She glanced around again, then whispered, "It's true, Abs. I saw my doctor last week."

"How far along are you?"

"Six weeks. Do you understand now why I need you to clear the family name?"

"Wait a minute. No one else knows? Not even Claymore?"

She nodded. "Please, Abs, you won't let an innocent child be hurt by a scandal, will you?"

I gazed into those wide green eyes and saw, not my gorgeous, twenty-six-year-old spoiled cousin, but the shy, withdrawn child whose back was so crooked from scoliosis, she had to be put in a body cast, and whose cheerless gaze had reflected her misery. Jillian had always looked up to me. How could I turn her away now?

I already had my next journal entry written in my head: *Bad luck supposedly comes in threes. So let's see. First Pryce called and tried to ruin my Monday. Then Jillian twisted my arm and did ruin my Monday. It's anyone's guess what the third misfortune will be.*

She put her finger against her lips to warn me to silence.

"Here's your water," Marco said, striding into the room.

"Thank you, Marco." Jillian smiled sweetly at him. Then when he turned away, she mouthed, *You swore!* And then mimed sticking a needle in her eye.

I gave her a quick nod. In my state of shock, it was all I could manage.

"What's up?" Marco asked, looking from me to my cousin, who was calmly sipping the water.

"Marco, I think"—*Take a deep breath, Abby*—"we should take Pryce's case."

There, I'd said it. And I had the knot in my stomach to prove it.

His eyebrows drew together. "Are you sure?"

"She's sure," Jillian said.

Marco kept his gaze on me, as though trying to peer inside my head. "What changed your mind?"

"I did," Jillian said. "I reminded her how upset Claymore gets when anyone in his family is in trouble. He has such delicate nerves that a situation like this can put him in a tailspin for months. He stops eating, and he doesn't need to lose weight."

Although Jillian hadn't lied about her husband's nervous condition, Marco still wasn't buying that as my reason. He studied me, his eyes narrowed. "Are you one hundred percent certain you want us to take the case?"

I made myself nod. I could almost hear my neck vertebrae screaming.

"Okay," Marco said.

"Oh, thank you, thank you, thank you!" Jillian said, placing her hands over her heart. "I'm so relieved. Can you come out to the cottage with me right now?"

"I can't leave the shop during the morning rush," I said.

"And I've got some business to take care of," Marco

said. "I can make it at noon, Abby, if you're sure you want to go with me."

"I'll arrange it," I said.

Jillian set her glass on the desk and took a shaky breath, looking pale now. "Then I suppose I'd better get back before someone notices I'm gone."

"Good idea," I said, trying to appear calm, although the thought of seeing the beach house—and Pryce—made me want to puke.

Jillian grabbed my waste can and did.

After Jillian's stomach had settled and she felt strong enough to leave, Marco escorted her to her car, while I took the waste can out to the alley and rinsed it with a hose. When I returned to the workroom, Marco had swiveled my desk chair around and was straddling it. For some reason he viewed sitting in a chair the right way an anathema.

"So Jillian is expecting a baby, huh?" he asked.

I paused in cleaning stray leaves off the worktable. "What would make you think that? She explained about getting sick on undercooked eggs."

"Her voice carries into the kitchen. I heard you two talking."

I brushed off my hands so I could give him a hug. "I'm so glad you know. Jillian made me swear I wouldn't tell anyone, and I really dislike keeping anything from you."

"I feel the same way, Abby." He chuckled. "Somehow I can't picture Claymore as a daddy. Messy diapers . . . middle-of-the-night feedings . . . colic. If you thought he was high-strung before, imagine what he'll be like with a newborn in the house."

"But you *can* picture Jillian handling it?"

"Nah. She'll have a nanny."

"Two nannies," I corrected. "One for Claymore, who'll probably be colicky, too."

We both laughed at that.

"Why would Claymore be colicky?" Grace asked, slipping through the curtain as quietly as a sailboat gliding into port.

"Um," I said, while I tried to come up with a plausible reason. My sixty-something British assistant was capable, efficient, and an inveterate eavesdropper, so I hoped that last bit was all she'd heard. I glanced at Marco for help, but he merely shrugged.

"Ah, so it's to be silence, is it?" She cleared her throat, placed her sensible beige pumps together, straightened her spine, and clasped the edges of her coral cardigan as though she were about to deliver the Gettysburg Address. It was the posture she assumed whenever she recited one of her myriad quotes.

"As that great American writer, historian, and philosopher Will Durant wrote, 'One of the lessons of history is that nothing is often a good thing to do and always a clever thing to say.' So brava, love, for your silence."

Whew. I was off the hook. "Thanks, Grace," I said, as Marco and I clapped. "Great quote."

She nodded regally. It was part of her performance.

The summer I clerked for attorney Dave Hammond, Grace had been his legal secretary, and we'd gotten along famously. Before that, she'd been, among other things, a surgical nurse, a school librarian, a tattoo artist, and a horse walker. She had decided to retire around the time I took over Bloomers, but two weeks of inactivity had her eager to become *She Who Rules the Parlor*. I credited Grace for the coffee shop's success.

Lottie pulled back the curtain and looked into the room. "Am I the only one working today?"

"Sorry, dear," Grace said, then turned to me. "Your mum phoned, Abby. She'll be stopping by after lunch to drop off her latest artwork."

There was a moment of silence followed by three heavy sighs.

"Okay," I said. "I'll prepare myself. By the way, I'm going to take my lunch break at noon unless one of you has a commitment. Marco and I have to go interview people."

"So you're going to take Pryce's case, then?" Grace asked. Not much got past her.

"Yep," Marco said.

"I suppose it was inevitable," Grace said with a heavy sigh. "Jillian *is* involved, after all."

"Speaking of inevitable, did Jillian tell you her news?" Lottie asked.

My heart gave a gallop, but then I looked at Marco and he signaled with a quick shake of his head that Lottie couldn't possibly have overheard from the front counter. So there must be other news.

"About her being with child, do you mean?" Grace asked.

Nope. Same news.

I exchanged stunned glances with Marco. "Who told you, Lottie?"

"Sweetie, anyone who's had a baby knows the signs, and that girl was about as green around the gills as I've ever seen."

"But how did you know, Grace?"

Grace, who had never had children, said, "Well, you know Jillian's voice is rather clamoursome, love."

Grace had the best words that none of us had ever heard of.

"But Jillian *whispered*," I said.

"Her whispers can split one's eardrums," Grace said. "Very high-pitched for what amounts to a hiss."

"You can't say a word to anyone," I told my assistants. "Jillian swore me to secrecy."

"It won't be a problem, love," Grace said. "None of

my friends would even care." Then she glided out as silently as she had arrived.

"Same here," Lottie said, and followed her.

Marco glanced at his watch. "Time for me to go. Pick you up at noon. And yes, I'll have a cooler packed with sandwiches."

The turkey BLTs were delicious, and I ate mine with gusto—until I thought about seeing Pryce and the beach house again, the scene of his marriage proposal. Then my mouth went dry and the food didn't go down so well. I took a swallow of bottled water, but that only made me cough.

"You okay?" Marco asked, turning east onto State Road 12, which wound around the southern tip of Lake Michigan. We were heading toward the exclusive village of Dune Haven, which had been built around tranquil Haven Lake.

"Food went down the wrong pipe," I rasped, pointing to my throat.

"According to my GPS, we're getting close to Elm Street."

According to the growing knot in my stomach, too. I rewrapped the uneaten portion of my sandwich and stowed it in the cooler in the backseat of Marco's green Prius. "I'll finish that later." Like maybe next week, when my tummy untangled.

After another ten minutes, we turned onto Elm, a private road that wound through a forest of cottonwood, maple, beech, pine, black walnut, and the ubiquitous elm trees. The tall deciduous trees formed such a heavy canopy that the hot August sun was nearly blotted out. The big two- and three-story vacation homes, set on acre lots, could be seen only in brief glimpses between the thick trunks.

"The houses look completely traditional from the front, but from the back, they're almost all glass," I explained. "Each one has its own sandy beach, pier, and boat dock."

"So you've been here before." Marco said it as a statement rather than a question, as though another fact to tuck away in his memory bank.

"Once—briefly—while I was in law school. I was still acceptable to the Osbornes then."

I didn't want to tell him why I'd been there. After all, how many guys could afford to have their soon-to-be fiancées serenaded by a string quartet on their private beach in the moonlight while they were proposing? And then afterward drink champagne in Waterford crystal glasses served by a butler?

However many there were, Marco wasn't one of them. Boy, was I glad.

"I didn't know it at the time," I told Marco, "but if I hadn't enrolled in law school, I would have been nixed from the get-go. Flunking out was the deal breaker."

"The Osbornes accepted Jillian," Marco pointed out.

"She met their criteria. Harvard degree. Father is a stockbroker. Mother golfs and lunches with the ladies at the country club. Jillian grew up in a big house, vacationed in exotic locales, and had cleaning people. Just the opposite of my upbringing."

I checked my watch. "This trip took longer than I thought it would, Marco. I'm not going to have a lot of time to interview the guests. I have to get back to Bloomers because the Monday Afternoon Ladies' Poetry Society meets at two, and it takes all of us to handle the shop when they're in residence."

"We'll just do some basic questioning, then. Mainly, I want to get a feel for the situation and everyone involved."

"There it is." I pointed to a traditional gray cedar three-story with white trim. Was my hand shaking?

"Not what I'd call a cottage," Marco said. "More like a mini-mansion."

The so-called cottage had four chimney stacks, two second-floor balconies on its front side, and a deep verandah that spanned the front and one side of the house. A matching four-car garage was situated close to the street, so Marco turned off the lane onto the driveway and parked in front of one of the bays.

As we walked up a brick path that wound through the wooded lot, I couldn't help but admire the cheerful verandah ahead. Pots of bright pink and white impatiens lined either side of the four wooden steps. Blue, green, and white print sofa pillows accented the bright green cushions that padded white wicker settees and chairs. And a rectangular teak table and six chairs with matching cushions filled the side verandah, with ceiling fans twirling overhead.

"Nice," Marco said, taking it in.

"Wait till you see the inside. Light wood floors, white cotton cushions on rattan furniture, with accents of bright blue and sea green . . . it's just what a beach house should look like."

He put his arm around my shoulders as we walked toward the verandah. "Are you sorry you didn't get to share in all this?"

"Not for a second. I'm the luckiest woman on earth for having met you. In fact, the next time I see Pryce's parents, I'm going to thank them for doing me a favor."

"There's no need to carry it that far, Sunshine."

Then why was there a pleased grin tugging at one corner of his mouth?

"Abs! Marco!"

I glanced up and saw Jillian waving from a balcony. She turned to motion to someone behind her; then moments later Claymore stepped up to the white railing.

"What are you doing here?" Jillian called down.

"Marco," I whispered, "please do your best to keep me from choking her today."

"Don't I always?"

"Point taken." I shaded my eyes to look up at her, wishing I hadn't left my sunglasses in the car. "Pryce asked us to come."

"Oh! I thought maybe you and Marco were just out for a ride—" Jillian paused, then clamped her hand over her mouth and fled inside.

Claymore watched her go, then said to us, "She ate something at breakfast that didn't agree with her. Why don't I meet you at the front door?"

"Is Clay covering for Jillian or is it possible she hasn't told him about the baby?" Marco asked, as we climbed the steps to the front door.

"According to Jillian, no one else knows. And just a word of caution. Don't call Claymore *Clay* in front of anyone but me. The Osbornes dislike nicknames."

"Any other rules I should know about?"

"Probably, but I can't think of them at the moment."

Marco took a long look at me. "Nervous?"

"Nah."

"Then why are you rubbing your arms?"

I shivered. "It's chilly here, don't you think?"

"It's eight-four degrees, Abby."

Okay, then it was chilly inside my stomach. Still. *Chilly!*

The door opened and Pryce's younger brother greeted me with a hug and Marco with a handshake. "Thank you both for coming. This is quite an awkward situation for us. We're simply at a loss as to what to do."

Like Pryce's, Claymore Osborne's light brown hair was always perfectly coiffed, his clothing neatly ironed—including swim trunks, from what I remembered—his fingernails manicured, his shoes impeccably shined, and his leather sandals conditioned. He was thin, nervous, and fussy, but had the genial disposition and generous heart that Pryce lacked.

As we stepped inside the foyer, I glanced around with growing disbelief. Could this be the same charming cottage I'd visited less than two years ago? Where had all the heavy, dark antique furniture and rugs come from? Had someone robbed a castle?

The shock continued as I looked up. In place of the large art deco, beveled-glass chandelier that used to illuminate the entrance, there now dangled an old wagon wheel from three thick, rusty chains. Chandelier bulbs tucked beneath small brown-fringed burlap shades provided illumination, which, considering the color of the shades, didn't amount to much.

A narrow table made from thick twigs and crude wooden planks stood against the side wall, replacing the sleek, white wood, cottage-style hall commode. And instead of the large black-rimmed schoolhouse clock that had hung above it, there now was a very small, elaborately carved cuckoo clock that appeared to have come straight from the Black Forest. Not exactly a beach look.

Fearing a similar fate had befallen the living room, I gazed through the wide doorway to my left and discovered that it had fared even worse. Instead of the crisp white cottage furniture with blue and green accents, the room was now done in Queen Anne–style furniture with fancy mahogany, curved-legged tables sporting ornate, burnished brass hardware.

High-backed camel sofas and wing chairs were arranged in conversational groupings, upholstered in a mix of solids, florals, and stripes in dark green, brown, and dusty coral. In the middle, a large, worn Oriental carpet in brown, black, beige, and rust nearly blocked all glimpses of the beautiful pale wood floor beneath. Large dark tapestries covered most of the walls, which were painted in a pretty sandy hue.

"Have a seat in the living room and I'll let Pryce know you're here," Claymore told us, then headed up the hallway toward the back of the house.

"Are you sure you've been here before?" Marco said quietly as we entered the living room.

"It's been redecorated," I whispered. "Isn't it hideous?"

"It isn't my taste."

Thank goodness. That might have been *our* deal breaker.

"From what I remember," I said, as we sat on a hard brown sofa, "it's not the Osbornes' taste either." I ran my hand over the rough fabric, amazed that anyone would find it comfortable, then glanced around the room. "Well," I said, letting out my breath, "here we are."

"You doing okay?" Marco asked. "Anger level down? Nerves under control?"

"Yep. All under control." I let out another heavy breath. "All. Under. Con. Trol."

He laid his hand across my shoulders, and I gave a start. "Sorry," I said. "I guess my nerves are a little frayed."

"Really? I hadn't noticed."

I heard footsteps coming down the hallway, and my stomach tensed. The last time I'd had to deal with Pryce had been at Jillian and Claymore's wedding, and then I'd avoided him as much as possible. How was I going to greet him now? Cool and distant? Stranger-friendly? *Just please, God, not nervous-babbly.* I was at my worst when I babbled.

"Marco," I whispered, "if I start babbling, squeeze my hand."

The footsteps were very close now. My hands curled

into sweaty balls on my lap. *Deep breaths, Abby. In to the count of seven, out to eight.*

Jillian strolled into the room, and I nearly slumped over in relief. She had on the same bright sundress as before, but had gathered her long copper locks into a twisted bun held in place with a tortoiseshell clip. Other than seeming a bit flushed, she looked model perfect.

"No one even suspected I left this morning," she said with a twinkle in her green eyes. "I'm as stealthy as a cat."

"That would explain why you ran into the bedroom a few minutes ago," I said. "Fur ball."

Jillian glared daggers at me. "Not funny."

Marco's phone beeped to signal a message. "Excuse me a moment," he said, and moved to one of the tall windows, turning his back to us.

"You better not have told him about you know what," Jillian whispered as she sat down beside me on the sofa.

"Calm down. I didn't tell him." I watched her whip out a wide-toothed comb and a large black hair clip. "What are you doing?"

"I'm about to make you presentable, silly. What did you think I was going to do?"

She reached for my head, and I jumped up. "Stop it," I whispered, casting a glance at the doorway. "I'm nervous enough without you fussing over me."

"I can't believe you're willing to leave your hair like that in front of Pryce."

"My hair is always like this, and I don't care what Pryce thinks. I can't help that it doesn't glisten like satin or lie perfectly straight like yours does."

"How many times do I have to tell you to switch to my brand of shampoo and conditioner? It'll strip away that dullness and tame your locks in no time."

"The only thing it'll strip away is the money in my wallet, Jill. Nothing works on this hair."

She stood up with a huff and guided me toward a gilt-edged mirror hanging over the fireplace. "Just give me two minutes," she said to my reflection. "I can work magic on you."

"What don't you understand about no?" I said, stepping out of reach.

"One minute, then."

With a defiant glare, I fluffed my hair with my fingers until it looked like tossed hay.

"Now we're back to two minutes," she said, and made a quick grab for my wrist. "You'll thank me later."

I jerked my arm away and my elbow sank into something spongy. Turning, I saw my former fiancé doubled over, grimacing in pain.

I'd wanted to do that for a long time anyway.

CHAPTER FOUR

"**G**reat Gatsby!" Claymore called melodramatically from the doorway, and hurried across the dark carpet to help his brother to the sofa. Jillian dashed to her husband's side to see what she could do to annoy them both.

Marco ended his call and strode toward me. "What happened?"

"I punched Pryce in the gut," I whispered. At Marco's startled reaction, I added, "Accidentally! Jillian and I were having a—difference of opinion—and he happened to be standing in the wrong place."

Marco eyed my hair. "Did the difference of opinion cause that?"

Oops. I turned back to the mirror and finger combed it as best I could. Through the glass I saw Pryce gently probe his diaphragm, wince, then take some deep breaths. Obviously feeling better, he ran his palm over his hair to make sure the part was straight, then adjusted the collar of his tan silk Tommy Bahama shirt.

"Pryce, I'm sorry," I said as humbly as I could manage. "I didn't know you had come into the room, let alone were standing behind me, or I would never have elbowed you in the stomach. It wouldn't have happened at all except that Jillian and I were having a disagreement over—well, that's not important now—but—"

Marco squeezed my hand.

I stopped. It was exactly as I'd feared—nervous babble.

"It's your fault for being so stubborn," Jillian said with a sniff, folding her arms.

"No bother." Pryce reached out to shake Marco's hand. "Thank you for coming. Would anyone care for coffee, tea, or iced tea before we get started?"

"We don't have a lot of time," I said. "Can we skip—"

"Tea for me, please," Jillian said, taking a seat on a brown and beige striped wing chair. "Claymore will have some, too." She smiled up at her husband, who was standing behind her chair as though to catch her in case she fell out.

"Nothing for me, thanks," I said, sitting on the end of the ugly sofa. Marco also declined, then sat down beside me.

Pryce used an intercom to put in the order, then took a seat in the other wing chair. It was a cozy conversation group with people who were anything but.

"I suppose you have a lot of questions for us," Pryce said. His eyes had dark circles underneath them.

"I usually talk to people individually," Marco said, "but in the interest of time, I'll run preliminary questions by all of you, then schedule a time to see you separately."

"Why separately?" Claymore asked. "We don't keep secrets from each other."

If I'd had coffee in my mouth, I would have spit it out. Jillian saw me holding back a laugh and squinted her eyes at me.

"It's just how we work." Marco pulled his small black

notebook and a pen from his pocket. "I'll be taking notes as we talk."

"Don't you want me to do that, honey," I asked, "as I usually do?"

Marco's eyebrows drew together as he handed the pad and pen to me, so I lifted mine in response. He knew I wasn't much into calling him endearing names in public. Today, however, I was prepared to lay it on thick, and my expression told him so. His only response was a slight flicker of amusement at the corners of his mouth.

"Would you spell your fiancée's last name?" Marco asked Pryce.

"H-a-z-e-l-t-o-n," Pryce said.

"Where does Melissa work?" Marco asked.

"She owns a home-decorating business called Pisces," Pryce said. "It's on West Lincoln Avenue."

"How many employees?" Marco asked.

"Just herself," Pryce said. "She subcontracts."

"Did she redo this room?" I asked. It wasn't part of the normal round of questions. I was just being nos— curious.

I saw Pryce's cheek twitch ever so slightly. "Yes, she did."

In that case, Melissa should have subcontracted the job out to a real decorator.

"When was the last time you saw her?" Marco asked Pryce.

"Sunday morning when I left to go for a run." Pryce templed his hands, fingertips under his chin. "You should know up front that it does seem I was the last one to see Melissa."

Cue the ominous music.

"Was Sunday yesterday?" Jillian asked me, and at my nod, she said, "Then I saw her yesterday morning, too.

She was leaving the cottage and had her Louise Green Laguna in her hand."

"What's a Louise Green Laguna?" I asked.

"It's a style of sun hat made by Louise Green. Duh."

"Don't say that like I should know, Jillian. I don't work in fashion."

"Obviously. Anyway, I was coming downstairs for breakfast and asked her where she was going, but she didn't even turn around to answer. Were you with me, Claymore?"

"No, my darling, I was poaching your eggs in the kitchen. And in answer to your question, Marco, the last time I saw Melissa was yesterday morning, as well. She and Jake were on the deck having breakfast."

"Wait. I'm confused," I said. "Who is Jake?"

"Jake Caldwell," Pryce said. "He and his wife, Lily, are staying with me for a few weeks while their house is being renovated."

I noted it, then started a timeline in the notebook. "What time did you have breakfast?"

"Eight o'clock, my usual time," Pryce said.

"So Melissa didn't have breakfast with you?"

"No, she did not."

"What time did you come downstairs, Jillian?" I asked.

She glanced up at Claymore, and he said, "It would have been shortly after nine, dearest."

"Shortly after nine," she told me, as though Claymore had been speaking Chinese.

"What time did you see Melissa having breakfast with Jake?" Marco asked Claymore.

"Let me think. I came down to make Jillian a cup of mint tea just after seven, and they were on the deck."

"Did Melissa seem angry or upset?" Marco asked.

"I couldn't tell," Claymore said. "Her back was toward me."

"Where was Lily Caldwell while Jake and Melissa were eating?" I asked.

"She had already eaten," Claymore replied. "She came in from the deck carrying an empty plate just as I got to the kitchen."

I tapped my watch, reminding Marco that our time was growing short. He nodded. "Will your other guests be joining us soon?" he asked.

"I alerted Jake and the Burches," Pryce said. "They'll be in shortly. They've been having coffee on the deck. Lily had to go to work."

"Have you had any trouble with crime in this neighborhood recently?" Marco asked.

"No," Pryce said. "This isn't an easy area to find, so we've never been a target for thieves. But even so, we all have alarms and use them religiously."

"Has Melissa mentioned whether she's had trouble with any of her clients?" Marco asked.

"None that I'm aware of," Pryce said.

"No dissatisfied clients?" I asked, trying to keep the disbelief out of my expression. Everyone had unhappy clients at some point. In fact, I was having a hard time believing Pryce's parents were pleased with what Melissa had done to their cottage.

He took a moment to brush a particle of lint off his pant leg before replying. "I don't believe she's mentioned any."

Jillian made a *pffft* sound. Claymore leaned down to whisper something in her ear, and she reacted by tilting her head back to give him a frown.

I wrote: *Ask J. about Melissa's reputation.*

"What day and time did each of you arrive for the weekend?" Marco asked.

"Friday at five p.m. for me," Pryce said. "Everyone else was supposed to be here by six."

"We arrived *promptly* at six," Jillian said proudly. Claymore patted her shoulder.

"Melissa was here by half past five," Pryce said. "Claymore, do you recall when the Burches arrived?"

"Ten minutes past six o'clock," his younger brother said. "They would have been here on time, but they went back to retrieve a bottle of champagne. Jake came in just after we did."

"And Lily, who's late to everything, arrived at six thirty," Jillian offered.

"Lily is a busy and highly successful restaurateur," Pryce said, giving Jillian a disgruntled look. "We're fortunate that she has any free time at all to spend with us."

Jillian rolled her eyes at me.

As soon as I finished marking the timeline, I made a side note as to how quickly Pryce had jumped to Lily's defense. I watched him now as he tapped his fingers on the arm of the chair, staring out the window as though he wanted to get moving.

"What's the name of Lily's restaurant?" Marco asked.

"Beached," Pryce replied.

"It's a chic bistro at the Key Club marina," I told Marco as I wrote.

"Have you ever been there?" Marco asked me.

I shook my head.

"You wouldn't be able to afford it anyway," Jillian said.

"Thank you for pointing that out in front of everyone," I muttered.

"I'm just saying."

She was right, though. Cost was half the reason I never went there.

"Lily does the cleverest things with shrimp," Jillian said. "Doesn't she, Claymore?"

"When it comes to shrimp," he replied, "Lily is a genius. Most of her menu is centered around shrimp dishes."

Which was the other half of the reason I didn't eat there. Not only had *Shrimp* been my nickname in middle school, but I'd seen those ugly creatures when they were alive.

"Beached is *très au courant*," Claymore added.

I refused to put that in my notes.

"What does Jake do for a living?" Marco asked.

"He teaches spinning classes at Up and Dune Health Club," Claymore said, "and does some acting in local theater productions."

"He also poses," Jillian said with a snicker.

"Poses for what?" I asked.

"Mirrors, picture windows, and anyone with a camera." She turned in her chair to imitate a bodybuilder's pose, flexing her arm muscles and casting a sexy glance over her shoulder.

"What do the Burches do?" Marco asked, ready to move on.

"Halston is a stockbroker and Orabell gives travelogue presentations," Claymore said. "They own the cottage to the right of us."

They're old, Jillian mouthed to me.

To Jillian, old could be forty, so I ignored her comment and wrote down the information Claymore had supplied.

The Osbornes' short, plump housekeeper entered with a tray that she placed on a coffee table in front of the sofa. When she straightened, she saw me and her eyes widened in a pleased way. "Miss Abby, it's so good to see you. How are you?"

"I'm doing great, Mrs. Ambrose, and you look fantastic, by the way."

She blushed and waved away my compliment. "You always say the sweetest things."

"I'd like you to meet my fiancé, Marco Salvare, Mrs. Ambrose."

There. I'd finally worked it into the conversation. Pryce didn't bat an eye, but the housekeeper smiled in delight. "I'm so happy for both of you. Oh, my," she said, shaking Marco's hand, "you're strong."

"Thank you, Mrs. Ambrose. That will be all for now," Pryce said tersely, dismissing her.

"Don't you want me to pour your tea?" she asked, looking surprised.

"We'll take care of it." He didn't even acknowledge her with a glance. How could I have forgotten how cold Pryce could be?

"Nice to see you again, Mrs. Ambrose," I called.

"A pleasure to meet you," Marco added.

The housekeeper gave us a grateful smile as she left the room.

Claymore stepped around Jillian's chair to fill the three china cups, then handed Jillian hers before taking his own to his place behind her. Pryce ignored his tea to walk to the window, where he stood with his hands clasped behind his back, staring outside.

"How well do your guests know each other?" Marco asked Pryce.

"Lily and Pryce were college classmates," Claymore said, "and Halston Burch is the Osborne family stockbroker."

Jillian glanced up at her husband. "Isn't he Lily's broker, too?"

"Yes, and also Melissa's," Claymore said.

"And Jake's?" I asked, writing down the names.

"Jake doesn't have money," Jillian said, as though I should have known that. "He depends on Lily for everything." She emphasized the word *everything*.

"We get together on most weekends in August,"

Pryce said without turning. "Halston has the month off and likes to entertain his clients on Saturday evenings."

"Thinking back over this weekend," Marco said to Pryce, "did you sense any tension between Melissa and any of the others?"

"No," he replied, at the same time Jillian said, "Yes."

I saw Claymore put his hand on Jillian's shoulder, as though to stop her from answering.

Marco's gaze flickered from Jillian to Pryce's back, as though assessing their responses. Then he said to Pryce, "You mentioned that Melissa arrived half an hour before the others. How was her mood when you first saw her?"

"Congenial."

"She wasn't congenial when we got here," Jillian said. "More like antigenial."

"Explain," I said. There was no point in arguing her word choice now.

"When we walked into the cottage, Melissa was coming down the stairs looking like she was ready to bite someone's head off." For my benefit, Jillian nodded in Pryce's direction to indicate who that someone was. Even with his back to us, though, Pryce caught it.

"We had a disagreement over a personal matter," he said in a brittle voice. "It has nothing to do with her disappearance."

Jillian raised her eyebrows at me, as though to say, *Oh, really?*

I took the cue and asked Pryce, "Are you certain it has nothing to do with her disappearance?"

"She stayed the weekend," Pryce said. "That should tell you something."

"That she was hoping to smooth things out between you?" I asked.

"I'd prefer to discuss this matter in private."

I made a note of his reply, because it was evident to me that Pryce had not wanted to smooth things out. It also reminded me so much of the horrible breakup scene we'd had that I found myself giving his back a steely glare. Too bad he couldn't see it.

"What did you do after your guests arrived Friday evening?" Marco asked Pryce.

"We went outside onto the back deck to have cocktails and enjoy the lake view."

I stopped taking notes to glance at my cousin in surprise. Jillian had a cocktail? In her condition? She gave me a scowl, as though to say she wasn't that dumb.

"Was Melissa friendly and conversing with everyone?" Marco asked.

"She was quite chatty," Pryce said, coming back to his chair.

"I thought Melissa seemed a bit tense," Claymore said. "Übertalkative, too."

"And we know why," Jillian whispered loud enough to scare snakes.

"Does Melissa normally get along with these particular guests?" Marco asked.

"Of course," Pryce said.

"Are you serious?" Jillian asked.

"Dearest heart," Claymore said, "let's let Pryce answer these questions, shall we?"

"He's not being honest," Jillian replied in one of her infamous whispers.

"With whom doesn't Melissa get along, Jillian?" Pryce snapped.

"You know very well with *whom*," Jillian shot back.

"Easy, dearest," Claymore said, patting her head. "Let's not get worked up."

"You'll have a turn to answer later," I said to Jillian.

"Does Melissa have any enemies that you're aware of?" Marco asked Pryce.

"How about everyone she's done any decorating for," Jillian muttered.

"Claymore!" Pryce said sharply.

His brother snapped to attention. "Jillian, shall we go upstairs? I believe we've helped all we can for now."

"No, we haven't," she replied. "And you know it's true, Pryce. Your own mother said Melissa's decorating—"

"Come, sweetness," Claymore said, lifting her by the elbow and removing the cup from her other hand. "I want to discuss dinner plans with you."

"I haven't even had lunch."

"Then let's go to the kitchen and whip up a bite for you. I was thinking of a refreshing gazpacho, something resplendent with raw cucumbers, tomatoes, cilantro, onions, garlic—"

Jillian jerked her arm away and, pressing a hand to her mouth, fled the room.

"Another fur ball," I murmured to Marco.

His cheeks coloring, Claymore said, "I should have remembered she's not a fan of my gazpacho."

As he followed in his wife's fleeing footsteps, I whispered to Marco, "I have to get back to Bloomers."

"I'm on it," he murmured. "Pryce, before we head back to New Chapel, I'd like to schedule times to meet with your other guests."

Pryce set his teacup on his saucer with a clatter. "You're leaving so soon? You've barely begun."

"We squeezed you in on short notice," I said. "We still have businesses to run."

"Is it possible for us to meet with everyone individually starting at five thirty?" Marco asked.

"The cottage is available for your use, certainly,"

Pryce said, "but I don't know whether Lily will be able to make it until much later." Shifting his gaze to me, Pryce added, "She has a business to run, too."

That would teach me for being snippy.

He headed for the doorway, calling back, "I'll round up the oth—"

At that moment, a tanned, square-jawed, exceptionally attractive white-haired man came striding into the room, nearly colliding with Pryce. He had on a Hawaiian-style print shirt and white shorts with black fisherman sandals. He appeared to be older than my dad, putting him in the fifty-five to sixty-five range.

Behind him was a bone-thin woman in a brightly colored gauzy dress that billowed out behind her as she moved, a big necklace made of red beads, a red-banded watch encircled with crystals, and multicolored strappy sandals. She sported a dark tan and had the leathery skin to prove it. Her hair was a shade of blond that reminded me of straw, and her eye shadow was a glittery blue that she'd swiped on in the middle of her lids, leaving a gap between her eyelashes and the color.

"Pryce, you simply must speed things up," the man said. He had an odd way of talking without moving his jaws. "We've been here for *hours* and Mummy is getting dreadfully tired."

"Pryce, darling!" the woman exclaimed dramatically, showing off three bulbous red rings and her glittering watch by raising her arms in the air. "Can't we please go home? We're just a stone's throw away."

She, too, talked without moving her jaws, and pronounced her short *a*'s as an *ah* sound. *Dahling. Cahn't.*

The man put his arm around her shoulders. "Don't get into a stew, now, Mummy."

"You'll be able to leave shortly, Halston," Pryce said. "Let me introduce you to the private detective."

"Oh, a private eye!" the woman exclaimed, pressing her hands together. "How exciting."

"Halston and Orabell Burch," Pryce said, "this is Marco Salvare."

"How do you do, Mr. Salvare," Halston said, giving his hand a firm shake.

"I'd prefer Marco," my intended said.

"And I'd prefer Halston, so we're good all around."

"So pleased to meet you, Mr. Salvare," Orabell said sweetly, taking Marco's hand with a smile, seemingly oblivious of his request. "Do call me Orabell."

She turned to me, hands pressed together at heart level. "And who is this de*light*ful young lady?"

"I'm Abby Knight," I said instantly. "Marco's fiancée and assistant."

"Ah, his fiancée!" she repeated, eyebrows raised. "So good to meet a woman who isn't chasing after someone else's husband."

A moment of silence followed her unusual comment. Then Marco stepped in.

"Abby also owns Bloomers Flower Shop," he said, gazing at me. My heart melted at the look of pride in his eyes. I gave him a smile that said, *Thank you for that*.

"How absolutely *divine*," Orabell said with a girlish squeal.

"A pleasure to meet you, Miss Knight," Halston said, taking my hand gallantly and kissing my knuckles. He was not only highly attractive for an older man, but also what my dad would have labeled *suave and debonair*.

"Thank you," I said, feeling my cheeks grow warm.

"So when are you going to release us, Marco?" Halston said. "I feel like a prisoner."

"I'll need just five minutes of your time," Marco said.

The Burches sat on the sofa and Halston took Orabell's hand in his. Marco and I sat in the two wing chairs, leaving Pryce to either perch beside the Burches or drag over a chair from the other conversation area.

He opted for a third choice—standing against the doorjamb, arms folded, glancing repeatedly at his watch.

"How well do you know Melissa?" Marco asked the couple.

"I'm afraid not very," Orabell said, as though it pained her to admit it.

"I know Melissa mainly through business," Halston said. "I'm her stockbroker, as I am to everyone who was here this weekend."

"Except for Jake," Orabell said. Putting her hand to the side of her mouth, she whispered, "He doesn't have two nickels to rub together. Depends on Lily for an allowance. So sad, really."

What was sad was that Orabell thought no one could hear her but me.

In a normal voice, she said, "Wait till you meet Jake. I'm sure you'll agree that he has untapped potential."

I checked my watch. I was overdue at the shop. "Is Jake going to join us?"

"I'll see what's holding him up," Pryce said.

As soon as he was gone, Orabell hurried to the doorway, peered out, then said to her husband in a whisper, "Shall I tell them?"

"Yes, Mummy, I think you should," Halston said in a serious tone.

Orabell hustled to her seat on the sofa. Taking a deep breath, her hands clasped in her lap, she leaned toward us. "We believe that Pryce had something to do with Melissa's disappearance."

"Not something, Mummy," Halston said. "Everything."

CHAPTER FIVE

It was at least three seconds before either one of us had the wherewithal to respond.

"Let me make sure I understand," Marco said, leaning toward them. I could tell by his expression that every brain cell in his head was at attention. "You're stating that Pryce is responsible for Melissa's disappearance?"

Orabell nodded vigorously.

"Would you clarify what you mean by that?" Marco asked.

I was practically on the edge of my chair.

"To start with," Orabell said in a hushed voice, glancing toward the doorway as though to be sure Pryce hadn't sneaked up on us, "he and Melissa had the most dreadful argument on Friday evening. We could hear them quite clearly from our porch. It runs along the front and side of our house facing this one, you see.

"Well, by the time Pryce was finished with her," Orabell continued, "Melissa was weeping uncontrollably. Then Claymore and Jillian pulled up, and the weeping stopped immediately. We assume Melissa went inside to compose herself."

"Did you hear what they were arguing about?" I asked, my pen at the ready.

"I caught only snatches," Orabell said, "and that mostly from Melissa, as her voice tends to be on the strident side when raised."

"Can't be of much help on this, I'm afraid," Halston said, tugging one earlobe. "Hearing isn't what it used to be."

"Would you share what Melissa said?" I asked Orabell.

"I can't believe you would do this to me," she said.

I was taken aback by the woman's sudden change of attitude. "It's just part of the interview process."

Orabell smiled. "No, darling, those were Melissa's words. 'How can I show my face in town? This will ruin me.' She was referring to their breakup."

"Their breakup?" I repeated.

"You didn't know?" Orabell asked. "Pryce called off their engagement."

I was shocked—and yet I wasn't, or shouldn't have been, since he'd done it to me. Why hadn't Pryce told us that up front?

Or had he? I recalled our first conversation, when he'd said, *Did you know that I'd planned to marry Melissa?* I hadn't caught it at the time, but now the use of past tense made sense.

"I'm saving the best for last," Orabell said eagerly. Her eyes sparkled as she whispered, "'You will pay for this.'"

"She threatened Pryce?" I asked.

"Yes, indeed," Orabell said, as if this were the most delicious gossip to hit the Midwest in decades. "And two days later"—Orabell snapped her fingers—"she vanished."

I'd wanted to vanish, too, after Pryce had dumped me. And, boy, had I wanted to make him pay. But for Pryce to have taken action against me because of that? I couldn't see it happening.

While I scribbled notes, Marco said to Orabell, "Are you certain of what you heard?"

"Yes, darling. My eyesight is horrible, but I have excellent hearing."

"That she does," Halston said drily, his teeth clenched even tighter than before.

"Abby and I will be here this evening around five thirty to conduct more thorough interviews," Marco said. "Will you make yourselves available?"

"We will for you, dear boy," Orabell said, rising. "Not here, though. You must join us for after-dinner cocktails in our home."

"Thanks for the offer, but we don't drink while we're working a case," Marco said.

"That won't stop us from enjoying them," Halston said, then guffawed.

"When you've finished talking to the others, trot across the beach to our humble abode," Orabell called as they left the room. "We'll be on the patio around back."

I heard Pryce say good-bye to the Burches; then he strode into the room accompanied by a blond-haired man in a navy tank top, low-slung white linen drawstring pants, and brown flip-flops. The man, who I assumed was Jake, appeared to be about my age, twenty-seven, and by the way he carried himself, I could see why Jillian poked fun at him. Even now, as Jake stood in front of me, he had locked his fingers together, turning his palms face out, and was stretching his arms to flex his muscles.

"Jake Caldwell," Pryce said, as Marco rose to meet him, "this is private detective Marco Salvare and his assistant, Abigail Knight. Jake, I'll leave you to talk to them. I have a business call to make."

"Dude," Jake said, sizing Marco up, "a for-real PI?"

"For real," Marco said.

"Awesome." Then, with a smile that revealed deep-set dimples, Jake gave me a leisurely once-over, returning to focus on my breasts. "Pleasure to meet you," he said.

I crossed my arms and narrowed my eyes at him. "Likewise." *He wished.*

"So is it true redheads have red-hot tempers?" he asked with a side curl of his upper lip.

"Yep," I said, "and a fast right hook."

Jake elbowed Marco. "Bet she's a wild one in the sack."

"She's my fiancée," Marco said with a deadpan expression.

Instead of taking the comment as an attitude correction, Jake raised his hand for a high five. Marco pulled out his iPhone to check his calendar instead. "When would it be convenient for us to meet with you and your wife?"

Jake scratched his head, as though that was what he'd intended to do all along. "Oh, right. You're here about Melissa. What time would be convenient for Lily and me? I don't know. How's ten o'clock tonight look?"

"Here?" Marco asked.

"Better make it at Beached. That's where Lily usually is."

Marco tapped it into his phone. "We'll see you there."

We were on our way out the front door when I heard my cousin call from up the center hallway, "Wait!" She was breathless by the time she caught up to us. "What did I miss?"

"Nothing," I said. "All we did was schedule interview times for this evening."

Marco pulled out his phone and opened the calendar

application. "Would you and Clay . . . *more* be able to get here by six o'clock?"

Instead of replying, Jillian hooked her hands through our arms and stepped outside with us. "Here's a better idea. Let's meet up at your bar after you've talked to everyone else so you can share their answers with me."

"You know we can't do that," I said.

She made her *pfft* sound again. "You could if you wanted to."

"In what world do private investigators share their information with outsiders, Jillian?"

She put one hand on her waist. "So you're pulling the anti-professional excuse?"

"It's *un*professional," I snapped. "Yes, Marco, I know my teeth are clenched, but can you blame me?"

"Calm down," Marco said, rubbing my shoulders. "What we find out is confidential, Jillian. By law, we can't divulge anything or I'll risk losing my license."

Jillian glanced over her shoulder, then whispered, "But I *know* these people, Marco. I can help you. I'll be able to spot their lies."

"We'll meet you here at six for your interview," Marco said.

"Thank you, Marco." Apparently believing Marco had capitulated, she gave me a smirk and went back inside.

"Is it any wonder that I grind my teeth at night?" I asked, as we walked to his car.

"Try humoring her, Sunshine. You know what Grace always says. You catch more flies with honey than with vinegar."

"I refuse to humor someone who makes up stupid words."

Marco opened the passenger-side door for me. "Will you humor someone who is crazy about you?"

My scowl left in a hurry. *That* sounded like an invitation for something yummy. "Always. Just name it, Salvare."

"Good. Then let's review your notes on the ride home."

"What do we have so far?" Marco asked, as he backed out of the driveway.

As soon as I was buckled in, I took out the notepad and flipped to the first page.

"I'll read everything I took down, and then we can go back over it. Okay, here goes.

"Pryce and Melissa had an argument before the other guests arrived, as witnessed by the Burches, who heard Melissa threaten him. Or rather Orabell heard her, because Halston seems to have a hearing problem.

"Jillian and Claymore noticed that Melissa was upset when they arrived, and later that she tried to hide it by being super friendly. I also noted that after Jillian made a comment about Lily's tardiness, Pryce was very quick to jump to Lily's defense, which makes me wonder if there's something going on between Pryce and Lily."

"Because he defended her?"

"Remember, this is Pryce we're talking about. He wouldn't jump to anyone's defense unless he genuinely cared about that person . . . or was hired to do so."

Which explained why he hadn't rushed to my defense when his parents attacked me.

"We'll have to dig deeper there," Marco said. "Go ahead."

"Okay, next up is the Burches. They seem nice but verge on snobbishness. Maybe that's because they don't open their mouths when they speak, like they have lockjaw. Anyway, I agree with them that Pryce has some accountability for Melissa's disappearance, but I don't think he did anything sinister to her, which is what I thought Orabell was implying."

"What about the scene they witnessed?"

"Well, if it's true that Pryce broke off his engagement on Friday evening, then I feel even more strongly that Melissa's gone MIA to lick her wounds and possibly to punish him by making him worry. I still don't understand why Pryce wasn't up front with us about their split."

"Sunshine, think about it. Would you really expect him to announce to you that he broke another engagement?"

"Yeah, you're probably right."

"Take the probably out of it."

"Okay, Mr. *Right*. Shall I continue?"

"Could I stop you?"

"Nope. But lucky for you, we have only one person left—Jake, who struck me as a player, and not a bright one. But we didn't get to talk to him for long, so I could be wrong. How about you?"

"I wasn't impressed with Jake, but maybe he'll grow on us."

An image popped into my head as I took out my cell phone to check for messages, making me laugh.

"What?" Marco asked.

"When you said 'maybe he'll grow on us,' the first thing that came to mind was a toadstool."

"A toadstool?"

"Toadstools grow by absorbing matter from their host. They're a fungus."

"And Jake's a toadstool because he lives off of Lily's money?"

"Correct. Also because toadstools look harmless but can be quite deadly."

"Is that a gut feeling about Jake?"

"No, my gut is telling me that if we're leaving at five

o'clock to come back out here for the evening, we should stop for a light meal on our way."

"How about if I bring roast beef and cheddar sandwiches from the bar?"

"Marco, have you ever known me to turn down an offer of good food?"

"I'll pack the sandwiches in the cooler."

Back at Bloomers, Marco's mom, Francesca Salvare, was playing hostess in the coffee and tea parlor while Lottie took care of the shop and Grace was at lunch. Francesca had started helping out back in June, when a murder involving Grace as a suspect had Marco and me working nearly around the clock to clear her.

Marco's mom was a cheerful, energetic woman who didn't know the meaning of relaxation. All her energy had worked in our favor when we were shorthanded, but after things settled down, I wasn't able to convince her to stay away. I didn't mind Lottie in the workroom with me, but three was definitely a crowd. I just didn't have the heart to tell Francesca.

What had consoled me in the past was knowing that she was going back to her home in Ohio. But had she gone? Nope. She had opted to stay in New Chapel instead, *purportedly* to babysit for her grandchildren. I knew it was really to oversee my bridal shower and wedding preparations as well as Marco's life. She hadn't exactly hidden her feelings on either subject.

Francesca currently resided with Marco's sister Gina, who had a toddler and a newborn, and a guest suite in her basement that was neither too hot nor too cold but just right for Mama Bear. That had been a relief for Marco, because his mom had been staying at his apartment. He still had the occasional nightmare about those weeks.

"Abby, *bella*!" Francesca cried upon seeing me enter the shop. With arms outstretched, she beckoned me to her and enfolded me in a hug. Then she gripped my arms so she could lean back and size me up. "Have you eaten lunch today? You look washed-out. Your freckles are jumping off your face. Come, I brought a pan of mostaccioli Bolognese fresh from the oven. It will make everything better."

Taking my hand, she led me through the purple curtain, through the workroom, and into the tiny galley kitchen in back, where she sat me on a tall wooden stool at the narrow bar along the wall and opened our small refrigerator, pulling out a baking dish covered with aluminum foil. "Do you have a serving spoon?"

"It's in the drawer. I'll find it for you."

I started to hop down, but she wasn't having it. "Sit, sit! You've had a busy morning."

So I sat as she dug through our cluttered kitchen drawer.

Francesca was in her mid-fifties but had the vibrancy, hourglass shape, and smooth skin of a woman much younger. Her eyes were dark brown and crinkled at the corners like Marco's, with dark brown arched brows and thick black lashes. Her gloriously full-bodied dark hair waved around her face and onto the tops of her shoulders. Her white silk shirt, paired with multiple silver chains and flowy black slacks, was impossibly clean for her having just made a dish with red sauce in it.

"So," she said, picking through an odd assortment of utensils, "I hear you and my son have a new case."

"Yes, we do."

"Aha! Here it is." She knocked the drawer shut with her hip. "This job is for your former fiancé?" She plopped a large spoonful of pasta smothered in a red meat sauce loaded with onions, garlic, oregano, basil, and—I sniffed the air; was that a hint of cinnamon?—onto a plate and set it in front of me.

"Yes, it is."

"The man who broke your engagement and your heart? And now comes to you for help? And you have agreed to this?"

Amazing how her voice rose with each question. It was the inquisition all over again. "I—sort of had to."

"You *had* to?" She dropped her voice. "Is this slime boy blackmailing you?"

Before I could answer, she leaned so close we were practically eyeball to eyeball. "You didn't *pose* for him for one of those *sext* messages, did you?"

My jaw dropped so fast I heard two pops near my ears. "No! I—*ew!*"

"Because I will have Marco break the slime boy's knees if he demanded that of you."

In the first place, Pryce didn't know what a sext message was. In the second, Marco would never break anyone's knees unless it was to save a life. In the third place, Pryce was as far away from something slimy as an über-fastidious man could be. And in the fourth, did she really see me as someone who would pose without clothes? If so, double *ew!*

"I truly wish I could tell you why I felt compelled to take the case, Francesca, but I promised someone I wouldn't."

She rose back up, her eyebrows lifting. "I see."

Translation: *You don't trust me enough to tell me.*

"As soon as I have permission, I'll tell you."

"Good." With a straight face, she said, "Now, are you going to eat my mostaccioli or sit there jabbering all day?" Then she broke into a wide smile and put her arms around my shoulders. "I'm teasing you, *bella.*"

Whew. She'd frightened me there for a second.

"How are the shower preparations coming along?" she asked.

"They're coming," I said cheerily, hoping she'd leave it at that. But did that ever happen in Abby's world?

"Do you have lists of what you need?" she asked.

"I keep a notebook and check things off as I order them."

"Are you still determined to do all the work for this big shower yourself?"

"I am."

"Even though it breaks your mother's heart not to be included? And your cousin's? And your guests will miss out on the best lasagna they've ever eaten in their lives?"

I blinked rapidly, trying to think of something to say. Then I saw Francesca lift an eyebrow, and I smiled. She was teasing again.

She put the baking dish in the fridge and walked to the doorway, pausing to give me a pitying glance. "I am afraid you will regret this decision one day, *bella*." Then with a heavy sigh, she left.

Not teasing.

Once Francesca had gone and Grace and Lottie were in their accustomed places, I turned my attention to the orders on the spindle. The first one was an arrangement for a woman's fortieth birthday. Her husband had requested brightly colored blossoms using anything but roses, which he considered extravagantly expensive, so I circled around the big slate-topped worktable in the middle of the room and walked over to the giant coolers where we stored our fresh flowers.

Inside the left cooler, I surveyed my stock and decided on an orange and yellow color scheme, perfect for late summer. I pulled stems of *Dahlia* 'Golden Charmer', with its wonderfully large flower head; the delicate, lily-like *Crocosmia* 'Rowallane Yellow'; the creamy yellow spikes of *Gladiolus tristis*; and *Chrysanthemum* 'Sunny Le Mans', a yellow flower with an orange center. I added green fern leaves to the mix, then carried them back to the table where my tools lay.

Nothing relaxed me as much as arranging flowers. While I prepared the pot, trimmed stems, and created my living masterpiece, I was in a zone, totally engrossed in what I was doing. In that state, I worked my way through seven orders, until a familiar "Yoo-hoo" from the other side of the curtain caught my attention.

Mom had arrived.

Correction: Mom *and* her latest work of art — my third piece of bad luck. The day was complete.

CHAPTER SIX

Before I could mentally prepare myself for her latest atrocity, the curtain parted and Maureen "Mad Mo" Knight burst into the room with a big box in her arms. She was followed by my thirteen-year-old niece, Tara, who bounced with excitement.

"Grandma has a surprise for you, Aunt Abby," Tara sang out.

The noun *surprise* never did Mom's creations justice. *Shock*, maybe.

I put down my floral knife and pasted on a smile. "Oh, boy. Can't wait."

"I hope we're not disturbing you, Abigail," Mom said, looking around for a place to set the carton.

Whether I was disturbed would depend greatly on what was inside the box.

You would never know it from her often outrageous creations, but my mother is a quiet, kindhearted, church-going kindergarten teacher who raised my two brothers and me with a firm hand. She stands five feet five inches tall, has light brown hair shot through with a few gray hairs, golden brown eyes, and creamy skin with nary a freckle to mar it. Lucky her.

Usually her outfit was geared to working with five-year-olds, but because she was still on summer break, she was wearing a short-sleeved floral-print blouse and light green capris with beige sandals.

Tara twirled around me. "Set it on the worktable, Grandma. Hurry! I can't wait to see Aunt Abby's reaction."

Being a teen, Tara took enormous satisfaction in viewing any form of torture, especially when it involved me. She's the only grandchild in our family, born when I was fourteen years old, which sometimes makes her feel like my kid sister more than my niece. She also looks a lot like me, with blunt-cut, shoulder-length red hair, short nose, freckles, and short stature. Today she had on a bold pink short-sleeved T-shirt over a plum cami, a stack of silver bangle bracelets on each wrist, skinny white ankle jeans, and silver flats.

"Calm down, Tara," Mom said. "Abigail, turn around and close your eyes."

"Wait, Grandma," Tara said before she could open the box. "Let's tell Aunt Abby what we named it and see if she can guess what it is."

"You tell her," Mom said. "You're the one who came up with the name."

"It's *Night Shades on Elm Tree*." Tara pressed her hands together, her eyes sparkling impishly. "Okay, now guess!"

"I give up."

"Come on, Aunt Abby, you didn't even try!" Tara whined.

"Aunt Abby is kind of busy," I said, giving my mom a pleading look.

Mom responded by opening the box. "We don't have time for games, Tara. Your aunt needs to get back to work so she can keep her business from going under."

She stuck her hands inside the box and lifted. Out

came a two-foot-tall elm tree made from brown and green clay. "*This* should help draw in the customers."

Okay. Nothing freakish about a tree sculpture, even one with the same name, coincidentally, as the street on which the Osbornes' cottage was located. Nothing that would scare away customers either—or draw them in.

Mom pulled out a handful of fabric and handed it to Tara. She reached in for another handful and the two set to work decorating the tree, their backs blocking my view.

With a "Ta da," they stepped back for me to see. What I saw were brightly colored, coaster-sized felt flowers strung on green cords, two blossoms per cord. Still nothing freakish about them, but what was their purpose?

Drawing a blank, I said, "Colorful!"

Tara giggled. "You don't know what they're for, and that's because you haven't thought about the name I gave them."

"Night shades on elm tree?" I plucked a green cord off the aforementioned tree. The cord was stretchy and had two daisies attached to it. "Is it a mask?"

"What kind of mask?" Tara asked, bouncing up and down on her toes.

"Put it on over your eyes," Mom said.

I did as requested. "Okay, not a mask because I can't see anything. And the cord is really tight. Ouch. Oh, wait! Is it a sleep mask?"

"Ding, ding, ding," Tara cried.

"Hold still," Mom said. "I'll take a photo with my phone."

"Lordy!" I heard Lottie cry. "What the hollyhocks is that?"

I snapped off the mask and saw her staring at me in amazement.

"They're night shades," Mom said. "Look at the cute picture I took of Abigail wearing them."

The two women stood side by side, gazing at the image on her phone. Lottie was trying hard not to laugh. Grace glided through the curtain and peered over Mom's shoulder; then Lottie and Grace looked at each other. The expression on their faces said it all.

"Come see, Abigail," Mom said, while Tara stood off to one side pinching her lips shut.

Heaving a resigned sigh, I took a peek. With my red hair sticking out at all angles where the cord pinched my scalp, and a big white daisy with a yellow center covering each eye socket area, including my eyebrows, I resembled a cartoon bug.

"Look how cute you are," Mom said.

Cute? Only if I'd been cast in a movie entitled *Cowboys and Alien Flower Heads*. Luckily, she'd made only a dozen or so.

Grace plucked another mask from a branch of the tree and held it up. "Are these petunias?"

"Yes, and they come in pink or purple," Mom said. "We also have oak-leaf masks for men and maple-leaf masks for our Canadian friends."

"You need anthurium masks, Grandma," Tara said, then giggled. "My friends would totally buy them."

"Stop that, Tara," Mom said sharply.

My niece dissolved into laughter. She found anthurium immensely funny because of its spadix, a cylindrical spike that protruded from the shield-shaped petal called a spathe.

"My sea glass sunglasses sold out, so I thought I'd keep the eye theme going," Mom said, slipping on a purple petunia mask to demonstrate. "These are better than anything sold in the drugstores because each flower operates independently, so if you need to reach for something on your nightstand, you needn't remove the entire mask. Just flip up one side."

"Clever idea, Maureen," Grace said.

"How much for a pair?" Lottie asked. "I could use some myself. Herman reads with his light on till all hours."

"What do you think, Abigail?" Mom asked.

"We sold the sunglasses for ten dollars a pair," I said. "We can't charge more than that."

"Six dollars and ninety-nine cents," Grace said.

Mom smiled. "That's perfect. I'll go get the other boxes. Come help me, Tara."

I could hear Lottie's and Grace's sharp intakes of air as Mom's words echoed through the shop.

Other boxes?

"She made night shades?" Marco asked, as we headed toward the Osborne cottage.

"More like fright shades," I said, blotting mustard off my lip. "And now we have fifty pairs to sell. Correction, forty-eight. Grace and Lottie each bought a pair. I think they took pity on Mom. And by the way, delicious roast beef sandwich."

"Thanks. Maybe I'll buy a pair of the shades for my mom and Gina, and then you'll only have forty-six to sell."

I leaned across the console to lay my head against his shoulder. "You'd do that for Mom?"

"I'm doing it for you, baby."

My heart did a cartwheel. Make that a pinwheel. One theme at a time. "Have I told you today that I love you?"

Marco's mouth turned up at the corners. When he gazed at me, I saw love shimmering in his dark eyes. He reached over for my hand and brought it to his lips.

Sometimes words weren't necessary.

I inhaled, expanding my lungs, feeling such happiness that I wondered if I could sustain it. If I thought too much about it, would I jinx myself?

My cell phone rang. I dug it out of my purse and saw Grace's name on the screen. "Hi, Grace. What's up?"

"Abby, love, I was checking our Web site for orders and saw a message for you from a party supplier. I thought you might want to act on it."

"What does it say?"

"They are low on the flower pinwheels for your shower. They can put them on back order, if you'd like, but it may take three weeks before they get them in."

"I'll have to order them from another supplier. Thanks for letting me know, Grace."

"Would you like me to ring up another company for you?"

I hesitated, wavering. If I let Grace help with my shower, would the others be far behind? But without a smart phone at hand, when would I have time to call around? "How about finding the numbers of a few other places so I can make the calls when I get back to the shop?"

"I shall leave them on your desk, dear. Ta."

I dropped my phone into my purse with a sigh. "Wonderful. I thought I had everything lined up except for the juggler."

Marco gave me a sidelong glance. "You're going to have a juggler at the shower?"

"You said no games, Marco, so I thought we should have some form of entertainment. I put in a call to a juggler I found in the phone book, so he should be getting back to me."

"A juggler."

"What's wrong with that?"

He hunched his shoulders. "Nothing."

Great. Marco didn't like it. What other kind of entertainment could I provide? "How about karaoke?"

Marco gazed at me with lowered eyebrows. Yet another time when words weren't necessary.

"Then you come up with something," I said.

"Why do we need a shower anyway?"

"I've already explained that, Marco. It's traditional. Part of our culture. Women expect to be invited to them—bridal, baby, retirement, even new-home showers on occasion. I wouldn't be surprised if they even had showers for—"

"The juggler is fine."

"Awesome."

Marco turned off the main highway and headed east. "Are you psyched up for this evening?"

"For another close encounter of the Osborne kind? I think so. I hope so. Make that a yes. Definitely yes. I am *psyched*, Marco."

"Coolheaded?"

"Yes! Psyched *and* coolheaded."

At Marco's skeptical look, I added, "For the moment anyway. I promise to try my best not to let Pryce get under my skin."

"You can always wait inside the cottage while I interview him."

"No way. I'm your wingman, Marco. I'll do Claymore's interview solo, though, if you want to take on Jillian."

A glance from Marco was enough to squelch that idea.

"Okay," I said with a resigned sigh. "I'll handle Jillian."

"Will it help if I throw in a foot rub for later tonight?"

"You are so on." I practically salivated in anticipation. Marco had the best hands in the world when it came to many things, but he was especially terrific at massages. And who knew where that might lead?

When we arrived at 5:25 p.m., Pryce was pacing the verandah as though we were an hour late. He had changed his clothes and was wearing a blue Tommy Bahama shirt instead of a tan one, with perfectly pressed brown walking shorts and brown leather sandals. He had us sit at the long teak table at one end of the side verandah and offered us iced tea from a white ceramic pitcher.

"Thank you," Marco said, accepting a tall glass. I merely nodded my thanks. We were sitting side by side, with Pryce opposite us.

"Will you be taping our conversation?" Pryce asked.

I held up my pen and the notepad. "This is it."

"Did you want your interview recorded?" Marco asked. "I have the equipment in my car."

"Whatever you deem appropriate is fine with me," Pryce said. "I understand that my interview is merely a formality anyway."

I glanced at Marco in surprise, but he showed no reaction, so I bit my tongue and let Pryce continue.

"Obviously I wouldn't have called on you to investigate if I'd had anything to do with Melissa's disappearance. Therefore I'm hoping we can move through this quickly so she can be found."

"I'll try to make it as expeditious as possible," Marco said.

In the face of Pryce's superciliousness, Marco was so calm and composed that he inspired me to be the same. I took a drink of the refreshing tea, determined to keep my cool.

"To start with, where does Melissa live?" Marco asked.

"On West Lincoln Avenue. I'm not sure of the exact address, but she has the second-floor apartment above Pisces. That's the name of her shop."

"I know where that is," I said to Marco as I wrote down the information.

"Do you have any credit card information for Melissa?" Marco asked.

"No," Pryce said.

"You stated earlier that you and Melissa had a disagreement after she arrived on Friday," Marco said. "What was it about?"

Pryce adjusted his platinum watchband. It was either to show how insignificant he considered that question or to make sure we noticed his display of wealth—or possibly both, not that it bothered me. Gazing at Marco, with his easy manner—and his simple Timex—made my heart double in size. What a wonderful contrast he was to Pryce's snobbishness.

"I'd prefer that to remain private," Pryce said.

"I understand how you feel," Marco said, "but the information helps me form a profile so I have a better feel for Melissa's situation. Rest assured that whatever you say will remain confidential."

I could tell immediately that my ex-fiancé didn't appear to be convinced by Marco's assurances. That was when my cool began to heat up. "Pryce, we're not going to ask you anything unless it will help us find Melissa."

"I understand that, Abigail."

"Good, then decide now whether you're going to cooperate—otherwise we're out of here."

Sensing my rising temper, Marco patted my knee under the table, while Pryce stared at me as though he'd never heard me speak before. "Of course I want to cooperate."

"Super. Then what was your disagreement about?" I asked.

"Melissa and I were discussing our engagement."

Snap. Just like that, I was taken back to that horrible evening when Pryce had said to me in an offhand way, *We need to discuss our engagement*, much like a person might say, *We need to choose entrées for our dinner party*. And then he'd pulled the rug out from under me.

Shaking off that memory, I said, "Wait a minute. You told us before that you and Melissa had a disagreement. Which was it, a discussion or a disagreement? There's a big difference between the two."

"Perhaps *disagreement* was a poor word choice. Let's just say we had a discussion about our irresolvable differences."

Did he *try* to obfuscate his answers?

"What was the outcome of your discussion?" Marco asked.

"By mutual agreement, Melissa and I decided to go our separate ways."

I knew exactly what Pryce's definition of a mutual agreement was: He spelled out the alleged offenses as dictated by his parents, then suggested the engagement be broken off quickly and quietly, and she reacted accordingly—with shock, disbelief, needing to cry but not wanting Pryce to know just how devastated she was, and finally with concession, ending with a tearful, *I guess it's over, then*.

Oh, yes, been there, done that, had the scars.

"That happened on Friday, and yet Melissa stayed for the weekend?" I asked.

"We weren't able to reach an accord until Sunday morning," Pryce said.

My mouth dropped open. Did he have to make it sound like two warring countries coming together for a summit meeting?

Marco gave my knee another pat, reminding me to sit back and relax. "What were the terms of your accord?" he asked, as though this were a situation he encountered all the time.

"We agreed upon who will initiate refunds on reception reservations, notify invitees of the event correction, cancel postwedding travel arrangements, and rescind exchanges of precious metals."

Yep, he was purposefully obfuscating. "What is an event correction?" I asked. "Is that Osborne-speak for calling off the wedding?"

"It's not Osborne-speak," Pryce said stiffly. "But yes, that's what it boils down to."

Then the metals he was rescinding had to be the engagement ring and wedding bands.

Marco's gaze shifted my way for a split second, conveying the message, *How did you ever get mixed up with this guy?*

Simple. I'd been naive and trusting and way too logical for my own good. I had learned a big lesson, though. My decision to marry had to be based on more than whether a man was financially responsible, although that was important. From Marco, I'd learned that any solid relationship had to come from love, friendship, mutual respect, and admiration. When any of those were missing, the relationship was doomed.

"Where were you and Melissa during your Sunday-morning meeting?" Marco asked.

Pryce took a drink of tea before answering. "In the kitchen."

"Were the two of you alone?"

"I assume we're not counting staff," Pryce answered.

"If by staff you mean other human beings," I said, "then count them, because on my planet we consider staff humans."

Marco nudged me ever so subtly, so I added, "Please?"

"The caterer and his helper were in the kitchen," Pryce said, "and Mrs. Ambrose was serving breakfast to the guests seated on the deck."

"Who would that have been?" Marco asked.

"I believe it was just Jake and Lily. The Burches had gone home Saturday afternoon and didn't return until lunchtime on Sunday."

"What happened after your meeting?" Marco asked.

"It was time for my run on the beach," Pryce said, "so I went upstairs to the bedroom to change into my running gear. While I was changing, Melissa came in for her hat and said she was going for a walk because she needed to cool down. That was the last time I saw her."

I wrote: *Pryce broke engagement / Melissa's heart, then went for scheduled run. Cold.*

"Did you and Melissa share a bedroom?" Marco asked.

"She shared *my* room," Pryce said, trying to see what I wrote down. I'd have to add *said the presumptuous bore* later.

"What was Melissa wearing when she left the house?" Marco asked.

Without pausing to think, Pryce said, "Coral tank top, white shorts, coral ankle socks, white sneakers, and a white panama sun hat with a straw visor."

"That was quick," I muttered as I wrote it down.

"I selected the outfit for her."

I looked up in surprise. "Why would you choose her clothes?"

Marco leaned close to whisper, "It's not relevant."

"If you must know," Pryce said, "it's because Melissa has . . . questionable taste in clothing."

Was that one of his deal breakers?

"Does Melissa have any family?" Marco asked.

"A brother in Chicago by the name of Harry Hazelton," Pryce said. "I've been in touch with Harry and he's heard nothing from her."

"We'll need his contact information," Marco said.

"I have it in my office," Pryce said. "I'll get it when we're finished, which should be shortly, shouldn't it?"

"Should be," Marco said. "Have you tried to call or text Melissa today?"

"Yes. Her phone goes straight to voice mail and my texts are unanswered."

"What do you think happened to her?" Marco asked.

"As I told you this morning," Pryce said, "she may have been abducted. She has a substantial portfolio, even with all the stock market losses she suffered."

"Were the losses due to investment mistakes?" Marco asked.

"Yes. She got some bad advice."

"From her broker?" I asked.

"Melissa would have to answer that."

Pryce was being very tight-lipped about it. Had he lost money, as well? Had Halston given them both bad advice or was another broker involved?

"If Melissa had been abducted for money," Marco said, "you or her brother would have received a ransom note or some other form of demand by now."

"I haven't received anything," Pryce said, stretching his arms behind his back, as though he was tired of sitting, "and I know Harry would alert me if he did. He knows I'm frantic."

Was that the picture of a frantic person?

"Does Harry know you broke off your engagement to his sister?" I asked.

Pryce's arms came forward. "Is there a reason you need to know that?"

"If Harry knows," I said, "he might not feel inclined to contact you."

Pryce glowered. "I didn't tell him about it. That's up to Melissa."

"Considering that you broke up with *her*," I said, "isn't it possible Melissa is cooling her heels somewhere to make you sweat?"

"Excuse me?" he asked.

I'd forgotten. Osbornes never sweated. They perspired. Besides, Pryce *was* the heel.

I started anew. "Did she run away to punish you for behaving like an a—"

"I know what you're asking," Pryce said sharply, "and I can't imagine her putting her family and friends through this."

I could imagine her putting Pryce through it, though.

My cell phone vibrated. I pulled it out of my purse and checked the screen. It was a text message from Jillian: *We R almost there.*

Alert the media.

"Did you notice any animosity or tension between Melissa and any of your houseguests at all this weekend?" Marco asked.

"I did not," Pryce said.

"Did Melissa mention any difficulties she might have been having at work?" Marco asked.

"She and I did not converse much between Friday evening and Sunday morning. We were out on the lake most of the day Saturday, with a party at the Burches' in the evening."

My phone vibrated again, causing both Marco and Pryce to glance my way. "Sorry," I said, checking the screen. It was another text from Jillian: *Found prfct baby name. W8 til U hear.*

Before I could reply to her to stop texting me, she sent another: *Get Xcited. We R here!* ☺

Yay. ☹

CHAPTER SEVEN

As both men seemed to be waiting for me to enlighten them on the interruption, I said, "That was Jillian. She and Claymore are here."

Pryce glanced at his watch. "Good. I'd like to get these interviews done and the search started as soon as possible."

"I understand," Marco said. "Let's go back to when Melissa arrived on Friday evening. Where were you and she sitting?"

"Over there." Pryce pointed to a group of chairs and a wicker love seat at the other end of the verandah.

"Where do the Burches live?" Marco asked.

Again Pryce pointed to the opposite end of the verandah. "The next cottage over. You can just make it out through the pine trees."

"If the Burches were standing outside their house having an argument, would you be able to hear them?" Marco asked.

"No. There's too much woodland between our cottages. Why do you ask?"

"Orabell claims to have overheard your argument with Melissa," I said.

"Impossible," Pryce said. "I've been vacationing at this cottage for most of my life and have never heard voices from their side. She must have heard gulls calling. Their cries can sound quite human at times."

At that moment, a woman, or possibly a gull, warbled from the house next door, "Hello-o-o, hello-o-o!"

Turning, I caught a flash of magenta, as though someone was waving a flag. "Like that gull?" I asked.

Pryce cupped his forehead with his palm. "That would be Orabell."

I hid my smile.

"Come one, come all!" the gull-woman said. "It's time for after-dinner cocktails."

"We'll be over shortly, Orabell!" Jillian called back cheerily, as she and Claymore came up the path toward the verandah.

Always the fashion plate, Jillian had on a V-neck mint green ankle-length sundress, a large-beaded necklace in mint green, bright peach, and silver, a stack of silver bangles on each wrist, and silver flip-flops with a kitten heel. She far outshone her husband, who had on a golf shirt and shorts in shades of cream and beige that blended with his sandy hair and fair skin. Had he been climbing a sand dune, he would've been impossible to spot.

"No, we won't be right over," I said to my cousin as she came toward us. "We haven't finished with Pryce's interview yet, and we still have all the others to do."

Claymore turned toward Pryce and said in a low voice, "I thought you told me your interview would take only five minutes."

"We got a late start," Pryce murmured back.

I glanced at Marco, and he pressed my knee to let me know he'd caught the lie.

"Hold it," I said to Jillian, who had just pulled out a

chair at the end of the table nearest to me. "You can't stay."

Jillian huffed, her cheery mood turning sour. "I hope you're not planning to keep us here all evening. The Burches have cocktails waiting."

"Calm down," I said. "You can't drink anyway."

I saw her eyes widen to the size of satellite dishes and immediately realized my gaffe. My *enormous* gaffe. Marco, too, was staring, as were the Osborne brothers, who were obviously baffled by my comment.

"What I mean is that you *shouldn't* have a drink," I said, "because . . . well, *you* know how mixed drinks have always affected your sleep . . . when you have them after seven thirty in the evening . . . as I recall."

It was lame but the best I could manage on short notice. I lowered my gaze and picked at the place mat, as Jillian was giving me the death stare.

"Abby's right, dearest," Claymore said. "You know how restless you get at night after an evening cocktail."

"That happens to me, too," Pryce said, as though it were a revelation. "I believe I read somewhere that it has to do with the body's circadian rhythm."

"I must have read that very same article," Claymore exclaimed.

Both men nodded, as though that was the most logical explanation for Jillian's alleged reaction, when, in fact, I'd always witnessed just the opposite. But as long as they bought it, what did I care?

Claymore took his wife's arm. "Let's go to the kitchen and have some tea while we're waiting. I believe there's even coconut fudge ice cream in the freezer with your name on it."

That not only didn't appease Jillian; it made her ill. Turning a sickly ashen color, she put her hand over her mouth, pushed him aside, and dashed for the front door.

"I forgot," Claymore said, his cheeks coloring, "she doesn't like coconut."

"It makes me queasy, too," Pryce said. "Perhaps you should toss it out."

As Claymore followed Jillian inside, Marco said to me, "Did you have any questions for Pryce?"

"Yes, a few."

Pryce checked the time, but I pretended not to notice. "How would you describe Melissa's relationship with Lily?"

"Amicable."

I jotted it down. "How was Melissa's relationship with Orabell?"

"Amicable, as she was with everyone who was here."

"How is the relationship between Melissa and your parents?"

I saw Pryce's spine stiffen. "You can't possibly think they would have anything to do with her disappearance."

"It doesn't matter what I think," I told him. "We're gathering information, remember?"

Somewhat mollified, Pryce replied, "My parents have a good relationship with Melissa."

"Even after the redecorating job Melissa did in the living room?" I asked.

Pryce placed his palms on the table and rose. "We're finished."

No, no, no! Not until I said so. Pryce Osborne II wasn't about to call the shots on my investigation. "Just a minute, Pryce."

He sat back down and waited, but wouldn't look at me.

"Where are your parents? I'm amazed that they're not here."

"They're traveling," Pryce said, his lips barely moving, as though he hated telling me anything about the elder Osbornes. "I haven't mentioned Melissa's disappearance to them because I know they'll interrupt their trip to come back." He started to rise, then paused. "Are we done now?"

"One more thing. We need contact information for Melissa's brother."

"I was on my way to get that, Abigail."

"Okay, then you can go."

Marco got up and reached across to shake Pryce's hand. "Thanks for your cooperation."

Pryce returned the shake, gave me a cool nod, then went inside.

"Were you trying to make him angry?" Marco asked quietly.

"No, I just didn't want him deciding when the interview was over."

Marco gave me a look that said he wasn't buying it.

"Seriously, Marco, that's all it was."

"Even the dig about Melissa's decorating skills?"

"It wasn't a dig. I was trying to get him to be truthful."

He studied me for a moment, which made me squirm, but at least he didn't belabor the subject. "Okay, let's get our interviews wrapped up. Do you want to talk to Jillian in the kitchen and send Claymore out here?"

"On my way," I said, pushing back my chair. I gave him a quick hug. "I couldn't resist that."

Marco put his hands on either side of my face and kissed me for a long moment. "Neither could I. Now you'd better go before I get serious."

Serious worked for me. My blood was coursing from that hot kiss. But we had a job to do, so I gave him a sheet of paper from the notebook for his notes, as well as a longing glance, and went inside.

Claymore was pouring tea into a gold-rimmed ivory china cup, while my cousin sat at the kitchen table with her chin in her hands, looking pale and unhappy. I pulled out a chair across from her and readied my pen. "Okay, you're next. Claymore, Marco is waiting on the por—verandah."

"Would you care for tea before I go?" Claymore asked me.

"No, thanks."

"Is there anything else I can get you before I leave, my darling?" Claymore asked Jillian.

"Just go away, Claymore."

Like a scolded puppy, he put his head down and quietly left the room.

"That was cruel," I said. "He was only trying to make you feel better."

Jillian sighed miserably. "I know. It's just that lately I can't stand his hovering. It makes me want to scream. Then I suddenly start to cry. For no reason. What's up with that?"

"Hormones," I said. "They'll even out by your second trimester."

She cast me a baleful glance. "How did you get to be such an expert?"

"Remember when Nikki's sister Diana was expecting? I think we were in our senior year of high school. Nikki was so excited about being an aunt that she updated me on her sister's condition ad nauseam."

Jillian sighed again. "That's the worst part."

"What is?"

"The nauseum."

"No, Jill, it's not naus—"

"And by the way, thanks for almost letting the cat out of the bag."

"I'm really sorry about that. It just slipped out."

"Let's talk in the living room. On second thought, I need fresh air, so let's take a walk on the beach. I can't stand to go in the living room. Talk about adding nauseam."

"What happened to the living room?" I asked, following her through the house. "It used to be so charming."

"Melissa happened." Jillian opened a sliding glass door and led me onto the wide cedar deck, where I saw four sets of teak tables and chairs shaded by large, tan umbrellas, a wicker settee, and a pair of chaise longues.

We headed down a set of concrete stairs that led from the deck to their in-ground pool. From there, we left the pool area through a gate at the back and walked out onto a wide swath of beach. Far ahead, I saw a dinghy and a motorboat docked at their private pier, the scene of Pryce's proposal to me. Farther out, a pair of sailboats raced each other, and gulls soared overhead. We both paused to take off our sandals.

"I understand Melissa happened," I said, trying to match Jillian's long-legged stride, "but how did her work ever pass inspection?"

"PJ and Evelyn gave Melissa free rein. *Big* mistake."

It took me a moment to remember who PJ was, but then it clicked. Pryce's father was Pryce Osborne, Jr., or PJ, as his own father had dubbed him, and Pryce's mother was Evelyn. Pryce, born after his grandfather had died, had apparently not needed a nickname, which was probably for the best. I couldn't think of a short moniker that fit him, or at least one that would be usable in polite company. "Why did they give her free rein?"

"It gets complicated, but basically it was because Pryce was going to marry her. They were trying to help him by promoting Melissa as this hot new designer. So to prove how talented she was, they told her to redo the foyer and living room and then they'd have a huge open house to show it off. And in their defense, they had talked with her beforehand and assumed she knew their tastes, especially since she'd been in both their cottage and their house."

"Shame on the Osbornes for assuming," I said.

"Shame on Melissa for believing she's an interior decorator," Jillian countered.

"Shame on the Osbornes for not checking her references."

"All I can say is, thank goodness they didn't have her go any further. Can you imagine the damage she could have done to the rest of the house?"

"What were PJ's and Evelyn's reactions after they saw the living room?" I said, starting to feel the heat of the sun on my freckled face.

Jillian stopped to pick up a white shell. "I wasn't there, but Claymore told me his mother nearly fainted. She said she'd been humiliated in front of their entire social set. PJ had to take her upstairs to lie down."

This was getting interesting. "Didn't they preview the room before inviting people over?"

"They'd planned the open house weeks beforehand. Then an opportunity to go to Australia came up, so they turned everything over to Melissa and Pryce. They didn't return until the evening before the party, and didn't come out to the cottage until the day *of* the party."

"Where was Pryce while Melissa was doing the redecorating?"

"Not here obviously. But that isn't all the Osbornes are upset about." Jillian threw the shell far out into the water. "Based on Evelyn's recommendation, a lot of people on Haven Lake hired Melissa to do cottage makeovers, including Halston and Orabell. Since they live next door, Melissa decided to do theirs and the Osbornes' at the same time."

"I'm guessing their redo didn't go well either."

"Orabell insisted on staying at the cottage to oversee the work, so it's probably okay, but why do you think I want to go over there for cocktails?"

"Because you're nosy."

"You say that like it's a bad thing."

Not when I'd inherited the nosy gene, too.

"Melissa was also hired to redo a cottage a few houses down from the Burches', way down that way," she said, pointing, "but the owners were so appalled by the design she presented them that they fired her on the spot and then complained loud and long to everyone at the country club.

"You can imagine Evelyn's embarrassment," Jillian continued. "There she was touting Pryce's new fiancée's amazing talent, and it turned into a fiasco, which, as we know now, turned into Melissa's broken engagement. Thank God I didn't disappoint them. And by the way, you know you're making a huge mistake not to let me choose your shower outfit, don't you?"

"This may sound off the wall, but is it possible Evelyn and/or PJ paid Melissa to leave town?"

"Well, duh. Of course it's possible. You know how the Osbornes are. You can't embarrass them in front of their peers and come out exscathed."

"Unscathed."

Jillian thought it over, then bent to pick up another shell. "My word sounds more terrifying."

I couldn't argue with that. "Did Melissa get along with the people who were here over the weekend?"

"Can you put *get along* in quotes? Because Melissa"— Jillian made air quotes with her fingers—"*got along* with everyone."

"Explain what you mean by"—I made air quotes—"*got along.*"

"It means she didn't."

"You could have just said she didn't."

"I'm a fan of satire."

"Jillian, you can't even spell sat—never mind. Who

didn't Melissa get along with—excluding Pryce, obviously?"

Jillian gasped. "How could I have forgotten?"

"Tell me."

"I haven't told you the baby's name yet! You're going to love it, Abs. It's totally unique. Okay, get ready. Here it comes. It's . . . Emerald!"

I blinked a few times, letting it sink in. "Emerald Osborne?"

"With emerald being the most expensive gemstone on the planet *and* the best color for redheads, it's perfect, isn't it?"

"For a munchkin maybe."

She tilted her head, catlike. "What?"

"Is it your intention to make people think of the Emerald City in *The Wizard of Oz* when they hear your baby's name?"

"You lost me."

"Emerald *Os*-borne, Jillian."

She thought it over, then tossed the shell over her shoulder with a frustrated huff. "You are so dejuvinating."

"You know that's not a word."

"And you know how to burst a person's bubble." At that, Jillian began to cry, covering her face with her hands. "I can't believe you hate my baby's name."

"I don't *hate* it."

Sniffling, she peered at me through her fingers. "Did you put *hate* in air quotes?"

"Marco is going to be finished interviewing Claymore and we've hardly begun. I thought you wanted to help me with this case."

"I'm sorry. I do want to be helpful, I really do, and I have a lot of information for you. I just feel so antijubilant now because I don't want my baby to be associated with little green people. I don't want her to be associated with anything. I want her to be her own person."

Jillian started sobbing again, so I didn't have the heart to scold her for making up another word. I fished a tissue out of my pocket and stuffed it in her hand. "It's okay. You'll find a name."

"No, it's not okay. I want to be here for you, Abs." She blew her nose, tried to hand back the tissue, and ended up stuffing it into her skirt pocket. After taking some deep breaths and wiping away her tears with the backs of her hands, she asked, "What was the question again?"

It had been so long ago, I'd nearly forgotten. "About Melissa getting along with the other guests."

"Oh, right. Okay, here's the scoop. Melissa has strong opinions about everything and hates anyone showing her up, but otherwise, she's really friendly."

Jillian could have been describing herself.

"I should amend that," Jillian said. "Melissa is"—she made air quotes—"*faux-friendly* to Lily."

"Why to Lily? And just a side note here. When you put *faux* in front of the word, you don't need air quotes. The sarcasm is implied."

Jillian looked at me as if I were speaking ancient Greek. She finally waved it off with a, "Whatever. Anyway, you knew Lily and Pryce were college classmates, right? Well, I've heard"—Jillian leaned closer and said in a low voice—"that they were lovers during their senior year. *And* that Lily moved to New Chapel after she finished her culinary apprenticeship so she could renew their relationship, but Pryce had just gotten engaged to you."

"Pryce never mentioned having a relationship with Lily."

"You know Pryce. When something is over, he moves on. But just wait. It gets juicier. After Pryce broke up with you, Lily set her sights on him again, and then Pryce got engaged to Melissa."

"Ouch. That must have hurt. But if Pryce and Lily have such a history, why did he choose Melissa over her?"

"To be honest, I think Melissa was chosen for him." Jillian glanced over her shoulder, then whispered, "By his parents."

"Melissa probably has a better pedigree."

"Way better. Her parents were blue bloods from Boston, and Melissa and her brother inherited a boatload of money when they passed away. Plus Melissa is attractive in a wholesome kind of way, and personable. She just doesn't have what it takes to be a great interior decorator."

"Poor Melissa," I said. "Now that the Osbornes have been publicly humiliated, her reputation will be in shreds, not to mention her heart. I wouldn't blame her at all for wanting to hide for a while."

"If she's hiding," Jillian said, stopping, "I'll be so annoyed."

"You'd rather something bad has happened to her?"

"Of course not, but she should have more concern for our feelings."

"I doubt whether she was thinking of everyone else's feelings after just having been dumped, Jill. Speaking of feelings, though, is Pryce aware that Lily still carries a torch for him?"

"I don't know how he could miss it." Jillian shivered. "Let's start back. Do you feel that chill in the air?"

I wiped perspiration off my forehead as we turned to head back. "Definitely no chill. Is Melissa aware of Lily's feelings for Pryce?"

"She has to be aware. Lily doesn't hide her feelings or edit her thoughts. Whatever she thinks comes straight out of her mouth. She has no tact at all."

"That reminds me of someone *else* I know."

"Me, too!" the clueless one said. "But Evelyn is my mother-in-law, so what am I supposed to do about it?"

I counted to ten silently, then took a deep breath. "How long have Lily and Jake been married?"

"Two, three, four months. My memory is a little foggy. Am I getting senile?"

"It's hormones. What is their marriage like?"

"Jake adores Lily. Lily adores Lily. In that respect, they're on the same page."

"Don't you think it's awkward for Lily and Jake to be staying here with Pryce?"

"If I were Jake, I wouldn't stand for it. I mean, surely he notices something! But he can't exactly demand that they rent a place while their renovation is going on, since he wouldn't be the one paying. So as long as Lily is calling the shots, of course she'll accept Pryce's invitation to stay here."

"Then you think Jake knows about Lily's feelings for Pryce?"

"I don't know what Jake knows, but anyone watching how chummy Pryce and Lily are would have to sense a bond between them. Okay, another amendment: Jake isn't the sharpest knife in the block, so maybe he doesn't know."

Jillian tapped her chin. "On the other hand, maybe he does know, because now that I think about it, Jake was flirting pretty heavily with Melissa this weekend, and that's unusual for him. He usually dotes on Lily, but since she supports him, he might feel obligated to dote.

"Then again, rumors have been flying all week that Pryce was going to break up with Melissa, and that helped restart old rumors about Pryce and Lily, so maybe Jake heard the rumors and figured it out and decided to make Lily jealous, and *that's* why he was flirting with Melissa. Then *again*, rumor has it that Pryce still carries a torch for you, so there you go."

Jillian was rambling. It was a good thing I wasn't trying to take notes. "If Jake senses anything at all, Jillian, I'd think he'd be worried about Lily leaving him."

"He should be worried! Everyone knows Lily married Jake on the rebound, so now that Pryce and Melissa aren't an item any longer, I'd bet that Lily will ditch Jake for Pryce."

"But is Lily being realistic? Besides the fact that Pryce has ignored her twice, would she meet the Osborne standards?"

"With the success she's had at Beached in the past several months, that would *not* be a problem, Abs. Lily is gorgeous, trendy, *and* making money. She's also tough as nails—a real tyrant at the bistro—which would be a plus for the Osbornes. As PJ always says, he didn't make his money by being the Pillsbury Doughboy."

Not being gorgeous, or trendy, or a tyrant, or making money, I must have been a big problem for the Osbornes. Was *doughy* how they had viewed me?

Jillian sighed. "It's a vicious world out there, Abs. You're fortunate you're so out of the loop."

"Thanks for that. Let's move on to the Burches."

Jillian fanned her face. "I'm boiling."

"It's hormones. Don't worry about it."

Jillian cast me an exasperated look. "Is that going to be your answer to everything now?"

"You were saying about the Burches?"

"The Burches . . . well, from the looks I saw passing between them, Orabell and Halston must have had words before we arrived at their house Saturday evening, because Orabell would barely speak to him. And she took every opportunity she could to get in nasty little digs about Lily's food, which Lily catered for our Saturday-evening meal. And PS, her dinner was excellent."

The weekend was sounding more and more like a soap opera. "Why would Orabell take potshots at Lily if she was angry at Halston?"

"I don't think those two things are connected, Abs."

"Then disconnect them for me."

"Unconnect."

Jillian never challenged me on a word, so for a moment, I was confused. "No, I think it's disconnect."

"Want to bet?"

"I don't care which it is. Just explain!"

Shivering now, Jillian hugged herself. "Well, along with her nasty food comments, Orabell kept hinting that Lily took one of her designer watches. And *those* two things *are* connected, because Orabell was obviously trying to get Lily to confess to taking the Piaget by making her angry about her food."

"I don't know Lily. Is she trustworthy, or does Orabell have a reason to suspect her?"

Jillian covered a yawn. "Lily has been catering parties around the lake all summer and nothing has ever been reported stolen by anyone else."

"Is it possible Lily's bistro isn't doing as well as you think?"

"It's jammed every night." Jillian yawned again. "I think I need a nap—and don't you dare say the *H* word again."

"What was Lily's reaction to Orabell's jibes?"

"She ignored them for a while. Then she began to mock Orabell. I thought they were going to come to blows before the evening was over."

"Didn't Halston try to mediate?"

"Halston's very protective of Orabell, but his way of handling discord is to make light of it. Unfortunately, it doesn't always solve the problem. I could tell Orabell was mad at him for not taking a stand."

"So we have Orabell and Halston at odds, Jake flirting with Melissa, Orabell and Lily exchanging insults, Halston cracking jokes, and Pryce and Melissa not talking to each other. This might seem like a foolish question, but why does everyone get together when it doesn't seem like anyone gets along?"

"For one thing, these weekend get-togethers take place only during August, when Halston has a month off. You might not realize it by the way he acts, but for the other eleven months, he's really a decent, professional, smart, business-minded guy, which is why we all use him as our broker. He likes to give back, so he and Orabell host a lot of parties for various clients. And if you watch closely, Halston doesn't drink much at all. He just likes to make it appear that he does so his guests feel comfortable drinking."

"What were you and Claymore doing during all the drama of Saturday evening?" I asked, as we approached the Osbornes' gated pool area.

"We got fed up and went out onto the deck to enjoy the cool evening. Let's go inside. I need a nap."

There wasn't anything more I needed to ask Jillian about the weekend, yet my curiosity about the missing watch had been roused. "Just one more question. If Lily has such a sterling reputation, what could have triggered Orabell's accusation? Could she be jealous of Lily for some reason? Her success, or her youth—"

Jillian sat forward. "Say that again."

"The whole question?"

"The first part."

"Is Orabell—"

"Stop!" Jillian clapped her hands together. "That's it!"

"You know why Orabell accused Lily?"

"No! You just gave me the perfect name for my baby."

"What?"

"Isabelle!"

"You got that from my question?"

Jillian gave me a pitying look. "You need to have more imagination, Abs."

"Isabelle," I said, trying it out. "I like it. Isabelle Osborne has a great sound to it."

"I wonder if Claymore will want me to use his mother's name as her middle name. Personally, I think Evelyn is too old-fashioned, but I can work on Claymore later." Jillian sighed dreamily as we climbed the steps to the deck. "Can't you just picture little Izzy in cute little red pigtails and a white pinafore?"

"You're going to call her Izzy?"

"I'll have to. Isabelle is too long for everyday usage. '*Isabelle*, it's time for your nap. *Isabelle*, your nanny wants to change your diaper. *Isabelle*, eat your caviar. *Grandmama* Evelyn had it flown in from Russia especially for you. *Isabelle*, put down that Waterford crystal candlestick before you kill your father.' See what I mean? Long."

"Jillian, think about it. Izzy . . . Osborne."

"Izzy Osborne. So?" Then her mouth dropped open in horror. "Oh, no! Everyone will associate her with Ozzy Osbourne." She put her hands over her face. "I did it again!"

Fearing she was on the verge of another crying jag, I said, "Wow. Look at the time! Let's gather the guys and head over to the Burches', okay?"

She opened the sliding glass door and stepped inside. "I don't think I can, Abs."

"Sure you can," I said, following. "You said you wanted to see their cottage. Come on." I started up the hallway to gather our men.

"Can't."

"Yes, you can, Jillian," I said, turning to motion her on. "Think positive."

"Thank you very much. Now I'm *positive* I have to puke."

I stepped back as she made a dash for the bathroom up the hallway.

"I'll wait on the verandah," I called, then headed toward the front door to see how the boys were doing.

But Marco and Claymore were nowhere to be found. Instead, I found Pryce and a slender, dark-haired woman sitting side by side on the wicker settee. By the looks of it, they were having quite a cozy conversation.

Probably not Melissa, then.

CHAPTER EIGHT

I cleared my throat as I opened the screen door and stepped outside, startling Pryce and the woman. Instantly, he took his arm out from behind her and got to his feet. The woman ignored me by pulling out her smart phone and tapping something onto the screen.

"Finished with Jillian's interview?" Pryce asked, pretending to smile. Or maybe it was a genuine smile. With Pryce, one could never tell. What I could tell was that he seemed to have lost his urgency to find Melissa.

"Yep. Are you finished with yours?" With a tilt of my head, I glanced in the woman's direction, letting Pryce know (a) I was waiting for an introduction, and (b) I had seen how intimate they'd been.

Blushing deep red, he said, "Lily Caldwell, owner of Beached Bar and Bistro."

Lily looked up from her tapping in annoyance. "What?"

"Lily, this is Abigail Knight. She's working with the investigator I hired."

"Just call me Abby," I said.

Lily tossed back her long hair, setting her silver chandelier earrings to dancing. She was wearing a long, strapless white sundress that showed off her light tan, flawless skin, and curvaceous figure. Her white gladiator sandals displayed glossy apricot toenails.

After a quick once-over, she pursed her full lips. "You're the florist?"

"Yes. I own Bloomers Flower Shop." I reached out to take her limply offered hand. "Nice to meet you."

"Pleasure," she said in a flat voice, letting me know it was anything but. I was surprised she didn't throw in a yawn. The stack of silver bracelets on her wrist jangled as she withdrew her hand and draped her long bare arm over the back of the settee.

"I was explaining to Lily," Pryce said, "that Jake had set up appointments for you and Marco to meet them at the bistro at ten tonight, but Lily never got the message. Turns out it wouldn't have worked anyway."

"I don't know what Jake was thinking," Lily said. "We're busy from eight o'clock until midnight all summer long. I rarely get home before one in the morning."

"She made an exception for us this weekend," Pryce added, as though he had to explain.

"No problem," I said. "We can interview them now."

"Jake isn't here," Lily said, brushing a fly off her arm. "He's at the gym, and I have to get back to the bistro to check on things."

I waited for her to offer more, but she didn't. "When will he be done at the gym?"

Lily started to turn her wrist, as though she was going to check her watch, then caught herself and gave me a shrug instead. I noticed a white area on her arm where a watch had obviously been.

"Would you mind contacting him to find out?" I asked.

Without replying, she picked up her phone.

"You can catch them here tomorrow morning, if you'd like," Pryce said quietly.

The screen door squeaked open, and Jillian emerged

from the house looking flushed, hot, and cranky. "Where's Claymore?"

"He and Marco took a walk on the beach," Pryce said. "They'll meet us at the Burches' later."

Lily put her phone down beside her. "I texted Jake."

By the way she'd said it, she considered her job done.

"Hello, Jillian," Lily said in that same bored tone.

Jillian gave her a half smile, then put her hands on her hips and looked at Pryce. "So are we going next door or what?"

"Excellent idea," Pryce said with his fake smile, clearly trying to humor her. "Let's join the neighbors for cocktails."

Jillian threw me a look that dared me to make a comment and then started down the wooden steps by herself. Pryce held out his arm for Lily, but she didn't take it.

"You know how I feel, Pryce," she said. "I refuse to step inside that woman's cottage until she apologizes to me. If anyone wants to interview me, it'll have to be done here and now because I'm leaving in five minutes."

Anyone being me, obviously.

Pryce glanced from Lily to me with an expression that said, *What do I do?* It was one of those rare occasions when he seemed unsure of himself.

I pulled a wicker chair up to the settee and took out my pen and notebook. "Let's get started, then. Pryce, will you tell Marco where I am?"

Looking relieved, he gave a nod and trotted off after Jillian.

"What does Orabell have to apologize for?" I asked, pretending I hadn't heard about the watch.

"Stupidity," Lily said drily, "to the point of my wanting to drown her."

Good thing for Lily that Orabell wasn't the one missing. "Would you elaborate?"

"No."

"Because . . . ?"

"Because it's none of your business."

I was not enjoying Lily's attitude. "Okay. Well, I'm guessing that Orabell did or said something to offend you, but if you don't want to tell me about it, the others will fill me in."

Lily folded her long arms under her bosom, letting me know with a sharp sigh that she was extremely put out. "*Orajel* accused me of taking her watch. Satisfied?"

"You mean Orabell," I said, pausing my writing.

"Or-a-jel," Lily said slowly. "It's a teething gel for babies. Works by numbing the gums."

Orajel. Great one. I'd laugh if I liked Lily more. "Why does Orabell think you stole her watch?"

"Seriously? Is this necessary?"

"We're gathering as much information about the weekend as possible, because we never know what tiny bit of knowledge will help us locate Melissa."

"I guarantee you that Orajel's inane accusation has nothing to do with Melissa, but, fine. Whatever. After I catered a party for the Burches, Orajel claimed her watch was stolen. Did she come right out and ask if I'd taken it? No. She just hinted at it. Repeatedly. In front of everyone. To make me feel even worse, she criticized every dish I prepared for last Saturday's dinner. And I'm not kidding. Every. Dish."

"Did you confront her about her accusation?"

"Absolutely. By the end of the evening, I'd had it with her. I said, 'Prove it, Orabell. Prove I stole your watch.'"

"What was her response?"

"She said she intended to do just that. So I left. Walked out of the house, got into my car, and drove back to my restaurant."

"Did she say why she suspected you?"

Lily twisted a long strand of hair into a tight, angry coil. "No. Someone else told me why."

"Who?"

"Halston. He felt bad about the way Orajel was behaving and said she was being a pain in the butt to both of us because she has some crazy notion that we're having an affair. As if I could ever find that crashing bore appealing. I mean, please. Halston is handsome, no doubt about it, but he's my stockbroker. Orajel knows I have to meet with him."

I glanced at her bare wrist a second time. "So Orabell made the accusation about her watch and the digs about your food out of jealousy?"

"I told you she was stupid."

"Did Halston do anything about Orabell's behavior?"

"Nothing." Lily let her hair untwist. "No surprise there. He's very protective of her and does whatever he can to please her, even though there's no earthly way to do that. I'd feel sorry for him if I respected him more, but how do you respect someone who lets himself be walked on? Throwing all those parties is expensive. Remodeling their cottage every few years is expensive. Providing her with designer clothes every season is expensive. But Halston does it without a complaint. I suppose it's better than incurring the wrath of *Orajel*."

I was getting really tired of that name. "How do you get along with Melissa?"

"Why is that important?"

"I've heard that there's some rivalry between the two of you over Pryce."

Lily laughed, but it didn't reach her eyes. "Jillian *does* remember I'm married, doesn't she?"

"I didn't say it was my cousin who told me that."

"You didn't have to. I know Jillian. She's a gossip."

No argument there.

"You two don't look anything alike, by the way," Lily added.

"I know. I'm the short, freckled one."

"I was going to say the smart one."

I scribbled on the notepad: *I might have to change my opinion of Lily.*

"So there's never been a rivalry between you and Melissa?"

"I was jealous of Melissa at first, but I was able to let it go."

"Do you still have romantic feelings for Pryce?"

"I've known Pryce since my college days. We've been friends forever."

"That didn't answer my question."

"I fail to see what your question has to do with Melissa's disappearance."

"Same response as before."

"So if I say yes, are you going to insinuate that I stuffed Melissa in a meat locker so I could have Pryce to myself?"

"I wasn't going to insinuate that . . . but now that you mentioned it, did you?"

That got the first genuine laugh from Lily that I'd seen. "There are certain people I wish I could do that to, but Melissa's not one of them."

"So you didn't have any hurt feelings when Pryce asked Melissa to marry him?"

Lily drummed her fingers on the arm of the settee. "Of course I did. But I don't hold that against Melissa. I got over it, just like I did when Pryce got engaged to you."

Zing. "Where do you think Melissa is?"

"I don't have a clue."

"Are you concerned?"

"I'd like to know what happened to her, but concerned? No. Melissa's been hurt. She's probably licking her wounds someplace where they sell umbrella drinks on the sand."

I heard footfalls on the ground and turned to see Marco come striding toward the verandah, looking hunkarifically hot.

Hunkarifically? Where had that come from? Was Jillian's word mania boring its way into my brain?

Lily took notice of him, too, flipping her long hair to one side, tilting her head, and giving him a catlike glance as he strode up to us. "You must be Marco." She held out her hand.

Bo-hunk took it, his mouth curling at the corners ever so slightly. "You must be Lily."

She batted her eyelashes. "You must be right."

I cleared my throat, in case I had suddenly become invisible, causing Lily to slide her hand from Marco's in a slow, sensual move. I wouldn't have been surprised to see her rub her head against his ankles and purr.

I was back to disliking her.

"I have to get to the bistro," she said, bending down for her white patent clutch purse, giving Marco a partial view of her assets. She rose from the wicker settee, the soft material of her sundress gliding down her long tanned legs.

"Thanks for your time," I called, as she sashayed down the wooden steps.

"Give Orajel my regrets," she tossed back. With a laugh, she headed toward the garage.

"If she uses that name one more time," I said, "I'm going to choke her."

"Interesting woman," Marco said, watching her. "How did the interview go?"

"Hey," I said, raising my hand. "I'm over here."

Before I could blink, he had pulled me into his arms. Gazing down into my eyes, he said in a sexy rumble, "*Now* you're over *here*." And then he kissed me.

A breathless minute later, I said, "Did I inspire that move or was it part of your Ranger training?"

"Both," he murmured, his lips against my neck. "Want to see another?"

At that moment, Claymore came pounding up the steps, breathing hard and looking worried. "Do you know where Jillian's purse is?"

"I think it's in the kitchen," I said, straightening my clothing. "Why? What happened?"

"She needs her mints." He flung open the screen door so hard, it banged against the siding.

"A breath mint emergency?" I sat down and gave Marco a come-hither glance, patting the cushion beside me. "I'll tell you about my interview with Lily if you tell me about your interview with Claymore."

"As fascinating as that sounds, let's compare notes later so we can interview the Burches while Orabell is still sober."

"Is she well on her way to sloshdom?"

"About halfway there. You realize you just made up a word, don't you?"

"Did I?"

"Sloshdom."

"Post-traumatic Jillian disorder."

"Sure." He took my hand and led me through the elm trees.

As we approached the Burches' two-story brown cedar home, Claymore overtook us, dashing up a stone path that ran up to their front porch and along one side of the cottage to the back.

"Here they are, my darling," he called, and disappeared around the far corner.

We stopped next to the screened-in porch at the front of the cottage, where Orabell claimed to have overheard Pryce's argument. I could just make out the Osborne home through the trees.

"Would Orabell have been able to identify who was arguing?" I asked Marco. "I can see only glimpses of Pryce's verandah."

"Let's be sure to ask her how she knew who it was."

We followed the path around the house to an expansive, quarter-moon-shaped patio that had been built from the back of the house right up to the edge of a bluff overlooking Haven Lake. There we found Halston, Orabell, Pryce, and Jillian sitting on the thick cushions of their black wrought iron deck furniture. A portable bar was set up on one side, with liquor bottles and a bowl of nuts on top. Everyone had a beverage but Jillian, who appeared pale as she tossed back a handful of mints, while Claymore hovered anxiously at her side.

The back of the Burches' cottage looked nothing like the traditional front, bowing out into a modern, two-story semicircle of glass windows and French doors. A two-foot-high brick wall ringed the patio except for an opening out onto a cedar boardwalk. The boardwalk led to wooden stairs down an incline to the sandy shore at the bottom.

"Now it's a party!" Halston called when he saw us. He rose with a martini glass in his hand and went over to the bar. "Anyone for a cocotini?"

"Just say coconut martini, Halston," Orabell said, giving the others an exaggerated eye roll. "No one knows what you mean by cocotini."

"What's the fun in that?" he asked. "Besides, one

should never question what's in one's drink. One should just drink it."

"How absurd," Orabell said, then downed the remainder of her drink.

"But isn't life itself absurd, Mummy?" Halston replied cheerily, as he refilled her glass. He seemed to be such a carefree person, I couldn't imagine why he talked with his teeth so tightly clenched.

"What may I pour you?" he asked us.

"Water is fine," Marco said.

"Do you have anything nonalcoholic?" I asked.

"Don't say you're still on the clock," Halston said, handing Marco a tumbler of ice water.

"Shut up, Halston," Orabell said over her shoulder. "They wouldn't be here otherwise." She turned to me with a smile. "I believe there's lemonade in the house, darling. Come along and I'll get you a glass." She rose unsteadily but didn't stumble or spill her drink as she walked toward the house.

Perfect. We'd be able to talk to Orabell alone, *and* I'd get to see the inside of her cottage. I motioned for Marco to follow.

"Wait for me!" Jillian called. "I want lemonade, too."

"I'll bring you a glass," I called back.

Orabell opened a pair of French doors to admit us, then led us through the two-story great room that opened onto the kitchen at the far end. The great room was filled with overstuffed sofas and chairs in floral prints done in beige, tan, ivory, brown, and peach, with a natural stone floor underneath.

Separating the great room from the kitchen was a semicircular, eight-foot, earth-toned granite island. More granite counters filled a side wall punctuated by stainless steel appliances. Near a bank of windows on one side of the kitchen was an oval, glass-topped table surrounded by high-backed chairs upholstered in ivory cotton.

I squeezed Marco's hand, whispering, "This place is stunning. I can only dream of living in a house like this someday."

"What are you dreaming about?" Jillian asked, coming alongside me.

"The day I can talk to Marco without you butting in."

"No, seriously, Abs, what?"

"You heard me."

"Jillian, darling," Orabell called, "do close the door, please. We don't want to cool the outdoors."

As Jillian backtracked to shut the door, a striking collection of native plants and blossoms caught my eye, so I walked over to a plant stand under a tall window for a better look. "This is a beautiful grouping," I said to Orabell, as she brought out a pitcher from the refrigerator. "Who did it for you?"

"I did," she said proudly. "I collected every single one of those stems from around the property."

"The arrangement of plants looks very professional," I told her.

"Thank you, darling. I did it purely on instinct."

"That's how I work," Jillian said. "Pure instinct."

"You have a degree in fashion design, Jillian," I reminded her as I looked over the mix of flora. "I recognize most of these, Orabell—hosta, mint, fern, sage, and eryngium—"

"Please, darling," she said, handing me a glass of lemonade, "use English."

"Sorry. I should have said sea holly."

"What's this one?" Jillian asked, touching a cluster of delicate orange and yellow blossoms.

"People around the lake call it Fireglow," Orabell said.

"Fireglow?" I took a closer look at the bright orange bracts and tiny yellow flowers of my diary's namesake, and fire*works* went off in my head. This was the perfect opportunity to put my plan into action.

I'd given my diary the odd name of Euphorbia to frighten off Jillian, who was so superstitious, she refused to carry a mirror in her purse for fear of cracking it. She had managed to find and read every diary I'd ever owned, and I was determined that she wouldn't read my new one. Now I had to plant the seeds of fear, pun intended, and hope she was gullible enough to fall for it.

"Wow, Orabell!" I exclaimed, moving back. "You have a *Euphorbia griffithii.*"

"Is that good?" Jillian asked.

"I've seen photos of this plant in my floral magazines," I continued, "but they certainly didn't do the blooms justice. This is amazing."

"So it's good," Jillian said.

"That depends. You know about the sap of the euphorbia plants, don't you, Orabell?"

"What's wrong with the sap?" Jillian asked, examining her fingertips.

"It's poisonous," I said. "It can cause severe skin irritation and even temporary blindness if it gets in your eyes—in any form, even vapors."

Jillian took a step back, whirled around, and darted to Orabell's sink to wash her hands.

"I've heard that the name *euphorbia* carries a curse with it," I added. "That's why people call it by its common name." Totally made-up, but, judging by Jillian's alarmed expression, effective.

"I believe I've heard that poinsettias are from the same family," Orabell said.

"That's right," I said.

Over Orabell's shoulder, I spotted Marco walking

around the room taking in all the details, no doubt completely bored with flower talk.

"But I love poinsettias," Jillian said in dismay, accepting a glass of lemonade. "They're my favorite flower—or were! Thanks, Abs. Now I'm never having another live poinsettia in my house as long as I live."

"You needn't go to such an extreme, darling," Orabell said. "Just be careful not to get the sap on your fingers."

"This flower," I said, touching a bright scarlet blossom, "reminds me of a poppy."

"Well done," Orabell said. "It's a California poppy." She hiccuped as she said *poppy*, then pressed her fingers against her lips. "Pardon me!" Then she hiccuped again.

"Are you feeling okay?" I asked.

"I'm—*hic*—fine, Addie. Do you know what these small violet flowers are?"

"Abby."

"I've never heard of an Abby flower," Orabell said, looking confused.

"I meant my name is Abby." I examined the woody vine that held light purple flowers with yellow stamens, purplish leaves, and red berries. "I hope this isn't a deadly nightshade vine, Orabell."

"Don't be a goose, darling. Why on earth would I have a deadly plant in my home? It's bittersweet vine."

Marco cleared his throat. I glanced around at him, and he tapped his watch, then nodded in Jillian's direction. He was ready to get on with the interview, but first we had to get rid of the Nosy One.

I gave him a discreet thumbs-up.

Step one: Enlist the aid of a bystander. "Orabell, do you ever buy fish from local fishermen?"

"I leave that to the restaurateurs," Orabell said with a light laugh, followed by a hiccup. "You couldn't pay me to gut a fish."

Jillian was about to take a drink of lemonade, but stopped, the glass touching her lips.

Step two: Up the ick factor. "What about the eyeballs?" I asked.

"It's quite the thing to leave them in, you know," Orabell said. "The fish is flash fried and put on the plate whole. It's up to the patron whether to eat or remove the eyes."

Step three: Wait for it.

Jillian set the glass on the counter with a clunk and hurried toward the open French door.

Orabell looked at me in astonishment. "Goodness. I didn't realize Jillian had such a sensitive nature."

"That's my cousin," I said with a sigh. "She loves all of God's creatures, even fish." I put out my hand behind my back, and Marco gave me a low five.

"Is it okay to get started on your interview now?" I asked Orabell, pulling out a chair at the end of the oval glass table.

"Absolutely, darling," she said. "May I get you some more water, Marco?"

"No, thanks. I'm fine." He sat at the head of the table while I took a seat at his left and Orabell at his right. I pulled the notebook and pen from my purse and nodded that I was ready.

"Have you had a chance to talk to Pryce this evening?" Marco asked.

"For a short while," she said. "The dear boy seems to be handling things quite well. Don't you think so, Annie?"

"Abby," I said.

"Do you still feel Pryce is responsible for Melissa's disappearance?" Marco asked.

Orabell shook her head. "Not at all, darling. Not. At. All. I've changed my mind entirely about who's to blame." She took a drink, then set the glass down and smiled lopsidedly before hiccuping again.

"Would you tell us?" Marco prompted.

"If you'd like, although I'm surprised you haven't figured it out, considering all the flirting going on beneath our very noses."

"Are you talking about Lily?" I asked.

Orabell made a sputtering sound. "Don't be silly, Aggie. Lily is a thief and a flirt, yes, but I'm talking about Halston."

CHAPTER NINE

"It's Abby," I said to Orabell, forcing a smile.

"No, darling, it's not Abby! Listen to me carefully now. It's *Halston*."

"You actually believe your husband is responsible for Melissa's disappearance?" I asked, giving Marco a quick, shocked glance. "This afternoon you were convinced Pryce was behind it."

"Some detective you are," Orabell said. "Everyone can see how distraught Pryce is."

I turned to gaze out the back windows and saw Pryce slap Halston on the back, laughing as if he'd been told a great joke.

"You see," Orabell said, leaning toward us on one elbow, "Halston has had a crush on Melissa for over a year now. How I wish you could have witnessed the delirium in his eyes when I told him that Pryce had broken off his engagement. Like a lovesick schoolboy, he was. Completely besotted with her." She shook her head pityingly. "And as soon as he heard the news of their breakup, he moved right in."

"To Melissa's apartment?" I asked.

She gave me a bleary-eyed stare. "Her apartment?

No, darling. You misunderstand once again. He moved in for the kill—or, in his case, for the catch. From the time we got together on Friday evening until Saturday after supper, the old goat wouldn't stop mooning over Melissa. It was disgusting."

"Then what makes you think he had something to do with her disappearance?" I asked.

"Isn't it obvious?" Orabell asked. "Melissa spurned his attention, so in a fit of jealous rage, he got rid of her." She made a slicing motion across her throat.

The woman was obviously drunk.

"Has Halston ever given you a reason to suspect him before?" I asked.

"Do you mean to ask if he's cheated on me?" Orabell's lips tightened in anger. "He's always had women after him. Loose women, that is. Married, single, widowed—didn't even matter to them that he wore a wedding ring. He was quite the young stud in his day, you see."

He was *still* quite a stud, if truth be told.

"Has Halston ever behaved in a way that makes you suspect he's capable of harming anyone?" Marco asked.

"Well," Orabell said slowly, "there was that one time he chased off a magazine salesman. If I remember correctly, he threatened to clean the miscreant's clock." She lifted her eyebrows to impress upon us just how dreadful that was.

"Have you ever seen Halston do anything violent?" Marco asked.

She hiccuped. "He's been violently ill a few times."

Marco gave me an exasperated glance. I could see by the flat look in his eyes, he considered the interview a waste of time, so I stepped in. "Did you actually hear Melissa spurn Halston?"

"Didn't have to, darling." Orabell tapped her temple. "A wife knows these things. I can't tell you how many women I've had to chase off over the years."

"Is Lily one of them?" I asked.

"You haven't figured *that* out either?" Orabell clucked her tongue at me, then turned to wave at her guests through the glass. "Hello-o-o, darlings!"

"Abby, she's too far gone," Marco whispered. "Let's talk to her tomorrow."

"But being drunk might be a good way to get Orabell to say things she might not say otherwise," I replied, very sotto voce.

"Darlings," Orabell said, turning toward us, "I should really be outside with my guests. Are we nearly finished?"

"Just about," I said. "But first, would you explain what you sensed about Halston on Saturday evening that made you believe he had something to do with Melissa's disappearance?"

"It's quite simple, really. After being seated next to Melissa at the dining room table, Halston was unhappy and out of sorts for the rest of the night. He couldn't even sleep. I had to lend him one of my sleeping pills. What else am I to attribute it to but that she spurned him?"

"Indigestion?" Marco said.

"Halston has a cast-iron stomach," Orabell countered.

"Are you sure there wasn't anything else going on during dinner or afterward that could account for his mood?" I asked.

"Nothing—*hic*—well, I shouldn't say that." She paused to hiccup again. "Halston knew I was upset about my piano . . . I mean Piaget. He heard me doing everything possible to elicit a confession from Lily, yet he refused to lift a finger to help me." Orabell tried to hit her fist against the table, but missed.

"By Piaget, are you referring to your missing watch?" Marco asked.

"We never refer to it as a *watch*, darling. It's a Piaget Altiplano, the world's thinnest automatic timepiece, in white gold. And I didn't *lose* it. As I just said, that spiteful Lily pilfered it. But would Halston address the issue? Absolutely not. He was so aggrieved over Melissa, he dumped the matter in my lap."

"Are you certain Lily took your wa—timepiece?" I asked, remembering the pale mark on Lily's wrist.

"The Piaget was in my jewelry closet before the party she catered and gone afterward. What else am I to think?"

"Is the closet easily accessible?" Marco asked.

"You've never seen my closets, have you? That's an experience not to be missed." Orabell rose unsteadily, finished her martini, set the glass down, and started toward the open stairway that was visible from the entire main floor. "Come with me, darlings, and I'll show you."

We followed her upstairs to a roomy walk-in closet that had white folding doors across the entire back wall. She opened a pair of louvered doors, and I stifled a gasp. In front of me were dozens of white, bald, faceless manikin heads, each in its own cubicle, each with its own display of a necklace and earrings. The entire closet was backlit, giving the heads an otherworldly glow.

"Don't be alarmed, Annie," Orabell said with a hiccup. "All that's in this one is costume jewelry." She pointed to another pair of doors at the far end of the wall. "*That's* where I keep my valuable jewels. Do you want to see, darling?"

"We're more interested in seeing where you keep your timepieces," Marco said.

She motioned for him to step aside. "This," she said, folding back another closet door, "is where I keep my timepieces."

White models' hands, at least two dozen of them, each in a cubicle, fingers pointing upward, displayed watches on slender white wrists. Orabell bent down and nearly plunged headfirst into a cubicle, catching herself at the last minute before she plucked one of the hands from its shelf. "You see? Bare where my lovely Piaget should be! Oh, the audacity of that Lily!"

"Why aren't these closets locked?" Marco asked.

"We have an alarm system that's turned on every night," Orabell said as she chose a photo from the cubicle. "And frankly, darling, there's never been a reason to have to lock up my jewelry." She held out the photo. "This is my lovely, lost Piaget."

Marco took it, so I leaned over to study it. The photo was a close-up of Orabell's wrist sporting the gold Piaget. It was elegant and thin, with a circle of pavé diamonds around the mother-of-pearl face. I couldn't have even guessed its worth.

"I keep photos of all my valuable jewelry for insurance purposes," she told us.

"Shouldn't you keep them in a safe?" Marco asked.

"That's where they all normally reside. I've needed this one."

"Do you have cleaning people?" I asked.

"During the summer, yes, but I monitor them religiously."

"Isn't it possible that one of your guests took the Piaget?" Marco asked.

She laughed. "My word, no! Our friends, as well as Halston's clients, are very wealthy people, darling, the one exception being Lily. Everyone else has their own valuable timepieces."

"How often do you check this closet?" Marco asked, examining the bare hand.

"When I need to match my timepiece to my outfit."

"Would that be daily?" Marco asked, as Orabell replaced the hand on its shelf.

"It depends on my mood. Today, for instance, I'm wearing red, so I chose this Movado." She held out her skinny arm, showing us a shiny red leather watch with a black face.

"So you didn't notice the watch missing until the morning after the party that Lily catered?" I asked.

"*Timepiece*, darling, and yes, the morning after the party, when I decided to wear platinum accessories. I can't begin to describe the sick feeling in the pit of my stomach." She belched and immediately apologized.

"Is it possible someone on Lily's staff came upstairs and slipped in here?" Marco asked.

"No, darling, I would have noticed, trust me. You surely saw that the staircase is easily visible. I'm telling you, it has to be Lily, because she was the only one allowed up here to use the guest powder room, which is right across the hall from this closet. The others on her staff had to use the servants' washroom off the kitchen."

"Why did you make an exception for Lily?" Marco asked.

"I wasn't the one who did," Orabell said, shrugging in exaggerated dismay. "Lily is Halston's client. He's the one who allowed it. I've never trusted the woman."

"Did you see Lily come up here?" I asked.

"Yes," Orabell said. "Clever, wicked Lily."

"Did you follow her upstairs?" I asked.

"I put Halston on it, as I was overseeing food placement at that time."

"Did you ask Lily whether she took your Piaget?" Marco asked.

"That would've been too rude, my dear. I did ask — politely — to see her wrist, but she refused to show me. Now tell me." Orabell waved her hand in the air and nearly toppled backward. "What more proof does one need?"

Her credibility as a witness evaporated completely at her last statement.

"How many parties has Lily catered for you?" Marco asked.

"Oh, dozens. At least eight this summer alone."

"Have you ever found anything missing before?" Marco asked.

"No, but the economy wasn't this bad, was it?" Orabell put her hand alongside her mouth, as though there were someone else in the room, and whispered loudly, "The word around the lake is that Lily's bistro isn't faring well. She probably sold my Piaget to keep her place running."

"I've heard Beached is crammed every night," I said.

"That doesn't mean people are spending a lot of money there," Orabell said.

"If I may ask," Marco said, "what is the average tab for one of your parties?"

Orabell took a moment to think. "Between six and eight thousand dollars."

And she'd thrown *eight* parties this past summer? I did a fast calculation and came up with an expense of between forty-eight and sixty-four thousand dollars. "Why would Lily jeopardize such a lucrative relationship?"

"People like her have no scruples, darling. They're opportunists. Lily saw her opportunity and seized it. Next thing you know, she'll have her claws into my husband, too. Not that she hasn't tried already. Lily is always after handsome, wealthy men. If she can't have Pryce, she'll take whomever fits the bill."

"So your theory is that Lily stole the Piaget because her bistro has fallen on hard times?" Marco asked.

"It's not just a theory, darling. There's simply no other explanation."

"If she took your timepiece for the money," Marco said patiently, "wouldn't she have sold it right away to pay her bills?"

"What are you getting at?" Orabell asked.

"She wouldn't have had the timepiece on her wrist if she'd sold it," I explained.

Orabell's eyebrows drew together as she pondered his question. "Then why wouldn't she show me her wrist?"

"Maybe you offended her by asking," Marco said. "Why would she wear it to your house and run the risk of you seeing it?"

I remembered Lily's bare wrist again and wished I'd mentioned it to Marco. Lily had obviously worn a watch enough to get tan lines around it, so why hadn't she worn one today? Was it possible Lily did take it?

"Lily stole it, I tell you. She stole my Piaget, and— *hic*—she has to pay for it."

As Orabell started for the door, I whispered to Marco, "You're right. Orabell is sloshed. Let's move on." He gave me a nod.

"One more question, Orabell," he said. "How did you know who you heard arguing on the verandah Friday evening?"

"By simple powers of deduction, darling. I saw Melissa's car in the driveway and—*hic*—I know her voice."

"Thank you for your cooperation," Marco said, offering her his arm. "May I escort you back to the kitchen?"

Orabell smiled. "Why, aren't you the perfect gentle— *hic*—man?"

Yep. That was my Marco. A gentle hic-man.

As we entered the kitchen, my cell phone beeped. I pulled it out of my purse and read the screen. It was a text message from Jillian that read: *I know what U did to me. Lame! :-<*

What I did to her? I turned to glance out the window and saw her make a face at me, her eyeballs bulging. Oh, right! The fish eyes.

Her head bent as she worked her phone. A few seconds letter, another text came in: *I M getting a tour. U R not invited.* It was followed by the symbol of a person sticking out her tongue. *:-p*

I was about to send a text back that said, *Too late!* when Halston came striding through the open French doors.

"My turn to play," he announced, giving me a wink, as Marco shut the door behind him. "May I sit across from you, my dear?"

"Please," I said.

He took my hand and bowed over it, an aging but still dashing Sir Galahad. Then he pulled out a chair, and dropped into it. Waving a hand in Marco's direction, he said, "Fire when ready, General. And please speak up so I can hear you."

Marco sat down and folded his hands on the table. "I'll try to keep this brief so you can rejoin your guests."

"Correct you are," he said. "Wouldn't do to ignore my guests. Mummy would have kittens." He guffawed so loudly, those kittens would have scattered like leaves.

"Halston, are you sticking by your allegation that Pryce is responsible for Melissa's disappearance?" Marco asked.

"Can't say that I ever believed it in the first place." Halston stretched out his legs and leaned back in his chair, his arms folded comfortably across his chest. "Had to go along with the missus to keep peace in the family, if you know what I mean."

"Then your wife still believes it?" Marco asked.

"Couldn't tell you what her latest allegations are," Halston said. "They change hourly, depending on her mood."

"Do you have any insights into what may have happened to Melissa?" Marco asked.

"Insights, is it?" Halston gazed up at the ceiling, rubbing his jaw. "I'd venture to say that if anyone would have insights, it would be Lily."

"Why Lily?" Marco asked.

"Wanted Pryce for herself, you know. Took his engagement to the girl hard. Barrels of resentment there. Married that wastrel Jake on the rebound and has regretted it ever since."

"In what respect did Lily take Pryce's engagement hard?" Marco asked.

"Not sure I understand what you're getting at," Halston said.

I tried to rephrase it for him by cutting to the chase. "Have you ever witnessed Lily taking out her resentment on Melissa?"

"Can't say that I have, but it's not like I look for that sort of activity." Halston glanced around. "Thought I brought my 'tini in with me. What a bother. Must have left it outside."

"We'll be done here in just a few minutes," Marco said.

"Best make it a few seconds," Halston said with his barking laugh. "My brain is starting to clear."

"How do you know Lily took the engagement hard?" Marco asked.

"That would be Orabell's department. I'm just repeating what she told me."

"Are you saying you have no firsthand knowledge that would make you suspect that Lily had a hand in Melissa's disappearance?" Marco asked.

Halston slapped his palm on the table. "You are one hundred percent correct, my good man."

"What kind of relationship do you have with Melissa?" Marco asked.

"Friendly. She's one of my clients. Reminds me of the daughter I wish I'd had."

"Do you have any children?" I asked.

"Sadly, no. Orabell never wanted any. Said they'd ruin her girlish figure and put a crimp in her lifestyle."

Lucky children. "Pardon me for asking, but why do you call her Mummy?"

"Started out as a joke," he said to me in a wistful voice. "She used to get a weekly spa treatment that had her wrapped up from head to toe. I called it her *Mummy time*, and it stuck. She'd tell you differently, tell you it's because I require mothering, but now you know the real story." Halston glanced at Marco and pretended to come to attention. "Sorry, General. Didn't mean to digress. Full speed ahead, then."

For a man pretending to be buzzed, Halston's clear, concise answers didn't support it.

"Have you ever had a relationship with Melissa outside of work or your social get-togethers?" Marco asked.

Halston gave him a puzzled look. "What other kind would there be? Surely you aren't suggesting romantic leanings."

When Marco didn't reply immediately, he sat upright, clearly indignant. "That's absurd. Who told you that?"

Before Marco could reply, Halston said, "Never mind. I'm sure it doesn't matter."

It seemed as though he'd guessed the answer and didn't want to know more, no doubt trying to protect Orabell. But I could tell by Marco's intent expression that he wasn't about to drop that line of questioning.

"What if I told you it was your wife?" Marco asked.

"I'm afraid Orabell has always had a jealous streak." Halston shook his head sadly. "Please believe me when I say I've never given her any reason for it, yet she persists in her belief that I'm on the hunt. You'd think by her age she'd have outgrown such nonsense, but there it is. She can't seem to shake her insecurity, even though I try continuously to reassure her."

"Tell me about the situation with your wife's watch," Marco said.

"The Piaget that Orabell claims Lily stole?" Halston sat forward and said discreetly, "Let me assure you that I don't believe Lily would have taken Orabell's timepiece. She's one hundred percent professional."

"Then why would Orabell make that claim?" I asked.

Halston sighed. "I wish I could give you a definitive answer."

"Why can't you?" Marco asked.

Halston pondered for a long moment, as though torn between telling the truth and protecting his wife. "Because I'm a loyal husband. All I can say is that Orabell has her own reasons for believing as she does."

"And you don't know what those reasons are?" I asked.

"I haven't asked and don't intend to bring up the subject."

"What do you think happened to the Piaget?" Marco asked.

"Misplaced, most likely. It's happened before is all I'll say."

"With her timepieces?" I asked.

"She takes them off before she goes outside to sun, swim, or work on her plant collection and then forgets where she puts them. As I said, it's happened before."

"Has she then recovered them?" Marco asked.

"Sadly, no."

"Do you use a cleaning service?" I asked.

"We do, and that's Orabell's department. Currently, she's trying out several new services to find one she likes." As though picking up on my thoughts, Halston added, "I agree that thievery among cleaning staff is a problem, but once again I must tell you that she's misplaced timepieces before. So"—he rubbed his palms together, as though eager to move on—"shall we get back to the main concern? Melissa?"

For some reason my inner antennae were waving. Something Halston said wasn't sitting well with me. Was it that the watches should have turned up when the house was cleaned? Was it his eagerness to get off the subject of the missing Piaget? I made a note to mention it to Marco.

"Where do you think Melissa is?" Marco asked.

"Tahiti, I hope," Halston said. "Living it up. Life is too short to waste mourning a failed relationship."

Hearing a door open, I turned to see Orabell and Jillian come inside. Orabell carried her martini glass in one hand while clinging to Jillian's arm with the other.

"Ah! Here come my rescuers," Halston said, donning his party-animal persona. "Mummy, did you bring my 'tini by any chance?"

"It was all I could do to carry mine, Halston," she said crossly. "You'll have to get it yourself. I'm leading a tour at the moment."

"Would you mind if I repaired to the bar?" Halston asked Marco. "I'm really quite dry."

"Not at all," Marco said, rising. "Thank you for your time."

"*Halston*," Orabell snapped, as her husband strode out the door, "don't leave it open!" She sighed loudly. "And there he goes without remembering to shut it. What an old fool."

An old fool who loved her more than she deserved.

"Orabell is going to show me the house," Jillian announced.

"You come, too, Debby," Orabell said to me, nearly

tripping on the edge of the sisal rug as they passed by. "The more the merri—"

At a sudden shout of "Where's Lily?" I turned to see Jake standing in the open doorway, looking at us as though he wanted to throw a hard punch.

Jillian gasped, and I glanced around to see her staring down at her sandals, which were now wet with the remains of Orabell's martini.

CHAPTER TEN

Jake was red in the face as he glared at us. "Where is my wife!" he demanded, clenching his fists. "She said she'd be here."

"Take it easy, man," Marco said in a calm voice, easing in front of me. "Your wife's not inside the house, but we'll be glad to help you look for her."

Clearly undisturbed by Jake's wild-eyed glare, Orabell said with a scowl, "Oh, for pity's sake, look what you did to Jillian's sandals. One would think wild dogs were after you the way you barged in here, Jake. Next time use a civil tone. Jillian, darling, I'm so sorry! Take one of the guest towels in the powder room to dry your feet."

"These are brand-new," Jillian whimpered, near to tears.

"Come along, darling," Orabell said to her. "We'll make it all better. Jake, sit down over there at the table and behave yourself. Lily's bound to show up eventually." Weaving slightly, she deposited her martini glass on the kitchen counter and walked with Jillian up the hallway.

Like a scolded child, Jake pulled out a chair and slumped down in it. He was wearing white athletic shoes and socks, navy biking shorts, and a navy and white tank top that was damp from sweat, as though he'd rushed right over as soon as his class had finished.

Taking pity on him, I said, "Lily told me earlier today that she was going back to the bistro. Did you check there?"

"She said to meet her here, dammit!" He muttered something under his breath that sounded a lot like *the witch*, although I had a feeling he wasn't being quite so generous.

"We finished her interview," Marco said. "Maybe she felt there was no reason to stay if she had something to do at her restaurant."

"No reason to stay?" Jake asked sarcastically. "Why? Did Pryce leave?"

Yikes. Sounded like Jake had heard those rumors after all. "Pryce is on the patio," I said, walking over to the windows to check. But Pryce was nowhere to be seen, so I returned to the table and sat down without commenting on it. "I'm sure Lily will be back soon. You and she are still staying at the Osborne cottage, right?"

Jake dropped his head back and covered his eyes with his palms. "Yeah, we're still there."

I could tell by the tone of his voice that he wasn't happy about it. I raised my eyebrows at Marco. His reply was to tilt his head a fraction, as though to say, *Leave it alone.*

"Would you like to get something to drink before we start your interview?" Marco asked.

Jake sat upright, placing his hands on the edge of the table. "No, let's just do this. What do you need to know?"

"To start with, when was the last time you saw Melissa?" Marco asked.

"Sunday morning."

"What was she doing?" Marco asked.

"Having breakfast."

"With you?"

Jake's knee was bouncing a mile a minute. "I'd already eaten."

"But she was with you at your table, correct?" Marco asked.

"Uh, yeah. Correct."

"Were you alone otherwise?" Marco asked.

"Well, Melissa was there."

Definitely not the sharpest knife in the block.

"What was her mood?"

"Pissed."

"Why?"

Jake threw himself against the back of the chair. "Are you kidding me? 'Cause that jackass pulled the plug on their wedding, that's why."

Wow. Quite a violent reaction to a simple question.

"Is this the same jackass who invited you to stay at his cottage while your house is being redone?" I asked, not that I felt the need to defend Pryce, but Jake's lack of gratitude annoyed me.

Jake scoffed, as though he couldn't believe what I'd said. "Inviting guests to stay at his cottage doesn't stop Pryce from being a jackass."

He had a point.

"Besides," Jake said, his lip curling in distaste, "Pryce invited Lily. I just get to tag along with her."

"Did Melissa talk to you Sunday morning about her broken engagement?" Marco asked.

"You mean like when we were all together or what?"

"When she had breakfast at your table," Marco said.

"Yeah, she talked about it."

"What did she talk about?" I asked.

"She was mostly complaining about having to return her wedding dress and send out notices to cancel the wedding." He shrugged. "You know, that kind of stuff."

Yep. Knew all too well about that kind of *stuff*.

"Did Melissa mention anything about taking a trip?" Marco asked.

"I don't remember her saying anything about a trip, but I kind of tuned her out after a while. You know how women get. Blah, blah, blah, until you want to stick your fingers in your ears."

Or in Jake's case, an electrical outlet would work.

"Where do you think Melissa is?" Marco asked.

"Man, I don't have a clue. Not a single clue. I wish I did know, 'cause I don't want nothing bad happening to her." Jake rubbed his knees with his palms, as though nervous. "I mean, it's bad enough what that jackass did to break her heart. When someone makes a promise, he should keep it, you know what I'm saying? A promise is a promise. A vow is a vow. It shouldn't be tossed away because of someone else coming into the picture."

"Do you think Pryce broke the engagement because of someone else?" Marco asked.

"I don't know," Jake said, "but I sure would like to find out."

"Why?" Marco asked.

"You know"—he rubbed his knees harder—"because I feel sorry for Melissa."

I had a hunch Jake felt sorrier for himself than for Melissa. There was no doubt in my mind that Jake suspected Lily was the *someone else* in the picture. What had really caught my attention, though, was how Jake claimed not to know where Melissa was. I kept remembering Grace's Shakespearean quote about someone protesting too much.

"Maybe Lily can tell you more," Jake said, "if you can find her. Are we done yet?"

I could tell by the watchful expression on Marco's face that Jake's behavior was raising red flags. "You don't think we'll find Lily at Beached?"

"Does it matter what I think?"

"The way you said it made me wonder," Marco said.

"Sure. You'll find her there. Whatever. Look, man, I thought you wanted to know about Melissa, not my marriage. So here's what I know about Melissa. Pryce pulled the plug, and now she's gone. End of story. See you around."

Jake got up and strode toward the French door, shutting it with a bang.

"I guess we're done." I tucked the pen and notebook in my purse and put the strap over my shoulder to stand up. "He was so on edge, he made *me* jittery."

Marco had a pensive look on his face as he walked over to the window to watch Jake. "He acted like he was in a big rush to get somewhere, and yet now he's camped out on the deck with a beer."

"Maybe his rush was getting out of answering any more questions. I'm surprised he didn't head to the restaurant to find Lily. For her sake, I hope she doesn't show up here with Pryce, because Jake clearly has a major jealousy issue with him."

"Everyone in this group has issues," Marco said, putting an arm around me. "I don't understand what holds them together. They don't seem to like or trust each other."

"From what Jillian told me, investment money holds them together. Did you catch how vociferously he claimed not to know where Melissa is?"

"I caught it. I didn't feel the time was right to pursue it, but it did make me wonder."

"I'll put an asterisk beside it in my notes."

Marco pulled me close. "What do you say we head home? It's been a long day."

"Not too long, I hope, because there's the little matter of a foot massage you owe me."

When we stepped onto the deck a few minutes later, Claymore and Halston were engaged in a lively dialogue.

"Come join us, you two," Halston called. "We were just discussing the play *The Iceman Cometh*."

Jake caught sight of us and immediately moved to the wooden railing to stare down at the shoreline. I glanced at Marco and saw him taking it in.

"We just stopped to say good-bye," Marco said.

"Surely you're not leaving without trying a cocotini," Halston said. "You can't still be on the clock."

"Oh, Halston, let these poor people leave," Orabell said, as she and Jillian stepped outside to join us. "They have more exciting things to do than to keep us company."

"Not Abby," Jillian said, carrying her sandals. "She is absolutimently boring."

I narrowed my eyes at her. "Fish eyes, Jillian."

"Stop that," she said, making fists, as though willing away the nausea.

"Fish *eggs*, do you mean?" Halston asked. "I've got an unopened jar of caviar in the fridge. Let me get them for you. They're outstanding on pita chips."

Jillian pivoted and ran inside, one hand over her mouth. Everyone watched her leave; then Halston said with a sigh, "Forgot the gal doesn't like caviar."

"Be more considerate next time, Halston," Orabell said crossly.

"Poor Jillian," Claymore said with a sigh. "She never has taken a liking to caviar."

"Gal doesn't know what she's missing," Halston commented.

They all nodded.

I grabbed Marco's arm and tugged him away before I burst out laughing.

"So where *did* Pryce go?" I asked, as we waited for a green light. "His car wasn't in his driveway."

"It's not important." Marco reached across to rub the back of my neck, which was getting more painful by the hour. "We got sidetracked today, Sunshine."

"By the missing watch?"

"Among other issues."

"Speaking of the watch, I wasn't satisfied that Halston was telling the truth about Orabell's Piaget. He seemed to be in a hurry to get off the subject."

"I caught that, too, but our job is to find Melissa, not to solve their problems."

"After listening to the interviews today, Marco, I don't think anyone knows where Melissa is, unless Claymore was able to shed light on her whereabouts."

"All Claymore knew was what Jillian told him."

"My gut feeling is still that Melissa has gone underground. She's too hurt and humiliated to show her face in town, that's all, not because anything bad happened to her."

"Pryce did make one good point, though, Abby. Melissa should have contacted her brother by now."

"Marco, I know you grew up with sisters, but sometimes I'm surprised by how little you understand the workings of the female brain. What makes you think she hasn't contacted her brother, then made him promise not to tell Pryce where she was?"

"Is that what you did?"

That stung. "No, I didn't do that. I didn't have contact with Pryce after he broke our engagement, but I never hid from him. What would you do if one of your sisters had just had her heart broken into tiny bits and asked you not to let the jerk who dumped her know where she was?"

"I'd honor her request."

"Of course you would, which is why I'm saying Melissa's brother may have done the same thing."

"And then I'd grind the jerk into a fine powder. Obviously we've hit a dead end with these people, Abby, so tomorrow I'll do an Internet search and see where that takes me."

He drove into the apartment's parking lot, turned off the engine, and pulled me close. "What do you say we go up to your place, work on that foot massage, and see where *that* takes us."

Straight to nirvana, I was sure.

Tuesday

When I walked into Bloomers the next morning, what greeted me was not the beautiful silk floral centerpiece that was usually placed on our round, antique oak table in the middle of the shop. No, it was Mom's new creation—the eye mask tree—and that wasn't the best way to start a day.

"Good morning, love," Grace said, coming out of the coffee parlor. "I have fresh vanilla scones this morning with raspberry-flavored coffee. Would you care to try them?"

"Sounds delicious, Grace. Thanks." I stopped to adjust one of the masks. "It doesn't look like we sold many of these eyesores yesterday."

"Not a one, sadly. I thought surely the lady poetesses would snap them right up, but they merely glanced at them and walked away."

"Did we price them too high?"

"They're significantly lower than sleep masks at the drugstores, dear. Perhaps we should wait a day or two before dropping the price. Interest may pick up. Let me get your coffee and scone and bring it into the workroom. I want to explain about your messages."

She had to explain them? That sounded portentous.

"Morning, sweetie," Lottie called as I stepped through the purple curtain. She was pruning mum stems with her floral shears. "We got a bunch of orders in overnight. Big funeral tomorrow. Isn't that great?"

"In a morbid way," I said, pulling out the chair at my desk.

"Here we are," Grace said, coming into the workroom with a cup and saucer in one hand and a plate with a scone on it in the other. "Lottie, dear, don't forget to help yourself to a vanilla scone. It's the first time I've made this recipe for the shop."

I picked up a stack of pink memo slips just as Grace set the plate and cup before me.

"Have a bite of scone, love," she said, and plucked the slips out of my fingers. "The butter in it will help calm your nerves."

My nerves were going to need calming?

I crammed a big bite in my mouth. "Okay, go ahead," I mumbled, spewing crumbs. "This is delicious."

"That does it," Lottie said, laying down her shears. "I've gotta try one."

"On to business," Grace said. "First of all, your Mr. Juggles called."

"Mr. Juggles?" Lottie asked, pausing at the curtain.

"That's the juggler I'm going to hire," I explained. "He was supposed to get back to me about a price."

"That wasn't why he called," Grace said. "Mr. Juggles is sorry to inform you that he has to have emergency shoulder surgery next week because he tore a tendon while performing last night and will be out of commission for at least eight weeks."

The morning was not going well. "Great. He was the only local juggler I found."

"There has to be more than one in the area," Grace said.

"Chicago," I said with a sigh. "I found a whole list of them there, but they were pricey, and I'd have to pay their travel expenses. I'll have to squeeze in a few minutes somewhere to search for someone closer."

Lottie came into the workroom carrying a scone wrapped in a napkin. "Did you tell her about the pinwheels yet?"

"I'm just about to do that now."

"There's another problem with my pinwheels?" I asked, reaching for my scone.

"I know you wanted to call around for them yourself, love, but when you mentioned yesterday that you'd be gone all evening, I decided to see what I could find out for you. Well, it was fortunate I did."

She placed a memo slip on the desk. "To start with, the sales representative from this company told me they don't carry flower pinwheels any longer, only solid-colored paper or miniature metallic ones."

She put down another slip. "This company sells happy-face pinwheels in addition to solid-colored paper ones."

Next slip came down. "This company carries ten varieties of pinwheel, including the flower kind, but they're twelve inches across, and I knew that would never work."

She put down another. "Now, this company had flower pinwheels at one time, but sold out at Easter and forgot to reorder because there's been no activity on that item lately."

"Wait, Grace," I said before she could put down another slip. "Did you find them anywhere?"

"I'm getting to that," she said, then laid out three more pieces of paper. "I found seven at this company, thirteen at this one, and five at this one. Apparently, flower pinwheels are a spring item, Abby. Everyone I contacted is either low or out of stock. Shall I continue?"

There went my pinwheel idea. "No. Thanks anyway, Grace. And thanks for making all these calls. That would have taken me a long time to research."

"Which is why I stepped in, dear. You have more on your plate than one person can handle. Now, let me think. . . . Yes, it was Antoine de Saint-Exupéry who said"—Grace took hold of the edges of her blazer and straightened her shoulders—"'One man may hit the mark, another blunder; but heed not these distinctions. Only from the alliance of the one, working with and through the other, are great things born.' Saint-Exupéry was speaking, of course, about teamwork."

I held up my thumb as I chewed another bite of scone. "Gotcha."

Then I caught Grace and Lottie exchanging glances. What had I missed? "Is there a problem?"

"Well," Grace said after some hesitation, "I don't want to talk out of turn, dear, but I feel I must speak my mind on the subject of your shower."

"You don't like my festival theme?"

"It's not that, sweetie," Lottie said. "Festivals are always fun. But sometimes . . . well, every so often . . . not always, by any means, but once in a while you seem to"—Lottie made a traveling motion with her hands—"and that just leads to—" She balled up her hands into fists and shook them.

"The only thing I got out of that, Lottie, is that I shouldn't travel so fast."

"What our Lottie is attempting to explain," Grace said, "is that trying to execute your plans by yourself, while it sounds admirable, may be your, shall we say, undoing?"

"It's not going to undo me," I said, wiping my fingers

on a napkin. "It's going to preserve my sanity. You know how Mom and Francesca are. They want to run everything. Believe me, I know, because they've already tried." I got up and gave each woman a hug. "I appreciate your concern, but don't worry about me. I'll substitute something for the pinwheels, find another juggler, and everything will be fine."

"Will you promise one thing?" Lottie asked. "Will you ask us for help if you feel like you're treading water?"

"Yes." But only if I was about to drown. Otherwise, Mom and Francesca would find out that Lottie and Grace were helping, and then there'd be hell to pay.

Lottie gave me a big hug, then turned to eye the stack of orders on the spindle. "You and I have our work cut out for us today, sweetie. But before I dig in to these orders, I'm gonna dig in to this sweet-smelling scone." She bit into the pastry and chewed for a moment, then sighed with delight. "Oh, my word, Gracie, these are the best you've ever made. What's your secret?"

"My grandmother's recipe," Grace replied cryptically.

"Come on, Gracie," Lottie said. "I know you used vanilla in it, but what makes it so creamy?"

Grace motioned for Lottie and me to come closer; then, in a team huddle, she said quietly, "Are we agreed that this goes no further than the workroom?"

At our nods, she said, "Very well. The secret ingredient is"—she dropped her voice to a whisper—"sour cream." Then she put her finger to her lips.

"I never would have guessed," Lottie whispered.

"Ladies," I said, "we're the only ones in the shop. Why are you whispering?"

The curtain parted and Jillian's head popped through. "What are you guys doing back here? You've got customers up front."

Grace stepped away with a knowing look.

CHAPTER ELEVEN

"How did you get inside?" I asked Jillian, as she came through the curtain. "The door is still locked."

She dangled a key in front of me, the same key I'd given her in a weak moment when I was desperate for help and she'd volunteered. "Not anymore."

Grace headed for the curtain. "I don't understand why the bell over the door didn't jingle."

"Shoot," Lottie said, hurrying after Grace. "I forgot to fix it. I saw it was stuck when I came in this morning."

"Thanks for opening the shop half an hour early, Jillian." I held out my hand. "Give me the key."

"How will I get in?" Jillian asked, pouting.

"The way everyone else does. You'll wait until the shop is open."

"Well, I'm *not* everyone else." Jillian leaned over my shoulder to sniff my half-eaten scone. "I smell vanilla."

She started to break off a piece, but I grabbed her wrist. "Give me the key first."

She dropped it on the desk and snatched the plate. Sitting on a stool at the worktable, she gobbled the rest of my scone, finishing within sixty seconds. "M-m-m. That was yummy. I was literally starving to death."

"You were not *literally* starving to death, Jillian. If you were, you wouldn't have had the strength to drag yourself out of bed."

She pointed to my cup. "Are you going to drink that?"

I picked it up and drank it down. "Coffee is bad for you. Why are you here?"

"Two reasons. A, I found the perfect name for *you know who*, and B, I found the perfect dress for you to wear to your shower."

"Tell me the name."

She clapped her hands together, smiling excitedly. "Okay, you know how cool it is that everyone calls Jennifer Lopez *J-Lo*? Well, if I name the *you-know-what* Jillian Ophelia, then I can call her Jill-O."

"You're going to give your child your name?"

"Yes, but as I just said, I'll call her Jill-O."

"Think about it."

She gave me a blank look. "What?"

"What do you always make for the family Thanksgiving dinner?"

"Rolls."

"No, you *buy* the rolls. What do you *make*? You know how to make only one thing."

"Strawberry cream Jell-O."

I smiled.

She blinked a few times, then let out a wail, laid her head on her arms, and sobbed.

I rubbed her back. "Don't worry. You have plenty of time to think of a better name. Want a cup of tea?"

She shook her head.

"Want another scone?"

As though suddenly inspired, Jillian raised her head, grabbed her shoulder bag, and slid off the stool. "I know just where to find the perfect name."

"Where?"

"You'll find out," she said, and slipped through the curtain.

At least I didn't have to hear about the perfect dress.

"Maybe I can still use my pinwheel idea," I told Lottie later that afternoon, as we put together funeral orders. "I just won't use the flower type."

"Whatever you use, you'd better get them ordered right now and have them overnighted. And call that juggler out of Chicago, too."

"I will as soon as I finish this." I stepped back to take a look at the arrangement so I could make final adjustments.

Doing a twist on a traditional wreath, I had used all white flowers—white 'Akito' roses, hydrangeas, carnations, and black-eyed gerberas—and aligned them to appear as if they spiraled around the circular green form. Then I looped steel grass loosely around the whole thing to suggest a continuous ribbon. To finish the effect, once we'd delivered the wreath to Happy Dreams Funeral Parlor, I'd place it on a white wooden easel.

I stowed the wreath in the walk-in cooler on the right side and sat down at my desk with Grace's stack of memos. Two phone calls later, my order of 150 colored metallic pinwheels was on its way. I wasn't as successful with the juggler, however.

The first one was busy on the day of my shower. The second didn't travel outside of Chicago. The third charged way too much. At that point I was out of names.

"My boys know how to juggle," Lottie said, as she stripped a stem of its leaves.

I swiveled to stare at her. "Why didn't you tell me that earlier?"

"They're not professionals. They juggle tennis balls mostly, but they're pretty good."

"Would they be willing to work up an act for me?"

"I can ask."

"That would be great, Lottie. I'll pay them for their time."

"I'm sure they'd like that, but are you sure you want four teenaged boys at your shower?"

"You've got great sons. Of course I want them."

I'd worked with Jimmy, Joey, Johnny, and Karl, Lottie's seventeen-year-old quadruplets, when I was hired to decorate for a massive Fourth of July party. The boys had behaved like normal teenagers, showing off as much as goofing off, but I'd never had any problems getting them to help me.

My cell phone rang. Fearing it was Jillian, I checked the screen and saw Marco's name.

"Hey, Fireball, how's it going?" he asked in his sexy voice.

"I think I have everything in hand as far as the shower goes, and I'm hopeful that Lottie and I will be able to get the funeral orders done by six thirty this evening. How about you? Any luck on tracking Melissa?"

"No. I talked to the renters in the apartment above Melissa's, but they haven't seen her or anyone else accessing her apartment, and the shop has been closed. There's also been no activity on her cell phone, which is problematic. I'm going to call her brother, Harry, and see what I can get him to tell me."

"What if Harry hasn't heard from Melissa either?"

"Then I hope he's called the cops."

"If Harry did that, the cops would have paid Pryce a visit, and he would have called us."

"That's why I have a strong hunch that you were right about Harry not telling Pryce everything he knows about his sister's whereabouts."

"Thank you. And good luck with that phone call. If Harry's protecting his sister, he won't tell you anything. Are we meeting later this evening for dinner?"

"Rafe just informed me that he's going to be short-handed at the bar, so I'll probably stay to help out. Why don't you come down here when you're finished?"

"It's a date, Salvare." I made a smooching sound into the phone just as the curtain parted and Grace peered in.

"Am I interrupting?"

I hung up the receiver. "Just finished."

"Perfect timing, then. Your mum's here for a tree inspection."

Perfect by whose definition?

I walked into the shop to see my mother trying to sell an eye mask to a pair of women who had just purchased a silk floral arrangement.

"See? They flip up independently," Mom said, following them to the door wearing one of her creations.

"Thank you," one of the ladies said. "We'll think about it."

"Be the first of your friends to own one!" Mom called as they scurried down the sidewalk, casting fearful glances behind them.

She turned back with a frustrated sigh. "They have no imagination."

Thank goodness there weren't any more customers in the shop. Mom would have buttonholed them, too.

She came forward to give me a hug and straighten the collar of my shirt, which gave her a few seconds to do a quick inspection. "Oops. You've got a little stain on the front here."

I looked down at my blue cotton shirt. "I spilled plant food earlier. I thought I'd wiped it all off."

"Maybe you can try again. So how's my newly engaged daughter today?"

Any mention my mom made of my status automatically made my palms sweat. I had to divert to another topic. "Busy, but doing fine, Mom. How about you? Enjoying the last weeks of your summer vacation?"

"I'm disappointed that most of my masks are still here."

"We didn't have as many customers as usual, Maureen," Grace said tactfully. "That could explain it."

"Did anyone look at my masks, at least?" Mom asked.

"Oh, any number stopped to look," Grace said. "Perhaps, as you said, they simply had no imagination."

I was waiting for Grace to deliver a quote on imagination, but she seemed more interested in watching Mom circle the tree, tapping her chin.

"What are you thinking, Maureen?" Grace asked.

"I wonder what would happen if you put the display outside the shop tomorrow."

Grace turned to me. "Abby? It's your call."

"We can try it," I said.

"Thank you, honey," Mom said, beaming.

I gave her a hug. "I have to get back to work. We have lots of funeral orders to get out this evening."

"Then I won't keep you. Don't forget to work on that stain."

"Okay." I started toward the curtain only to be stopped by, "Oh, Abigail, I nearly forgot. Have you spoken with your cousin today?"

Instantly, my inner antennae quivered. The only reason Mom would ask me that is if there was a plan afoot and Jillian was in on it. Apparently, Grace's antennae had quivered, too, because she quickly back-stepped into the parlor.

"As a matter of fact," I said, "Jillian was here a little while ago."

"Did she mention anything about, oh, I don't know, a dress perhaps?"

The plan began to unfold. "What kind of dress?"

"Well," she said, her eyes sparkling, "your father and I want to give you a special shower gift, something just for you, so I thought, why not a lovely dress for the occasion? Then Jillian happened to mention that she'd found one that would be just right for you, and *bingo*! There it was! The perfect gift."

"That's generous of you, Mom, but I have an outfit already."

"Oh." She waited a beat. "A nice one?"

"All under control, Mom," I said, walking her to the door. "Tomorrow we'll put out your tree and see what happens, okay?"

When she was gone, I turned the sign to CLOSED and locked the door.

"I didn't realize you'd purchased an outfit for the shower," Grace said, carrying a fresh arrangement out of the parlor to store in the cooler. "You hadn't mentioned it anyway."

"I didn't buy an outfit for the shower. All I told Mom was that I *had* an outfit."

"Ah, splitting hairs, are we?" She closed the glass-fronted cooler and turned to give me a smile.

"I've worn the dress only twice, Grace. I might as well get my money's worth out of it."

"Do you have proper shoes for the dress?"

I did a mental search of my shoe collection, which took approximately three seconds. I had one pair of high heels, black, that probably wouldn't look all that good with a brown and white halter dress. "No."

"When do you plan to shop for new shoes?"

Sometimes it felt as though I had way too many mothers. "Maybe I'll order shoes online. I can overnight them."

"If they don't fit and you have to send them back,

you'll be cutting it very close, love. As your wise President Lincoln famously said, 'Leave nothing for tomorrow which can be done today.' Why not trot down to Olcott's Shoe Store as soon as you finish this evening? I believe they're open until nine."

"Sounds like a great idea," I said, and headed for the curtain.

The phone rang and I heard Lottie answer from the back, "Bloomers Flower Shop. How may I help you?"

As I walked into the workroom, Lottie put her hand over the receiver and said, "Did you order a thousand feet of lei flower garland? Because the price just went up sixty percent. The salesman wants to know if you have a problem with that."

Oh, yes, I had a problem with it. "Who raises a price by sixty percent? Someone has to be selling garland for less than that. Tell him to cancel it." With a scowl, I plucked another order off the spindle and headed to the cooler to gather my stems.

No professional juggler, and now no lei garland. The water was rising, but I wasn't treading yet.

I didn't get to Down the Hatch until eight o'clock that evening, and by that time, the place was jammed. Marco was working behind the bar with a new bartender, Rafe was delivering drinks and busing tables, and Gert was serving up sandwiches from the kitchen.

Marco saw me and winked, then motioned for me to come to the end of the bar.

"Hey, baby, how are you?" he asked, pulling me into his embrace. That got a loud cheer from the patrons on the stools.

"I'm fine, but it looks like you'll be here for a long while," I said.

"Yeah, looks like it. Have you eaten?"

"No, and I'm famished."

"How does this sound? Ham and Swiss sandwich, sweet potato fries, and one of our new, mellow microbrews?"

"I'm salivating already."

Marco arched one eyebrow. "For me or for the food?"

"Hey, hot stuff," Rafe said, as he came around the end of the bar. "How's it shaking?"

"Would you find Abby a booth?" Marco asked his brother. Then to me he said, "I'll be back in a few."

Rafe motioned for me to follow him, then picked up a tray of drinks and led me through the crowd. He was ten years younger and slightly lankier than Marco, but otherwise he was the spitting image of his brother. On top of that, he was single and proving to be quite a draw for the college students who went to New Chapel University. Rafe had dated a few women since he'd arrived in town and had come dangerously close to a really bad marriage, but now he was back to being footloose and loving it.

Rafe had dropped out of Ohio State one semester shy of graduating in order to "find himself," then hung around his mother's house until she got so frustrated with his so-called self-discovery that she sent him to live with Marco, hoping big brother would straighten him out. After a few false starts, Rafe had finally become industrious and was now learning how to manage Marco's bar so that after we were married, Marco could focus solely on private investigations.

"Here we are," Rafe said, stopping at a booth.

I edged through the crowd and slid onto the upholstered bench, then realized the booth was already occupied.

By Francesca Salvare.

I was going to have to choke Rafe later.

Francesca had finished a bowl of soup and was calmly

sipping a glass of red wine. She was wearing a cowl-necked, black silk top with at least five different silver chains, silver and turquoise earrings, and heavy turquoise bangles on both wrists. She looked amazing.

That was when I remembered the stain on the front of my shirt, so I quickly turned my body at an angle, hoping she wouldn't see it.

"Bella!" she cried. "What a pleasant surprise. I'm so glad you're joining me."

Surprise, yes. I wasn't so sure about the pleasant part. That would all hinge on her topic of conversation.

"How fortunate that you came in tonight," she said with a big smile. "I was going to call you anyway. I have been thinking about your shower."

Surprise!

"I understand that you want to choose the menu yourself," Francesca said, "so here is what I'm thinking. You tell me what you have in mind, and I will make it using only the freshest ingredients, so you will have the most delicious, nutritious food around with no cost to you and my son."

That sounded reasonable enough.

"So, tell me," she said, folding her arms on the table, "what will it be? Pans of golden brown, bubbling, meaty lasagna? Rich, creamy mushroom risotto? Steak Pizzaiola? Osso buco? Or maybe something French, such as chicken in Dijon sauce?"

"Well," I said, as Rafe delivered my microbrew, "as delicious as those sound, I was planning a Chinese theme."

Her smile stiffened slightly. "Chinese?"

"Yes, with miniature egg rolls, pot stickers, tofu fingers, and chicken skewers with a peanut dipping sauce."

"Pot stickers? This is a food?"

"It's a Chinese dumpling."

"I see." She tossed back the rest of her wine as though it were a shot of whiskey. "And for your cake?"

"Fortune cookies."

"Fortune cookies?"

"Sure. Everyone does the standard white, banana, or chocolate cake, but I want to mix it up, so I'm going to arrange the cookies on a three-tiered holder to make them look like a cake."

Francesca picked up the cloth napkin that had been on her lap and carefully patted her lips, then folded the napkin and set it beside her glass. After placing her hands on the tabletop, fingers laced, she said in a serious voice, "*Bella*, have you thought this out carefully?"

"I know it's not a traditional shower meal, but that's why I chose it. I don't want to do the usual things. I want my shower to be unique. I hope you understand."

"I understand your wanting this to be . . . unique, but will your guests understand?"

"Who doesn't like Chinese food?"

"And my son likes this idea?"

"Marco said he wants whatever makes me happy."

"An admirable quality in a man," she said in a flat voice, glancing toward the bar with narrowed eyes. I had a feeling Marco would hear about this conversation later.

Rafe delivered my sandwich and fries. "There you go, HS." He paused to say to Francesca, "Anything I can bring you, *Mamma*?"

"No, thank you, Raphael. *Bella*, will you excuse me, please? I must be going now. It was good to see you, as always." She gave me a hug, then started through the crowd, which parted before her like the Red Sea.

Rafe waited until she was gone; then he said, "What did you do? She didn't look pleased."

"I informed her I was going with Chinese food at the shower."

"You know she doesn't have a clue how to make Chinese food, right?"

I smiled.

Rafe nodded. "Smart girl." With a chuckle, he turned and left.

Wednesday

My cell phone rang early the next morning, before I was fully awake. I was sitting at the counter in my apartment's small galley kitchen, sipping my first cup of coffee and waiting for my toast to pop up, when my phone began to play Pink's "So What." I'd chosen that ringtone around the time of Jillian's wedding, but now I couldn't remember for whom.

One look at the screen said it all: Pryce Osborne II. I should have known by the knot in my stomach.

Marco came into the kitchen wearing navy and maroon plaid pajama bottoms, took a coffee mug from the cabinet, and sat on the stool beside mine. He'd come in some time after one o'clock in the morning and had camped out on the sofa so he wouldn't wake me. "Aren't you going to answer that?"

"It's Pryce," I whispered, giving him a pained glance.

"He can't hear you," Marco whispered back. "Want me to get it?"

And make me feel like a coward? "No, that's okay. I can do this."

The phone stopped ringing. Problem solved.

"Are you going to call him back?" Marco asked, because clearly that was what he would've done.

"If it's important, I'm sure Pryce will try again."

The stupid phone rang. Marco waited. I sighed and reached for my cell phone just as my roommate Nikki's white cat, Simon, leaped onto the counter and began to wash his face to remove all traces of breakfast tuna. "Down, Simon!" I said.

The cat stopped washing to give me a *Surely you don't mean* moi look, then went back to his ablutions. He was cranky because Nikki was out of town for a five-day medical conference.

Marco put Simon on the floor, then got up to pour himself a cup of coffee. "You sure you don't want me to answer?"

I hit the green button and said, "What's up, Pryce?"

"Sorry to phone so early," he said in a quiet voice, "but there's been a serious development."

I wanted to give him some kind of flip comment, one of the many I'd saved in my head just in case I should ever have the opportunity to use one, but the anxiety in Pryce's voice had my full attention. "How serious?"

There was no sound from the other end of the line, as if the call had been dropped.

"Pryce? Are you there? Hello?"

Marco was instantly on full alert. "What's going on?"

"He said there'd been a serious development—then the line went dead."

The phone trilled and I quickly hit the green button. "Pryce?"

"Weak signal out here," Pryce said. "There are police swarming all over my property. Would you call Marco and have him phone me immediately?"

"Police are swarming your property?" I repeated for Marco's benefit. "Why?"

"Just tell Marco a woman's body washed up onto the sand near our boat dock this morning, and to get here right away. Please!"

CHAPTER TWELVE

That was serious enough to put my animosity aside. "Pryce, hold on."

"What is it?" Marco asked.

I held my hand over the receiver. "A woman's body washed up on the beach by the Osborne boat dock. Pryce wants to talk to you." Taking my hand off the mouthpiece, I said, "Pryce, Marco is here with me now. I'll put you on speakerphone so we can both listen."

"Abigail, the police are pounding on my door! Please hurry."

I pushed the speaker button and laid the phone on the counter. "Okay, Pryce, go ahead."

"Has the body been identified?" Marco asked.

"I don't know," Pryce said, sounding panicked, "but I'm afraid it's Melissa."

"Calm down and listen to my voice," Marco said sternly. "Have you let the cops enter your cottage?"

"No."

"Okay, good. Listen to me carefully. They cannot come in if you don't open your door. Do you understand? They cannot come in without a warrant. Do you know if they have a warrant?"

"I—I don't think so. They didn't say anything about a warrant."

"Have any detectives spoken to you?"

"Yes."

"Did you give them any information at all?"

"Yes, I told them I didn't know anything."

"Good. Then they have nothing on you. Do you understand?"

"Yes."

"How did you find out about the body?"

Pryce's voice was shaky and hoarse, as though his throat had closed up, and I could hear him breathing shallowly. His anxiety came as a surprise. I'd never heard him sound anything but arrogant.

"A cop was standing out on the back deck," he said, "so I opened the door to see why and that's when he told me about the . . . woman."

"Then don't worry," Marco said. "They're simply informing you they found a body on your beach. Do you understand?"

"Why do you keep asking him if he understands?" I whispered.

Marco held his hand over the speaker and said near my ear, "He's frightened, and that means he might not be getting what I'm telling him. If I keep repeating the question, it forces his brain to pay attention."

"How do we know he isn't responsible for whoever is on the shore?"

"I can tell by his voice, Sunshine. That's not the voice of a guilty man."

Marco uncovered the speaker. "Who's out there now, Pryce?"

"I don't know. Cops, investigators, medics, a police photographer, the coroner . . . Dear God, two television vans just pulled up. I've got to keep this from hitting the news, Marco."

"Pryce, listen to me. Are any of your friends at the house with you now?"

"No."

"Do you know who discovered the body?"

"I don't know and I don't want to ask. You have pull with the police, don't you? Would you please find out what's going on? I'm desperate."

"I'll do that now and let you know. Hang in there, Pryce. At this point, the cops are talking to everyone in the vicinity to see if anyone saw or heard anything, that's all. Understand what I'm saying? No one is accusing you of anything, okay? I'll get back to you shortly. Keep your phone with you."

Marco ended the call, then texted his buddy Sergeant Sean Reilly of the New Chapel PD. As we waited for a response, Marco said, "I'm not sure how much Reilly can help, because some police departments don't talk to anyone outside their own force."

While we waited for Reilly's call, I made the two of us toast with almond butter and honey on it; then we sat back down at the counter to eat. Simon stood on his hind legs to give Marco a tap on the arm, which earned him a gentle head scratching. He rewarded Marco with loud purring.

"Who's my bud?" Marco asked, leaning down so Simon could rub his cold little nose against his forehead.

Simon had never taken to any male before Marco. The only attention he'd given Pryce was to puke on his Ferragamo loafers. Nikki's boyfriends were ignored completely.

Marco's phone buzzed, so he grabbed it. "Hey, Sean, thanks for getting back to me. I need a favor."

I left him talking so I could get ready for work. When I returned to the kitchen, Marco was rinsing out the coffee-pot.

"Well?" I asked.

Marco put his plate in our minuscule dishwasher. "The only information Reilly had was that a man out jogging along the shore at dawn phoned in the report of a woman's body. There's been no identification made yet, so there's a good chance it's not Melissa. For all we know, the victim could have been pulled under by a riptide or drowned in a boating accident."

"So what happens next?" I asked.

"What happens next is that I'm going up to the lake to see what I can find out. I don't think there's any danger to Pryce, but I'd feel better talking to him face-to-face and maybe seeing what I can find out from the cops."

"Do you want me to come along?" It was a question I had to ask because half of me dreaded going out to that cottage again and spending more time in Pryce's company. The other half was burning up with curiosity.

Marco pulled me close. "I always want you along, butter-cup, but we may be there for a couple of hours. Do you have that much time free?"

I glanced at the clock. Figuring on half an hour of travel time each way, and a few hours at the lake, I wouldn't get into Bloomers until ten o'clock or later. Dilemma over. "I'll take a pass. I don't want to leave Lottie and Grace shorthanded."

Marco put his forehead against mine. "You could ask my mom to help out, you know."

"That would definitely solve one problem. But I'm afraid it would foster a new one."

"Which is?"

"Promise you won't laugh."

He made a cross over his heart. "Promise."

"Your mom might ask me to employ her."

Marco covered his mouth, trying to squelch a smile, so I playfully punched his arm. "You promised."

"Sorry. I couldn't help it. Why do you think my mom would want to work for you?"

"Because she loves Bloomers as much as I do. She calls my workroom her paradise. *Her* paradise, Marco. My workroom."

"Okay, Abby, let's put that fear to rest right now. Francesca Salvare works for no one. If she can't call the shots, she doesn't want the job."

"*Her paradise*, Marco, as though she owned the shop."

"Do you trust that I love you?"

I knew this was going to be a trick question. "Of course."

"Then trust me when I say she doesn't want to own Bloomers. She just likes the atmosphere there."

When it came to understanding mothers, Marco was too naive for his own good. "How much do you love me, Marco?"

His voice dropped to a husky growl. "Want me to show you later?"

"Yes. But how about a quick demonstration now?"

"Now?"

"No time like the present, as Grace likes to say." I reached into his pocket and slid out his cell phone. "Call your mom for me and ask her to help out at *my* flower shop. I'll phone Lottie to let her know we're on our way to Dune Haven."

"You didn't tell me you and *Mamma* had a confab last night about the shower food," Marco said, glancing at me with a flicker of a grin as we drove north.

"I blocked it from my mind. She wasn't happy with our selection."

"Which is why you chose it."

"No! I chose it to be unique."

"Abby."

"I'm absolutely serious."

"Two weeks ago, you asked if my mom had ever made Chinese food, and I told you she hadn't because she didn't care for it."

"Okay, that might have been a *minor* reason for my choice. Did I tell you my mom and Jillian are conspiring about my shower outfit?"

"Yes. Twice. Please, sweetheart, don't go with Chinese just to keep my mom from preparing it. If you'd rather do it yourself, which I still think is taking on too much responsibility, just be up-front about it. Mom will get over it."

"Are you hinting that you don't want Chinese food?"

"Abby, be straight with me. Do you really want Chinese food or are you only choosing it to keep my mother from interfering?"

"The answer is both of the above. I can't hurt your mom's feelings by saying she can't make the food, Marco, and you know she will insist upon making it. *And* I think Chinese food will be fun. I've already researched it and have my list made out. I just need to buy egg rolls, pot stickers, chicken skewers, and fortune cookies, and make the peanut dipping sauce myself, and voilà! A finger-food fun shower."

Marco sighed and shook his head. "You're taking on too much work, Abby."

"If you help me, it shouldn't be a problem."

Marco glanced in his rearview mirror, then immediately turned on his signal and pulled onto the shoulder to let an ambulance pass. "You know I'll help, but I still think you're trying to do too much."

"Not a problem. I can handle it." Or at least die trying. I just hoped it wouldn't come to that.

"Okay, Superwoman," Marco said, laying his hand across my shoulders, "we'll see. How painful is your neck right now?"

I sighed miserably and reached my hand around to massage a tender spot. "Let's just say it's been better." It had also been worse. I'd developed a horrendous pain in my neck when I was engaged to Pryce. Coincidence? I thought not.

We followed the ambulance onto Elm Street, stopping at a roadblock set up just before the Osborne cottage. Marco had to show his driver's license and PI badge so we could park and get out of the car.

Pryce was waiting for us by the front door and greeted Marco with a vigorous handshake. I would have shaken his hand, too, if pushed into it, but he was so agitated, I didn't think he even noticed me.

"Thank you for coming, Marco. I'm an absolute wreck. Hello, Abigail."

So he had noticed me.

Pryce opened the door for us, then followed us inside. "Were you able to find out anything?"

"I'm still waiting for a definitive word," Marco said. "All I could learn was what you'd already told me."

"Let's go to the back deck so you can see what's happening."

"Did you call your attorney?" I asked, as Pryce led us through the cottage.

"I wasn't able to reach him. He's at a legal conference, and his associate hasn't returned my call."

"You know other lawyers," I said.

"I don't trust anyone else. If it comes down to it, I'll represent myself."

"You're a corporate attorney, Pryce," I said, rubbing a spot just above my left shoulder blade. "You don't have any experience in this realm. You've heard that saying about a doctor who treats himself has a fool for a patient? That applies to lawyers, too."

"Seriously, Pryce," Marco said, "*if* the body is Melissa's, and I'm just saying *if*, then you'll need an experienced lawyer at your side, because they will probably want to question you. It would be for your own protection."

We stepped onto the deck and walked across to the railing to look at the scene below. It looked like the movie set for a disaster flick. Red and blue lights flashed on a dozen different vehicles parked close to the sand; men in uniform combed the beachfront in a straight line, looking for evidence; a photographer knelt on the dock taking pictures; reporters and their cameramen did live broadcasts; and two EMTs lifted a black body bag onto a gurney and wheeled it to the back of an ambulance. Minutes later, the ambulance pulled slowly away.

Pryce raked his fingers through his hair, a gesture he would never have made unless he was really freaking out. "Do you see what I mean about the media? My parents are bound to find out."

That was Pryce's main concern?

As we watched, two men in navy blazers and khaki pants entered the fenced-in pool area, circled the pool, and came toward us, climbing the steps to the deck. Both displayed their detective badges. "Do you folks live here?" a tall, gray-haired man asked, wiping perspiration from his forehead with a handkerchief.

Pryce's Adam's apple bobbed in his throat as he replied hoarsely, "I do."

The other detective, a stocky, dark-skinned man, took out a small tablet and pencil. "Can I have your name?"

"P-Pryce Osborne. The S-Second." He was breathing so shallowly, I was afraid he would pass out.

"How about you?" the gray-haired detective asked, looking at Marco and me.

"Marco Salvare," Marco said calmly, pulling out his PI badge. "This is my fiancée, Abby Knight."

"Any relation to Sergeant Jeffrey Knight?" the gray-haired man asked.

"My dad," I said proudly.

"Good man," Detective Gray Hair said with a nod. "Great cop, too."

"Thanks." I loved hearing that.

"Did any of you notice any suspicious people or activity or unusual noises last night?" the second detective asked.

"I heard n-nothing," Pryce said shakily. "It was a quiet evening."

"We just got here," Marco said, slipping his wallet into his back pocket.

"Wh-who is" — Pryce swallowed hard as he nodded toward the lake — "the woman?"

Seeing Marco's quick shake of the head, Pryce tucked his hands into his armpits, no doubt to keep the cops from seeing them shake.

Marco moved forward, putting himself between Pryce and the detectives. "Can you tell us what happened?"

"All we know at this point is that we've got an unidentified body," the second detective said. "We're talking to all the neighbors along the lakefront to see if anyone has helpful information on that subject."

"Okay, then," the gray-haired detective said, tucking his tablet into his blazer's chest pocket. "Thanks for your help."

"Thank you, Detectives," Pryce called as the men walked back down the steps. He turned toward us and sighed in relief. "Let's go inside. I need a drink."

"A cup of coffee sounds good to me," I said. "Marco, anything for you?"

"Coffee sounds good to me, too."

"In that case," Pryce said, "Abigail, you'll have to operate the coffeemaker. Mrs. Ambrose is off today."

While I was in the kitchen waiting for the java to finish dripping, I heard the front door open and the click of high heels come toward me. A few seconds later, Jillian came around the corner carrying two giant shopping bags. Her eyes lit up when she saw me.

"Oh, good, you *are* here. Lottie said this is where I'd find you, but I seriously didn't believe her. I mean, why would you be here so early in the morning?"

Her questions, along with her curiosity, ended there. She set down her bags and straightened, her hands on her hips and a smile on her face as she looked me over. "I knew it."

"What?"

"You'll see in a minute. Turn around and don't peek. I've got a meeting with a client, so I can't stay long."

"Don't you want to know what I'm doing here?" I asked her.

"Later."

I heard tissue paper rustling and got a queasy feeling in my stomach. "Jillian, if you brought a dress for me to try . . ."

"You can look now."

I turned, and she handed me a mint green dress on a hanger. "Here. Go try it on."

I took one look at the ruffle trim around the V-neck and the big bow that tied at the waist in the front, and thrust it back into her arms. "Not my style. Too chic. Besides, I already have an outfit for the shower."

"I hope you're not talking about that old brown and white floral thing you had back in college. No one is wearing that color or style anymore, Abs. This is what's in now. It'll look fabutastic on your short little body. Trust me." She tried to hand it back, but I wouldn't take it.

"Jillian, what don't you understand about the word *no*?"

"Would you just try it? Trust me, Abs, this is *the dress* for you."

"You're going to have to take *the dress* back, Jill, because I'm not wearing it. I'm not a fashionista like you are, and I probably couldn't afford it anyway."

"But it's a gift from your parents!"

I folded my arms. "No. Way."

She stamped her sandaled foot on the floor. "What's wrong with you?"

"I don't like people dictating what I should wear or do or eat for my shower. It's *my* shower, Jillian. My. Shower."

She huffed as she knelt to put the dress back in the shopping bag. "You're being anti-tractable."

"It's *in*tractable, and *you're* being anti-observant. Look out the windows. What do you see?"

She stood up with a frown. Her gaze moved over my shoulder to the view outside and instantly her eyes widened. "What happened?" she cried, hurrying to a window.

"A woman's body washed up on the beach this morning."

Jillian gasped. "Melissa's?"

"We don't know."

She pulled out her cell phone and began to tap in numbers. "I have to let Claymore know. He'll want to be here for his brother, just in case. I'll have to cancel the meeting with my client, too."

"Jillian, wait. Canceling your meeting isn't really necessary at this point because it might not be Melissa."

"Claymore? Hi, it's me. You'd better get out to the cottage *immédiatement*." She held her hand over the phone and whispered to me, "Run along. I'll meet you outside."

When I stepped onto the Osbornes' deck carrying two mugs of hot coffee, Halston and Orabell had joined the party, or so it seemed from their buoyancy. Halston had taken a seat at a table with Pryce and Marco, while Orabell had parked herself on a wrought iron bench near the railing where she could watch both the people on the deck and those on the beach.

Unlike Halston, who wore a casual gray linen shirt and white shorts, with sandals and a straw hat, Orabell had on an ankle-length red sundress made of a flowing gossamer cotton, over which she'd tied a multicolored silk wrap, red gladiator sandals that gripped her skinny ankles, and a bright red floppy sun hat. Her earlobes sported large red feather earrings that brushed her shoulders and, in combination with the rest of her attire, made her look like a large crimson parrot.

Both Burches had margarita glasses filled with a pinkish brown drink. An insulated pitcher sat on the table in front of Halston, no doubt holding refills.

"Come sit, darling," Orabell called, patting the bench. "Halston, pour Ally a drink."

"It's Abby," I said, "and I've got coffee. But thanks for the offer." I handed Marco his mug, then leaned against the side railing.

"Look at all the excitement down there," Orabell said with a girlish squeal, jumping up to join me. "We haven't had so much activity in eons, have we, Halston?"

"Say what?" he asked, cupping his ear.

"Buy a new hearing aid, you old fool," she said, throwing him a scowl.

"Wish I could hear you, Mummy," he said. Then, when she glanced away, he gave her a smirk and took a drink from his glass, making me wonder if he didn't prefer not to hear her.

"Who do you think drowned?" Orabell asked Pryce.

He stiffened, saying nothing, his gaze never leaving the beach.

Orabell tapped my shoulder with a pointed red fingernail. "He's worried it's Melissa, you know."

"I think we're all worried that it's Melissa," I said.

"Well, of course we are, darling, because Pryce would be numero uno on the suspect list." She sighed dramatically as she flounced over to the bench. "Poor dear."

"Who's the poor dear?" Halston asked, tapping his hearing aid. "Pryce or Melissa?"

Orabell glared at her husband. "Both, of course." To Pryce she said, "If it is Melissa, do you think she threw herself in?"

I could see the shock on Pryce's face as he rose and strode toward the sliding glass door, meeting Jillian on her way out of the house carrying a steaming mug of what was undoubtedly tea.

"Pryce, I was just coming to tell you that Claymore is on his"—she stepped aside as he brushed past her—"way." She turned to give me a puzzled glance.

"Jillian, darling!" Orabell called. "Come join me over here." She patted the bench.

"Oh, bother," Halston said. "Here come those blasted police again."

The same two detectives strode toward the deck stairs. At once, Marco got up and walked down to meet them. He listened to what they had to say, then came back and headed straight for the sliding glass doors.

"What's the story, General?" Halston called.

"I'll let you know in a minute," Marco replied.

"What happened?" I asked breathlessly, hurrying inside after him.

He closed the door and said in an undertone, "The detectives have an ID on the victim. They want to talk to Pryce, but I told them he was on the phone with his attorney and would be unavailable until the attorney arrived. That will stall them for a while, but not forever, if they're determined."

My heart started to race, imagining Pryce's shock. "Then the body has to be Melissa's."

"That's my guess. I tried to get them to say more, but they wouldn't budge. We need to find Pryce and warn him."

We found Pryce sitting on the front verandah, staring blankly into space. Hearing the screen door creak open, he jumped. "Do you have news?"

"There's been an ID on the body," Marco said.

Pryce lost all color in his face. "Who is it?"

"They wouldn't tell me. They wanted to speak with you, so I told them you were talking to your attorney. They're gone for now, but they'll undoubtedly be back."

"Dave Hammond could help you," I said. "You remember Dave, don't you? Public defender? The lawyer I clerked for?"

Pryce rubbed his forehead. "I remember him vaguely, but I'd prefer not to complicate matters more by switching law firms."

He thought *that* would complicate matters?

"Do whatever it takes to protect yourself, Pryce," Marco said. "Dave would be a good man to call. And remember what I told you before. Mum's the word. Listen to what the cops have to say, because they just may want to inform you of what they know. But if you feel at all as though they're trying to get information from you, then tell them your lawyer gave you instructions to wait until he arrived. Got it?"

"Wouldn't that merely serve to make me look guilty?" Pryce asked.

"Don't analyze it," Marco said. "The cops know it's routine procedure. Now get on the phone and call your attorney's associate and tell him it's urgent that you speak with him."

Pryce stared out at the trees for a few moments, then seemed to gather his strength and rose, straightening his shoulders. "Thank you for the advice. Forewarned is forearmed, so they say."

He opened the screen door and waited for us to enter. "Anyone for a glass of tea? I have a pitcher in the refrigerator."

"I think I'd rather have coffee," I told him.

"In that case . . . ," Pryce began.

"I'll make a fresh pot," I finished with a sigh.

"Think I'll go down to the wine cellar to pick out a fine Bordeaux for lunch," Pryce said.

I started a fresh pot brewing while Pryce went to the basement to get his wine. Holding full cups, Marco and I stepped out onto the deck, where we found Jillian and the Burches watching the somber scene on the beach below. No one spoke. Even Orabell had settled down, sitting with her shoulders hunched and elbows propped on her knees.

Marco and I walked to the side railing and stood sipping our coffees. Hearing the sliding door open behind me, I glanced around and saw a blond woman of about my age step outside.

Her highlighted hair was long and straight, with bangs that covered her eyebrows and half of her eyes. She wore a long pink halter dress, shiny tan flip-flops, a big green plastic watch, and a black patent leather tote bag over one shoulder.

"Why is the road blocked?" the woman asked, dropping her glossy bag onto an empty chair. "I had to park a mile away."

Orabell's head swiveled and she let out a gasp. "Melissa!"

CHAPTER THIRTEEN

I glanced at Marco in surprise. *Melissa is alive!*

"Where on earth have you been?" Jillian demanded,
standing with her hands on her hips, giving the prodigal
ex-fiancée a once-over. She took in Melissa's choice of
clothing and gave a shudder.

"I had to get away for a while," Melissa said, as if pulling a disappearing act was no big deal. She caught sight
of the activity on the beach and walked toward the railing for a better look. "What's going on down there?"

"A woman drowned this morning," Halston said, his
teeth clenched even tighter than usual. "We thought it
was you, didn't we, Mummy?"

Orabell stood up, swaying slightly, and pointed a
shaky finger at Melissa. "Yes, we thought it was *you*."
She muttered something afterward that sounded like
"You ingrate" as she tottered toward the bar.

"Why did you scare us like that?" Jillian demanded.

"Scare *you*?" Melissa said with a sarcastic laugh. "As if
you cared about anyone but yourself to be scared,
Jillian." Holding out her arms, Melissa said, "Take a look,
everyone. As you can see, it's not me down there, although
I imagine a couple of you were wishing otherwise."

I checked Halston's and Orabell's faces to see their reactions, but neither impressed me as feeling ashamed or guilty. Jillian just looked hurt. Melissa strutted over to the portable bar and scanned the liquor bottles on the shelves below. She didn't even seem curious about who the victim might be. Then again, she was probably feeling like a victim herself. I'd been in her shoes and remembered exactly what she was going through—an emotional roller coaster, up one moment and down the next. It hadn't been easy to get my life back on track, and I knew the same would hold true for Melissa.

Still, my inner antennae quivered a warning that something other than a broken engagement was on Melissa's mind. I glanced at Marco and found him observing Melissa, too, as though he shared my thoughts.

"Why didn't you let one of us know where you were, gal?" Halston said loudly. "Had us all concerned."

"Didn't give us a thought, I'm sure," Orabell added, sniffing contemptuously. "Doesn't care a whit about our distress."

Jillian started to chime in, but before she could speak, Melissa swung on Orabell, her fingers curling into fists. "I'm *sorry* if I caused you *distress*, Orabell, but I had a lot on my mind, so forgive me for being so inconsiderate of your feelings." Then she burst into tears and turned away, covering her face with her hands.

Orabell fluttered a hand at her husband. "Don't sit there like a lump, Halston. Pour the girl a martini. That'll fix her right up." With a huff, she returned to the bench and smoothed the dress around her legs.

"How about a margarita instead, gal?" Halston asked. "'Fraid my cocotinis are running low and Pryce's martini fixins ain't what they should be. There's a bottle of fine rum here if you prefer a stronger drink. That'll put some starch in your shorts."

"It's not rum that starches the shorts, Halston," Orabell said snidely. "It's whiskey."

"Doesn't matter which it is," Halston said, giving her a glare so subtle I would have missed it if I'd blinked. He handed a full glass of rum to Melissa. "Here, gal. You'll feel better afterward. Take my word on it."

Melissa took it with an uncalled-for flirtatious smile. "Thank you, Hals. I'll need this before I face Pryce again."

Jillian looked stunned, and Halston quietly withdrew, while Orabell went on the attack, asking accusingly, "Why do you have to face him? Your engagement is over."

Melissa turned on her, giving her a fierce glare. "So just like that"—she snapped her fingers—"it's over, Orabell? What do you know about what I'm going through? Have you ever been stomped on by your husband? Because that's what Pryce did to me. He stomped on my heart."

I glared at Orabell, too, for her insensitive comments. Oh, man, did I know what being stomped on felt like. Despite my initial wariness, I empathized with Melissa.

"Then why'd you come back?" Orabell fired back. "What's the purpose in belaboring the point? You think we're going to convince Pryce to take you back when it'd be best for everyone involved if you moved on—as far away as possible?"

Jillian let out a small gasp of surprise, while everyone else waited for Melissa's reaction.

"You don't know anything about what's best for Pryce and me!" she cried, then took a drink and looked around. "Where's Pryce? We need to talk."

"He's in the cottage," I told her. "I'm surprised you didn't see him when you came through."

"And who are you?" Melissa asked.

I walked toward her and held out my hand, which she didn't shake. "I'm Abby Knight and this is my fiancé, Marco Salvare. You probably don't remember, but we met once at the country club."

She looked me over, and suddenly her eyes narrowed into icy slits. "You're Abigail?"

"Yes, but I prefer Abby. I own Bloomers Flower Shop, on the square."

"I knew I'd seen you somewhere before. You were engaged to Pryce before I was."

"That's right."

Rather than realizing we had something in common, Melissa reacted as though I were a threat. She swept her bangs out of her eyes. "What are you doing here?"

"Pryce hired us," Marco said evenly, drawing her eye.

"And you are?" Melissa asked, ignoring my earlier introduction, her tone softening as she absorbed Marco's attractiveness.

"Marco Salvare. I'm a private investigator."

Melissa's eyes narrowed. "What are you investigating?"

"Your whereabouts," Marco replied.

At once, Melissa seemed to relax. With a fey smile, she said, "So Pryce actually hired an investigator to find me."

By her expression, I could tell this was good news. Melissa walked over to the railing on the other side of the bar and turned her back on the beach. A flicker of a smile played across her face as she sipped her rum. "What do you know, Orabell? Maybe Pryce cares after all." She made a sweeping gesture with her drink. "My apologies for the worry, everyone. That was not my intention."

Clearly her intention had been to make *Pryce* worry, and now that Melissa knew she'd succeeded, she seemed almost jubilant about it.

"Mystery's solved," Marco said quietly to me. "Pryce can take it from here. Let's get you back to the flower shop."

Leave before Pryce returns to find Melissa resurrected? I wasn't about to miss that. "Why don't we wait until Pryce comes outside? You know. Just to be sure everything's wrapped up."

Marco wasn't buying it. He leaned closer to say, "What is it that Grace always says about curiosity killing the cat?"

"Just another five minutes," I said. "Pryce has to come out soon."

"Unless he's stamping the grapes to make the wine," Marco grumbled, ready to be on his way.

"I could use more coffee," I said to the group. "Anyone else want a cup?"

"I'll have tea," Jillian said. "One for Claymore, too. He should be here any minute now."

"Here's a better idea," Halston said cheerfully. "Why don't we all repair to my deck for some of my new Bontinis? I have a pitcher chilling in the Frigidaire."

Didn't these people believe in coffee in the morning?

"What's a Bon-tini?" Jillian asked.

Halston rubbed his hands together. "Got the recipe from the owner of Belle Femme restaurant back in New Chapel. Interesting combination of flavors. Svedka Citron, Chambord, Triple Sec, Rose's lime, and a splash of cranberry juice. Doesn't it sound enticing?"

Jillian's response was to cover her mouth and head for the sliding glass door.

"Ah," Halston said. "Should have known beforehand that the gal doesn't have a taste for martinis, right, Mummy?"

"Gal should speak up about what makes her sick," Orabell said grumpily, rising. "We're not mind readers."

"Where you heading, Mummy?" Halston called, as Orabell navigated the steps.

"Where d'ya think?" she called back. "To get your silly pitcher of martinis."

"A Bon-tini sounds delightful, Hals," Melissa said, laying her hand on his arm in a way that seemed too familiar. It made me wonder if their relationship did go deeper than broker-client, as Orabell had claimed.

"Who do you think fell into the lake?" Melissa asked Halston. "Pryce's mother, I hope?"

As they continued conversing quietly, I tugged Marco's arm, leading him along the railing until we were closer to the house. "That was cold," I said softly.

A voice near my ear made me jump. *"Exactement,"* Jillian said, her face still looking wan. "I remember very clearly that you were furious with Pryce for dumping you, but you never wished his mother any harm. But that's because you're a good person, and Melissa isn't." She shrugged. *"Chacun à son goût."* For my benefit, she added in a whisper, "That means to each his own taste."

"Seriously, Jillian?" I asked. "French now? And how did you get out here so quickly? I thought you were sick."

"False alarm," she said with a happy sigh. "But I still want that tea."

Marco began to massage my neck, no doubt to remind me to relax my shoulders—or that he was ready to stop me if I tried to grab her by the throat.

"Remind me to tell you later about the new"—she whispered in my ear—"name I came up with, inspired by the British royal family."

"Just tell me now and get it over with," I said quietly.

"Not in front of"—she whispered in my ear— "Marco."

"Whatever."

Another whisper. "It's Beatrice. Beatrice Osborne."

"Initials, Jillian. B.O."

My pale-faced cousin repeated the initials, then sank onto a chaise longue with a pout. "I'll never come up with the right name."

"A name, you say?" Halston asked, turning. "A name for what?"

Jillian's response was to turn to me for help, so I blurted the first thought that came into my mind. "A horse."

Jillian nodded at Halston. "A horse."

Halston pondered it, sipping from his glass. "Pegasus would be a fine name, wouldn't it?"

Jillian sat upright, her eyes brightening. "Pegasus . . . Peggy!"

I shook my head and she flopped back down again, laying her arm over her eyes.

"Come on, Jillian," Melissa said, her lips quivering as she tried not to smile. "Pegasus would be a great name for your *horse*."

I eyed Melissa skeptically. Had she guessed about Jillian's pregnancy?

"A fine name," Halston continued. "I won money on a horse by that name. Long time ago of course. Filly's probably dead by now, but I'll never forget it. Pegasus. Yes, ma'am. A fine name."

"Weren't you going to see about more coffee?" Marco said to me.

"And my tea," Jillian found the strength to mutter.

"Hey!" someone called. "I didn't know we were getting together today."

I turned toward the glass door and saw Jake step out. He had on a pair of torn denim shorts with a white T-shirt and thick-soled canvas flip-flops, and his hair was sticking up as though he'd just tumbled out of bed.

"Did you guys know there's a roadblock down the street?" he asked, looking puzzled.

Catching sight of Melissa, Jake stopped dead in his tracks. "Hey, Melissa! You're . . . here!"

He seemed more shocked by Melissa being on Pryce's deck than by her return from the dead. A quick look passed between the two of them as Jake added, "You're okay!"

She held up her glass and said with a smile, "I'm okay now."

"Awesome," Jake said with what seemed to be forced cheerfulness, almost as though he was playing a role. I made a mental note to mention it to Marco.

Jake strode over to give Melissa a high five, then turned to gaze at us. "Where's Pryce?"

"Pryce is inside," Melissa said. "I haven't seen him yet."

"In case you're wondering, Claymore is on his way," Jillian said. "He had to go to the market to buy more organic eggs."

"Where's Lily?" Halston asked loudly, cupping one ear. "Didn't she come with you?"

Jake gazed around at us, as though he'd missed her the first time, then said with a careless shrug, "I figured she'd be here with you guys."

His behavior was a marked contrast to the way he'd burst into the Burches' house the evening before. This time he didn't seem at all upset by her absence.

"She must be at Beached," Jillian said, "where she always is."

"Where else would she be?" Orabell asked, climbing the steps with a green insulated pitcher in her hands. "Here's your martini mix, Halston."

"Why, thank you, Mummy," he said, and rose to take it from her. "Think I'll put it in Pryce's fridge for now."

"Not before you pour me one," Orabell said, holding out her glass.

I rolled my eyes at Marco. The thought of a martini that early in the day was nauseating.

Jillian held her hand over her cell phone and whispered loudly, "Lily's not at Beached. I've got one of her kitchen staff on the phone. She says Lily hasn't been in yet this morning."

"She might have gone to the hair salon," Jake said. "I think I remember her mentioning an appointment." Finally catching sight of all the flashing lights on the shore, he strode to the railing. "What happened down there?"

"A woman's body washed up on the shore this morning," Jillian said, putting away her phone.

"Wow. No kidding. I keep hearing how dangerous those riptides have been this summer."

Marco's gaze followed Jake as he left the railing and went up to Halston, who was standing beside Melissa. "What'cha drinking, Hals?" Jake asked, putting an arm around the older man's shoulders and giving them a squeeze.

"Not tea, that's for sure," Jillian said, throwing me an accusing glance.

"A Bloody Mary," Halston said lightly, though his jaws seemed more tightly clenched than usual. He inched away from Melissa and said with false cheer, "Orabell brought over a fresh pitcher of Bon-tinis, if you're of a mind to try one."

"Not for me, dude." Keeping one eye on Halston, Jake moved back and flexed his biceps. "Don't wanna drug my system or dull my mind."

"Too bad, Jake," Melissa said, holding up her nearly empty glass. "Alcohol works wonders on a broken heart." She nodded to us, then to Jake. "Cheers." Then she downed the remainder of her rum and set the glass on the bar with a bang.

A look passed from Jake to Melissa that I couldn't read. A threat? A chiding glance? There was an undercurrent to their silent conversation that I couldn't put my finger on. Whatever it was, Melissa scowled as though she was angry at him, while Jake merely made himself comfortable on a chaise longue near the cottage door and took out his cell phone.

"You never did say where you went off to, Melissa," Orabell said with a snide smile.

"Mackinac Island," Melissa replied. Again, a look passed between her and Jake that baffled me. Did Jake know she'd been to Upper Michigan?

"Mackinac Island, did you say?" Halston asked.

"That's right," Melissa answered. "No cars there at all, only bikes and horse-and-buggies. It's a great place to get your head together."

"No cell phone service there either, apparently," Orabell said drily.

"Did you stay at the Grand?" Jillian asked, taking a bottle of water from beneath the bar, obviously having given up on my bringing her tea.

"I sure did," Melissa replied, her gaze shifting toward Jake and then away. I wondered if Marco was catching all their quick glances.

"Did you have a reservation?" Jillian asked.

Melissa narrowed her eyes at Jillian. "Are you questioning me?"

"Someone's testy," Jillian said, then glanced at me and raised her eyebrows, as if to say, *What's going on here?*

"I'm not testy," Melissa retorted. "Why do you care if I had a reservation?"

"I was just curious," Jillian said. "Claymore and I

tried to go up to the island for a weekend, but we couldn't get in. They book months in advance."

"Why don't you go wait for your husband in the kitchen," Melissa said, "so he can fetch you a cup of tea with your egg sandwich?"

Jillian's mouth dropped open. She wasn't used to sarcasm directed at her. "I don't want tea anymore," she said, folding her arms. "Why don't you go find your ex-fiancé and"—she gestured toward the cottage—"have him fetch you a more believable alibi."

Go, Jillian!

"Alibi for what?" Melissa demanded.

"How did you manage to get a room so quickly?" Jillian asked, on the attack now.

"They had a cancellation," Melissa snapped. "If it's any of your business."

"Isn't that convenient?" Jillian retorted, giving Melissa her death stare. "Like anyone just drives up there and gets a room. And do you really think Pryce will take you back because you disappeared for two days?"

"You don't know what the hell you're talking about," Melissa said, moving toward Jillian, "so be careful what you say to me."

Marco stepped forward to block her path. "Let's leave it there, ladies. Abby, would you take Jillian inside to wait for Claymore?"

"Claymore, is it?" Halston asked. "Haven't seen the dear boy in some time. Pryce either, for that matter. Where'd he go off to, d'you suppose?"

As if he suddenly woke up, Jake rose halfway from the chair to point toward the beach. "Pryce is down there."

I turned to look below, my eyes searching the figures on the sand just as a cop strode toward the two detectives with a piece of glossy paper in his hands. Standing across from them was Pryce. "What the heck is he thinking?" I asked Marco.

At once, Marco strode toward the deck steps and hurried across the pool area, while Halston, Melissa, Jillian, and Orabell joined me at the railing to watch. Jake stayed back to make a phone call, then stepped inside the cottage to talk.

Before Marco could reach the group, the detectives showed the glossy paper to Pryce, who looked at it, then seemed to crumble, buckling at the knees. The detectives went to grab his arms, but he shook them off, then braced his arms on the side of the squad car and bowed his head as though he was going to be sick. Marco stood beside him, talking to him.

"Maybe it *is* his mother," Jillian whispered to me.

CHAPTER FOURTEEN

"**H**is mother isn't a young woman," I reminded my cousin.

"Then there's only one other person that I know of who'd get that kind of reaction from Pryce," Jillian said, then suddenly brightened. "Claymore!"

"It can't be Claymore," I said, then realized she was talking to her husband.

"I'm right here, my darling," Claymore replied, stepping out of the cottage.

She hurried toward the sliding glass door to hug him, then straightened the collar of his polo shirt. "I was beginning to worry about you. What took you so long?"

"I couldn't get off the phone with my mother," he said, kissing her forehead.

At least now I knew for certain that the body wasn't Evelyn Osborne.

"You know how she goes on," Claymore continued, as Jillian led him toward me. "Then I had to park all the way down the road and hike here. It was grueling." He gave a shudder. "Does anyone know where Pryce is?"

"On the beach," Melissa said.

Claymore spotted Melissa and his eyes widened. He

immediately went over to give her a hug. "I'm so glad you're safe. We were all worried about your well-being. Where were you?"

"In recovery," Melissa said, holding up her glass.

"She said she stayed at the Grand Hotel on Mackinac Island," Jillian said with an eye roll. "I'll tell you about that later."

Melissa gave Jillian a furious glare. "I stayed there, Jillian."

"I don't believe her," Jillian whispered to me.

"Look down on the beach, Claymore," Orabell said. "There's your brother. If you asked me, Pryce shouldn't have gone down there. Going to make those detectives think he's guilty as sin, isn't he?"

"Claymore, don't worry," I said, as Pryce's younger brother rushed to the railing. "Marco's with him."

"Why did Pryce go down there?" Claymore asked Jillian. "You told me on the phone he'd been advised against it."

"Wanted to find out who drowned," Orabell said. "The detectives are grilling Pryce about it now." She lifted her eyebrows to emphasize the importance of her statement.

"How do you know what they're doing?" Melissa snapped.

"What do you suppose they're doing?" Orabell retorted. "Having punch and cookies? Of course they're grilling him. That's what cops do. See if they can force a confession out of him is what they'll try."

"For what?" Jillian asked. "What do you think Pryce could confess to, Orabell?"

"Don't get your panties in a twist," Orabell replied. "I call them like I see them."

Before Jillian could retort, Halston held up the bottle of rum. "Want some, Mummy?"

"No." Orabell shrugged unhappily. "It's not fun over here anymore, Halston. Let's go home."

"Jake, have you tried calling Lily's cell phone?" Jillian asked, a worry wrinkle forming between her eyebrows.

"She hates it when I interrupt her while she's busy," Jake muttered, not looking at her.

"Fine. I'll call her," Jillian said.

"Never mind, I'll do it," Jake grumbled. He hit a speed dial number, then put the phone against his ear and waited. After a minute, he said, "Hey, Lil, it's me. Call me back, okay?"

Ending the connection, Jake said tensely, "It went to her voice mail. You know how calls get dropped around here. Right?"

No one replied.

"Who else might know where your wife is?" I asked.

"What is this?" Jake said, gazing around at us. "Do you guys know something I don't know?"

"Here come Pryce and Marco," Claymore said with relief, and started toward the steps, only to stop and stare at his brother as he approached, head down, shoulders slumped.

"Did they tell you who it is, Pryce?" Halston called.

"Shut up, Halston," Orabell called. "Can't you see he's got things on his mind?"

At the top of the stairs, Pryce drew in a breath and blew it out, as though gathering his strength.

"What happened?" Claymore asked.

Pryce's gaze moved slowly toward Jake, who had gone absolutely still. As Pryce walked over to him, Jake rose slowly from his chair, his Adam's apple bobbing as he swallowed. I put my hand in Marco's and gave it a squeeze.

Laying his hand on Jake's shoulder, his voice breaking, Pryce said, "I'm sorry, Jake. It's Lily."

There were gasps all around. Halston fell back into his chair, while Jake merely stared at Pryce in shock. After a long moment, he cried, "What are you saying, dude?"

Pryce just gazed at him forlornly.

Jake pushed Pryce's hand off his shoulder and backed away, as though ready to fight or flee. "You're insane, you know that?"

"Take it easy, Jake," Marco said.

"You'd better sit down, Jake," Claymore said kindly.

"No!" Jake shouted. "It's not true!" He got out his phone again, hit a number, and listened. A few seconds later, he threw down his phone. "Why can't I ever get a signal here, dammit!"

"Jake," Pryce began.

"Hey," Jake said sharply, "I don't know what the detectives said to you down there, man, but they lied. That dead woman isn't Lily." Jake gazed at all of us. "It's not her!"

Pryce sighed. "They showed me a photo of her body. She was wearing the clothing she had on yesterday."

Jake didn't move. He simply stood there, blinking slowly, as though trying to absorb the news.

"I'm sorry," Pryce said in a hoarse whisper.

His face turning red from rage, Jake pulled back his fist, ready to throw a punch at Pryce, who stood there as though he wanted to take it. Before Marco could get between them, Jake's arm went limp and then he collapsed onto his knees on the deck, covering his face with his hands and sobbing.

"Halston, pour the boy a drink," Orabell commanded. "He's about to fall apart."

It was Jillian and Claymore who coaxed a red-eyed Jake inside. Meanwhile, the drama on the deck continued when Melissa stepped forward, catching Pryce's eye.

"I'm back," she said softly, giving him an innocent head tilt and a hopeful glance.

Pryce seemed to freeze. Then, after delivering his haughtiest nose-in-the-air look, he stalked across the deck, slid the door open with a bang, and went inside, closing the glass door so hard, I was afraid it would shatter.

And Marco had wanted to miss all this drama.

"He'll come around," Melissa said, lifting her chin as she gazed around at the onlookers. "Just wait and see." She curled up in a chair and gazed out at the water.

Her reaction didn't come close to mine when Pryce broke up with me. I'd run and hidden at my parents' house. Melissa was definitely a different sort of bird.

Speaking of birds, Orabell flitted toward the sliding door as though about to follow Pryce inside. Halston caught her arm and said with a somber sigh, "Let's go home, Mummy. Time for your nap."

Orabell jerked her arm away from him. "How am I supposed to nap with all this activity going on? You can go if you want, Halston, but I'm staying put."

"Abs," Jillian called from the doorway. "Could you and Marco take over in here? I'm feeling a little *mal à l'estomac*." She pointed to her stomach and made a sour face.

Marco and I sat on the sofa in the family room as Jake paced, his eyes haunted, his fists clenched, clearly too distraught to sit.

"Why didn't the cops tell me?" Jake ranted. "I'm Lily's husband! Me! They should have come to me! I have my rights!"

"Pryce already explained that," I said. "The police needed an ID and Pryce didn't realize you'd come back."

"They could have phoned me. I mean, who doesn't

have his cell with him? Why go to Pryce before me? It makes no sense, man!"

"They found her body in his backyard," I said. "It makes perfect sense. Maybe they tried your phone and couldn't get a connection."

"It's a moot point, Jake," Marco said. "They did it, and it's over."

Jake stopped at the window, bracing his hands on the sill to stare out at the water. After a long moment, he sighed heavily and in a voice devoid of emotion asked, "So what happens now?"

"Lily's body is on its way to the county morgue for an autopsy," Marco said. "The police should be contacting you shortly."

"For what?"

"To explain what to do about funeral arrangements," Marco said, "and to ask you some questions."

"What kind of questions?" he asked, glancing over his shoulder at us.

"Just routine stuff," Marco said.

Jake strode back into the family room and sat down in a nearby chair, resting his elbows on his knees. "Like what?"

"Such as, did Lily say anything to you about going down to the water?"

"You mean like for a swim?"

"Pryce said she still had on yesterday's clothing, so maybe for a boat ride?"

"Not to me she didn't," Jake said tersely. "Maybe that's a question they should be asking Daddy Big Bucks. Maybe they should also ask him how Lily drowned."

"Daddy Big Bucks being Pryce?" I asked.

"Who else?" Jake said, his upper lip curling in distaste.

"Why would you think Pryce had anything to do with her death?" Marco asked.

Jake shrugged but didn't reply. Did he know more, or had he spoken out of spite?

"When was the last time you talked with Lily?" Marco asked.

Jake picked at a thread on the cotton cushion. "Yesterday before dinner."

"Did she come home last night?"

"I don't know. I fell asleep around midnight, and she wasn't there this morning when I got up, so I figured she got up early, had breakfast, and went straight to Beached."

"Would she have worn the same outfit two days in a row?" I asked.

Jake shrugged his shoulders, a miserable look on his face. "Lily did what Lily wanted to do."

The sliding door opened and Halston peered inside. "Jake, two detectives are here to see you."

Jake stared at him as though the statement hadn't made sense. "Right now?"

"They're waiting by the pool."

Jake rubbed his hands on his shorts, as though drying his palms, then got up, but seemed hesitant to move. "Can they question me?"

"They can," Marco said. "That doesn't mean you have to answer them. You can tell them you want a lawyer present or you can see what kind of questions they're asking first and take it from there."

"Are you saying I'll need a lawyer?"

"Yes," I said.

"It would be a good precaution," Marco replied. "That's all."

Jake studied us for a second, then followed Halston outside, sliding the door shut behind him.

"He shouldn't be talking to the cops at all," I said. "The husband is always the first to be suspected."

"It's out of our hands, Sunshine. Besides, Jake won't need a lawyer unless the cops find evidence of foul play. As of this moment, all we know is that Lily drowned."

"Wearing her clothes, don't forget."

"Did you ever walk along the sand in your clothes?" Marco countered. "Or sit on the dock with your bare feet dangling in the water? Or go for a boat ride?"

"Are you saying she fell in accidentally?"

"I'm saying we were hired to find Melissa, not investigate Lily's death."

"You're right," I said. "I've been hanging around you too long, Salvare. I see mysteries everywhere I look."

Marco pulled me onto his lap. "So what do you see now?"

I put my hands on either side of his face and pretended to study him. "I see a potential suspect."

Marco laid me back onto the sofa and leaned over me. "What am I suspected of?"

"Kissing your redheaded fiancée slash assistant."

Giving me that devilish flicker of a grin, he proved me right.

"Ugh. Get a room," Jillian said, flopping down on one end of the sofa.

Marco and I sat up as Jillian propped her feet on the coffee table and sighed. "I'm so hungry I'm sick to my stomach."

"I thought Claymore was making you an egg sandwich," I said.

"He's just now peeling the hard-boiled eggs."

"You mean you're waiting on an egg *salad* sandwich? Why didn't you just have fried eggs on bread?"

"Do not mention the word"—she used her fingers to make air quotes—"*fried* ever again. You know my fragile stomach can't handle grease. Now, do you mind?" She made a shooing motion. "I really need to lie down."

Taking my hand, Marco pulled me up. "Come on, Sunshine. We're done here."

"Abs," Jillian said, stretching out her arm, "here's your purse. You left your cell phone in it and the phone's been beeping."

I pulled out my phone and checked the screen. "It's Bloomers," I told Marco. "I'd better see what's going on." Especially with Marco's mom being at the shop.

"Go ahead," he said. "I'm getting a glass of water from the kitchen. Want some?"

"No, thanks." I dialed the shop, then walked up the hallway toward the front of the cottage as I waited for someone to pick up. Finally, I heard Grace say, "Bloomers Flower Shop. How may I help you?"

"Hi, Grace. It's me. Is everything okay?"

"Lovely, dear."

I stopped at the doorway to the redecorated living room but couldn't bring myself to go inside. With a shudder, I turned away. "Okay. I just noticed I missed your call, so I thought I'd better check in."

"It wasn't my call, love. Hold on a moment."

Please don't let it be Francesca's call. I wasn't in the mood to be hounded about the shower.

I heard Grace cover the phone to say, "Maureen, did you ring up Abby?"

My mom was there, too?

"Your mum would like a word," Grace said.

"Abigail, it didn't work," Mom said, "and I don't know what to try next."

"What didn't work?"

"Putting my elm tree display outside. The wind kept blowing masks into the street, and when we moved it farther back, people just stepped around it to get inside. Do you have any ideas?"

I had a few, but I was pretty sure she wouldn't want to

hear them. "How about"—I couldn't believe I was about to say this—"the bay window?"

"I thought of that, but the sun is so hot, I'm afraid it will melt the tree."

"Then I guess you'll have to move it back to where it was, Mom. I don't know what else to tell you."

"Okay," she said in a disappointed voice. "Thank you, honey."

"You're welcome. Can I talk to Grace again?"

A second later, Grace came back on the line. "Yes, love?"

"How is everything else going?"

"The parlor is humming along quite nicely, Lottie is busy in the workroom, and Francesca is taking care of the customers in the shop."

I dropped my voice to ask, "How is *that* going?"

"Splendidly, dear. Francesca gives everyone who comes in a small plate of Italian hors d'oeuvres, and you'll be pleased to know they've become quite a hit. We've had a steady stream of people since we opened, the cash register has been ringing like mad, and Francesca is having a delightful time. I have to say, Abby, Marco's mum is a fine complement to our shop."

"Well," I said, forcing a cheerful tone, "that's terrific, Grace." A complement to our bottom line, maybe, but not so much to my self-esteem.

"Did you want to speak with her, love?"

"No! I mean, it's not necessary—unless Francesca needs to speak with me."

Grace murmured something I couldn't hear, then said, "She sends her love, dear, and says to take good care of her boy."

I ended the call with a scowl. Did Francesca really need to remind me to take care of Marco? And handing out hors d'oeuvres at a flower shop? Really?

"Everything okay at Bloomers?" Marco asked, walking toward me.

"Everything is splendid, according to Grace."

"Then why don't you look happy about it?"

"What's not to be happy about? Your mom is wowing my customers with free appetizers, and the cash register is ringing like mad."

"*Mad* and *splendid* are Grace words, and that tells me there's trouble in paradise. What did my mom do?"

"Nothing, Marco. In fact, according to Grace, your mom is a complement to the shop."

"Ah."

"Ah?"

"Now I get it."

"What do you get?"

He put his arm around me. "That it's time to return you to Bloomers to claim your territory."

We were on the same page. What a relief. I leaned in to him as we passed through the kitchen on our way to the back deck to say our good-byes. What had I done before Marco came into my life?

Got engaged to Pryce, for one thing.

Claymore was humming softly as he chopped eggs, while Jillian stretched out on the sofa in the next room with her eyes closed, a contented smile on her face. It struck me then how perfectly suited to each other they were and how happy they were together. If they could be that satisfied with married life, then Marco and I should have it made.

I put my arm around Marco's waist, letting his energy and love flow into me, easing my frustration. Why was I angry anyway? Francesca was drawing customers into Bloomers. And thanks to her love of cooking, we were making money. Surely it wasn't jealousy. Surely I wasn't that petty.

"Penny for your thoughts," Marco murmured in my ear.

I stuffed my frustrations back inside to work on later. "I was just thinking how suited Jillian and Claymore are. Let's go say good-bye and get out of here."

When we stepped outside onto the deck, I was surprised to see that Jake had returned from meeting with the detectives. He was sitting at a table with Halston, working the keypad of his cell phone, while Melissa stood at the railing observing the happenings below, an odd, Cheshire-cat grin on her face. Orabell sipped her drink and studied Melissa from the wicker settee. Halston had his eye on the activity on the beach, too, but with an intense frown marring his normally jovial countenance.

Hearing the sliding door close, Melissa turned, her expression changing instantly to one of concern. "The detectives came back for Pryce a few minutes ago," she said, her hands clasped tightly together as she walked toward us. "What do you think that means?"

"That he wasn't listening when I told him not to talk to the police without his lawyer," Marco said, walking over to the railing for a look. I followed and so did Melissa, Orabell, and Halston. Jake seemed oblivious.

"How did it go, Jake?" Marco asked.

Jake shrugged. "Just routine questions, like you said. Luckily I have a solid alibi."

"Which is what?" I asked.

"I was here all night. Pryce can vouch for me."

He certainly had that all worked out. Almost. "Pryce's bedroom is at the end of the hallway," I said. "And—"

"Abby, come look," Marco said, and ushered me over to the railing, saying quietly, "Leave that to the detectives, okay? It isn't our case."

"Sorry. I told you I've been hanging around you too much," I whispered back.

Down below, the beach had practically emptied out. The news vans, the emergency vehicles, and all but two police cars, one unmarked—except for the half dozen antennae waving from the trunk—had departed. Two uniformed officers stood guard over a wide area marked off by yellow crime-scene tape, while curious neighbors looked on from a distance.

The yellow tape closed off half the shoreline in front of the Osborne cottage, along with their pier and the boat moored there. Pryce and the two detectives stood on the pier talking, and I could tell by the way Pryce held himself that he was agitated. I glanced at Melissa and saw that her sly grin had returned, as though she was enjoying what was happening to her ex-fiancé.

"Doesn't look good for Pryce," Orabell remarked. She clucked her tongue to suggest that she thought it was a pity, but her expression didn't register that same emotion.

"He's going to need a stiff drink when he comes back," Halston said.

"Unless they arrest him first," Orabell said.

"Why would they arrest Pryce?" Melissa asked.

"Why do you think?" Orabell snapped. "*Someone* pushed that woman into the lake."

Jake's head bobbed up again. "How do you know Lily was pushed?"

"I didn't say I knew," Orabell answered.

"Yes, you did," Melissa retorted. "How do we know it wasn't you who pushed her?"

"Me?" Orabell tipped back her head and brayed out a laugh. "Did you hear that, Halston? Here's a pot calling a kettle black. How do we know it wasn't *you*, Miss Priss? We all know how jealous you were of Lily, and then you conveniently disappeared, only to reappear after the body was found."

"There's your likely culprit," Halston said, pointing at

NIGHTSHADE ON ELM STREET **183**

Jake, his jaw locked tighter than usual. "Think he'd be a bit soggy around the eyeballs from losing his wife instead of busy playing with his techno-toy."

"You want to take me on, old man?" Jake called, hands braced on the wooden chair arms as though he was ready to spring up.

A parrot lady, a vindictive ex-girlfriend, a gym jock, a lock-jawed neighbor, a high-strung brother, and Jillian. These were the people Pryce chose to spend August weekends with?

Marco linked his hand through my arm and led me toward the door. "Time to get away from the craziness here."

Right. And back to the craziness at Bloomers.

I had Marco drop me at the corner so he could park his car; then I headed up the sidewalk, slowing when I saw half a dozen men standing outside Bloomers, peering through the big bay windows, hands cupped around their eyes.

"Did something happen?" I asked one of the men, recognizing him as the husband of one of our best customers.

He glanced around at me, then immediately turned red in the face and began to stammer. "N-no . . . we were just admiring your . . . flowers."

"You're welcome to come inside and browse," I said, opening the yellow door.

"We've already been inside," one of the men said with a sheepish grin.

"We were just enjoying the . . . scenery," another one said.

Several more men came out of Bloomers carrying small white paper sacks. "We'll be back tomorrow, Francesca," one of them called over his shoulder.

Francesca?

"Bene," I heard Marco's mom call. "I will see you then, Carlo."

"Carlo," the man said to his friends with a proud smile. "That's Charlie in Italian."

I let them pass, then stepped inside and stopped in surprise. Make that shock.

Customers, most of them male, filled the shop, all of them holding small paper plates loaded with food. Francesca was moving among them carrying a platter of bite-sized appetizers, flirting and laughing and having a great time; Lottie was at the cash counter ringing up purchases; and Grace was in the parlor weaving among the tables, refilling cups of coffee and tea.

For a full minute, I simply stood there, feeling like a foreigner in my own country, an alien life-form dropped in from a different dimension. Or maybe I was in the thick of my worst nightmare, because it certainly appeared as though Marco's mom was taking control of Bloomers—and Grace and Lottie were helping her. The only reminder of the peaceful flower shop I'd left behind that morning was Mom's elm tree on the table in the middle of the room, its branches still covered with sleep masks.

"Bella!" Francesca called above the melee. "Look how busy we are. *Fantastico*, no?" She paused to let a man take food from the platter. "Eat, eat! There is more where this came from."

Moving in a daze, I darted between people, aiming for the purple curtain and the sanctity of my small slice of paradise behind it. I lifted one side of the curtain and stepped through, ready to inhale the soothing scents of my blossoms and exhale the chaos behind me. And there I stopped, as the second shock wave hit me.

Marco's sister Gina was putting together a bouquet of roses at my worktable.

Wearing *my* florist's apron and wielding *my* floral knife.

The takeover was complete.

CHAPTER FIFTEEN

"Hi, Abby," Gina said, glancing up, as if there were nothing unusual about what she was doing. "How do I wrap these once I get them all trimmed?"

What could I do but show her? I didn't want to stand there with my hands on my hips and a perturbed look on my face, demanding to know why she not only had invaded my space but was also touching my personal items. It wouldn't do to have Gina think her brother was marrying an unappreciative stick-in-the-mud devil-witch, even though that was exactly what I felt like.

Gina Salvare Ferraro was two years younger than Marco, with the same glossy dark hair, dark eyes, and olive complexion that Marco, Rafe, and Francesca shared. She was a strikingly attractive, curvaceous woman a year older and a few inches taller than I was.

Gina and I had been on shaky footing at first because I hadn't been in a rush to get married and have a baby, making her suspicious of my intentions. Over the course of the past six months, our relationship had evolved, and although we weren't best friends, we also weren't enemies, and I didn't want to rock the boat now.

"Use this clear wrap," I said, and tore a sheet off the

roll hanging under the worktable. "Then tie it with the ribbons from the spool on the wall. It has a cutter on one side."

"Thanks."

"So, Gina, how long have you been working here?"

Why did I sound like I was trying to pick her up?

"Just about an hour. Things got so hectic, *Mamma* asked me to come lend a hand. And I hope you don't mind, but I had to bring—"

Her words were drowned out by an ear-piercing happy-child scream. That was followed by a small whimper from beneath the worktable that turned into a full-blown baby cry. "Christopher!" Gina called sharply, kneeling down in front of the table, "you woke your sister."

"Christopher is here, too?"

She stood up cradling Rosa, her eight-month-old daughter, dressed in a pink baby outfit, and began to pat the infant's back. "Chris is playing around here somewhere," she said with a shrug, apparently unconcerned about her three-year-old's whereabouts. She sniffed the baby's midsection, then, with a wrinkled nose, walked over to the back counter, where a large pink and green quilted bag lay and began to dig around inside until she found a diaper.

"Someone did a big ol' poops," she cooed, laying Rosa on my counter.

I glanced around for Marco's nephew and spotted one of the cooler doors standing partway open. I darted over to the cooler and pulled it open all the way. There sat Christopher in the midst of my buckets of fresh flowers, splashing water and laughing at the mess he'd made.

"I found him," I called. "He's in my cooler . . . playing with my flowers." More like destroying them.

"Oh, wait! Let me get a photo!" Gina said, and came

hurrying to the door with her cell phone ready, the baby over her shoulder, bare butt in the air. Gina laughed as she snapped a picture. "You are too cute, Chris," she said, and walked away chuckling and shaking her head.

"It's really cold in the coolers, Gina," I told her.

"It's okay. Chris loves the cold," she said, then began talking baby talk to Rosa.

"He's getting wet," I tried.

"Yeah, he does that a lot," she replied.

Realizing there'd be no help from that source, I lifted the boy under the arms and set him on his feet. "Come on, Chris. This isn't a place for little boys."

"I wanna stay!" he said, stamping his little sports shoe in the puddle for emphasis. "I." *Splash.* "Want." *Splash.* "To stay!"

"Okay, that's it. We're going now. Your mama wants to see you."

"No!" He stamped his foot again, spraying my clothing with water. That seemed to please him no end, so he stamped again until I lifted him out of the water and carried him outside. I shut the door behind me and leaned against it. "Sorry. This is off-limits."

Christopher squeezed his small hands into fists and had a tantrum—right there in my oasis—screaming until his face turned beet red and stamping both feet so hard, they had to hurt.

"Stop," I yelled over the noise. "How would you like it if I screamed?"

He couldn't hear me and wouldn't look at me. I was at a complete loss.

"Don't worry. This happens all the time," Gina said, as she put her daughter back in her traveling seat beneath the table. She pulled a candy bar from a side pocket of her diaper bag and held it out to her son. "Look, Chris. It's your favorite."

"No!" he cried, and slapped it out of her hand.

As the bar slid beneath my worktable, Gina fished a packet of cookies from another pocket of the bag and tried to entice him with it. "How about this, Chris?" she cried over his earsplitting screams. "Yum. You like these."

"No!" he said, and smacked her hand as hard as he could.

I was expecting her to give him a swat on the behind, but instead, in growing consternation, Gina dug through her bag and came out with a small bottle of apple juice. "How about *this*, Chris? You love apple juice. Don't you? Right?"

"No!" he cried, and began stamping and screaming again.

At that point, Gina panicked. "Do you have any peanut butter?"

Dear God, I hoped so.

I headed for the tiny galley kitchen at the back of the shop and opened the refrigerator door. Gina squeezed in beside me, scanning the shelves for anything her son might like. She grabbed a package of Lottie's deli-sliced cheddar cheese and ripped off a piece, running back to the workroom to try tempting him with it, but that didn't stop the boy either.

As she returned to ransack my small kitchen, I said loudly, "Maybe you should isolate Chris until he stops screaming. My mom used to stand us in the corners when we misbehaved."

"No, he'd hate that," she shouted back, uncapping a jar of strawberry jelly to sniff the contents.

"That's the whole point," I called. "If he hated it, he'd stop."

"That's just cruel."

Making someone's ears bleed was cruel, too.

Gina shoved the jar into the cabinet, slammed the

door, and headed for the workroom. "Do you have food anywhere else?"

I was considering whether to shut myself inside the cooler when the curtain parted and the SS *Grace Bingham* sailed in, obviously hearing my silently screamed SOSs. She took the child by the hand, led him into the bathroom, and closed the door. Gina glanced at me in horror, as though she feared Grace was going to flush Chris down the toilet. She rushed toward the bathroom and lifted her fist to knock when at once the tantrum stopped.

I was halfway expecting to hear a toilet flush when the bathroom door opened and Grace led a subdued Christopher out.

"Tell your mum you're sorry," Grace said, pushing the boy forward. "Go on, now."

"I'm sorry," Chris said, sniffling back tears, one finger in his mouth, his gaze on the floor.

"There's a good boy," Grace said. "Now tell your mum you won't do it anymore."

Chris mumbled something that sounded close enough, so Grace said, "That'll do," and sailed back through the curtain. Tallyho. Mission accomplished.

God bless the English navy.

By one o'clock, Gina and her kids had left Bloomers— forever, I hoped—and Francesca had gone to the grocery store to buy more ingredients for the appetizers she planned to bring in tomorrow. Somehow I had to find a way to dissuade her—I didn't want my flower shop turned into an Italian eatery—but that was a subject I would have to tackle after I'd cleaned up the cooler.

I was mopping up the water when Lottie and Grace poked their heads in.

"Are you still speaking to us?" Lottie asked, then saw

the floor of the cooler and gasped. "What on God's green earth happened here?"

"Christopher made this his playground," I said, sweeping a big pile of flower petals and crushed leaves onto a dustpan.

"His mom let him get away with that?" Lottie cried. "I'd have paddled his backside."

"Paddled whose backside?" my mom asked, stepping in between my assistants.

"Marco's three-year-old nephew's backside," I said.

Mom gasped at the disarray.

Lottie shook her head. "I can't believe his mother didn't stop him."

"Gina didn't seem to mind," I said. "In fact, she thought it was so cute, she took photos."

"I'm sure of one thing," Mom said. "Francesca would never allow her grandchild to get away with such bad behavior."

"Francesca wasn't back here," I said, and possibly for the first time, I wished she had been.

"I know what I would have done if this was your child, Abigail," Mom said.

"Stand him in the corner with his nose against the wall," I recited, remembering the feel of cold plaster against my so-called "perky" proboscis.

"It worked, didn't it?" she asked.

Grace shook her head sadly. "I'm afraid Christopher's mum is one of those parents who thinks everything her child does is cute and therefore permissible. It's quite unfair to the child, really, to grow up believing that. Doesn't prepare them at all for life in the real world, does it? As your American jurist Clarence Thomas once said, 'Good manners will open doors that the best education cannot.'"

"Thanks for coming to my rescue, Grace," I said.

"You're welcome, love. I didn't work as a nanny for one of the most prominent households in London for nothing, you know."

"You were a nanny?" I asked. Grace never failed to amaze me. "For whom?"

"I'm not at liberty to say," she said. "Confidentiality clause in my contract, you know."

"So how did you get Chris to stop screaming?" I asked.

"It was simple really," Grace said. "I told him if he didn't stop at once, I would flush him feetfirst down the toilet."

Better than standing in the corner for half an hour.

I shut the cooler door behind me. "We're going to have to order more daisies, Lottie. Chris pulled the petals off ninety percent of our supply."

"I'll get on it," Lottie said. "Our flower stock in the display case is wiped out, too. I don't think I've ever seen so many customers in one morning."

"I'm completely out of scones and clotted cream," Grace said. "It was a madhouse."

"And yet," Mom said, "my elm tree is still full."

Silence followed. Having no gentle way to explain that her sleep masks had bombed, the three of us stood there mutely, gazes meeting, then dropping, until Grace started for the curtain, saying, "I should make more coffee for the midafternoon crowd."

"I'd better get those flowers ordered," Lottie said, and scurried toward the computer.

Rats deserting a sinking ship.

Mom turned toward me, a look of bafflement on her face. "I don't understand why they're not selling, Abigail. What's wrong with my masks?"

So there I stood, the full dustpan in one hand and

broom in the other, wishing someone would flush *me* down the toilet.

Then the bell over the door jingled in the outer room and a moment later my cousin swept through the curtain, singing, "I found the perfect name!"

Saved by the Jill.

"Perfect name for what?" Mom asked, as Jillian came to a dead stop, a look of shock on her face.

"For"—Jillian glanced around wildly, her gaze landing on me—"Abby's baby."

Statement retracted.

Mom's eyeballs grew so big, it was a wonder they stayed in their sockets. Even Lottie swung around in the desk chair to stare at me wide-eyed.

"Abigail," Mom said, her voice choking up, "are you—?"

"No!" I cried. "Jillian, tell them what you meant! Now!"

Jillian swallowed. "What I meant?"

My cousin was not known for thinking fast on her feet. "What. You. Meant, Jillian."

"I meant that . . . *someday* Abby will have a baby," Jillian said. "And when she does, I have the perfect name for her—him—it."

My mom put her hand over her heart. "Don't ever do that to me again, Jillian."

"I'm sorry, Aunt Mo," Jillian said, and wrapped her long spider arms around my mother. "I didn't mean to scare you."

"Good." Mom leaned back to study her suspiciously. "Now tell me why you're thinking of baby names for Abby."

"Because—" Jillian looked at me in alarm, realized I wasn't going to throw her a rope, and then finished with, "Abby asked me to."

I was going to stuff *her* feetfirst down that toilet.

"For a game," I said immediately. "A shower game. But judging by your reaction, I can tell that it's a bad idea, so let's just drop it."

"Now you've got my curiosity up," Lottie said, playing along. "What's this perfect baby name you found for Abby?"

"Well," Jillian said with a smile, "Abby has always loved poinsettias—until recently, when she told me they're poisonous—so I thought, what's close to a poinsettia? And then I thought, how about Poinciana?"

Mom and Lottie looked at each other. "Poinciana?" Mom asked, shifting her gaze from Jillian to me.

"I wouldn't do that to a child, Mom," I said. "Jillian, tell them it's actually a game you've been playing since you were young."

Jillian snatched the idea and ran with it. "We've all played it since we were kids, Aunt Mo." She stopped to dig for her iPhone in her extravagantly expensive Prada bag, then showed both women a short list she'd made.

"Isabell slash Izzy," Mom read. "Jell-O?"

Jillian took her phone back. "That was a mistake."

"Why is the list in your phone?" Lottie asked her, giving me a quick wink.

"Because I'm the Bearer of the Records," Jillian said. "These are just the latest names we've come up with." With a secretive smile, she dropped her phone back in her bag.

Mom studied her for a moment, then asked, "Jillian, is there something you want to tell us?"

My cousin folded her arms and gave Mom a stubborn stare. "No, Aunt Mo, and I take umbrage with your *antisinuation* that I'm hiding some thing." She separated the last two words with such subtlety that Mom missed the little white lie.

Lottie hid her grin with a cough. "I've got to get back out front."

Mom gazed at Jillian skeptically, then checked her watch and came over to kiss my forehead. "I've got to get going. Are you sure there's nothing you need me to do for the shower?"

"It's all under control, Mom, but thanks."

Mom's forehead creased. "That's what you kept telling me when you were in law school, and we know how that turned out." She patted my shoulder. "You know I'm here if you need me."

"Thanks, Mom."

She hugged me, then whispered in my ear, "And please see if you can come up with a more creative way to display my masks."

She gave Jillian a hug, seemed about ready to say something to her, then pressed her lips together and walked out of the workroom.

Jillian pulled out a stool and sat down beside me, dropping her ginormous bag on the floor. "That was close."

"Don't ever put me on the spot again, Jill."

"It turned out well. So what do you think of my new baby name? Isn't it perfect? Poinciana Ophelia Osborne," she said in a wistful voice. "Doesn't that have an elegant ring to it?"

"Are you sure you want to go with that name? Have you really thought about it? I mean, *really* thought about it?"

She glowered at me. "What's wrong with this one?"

"Don't you remember that when we were kids, you insisted we go by names made from our initials? I was ACK, Jonathan was JAK, Jordan was JRK—"

"Fitting, by the way. He teased me anti-mercifully."

"—and you were JOK?"

"You're not using the French pronunciation."

"Whatever. The point is, you still call my brothers JAK and JRK, don't you?"

"I call you ACK, too, but only behind your back. Affectionately."

"Think about it for a minute, Jill. What would Poinciana Ophelia Osborne be?"

Jillian pondered it a second; then a look of horror spread across her face. "POO!"

"I rest my case."

She looked like she might cry, then suddenly turned pale and waved a hand in the direction of my desk. I handed her the wastebasket just in time.

"Why did you leave the cottage without saying good-bye?" Jillian asked, after her stomach had settled down. She had moved to my upholstered desk chair, slipped off her wedge sandals, and propped her bare feet on my desk.

Jillian and I came from a family that placed great significance upon the act of saying good-bye. Our big holiday get-togethers took forever to end. No one had ever come right out with the underlying fear that we'd never have another chance; it was merely implied, mainly through constant reminders of all those ditches along the roads just waiting to swallow us up.

I handed her the glass of water she'd requested, then began to lay out my supplies for the next flower order. "You were sleeping so peacefully, I didn't want to disturb you." With my cousin, the simpler the explanation, the less chance there was of flustering her.

It was just the two of us in the workroom now. Mom had taken her wounded pride home, Lottie had placed the flower order and gone back to the shop to wait on customers, and I was once again master of my space. The only good thing I could say about the frantic morning was that everyone seemed to have forgotten about my bridal shower.

"You missed the big scene," Jillian said.

"What happened?"

"Orabell and Melissa got into a humongous argument and nearly came to blows. Halston had to drag Orabell home to keep the two apart, which was quite a sight to see considering how unsoberfied Orabell and Melissa were."

"Again, Jillian, *unsoberfied* is not a word."

"You know what I mean."

Sometimes I couldn't believe Jillian and I shared the same DNA. "Sadly, I do. Go on. What was the argument about?"

"Which one of them might have pushed Lily into the lake. Can you believe that? Right in front of Jake!"

"What did Jake do?"

"He said he was heading to the gym to work out because he couldn't stand their bickering." Jillian cupped her hands over her abdomen as though they were headphones, and then, in a whisper, added, "He used a different *B* word, but I don't want *you know who* to hear it coming out of my mouth." In her normal voice, she said, "Then Jake said it was a"—she dropped her voice to a whisper again—"insert the *B* word here, too—just sitting around waiting for the other shoe to drop."

"Did you ask him what shoe he was expecting to drop? And don't remind me that he had on flip-flops, because I was being metaphorical."

"He wasn't speaking to me at the time, and I couldn't exactly butt in, could I?"

I wasn't even going to comment on that remark. "Who was he speaking to?"

"Everybody but me."

"So he wasn't on the phone—he just wasn't talking to you."

"Right. I told him he should be planning a funeral,

not a workout, and he got all bent out of shape. Abs, there's something not right about Jake. He should be in deep mourning. Halston appeared to be in more shock over Lily's death than Jake did."

Wow. For the first time in recent history, Jillian and I were on the same page. "I was thinking the same thing about Jake. When Pryce informed him that Lily had drowned, Jake seemed to fall apart, but later, while we were inside, when he heard that the detectives wanted to see him, he snapped out of it. For a man who was supposedly crazy about his wife, he doesn't seem all that fazed by her death."

"Some of it could be explained by the shock of hearing about Lily."

"True. People do go into shock when they lose someone close to them."

"Still, Abs, I've felt for some time that Jake isn't what he seems."

"And that's what?"

"A dumb gym jock. I think he's smarter than he acts."

"Because?"

"Because I caught him playing chess on his cell phone."

"And that means?"

"Can you play chess?"

"Not on my cell phone."

"Not even on a regular chessboard, Abs. Remember how we used to try and ended up bringing out the checkerboard? Playing chess takes a clever mind, which is why Claymore is so good at it. So what does that tell you about Jake? He's smarter than he lets on."

"That's actually a good observation. So what happened next? Did Jake leave?"

"He left; Halston took Orabell through the trees to their cottage; I was sitting on the sofa eating my egg salad sandwich; Claymore was cleaning the kitchen sink—you know how particular Claymore is about having a spotless kitchen. I mean, really, he couldn't even leave it one day for Mrs. Ambrose to handle?"

"And Pryce?"

"Pryce came into the kitchen to get his car keys."

"Did he say anything about what happened on the beach?"

"Not while I was there, but Claymore told me he'd get the scoop when Pryce got back. So that's all I know until I hear from Claymore. May I have more water, please?"

I took her glass and headed for the kitchen. When I came back, Jillian was nodding off, her head on her arms on my desk.

"Jillian," I said gently.

She jerked awake, took the glass, and drank thirstily. "Thanks. I don't know why I crave so much water—and if you tell me it's hormones, I'm going to douse you with this."

Her phone pinged, so while she read and responded to a text message, I started prepping a pot for a twenty-fifth wedding anniversary arrangement.

"Thank God," Jillian said on an exhale. "PJ and Evelyn came back from their trip, but they're staying away from the cottage because of the possibility of the media being there. What a handful they would've been."

Just thinking about Pryce's parents made my neck tighten.

She got up and stretched. "I'm going to call Claymore back and have him meet me somewhere for dinner. Do you and Marco want to join us?"

"Thanks, but we've got plans."

Jillian blinked at me, as though she couldn't understand why I'd pass up such a golden opportunity. "Okay," she said, drawing out the word.

While she made her call, I pulled stems. I was currently favoring simple but elegant designs, so I kept my floral choices to a minimum. Silver was the designated color for a twenty-five-year-old marriage celebration, so I chose a silver Revere Ware bowl for the vase, and *Cosmos bipinnatus* in a deep pink, *Cosmos sulphureus* in a dark red, and enough baby's breath to form a soft cloud of white for the blossoms.

For interest and height, I had tall, wispy, silver blue wild grass that would curl as it dried. I'd harvested the grass from my mother's garden bed, and it had instantly become one of our shop favorites.

Jillian came out of the kitchen carrying another glass of water. "Claymore said Pryce wants to keep Marco on a retainer in case things get complicated."

"What does that mean?"

She sat in my chair and tucked her long legs beneath her. "You'll have to talk to Pryce about that."

I pushed on that tender neck muscle and winced. "Better yet, just have Claymore tell Pryce sorry, no way. We're out of it now. He can find another investigator to keep on retainer."

"You are not seriously going to turn Pryce down in his hour of need."

"His hour of need?" I asked, putting down my shears. "He hasn't been charged with anything."

"Why are you being so stubborn?"

I picked up a red cosmos stem and began to trim it. "Because I don't feel like dealing with any more Osborne drama."

"Of course you can deal with it, if you wanted to. But you'd rather stay angry at the Osbornes."

"Would not."

"Would, too. It was obvious at my wedding how you

felt about Pryce and his parents. If it wasn't for me, you'd feel the same way about Claymore, too."

"That's not true. I like Claymore. And what was so obvious about my behavior at your wedding?"

"Nobody can freeze out a person with a killer glance like you can, Abs. You've got to let it go, wittle cuz. Grow up."

Jillian was telling *me* to grow up? "Do not talk baby talk to me, Jill. I've got a lot going on right now. Do you understand how stressful it's been trying to manage the shop, Marco's mother, my mother, and my—" Realizing I was about to say *shower*, I stopped.

Jillian tilted her head like an Irish wolfhound listening for a fox. "And your what?"

"Finances."

Jillian heaved a loud sigh. "Abs, you clearly don't understand the husband's role. The day you get back from your honeymoon, give Marco a shoulder rub, kiss his ear, hand him the passwords and user names for your bank accounts, and you're good to go. As for your work here, that's why you have helpers. Besides," she continued, "all my friends think that you and Marco should stay on the case."

"What friends? All you have are me, your social acquaintances, and your clients."

"Excuse me? I have two hundred ninety-nine friends, and if you *friend* me, it'll be an even three hundred."

I turned to stare at her in disbelief. "Are you telling me you posted about what happened at the cottage on Facebook? What's wrong with you?"

"What's wrong with you?" she countered. "Facebook is a great place to get advice. So I took a poll, and eighteen people responded affirmatively that you and Marco should continue to help Pryce. Have you checked your

Facebook page lately? I'll bet you're getting the same advice."

I held up the cosmos. "Does it look like I have time to play on the computer? The only reason that page exists is because Tara set it up for me."

"Then I'll show you." Jillian swiveled toward my computer, logged on, and brought up her Facebook page. She scrolled down to show me her postings, then ran through the comments.

"See?" Jillian said, tapping the monitor. "Everyone says you should help Pryce. Here's one that says helping him will get rid of the hostility you're harboring and re-balance your karma."

"You posted about Pryce dumping me?"

"How are they supposed to give advice without all the facts?" She turned around to gaze at me. "I didn't realize your karma was unbalanced, but it makes perfect sense. Fortunately for you, it doesn't show."

"There's nothing wrong with my karma, and you can poll your so-called friends all day. I'm still not taking Pryce's case."

"Shouldn't Marco be in on that decision?"

"I meant we. *We* will not get sucked into another Os-borne mess."

"So," she said slowly, "you've already asked Marco?"

Sometimes, just sometimes, Jillian was too perceptive. "He'll back me up."

Jillian's phone signaled another incoming message, so when she began to read it, I took a deep breath and re-turned to the arrangement. There was nothing as sooth-ing as working with flowers.

I focused on my arrangement for a good ten minutes before I realized I hadn't heard one peep from Jillian behind me. I assumed she'd nodded off again until her gasp of surprise.

When I turned, she shook my diary at me. "You did that on purpose! You named your diary Euphorbia thinking that you could frighten me off because I'm superstitious! You're playing mind games with me and that's just cruel to do to someone in my condition. See if I help you ever again." She slid the strap of her purse over her shoulder and stormed from the work space through the dividing curtain.

As soon as I heard the bell on the front door jingle, I sat down at the desk, opened the diary, and wrote:

Dear Euphorbia,
It didn't work. Jillian was savvier than I thought.
Now I have to find a good hiding place for you.

The curtain parted, and Jillian marched back into my space. I quickly closed my journal and slid it under a floral catalog.

Mental note: Don't trust the bell.

Jillian pulled a velvet sack out of her gigantic Prada bag and tossed it onto my desk in front of me.

"Your heels," she said with a glare. "And when you finally come to your senses, the dress is in my car."

Apparently, not everyone had forgotten about the bridal shower.

CHAPTER SIXTEEN

I dumped the contents of the bag onto my desk, picked up one of the shoes by its silver heel strap, and let it dangle from my fingertips. They were Jimmy Choos, with a pebbled-leather silver platform that raised the sole at least an inch, a heel that had to be nearly five inches tall, and a peep-toe leather upper covered in multicolored glitter. All I could think of was Bride of Frankenstein on steroids.

Remembering how I'd disastrously sprained my ankle the last time I'd tried to wear tall spike heels, and ended up on crutches for several weeks, I put the shoes back in their bag and set them aside. But then my curiosity got the better of me, so I logged on to the Internet and did a search for the brand.

"Six hundred dollars!" I wheezed.

"What's six hundred dollars?" Lottie asked, coming through the curtain.

"The shoes Jillian wants me to wear to my shower. Can you imagine spending that much on a pair of shoes? On my income?"

"My first car didn't even cost that much," Lottie said, stepping inside the fresh-flower cooler.

"They'll have to be returned, that's all. Even if I felt safe walking in them, there's no way I could afford them."

Lottie came out with a bundle of multicolored roses in her arms and pushed the heavy door shut with one hip. "Did you see the note I left about my boys? They said they'd work up a juggling act for you."

"Terrific." I grabbed my list and crossed off another item. All that remained was to pick up groceries at Costco, take delivery of the pinwheels, and make sure Friday was cleared on Marco's calendar so we could prepare food and decorate the Fraternal Order of Police hall.

Lottie was just about to step through the curtain when she paused, her mouth puckered the way it always was when she was deep in thought. "What did I want to ask you? Oh, I know. What do you want to do about Francesca? You know she's planning to bring in more goodies tomorrow, and I could tell by your face when you came in earlier that you weren't happy about her doing that."

Yet another problem on my plate. I rested my chin on my hand and sighed. "How do I tell her no more food without hurting her feelings?"

"You sure you don't want her to bring food? It was a big hit."

"Lottie, I don't want Bloomers known for its food. We'll have people in here from nine until five wanting to eat."

"Yeah, I suppose it isn't the smartest marketing idea. Sure was good to hear that cash register ring all morning, though."

"What can I say to Francesca?" I mused.

"As writer and professor Arthur Dobrin wrote," Grace said, slipping into the room, "'There is always a way to be honest without being brutal.'"

Grace had to have internal radar. "Okay," I said, "and what way would that be?"

She pondered the topic for all of ten seconds; then, placing her feet just so, she straightened her shoulders and said, "'Appreciation can make a day, even change a life. Your willingness to put it into words is all that is necessary.' And in case you're wondering, that was from the late, great author Margaret Cousins."

Lottie clapped. "Good quotes, Gracie. Now translate for us mortals."

"I think Abby understands what that means," Grace said.

Great. A test. "How's this? I should tell Francesca that I appreciate her efforts, but I'm concerned about turning the shop into an Italian café."

"Lovely, dear," Grace said. "As the old maxim goes, honesty is always the best policy."

"And what do I do when Francesca tells me there's nothing wrong with having an Italian café inside Bloomers?"

"Shall I repeat the first quote?" Grace asked.

"No need, thanks."

"You're welcome," Grace said, and left, her mission fulfilled.

As I tagged and wrapped the arrangement, I tried to imagine myself having that heart-to-heart talk with Francesca, but every time I got to, *So, as much as we all love your cooking, I really don't want you to bring in food anymore,* I could feel my blood pressure hit the ceiling.

Out front, the bell over the door jingled frantically, and a moment later, Jillian came rushing into the workroom. "Abs, the absolute worst has happened." She pulled out the desk chair and eased herself into it, then fanned her face. "Water. I need water."

"First tell me what happened."

"I was all the way around the square when Claymore

phoned." She drew in a few breaths. "It's Pryce. He's a suspect. The police want him to come in for an"—she made air quotes—"*interview*. Now, water, please!"

I grabbed a bottle from the fridge in the kitchen and hurried back, twisting the cap off as I went. "How did Pryce find out he's a suspect?"

"It's awful, Abs," she said between gulps. "Pryce said the preliminary autopsy indicated that she died between eight p.m. and midnight, and there were bruises around Lily's throat, as though someone held her underwater. How horrible would dying that way be?"

Jillian teared up, so I grabbed a tissue and handed it to her. "So, in other words, Lily was murdered."

"That's what the police are saying."

"Is that all they have?"

Jillian blew her nose, then would have given the tissue back had I not held up a waste can. "Pryce didn't tell Claymore any more than that, and even then, Claymore had to pry it out of him. Abby, my baby's uncle is a murder suspect." She laid her head on her arms and sobbed.

"It's okay, Jillian. I'm sure the police are interviewing everybody involved. That doesn't make Pryce their main suspect."

"Right. Wink, wink." She raised her fingers as though to make air quotes, then dropped her hands in her lap. "Pryce also asked Claymore to ask me to ask you for the name of that criminal attorney you told him about."

"It's Dave Hammond, Jillian. Pryce knows who Dave is."

"Abs, come on! The poor guy isn't thinking clearly. I mean, how would you feel if the cops accused you of killing someone?"

"They did accuse me. Remember when one of my law professors was murdered? Remember that I had just delivered flowers to his office?"

She brushed a couple stray leaves off my desk. "Do you want to clean off the desktop now?"

That was Jillian—all sympathy. "Call Claymore and give him Dave's name."

"I've already done that."

"Good. So here's how we'll leave it. *If* Pryce hires Dave, and *if* Dave feels the need for an investigator, he'll let Pryce know, and they can work something out with some other PI."

She folded her arms tightly in front of her. "I thought family meant something to you, and yes, I forgot to put air quotes around family. That's how upset I am."

The phone rang, so I reached around Jillian to pick up the receiver, then put my hand over the speaker and whispered to her, "I'll talk to you after business hours, and yes, there should be air quotes around *after*."

Jillian stood up with a sharp huff and put her bag's wide leather strap over her shoulder.

"Bloomers. How may I help you?" I wiggled my fingers good-bye to my cousin, hoping she'd take the hint. Which she didn't.

"Hey, buttercup, how's it going?"

Just hearing Marco's reassuring voice helped bring my blood pressure into the normal range. "Fair," I replied.

"I know Jillian is there. I saw her rushing toward Bloomers about five minutes ago. So just listen, okay? I got a call from Dave Hammond. The cops are preparing to draw a bull's-eye on Pryce's forehead and he wants us on the case."

So Pryce had contacted Dave after all. "If I say I'm not thrilled, are we going to have the same discussion we had the first time?"

"Yep."

"Is that Marco?" Jillian asked suspiciously, hovering near the curtain.

"It's one of my floral suppliers," I whispered, then said into the phone, "I'm sorry. Go ahead, please."

"I'm going to give Pryce a call," Marco continued, "to see if we can meet with him here at the bar after dinner this evening."

"I don't know if that's a good idea, Mar—tin. I'm well stocked on mums right now."

"Listen, babe, I get it that you can't talk, so let's just leave it that if you're swamped with orders, I'll meet with Pryce alone."

"Okay, look, it's not just that I'm well stocked. . . ." I paused, searching for words to explain my feelings but not quite finding the ones I needed, especially with Jillian listening in. All I knew was that sitting in our special booth with Pryce that evening wasn't on my bucket list. "It's more that I was hoping I wouldn't have a need for *more* mums in the near future."

"Look at it this way, Abby. Since we've already interviewed Pryce's guests, we're way ahead of the game. Plus, think about that romantic honeymoon we want to have."

"I don't want this to be about money," I said a little sharper than I'd intended.

Jillian sighed sadly. "It's always about money, Abs. That's what makes the world go 'round." She put her hands on my shoulders and bent at the knees until she and I were eyeball to eyeball. "I've got to meet with a client," she whispered. "Think about taking Pryce's case. It's the right thing to do." She brushed a lock of hair away from my eyes. "And next time I see you, let's try that updo."

I counted to ten, waiting until she was gone, then sat down in my chair and rubbed my aching neck. "Jillian is gone finally. And I'm sorry about snapping at you, Marco. I'm a little on edge."

"A *little*? What's wrong, Sunshine? This isn't like you. You're always up for a challenge. Is it still about those hurt feelings you've been sitting on?"

"It's more about having reservations about taking on—you know—*more Pryce*." I tried to make that sound lighthearted, but I wasn't fooling Marco.

"Then don't work this case with me, sweetheart. You always have that option."

"But don't you see? That's part of my dilemma. I love it when we work together."

"Then listen to me, Abby. I'm telling you this because I love you. You've got too much on your plate. You've got to step back from something. Remember, this is just one case, okay? There'll be more. And let your mom and my mom help with the shower details. It'll make them happy and take the pressure off you so you can get back to what you love best—arranging flowers."

I took a deep breath, trying to analyze my worries about taking Pryce's case. What was I up against anyway? A little more of being around my ex? No big deal. As long as I was working with Marco, I could do that.

"Marco, trust me, I've got the shower under control and I've got two capable assistants to help me here at the shop, so get the meeting set up with Pryce and I'll be there."

"That's my fireball."

"But I've got a really busy day tomorrow, Marco, so would it be all right if we worked on the case after dinner? A bunch of funeral orders came in this afternoon. I'm going to have to come back to Bloomers for another two hours tonight, in fact, after our meeting with Pryce."

"That'll work. I have plenty to do to keep myself busy, including doing some Internet searches on our suspects, and I can always use extra time to catch up on my bookkeeping. So I'll see you down here at five o'clock, okay?"

"I wouldn't miss it." I looked at the reminder Lottie had left on my desk. "On a different subject, Marco, Lottie's boys are going to perform a juggling act at our shower."

Marco said very slowly, "Okay."

I glanced over my shoulder to make sure Lottie wasn't nearby. "It'll be fine. Lottie wouldn't steer me wrong."

"Whatever makes you happy, Sunshine. If you want jugglers, have jugglers."

"*You* make me happy, Marco."

"And I'm fine with that, too."

I finished the call, then opened my diary and wrote:

> *Do you appreciate what a great guy I'm marrying, Euphorbia? All those doubts I had about taking that big leap into commitment? Gone. With Marco's help, I'm going to make this the greatest shower to ever hit New Chapel.*

By 5:50 that evening, Marco and I had not only prepared for our meeting with Pryce but also managed to polish off juicy pulled-pork sandwiches and a green salad beforehand. So when Pryce arrived—early, as usual—we had our questions ready.

Marco rose to shake his hand, then indicated the bench opposite us in our favorite booth. "Have a seat."

I still had nervous butterflies in my stomach—being in such close proximity to Pryce did that to me—but all I had to do was reach for Marco's hand beneath the table and the butterflies fluttered off.

Pryce was wearing an ivory linen blazer over a blue shirt, open at the collar, with light brown pants and brown tasseled loafers, slightly overdressed for the college crowd that filled the bar most nights. Marco, on the other hand, looked super sexy and casual in his black T-shirt with *Down the Hatch* printed in pale gray along the length of one sleeve, lean gray denims, and black leather Pumas.

"What can I offer you to drink?" Marco asked.

"A glass of champagne would be appreciated," Pryce said.

He was sitting with his hands flat on the table, elbows against his sides, his spine barely touching the upholstered back of the booth. His body language telegraphed his tension, but judging by his expression alone, no one would know a thing.

I sat there silently while Marco and Pryce made small talk, and then once our microbrews and Pryce's bubbly arrived, Marco got down to business, while I sat with notebook and pen at the ready.

"When I spoke with Dave Hammond earlier," Marco said, "he indicated that the police are now calling Lily's death a murder and are looking at you as a suspect because of evidence that points to you. So let's start there. Tell me what they have."

Pryce ran a trembling hand through his hair. "They found Lily's car in a stand of pine trees on Elm Street a quarter of a mile up the road from my house. Inside the car, police discovered a handwritten note"—he shook his head, as though he couldn't believe it—"asking Lily to meet me on the pier at midnight."

"Did you give them a sample of your handwriting to disprove it was your note?" I asked.

Pryce glanced over his shoulder, then leaned in to say quietly, "That's the thing. It *is* my note. My handwriting. My stationery."

My goodness.

"Let me make sure I understand," Marco said, as I jotted it down. "On the night before Lily was murdered, you wrote her a note asking her to meet you at midnight on your pier?"

"No," Pryce said. "I wrote the note, but gave it to her over two weeks ago."

"How did you deliver the note?" Marco asked.

"I handed it to her before she went up to her room for the night."

"Did she meet you?" I asked.

On a heavy sigh, he nodded, but offered no comment.

"Did Jake ever find out about this meeting?" Marco asked.

"As far as I know, he did not," Pryce said, looking down at his hands.

"Did Jake ever drive Lily's car?" Marco asked.

"Yes, about as often as Lily did," Pryce said. "Sometimes he'd drop her off at work in the morning, then use the car to go back and forth between the gym and their home."

"Is it possible that Lily placed your note in her car to make her husband jealous?" Marco asked.

"No," Pryce said on a sigh. "She wouldn't have done that. Lily regretted marrying Jake, but she wouldn't have done anything that would lead to a split, because she didn't want to divide her assets."

That Lily had been all heart. No wonder Pryce had been attracted to her.

"She told you that?" Marco asked.

"It was a conversation we had, yes. Besides, she told me she kept all my notes in a well-hidden compartment in her overnight bag."

"*All* your notes?" I asked.

Pryce gave me a single nod, then looked away. Who knew he had a romantic side? I sure wouldn't have guessed it. Other than his over-the-top wedding proposal, which I'd always suspected had been orchestrated by his parents, he'd never paid that much attention to me.

"Except for that time two weeks ago," Marco asked, "did you write any other notes suggesting a midnight talk?"

"No. Absolutely not."

"Did Lily bring this overnight bag with the hidden compartments to your cottage?" Marco asked.

"Yes," Pryce said, reaching for his glass.

"Did Lily share a bedroom with Jake?" I asked.

Pryce nodded.

"Would anyone other than Jake have had access to their bedroom?" Marco asked.

"Anyone would during the day," Pryce said. "The bedroom doors don't lock from the outside."

"Do you remember a time when any of your guests were at the cottage while the rest of you were out?" Marco asked.

Pryce thought for a moment, then shook his head. "I don't recall. Perhaps Mrs. Ambrose would know."

I wrote: *Interview housekeeper about guests in cottage alone.*

"How do you think that note got into Lily's car?" Marco asked.

Pryce leaned in to say in a hushed voice, "The only thing that makes sense is that Jake planted it."

"For what reason?" Marco asked.

"My guess is to make it appear that she died by my hand."

"Then you think Jake is responsible for Lily's death?" Marco asked.

Pryce leaned in again. "Who else would be searching through Lily's bag? Who else would have that kind of access to her car?" He sat back and reached for his champagne again.

"Did Lily keep her car locked when she stayed here?" Marco asked.

Pryce didn't know.

"Do you know where Lily kept her keys during her stay at the cottage?"

"In her purse."

"And where did she keep her purse?"

"In the kitchen, on a small counter I use as a desk. It's where Melissa kept hers, too."

"So," Marco said, "it's possible that any one of your guests could have slipped Lily's keys out of her purse and back in again without anyone noticing."

"I suppose so," Pryce said, clearly unhappy that he hadn't thought of it himself.

"Did any of your guests harbor any ill will against Lily?" Marco asked.

"Absolutely not," Pryce said. "Everyone respected Lily for her accomplishments."

I didn't want to start an argument with Pryce, which was exactly what would happen if I were to contradict him, but Marco had asked about ill will, not respect. An enemy could have both respect and ill will, and based on what I'd seen at the cottage, I jotted down three names: *Melissa. Jake. Orabell.* I left off Halston's name because he didn't seem to harbor bad feelings toward anyone, other than maybe his wife. Jillian and Claymore weren't even in the picture.

"Why do you think Jake might have wanted to kill his wife?" Marco asked.

"He operated under the fear of having his meal ticket taken away," Pryce said.

"Is that a conclusion you drew or did Lily tell you that?" Marco asked.

"Lily had mentioned a few times that Jake viewed her as a source of money. But it was my brother who pointed out to me just this morning that he'd witnessed Jake observing Lily and me speaking privately on a number of occasions last weekend, all of which could have fostered resentment and incited jealousy."

I stopped writing word for word and put down instead, *Pryce just realized his behavior with Lily was wrong.*

"We'll need to interview everyone again," Marco said.

"Jake is staying with the Burches now," Pryce said.

"Why did Jake move from your cottage?" I asked.

"If I answered," Pryce said, "I would be assuming. All I know is that when I got to the cottage this afternoon, his belongings had been removed. He left a note."

"How is your relationship now with Melissa?" I asked.

"Amicable."

"For both of you?" I asked.

"I'm making an effort," he said stiffly.

"What was the last contact you had with Lily?" Marco asked.

"The last contact?" Pryce pulled up his calendar on his phone. "That would have been yesterday morning at breakfast."

"Ah, here you are!" I heard, and looked up to see Marco's mom push through people standing two deep at the bar to get to our booth. "Raphael said you were back here. *Mamma mia*, what a crowd tonight, Marco!"

Marco rose to give her a hug, then whispered something in her ear.

"I won't stay long," Francesca said, giving his face a pat. She leaned over to hug me next. "Abby, *bella*, how pretty. You look like a peach tonight."

I gazed down at my short-sleeved shirt and khaki pants in dismay. If I were a peach, Francesca was bananas Foster. Looking as elegantly put together as always, she wore an ivory-colored blouse with a yellow, black, and ivory silk scarf around her neck, gold and black hoops in her ears, and black slacks with black leather peep-toe pumps.

She turned toward Pryce. "And here we have one of your friends, Marco. Hello, I'm Francesca Salvare, Marco's mother," she said, offering her hand.

As Pryce squeezed her fingers, Marco said, "Mom, this is Pryce Osborne."

Francesca withdrew her hand. *"This"*—she glanced at me in surprise—"is Pryce Osborne?"

"We're working on a case for him," I said, trying to signal with my eyes that it was okay. Too late.

She said to Marco in a stern voice, "Go get your mother a glass of Chianti," then slid onto the bench beside Pryce and turned toward him, her hands folded on top of the table, a steely glimmer in her eye. "So, *Mr.* Osborne—"

"Ma," Marco said firmly, "we're having a meeting."

Francesca didn't respond. She was focused on Pryce. "—*you* are the man who broke this young woman's heart."

"Ma!" Marco said sharply. "Not appropriate." Hooking his arm through hers, he lifted her from the bench and practically dragged her away from the booth.

I looked at Pryce and saw him pretending to study the bar menu, his cheeks on fire. He felt my gaze on him and darted a look at me. Was that remorse in his eyes? Or was I just wishing to see some kind of sign that he felt bad about breaking our engagement?

He gave me a weak smile, then went back to reading the menu.

Awkward! Shifting toward the bar, I began to shred my napkin beneath the table, willing Marco to hurry. After another long minute of wishing I were anywhere else, I reached for my beer just as Pryce reached for his champagne. Our gazes met again and quickly darted away. Nope, no remorse there, only avoidance. But that was undoubtedly for the best. Now would not be a good time to delve into our past.

Thankfully, I saw Marco coming toward us, but then, with a frown, he changed directions and headed around to the inside of the L-shaped bar. I stretched my neck to see what was happening, and caught a glimpse of Rafe standing at the far end, his elbow on the counter, his chin propped on his hand, engrossed in conversation with an attractive young woman, completely ignoring the other customers.

Meanwhile, here I sat, trying to act as if the man who had privately destroyed what I thought was my future and publicly humiliated me was invisible. I sighed inwardly. The bar was noisy, but the silence at our booth was deafening.

"Look, Abigail," Pryce said suddenly, "there's something I've been meaning to bring up."

I froze. Where the hell was Marco? "No need," I said in a light voice.

"You don't even know what I was going to say."

"Look, Pryce, you don't need to explain anything. It's taken a while, but I've moved on. I've got a wonderful man in my life now who I wouldn't have met if you and I had . . . well, you know . . . stayed together."

"Whom."

"What?"

"*Whom* you wouldn't have met."

He was correcting my grammar *now*? To think I had been toying with the idea of forgiving him. With great effort, I clutched my mug in both hands and brought it to my lips. Better to drink the beer than to fling it at him.

He went back to reading the drinks list. I went back to shredding my napkin.

"Sorry," Marco said, sliding onto the bench beside me. "Little problem at the bar. I apologize for my mother's behavior, Pryce."

"No need for apologies," Pryce said. "I know how impossible mothers can be. Would you excuse me?"

As Pryce headed toward the men's room, I wrapped my arm around Marco's arm and snuggled close. "I'm really, really glad you're back."

"Did something happen?"

"It's just awkward being, you know, *alone* with Pryce." Ye Gods, I'd almost made air quotes.

"Just awkward?" He pointed to my lap, where my paper napkin lay in shreds. I balled it up and set it aside.

"You've got to let go of that anger, babe."

"I'm not angry, Marco. Seriously. It was just awkward. But you're here now, and all is right with my world."

He put his arm around my shoulders. "Sorry if my mom embarrassed you, sweetheart. She means well. She's just protective of her cubs, and you're one of the den now."

"And I really do appreciate that, Marco." I laid my head against his shoulder. Everything *was* fine now.

"Just so you know," he said, "Mom is still in the bar."

The earth tilted once again and I fought for balance. "I thought you walked her out."

"She saw an old friend sitting in a booth up front and stopped to chat. I doubt she'll come back here, but I wanted to prepare you, just in case."

That little voice of conscience whispered, *Here's your chance for that heart-to-heart talk with Francesca. Catch her before she leaves.*

Stupid, annoying voice. I couldn't speak to Francesca yet. I hadn't had time to rehearse anything.

"Why the frown?" Marco asked.

Pryce slid onto the bench opposite us, so I just smiled at Marco and gave him a quick shake of my head to let him know it was nothing.

Are you really going to let this golden opportunity slip by? the little voice of conscience whispered. *Francesca will be gone in a minute, and the next thing you know, it'll be tomorrow, and you'll be whiny and out of sorts all day because you didn't talk to her.*

I massaged my temples. I hated it when my conscience nagged.

"Sorry for the interruption," Pryce said. "What were you about to say before I left?"

I wasn't sure about Marco, but I was about to say something really dumb.

CHAPTER SEVENTEEN

"Would you excuse me for a few minutes?" I said to the men, and exited the booth before I changed my mind.

Francesca was just about to leave the bar when I caught up with her. I tugged on her sleeve and when she turned, I said with a tentative smile, "Could I have a word with you?"

"Of course, *bella*," Francesca said. "Would you like to sit inside and have a glass of wine?"

I fanned my face. "Outside, if you don't mind. I'm a little overheated."

We crossed the street to the courthouse lawn and sat on a cement bench facing Bloomers and Down the Hatch.

Francesca patted my hand. "What is it, *bella*? You look troubled."

I leaned down to tear off a blade of grass, trying not to give away my nervousness. "I need to talk to you about something . . . personal."

"Is it about that man who broke your heart? I know Marco doesn't want me to interfere, but just say the word and I will go back inside to give him a piece of my mind."

"I appreciate that, Francesca, but I need to discuss what happened today at Bloomers."

Francesca looked alarmed. "Did something happen that I don't know about?"

"What I mean is that I need to talk to you about the customers who came in—and the goodies you made, which everyone said were delicious, not that anything you make isn't always delicious, or that we don't appreciate the effort it took, the hours of preparation . . ."

Rambling. *That* was why I should have rehearsed. *Can you hear me, voice of conscience?*

"No need to thank me, *bella*. I am more than happy to help. You want me to make more appetizers for tomorrow, yes?"

"Actually," I said, shrinking down on the bench, "less."

"A smaller amount? You know we ran out today, don't you?"

I realized I'd now shredded the blade of grass and quickly tossed it away. What was it about shredding that was so therapeutic? "Yes, I do."

"Then I don't understand, *bella*."

"Okay, let me start over." I took a slow breath and let it out. "What I'm trying to say is that I really appreciate the tremendous effort it took to make all those delicious Italian appetizers and then cart them down here to the square, find parking—" I paused as an ambulance raced up West Lincoln Avenue. That was followed by a fire engine, two police cars, and an emergency rescue van.

When I glanced back at Francesca, I realized she was talking.

"I'm sorry. What did you say?" I asked.

"I said I understand." Francesca patted my hand. "No need to explain further."

I smiled as a wave of relief washed over me. That was way easier than I'd expected. "Thank you, Francesca."

Marco's mom put her arm around my shoulders and leaned her head against mine. "You are like my own daughter already, Abby." She kissed my temple, gave me another hug, and then rose. "Now you go back to my son, and I will go home and get started."

Wait. What?

She put her cell phone to her ear and headed across the courthouse lawn toward Indiana Avenue, turning to give me a wave. "Ciao, Abby! See you tomorrow, eh?"

"Get started on what?" I called.

She waved again, then rounded the corner of the big limestone courthouse, disappearing from view.

When I returned to Down the Hatch, Marco and Pryce had just finished their meeting, and Pryce was preparing to leave.

"You'll be in touch tomorrow?" Pryce asked, rising from the booth.

"As soon as I have some new information," Marco said.

"Thank you." Pryce shook his hand, nodded to me, and eased through the crowd.

"What did I miss?" I asked, scooting in beside Marco.

"Not much new except that Pryce admitted he couldn't verify Jake's alibi. As you almost pointed out, Jake could have slipped out of his room without Pryce knowing." He handed me the notebook and pen. "Let me give Rafe some instructions, and then I'll walk you back to Bloomers."

With his hand on my shoulder to guide me through the crowd, Marco said, "By the way, where did you go earlier?"

"To talk to your mom about the food she brought to Bloomers today."

"How did it go?"

"I'll tell you outside."

"That bad, huh?"

"I wish I knew."

"You told her to stop bringing food—and she was okay with that?" Marco asked, as we headed up the block.

"I didn't get that far. I was telling her how much I appreciated her appetizers when a half dozen emergency vehicles raced by us. I paused to let them pass, and the next thing I knew, she was telling me not to worry. She understood. All I know for sure is that she seemed pleased, so who knows what she'll show up with tomorrow?"

"Want me to call her and tell her not to bring anything?"

"And make me look like I can't handle my own problems? No way." We stopped in front of Bloomers while I dug for my key. "The way it is now, she might think you're marrying an ungrateful brat, but at least she won't think I'm a chickenhearted one."

"I don't think anyone would call you an ungrateful brat, chickenhearted or not."

"Hey, Marco, look across the square." I pointed to the next corner on West Lincoln, where a sign in large bold script read PISCES. "Melissa's shop has lights on. She must be working late. Why don't we see if she's available to talk to us? I've got a whole list of questions I'd like to ask her."

"I thought you had flower arrangements to make."

If I'd been Grace, I would have had a quote for Marco that explained why I felt we should seize the moment. Being me, I said simply, "So what? Let's do this."

Pisces occupied the first floor of a building on the corner of West Lincoln and Lafayette, with apartments on the second and third floors. Melissa's apartment was on the second floor. The facade was undergoing a major face-lift, so we had to dodge a few orange cones and stacks of new face brick to reach Pisces's front door.

Marco tried the door and found it open, setting off a distant bell. "She must be in the back," I whispered, pointing to a doorway at the rear.

Typical of a decorating store, Pisces was stuffed with racks of fabric samples, wallpaper books, area rugs stacked three deep under various items of display furniture, high-end lamps, paintings, large ceramic vases, and even some very large, expensive, silk floral arrangements that had not come from Bloomers.

I was checking out one of the arrangements when I heard, "Welcome to Pisces."

I glanced around as Melissa came toward us. She wore a short, fitted black leather jacket, brown cotton tank top, blue plaid pencil skirt, Frankenstein high heels in pebbled black leather, and chunky natural stone jewelry, making me understand why Pryce felt a need to choose her outfits. Her hair was twisted in back and pinned with a comb, letting the ends fan out around her head.

She took in our faces and her smile froze in place. "Well," she said, making a bad attempt to be casual, "look who's here."

"Evening," Marco said.

"Beautiful shop," I added, thinking that I could really go crazy in a place like that—if I were independently wealthy. "I'm surprised you're open so late."

"I was supposed to meet with a client," she replied. "Unfortunately, she canceled at the last minute."

"Is Pisces your sign?"

"Yes," she said with forced politeness. "I'm a Pisces. So how can I help you?"

"We'd like to talk to you about Lily," Marco said.

She gave him a perplexed frown. "I'm not sure what kind of help I can be. I didn't know her all that well. Are you"—she shrugged, as though she were pulling the idea out of thin air—"investigating her death?"

"We've been hired by Pryce's lawyer to look into it," Marco said. "Since you don't have any customers at the moment, is it okay if we talk?"

Melissa checked the chunky blue rubber watch on her wrist. "I'll be closing in twenty minutes and then I have to be somewhere."

Marco gave her one of his charming smiles. "Then would you give us just a few minutes of your time?"

She seemed ready to decline, but, in a sudden change of mood, indicated two hard-backed chairs facing a tan love seat. "Make yourselves comfortable."

"An office or somewhere private would be better," Marco said, "in case a customer comes in to browse."

She chewed her lower lip for a moment. "I guess we can use my office. This way, please."

We followed her through the doorway into a small office crammed with more samples. She moved a pile of decorating books from a cherry side chair with curved arms and scooted it up to her desk beside a wicker chair with wrought iron arms.

"If you'd like coffee or tea, help yourself," she said, pointing out a slim commode against the wall. She picked up her cell phone and headed for the door. "There's water in the electric teakettle. Cream, sugar, and tea biscuits are in the cabinet. I'll be back as soon as I make a phone call."

I waited until she was gone, then walked over to make myself a cup of tea. "Any chance Melissa will take off again?"

"She won't run," Marco said, stretching out his legs. "It's in her best interests to convince us of her innocence."

I picked up a coffee mug. "Want something?"

Marco's eyes narrowed devilishly and one corner of his mouth quirked. "Not now."

Giggling like a teenager, I dropped a tea bag into a cup of hot water, then crouched down to find the sugar. "Didn't Melissa say there were tea biscuits here?"

Marco had pulled out his cell phone and was checking messages. "I thought she said they were in a cabinet. Grab one for me if you find them."

I stood up and opened the doors of the small armoire beside the commode. Inside I found a box of English-style tea biscuits. I also saw four designer purses sitting on an upper shelf. One of them was a black patent leather hobo bag with a long thin shoulder strap, the purse she'd had with her when she'd returned to the cottage that morning.

I darted a quick glance at the doorway, then pulled the black purse off the shelf and unzipped it. Inside was a matching black wallet, a silver makeup bag, a packet of tissues, and a business card holder. I opened the wallet and took a quick peek at her driver's license and credit cards. All were in the name of Melissa D. Hazelton, with her local address.

I tucked the purse back on the shelf and removed the next one, a Coach bag in the traditional brown and white logo pattern. The purse was empty except for a folded piece of paper at the bottom. Curious, I opened it.

It was a note from Pryce, on his stationery, in his handwriting that said simply, *I love you.*

"What are you doing?" Marco asked, startling me.

"Looking for biscuits."

Footsteps came toward the office. Quickly, I shoved the purse onto the shelf and quietly closed the armoire. With my cup in hand, I headed back to my chair just as Melissa stepped into the room.

She smoothed her short skirt underneath her as she sat down behind her desk. "So," she said evenly, "what do you need to know?"

"I'm hoping you can provide us with some missing information," Marco said, as I got out the notepad and pen.

"As I told you earlier," Melissa replied, "I didn't know Lily well."

"Have you talked to Pryce today?"

"You're wanting to know if I've heard that the police are calling Lily's death a homicide," Melissa said. She had a coy grin on her face, as though she thought herself one step ahead of us. "Yes, I've spoken with Pryce. So, does your presence here indicate that you think I'm a murderer?"

"We're investigating a death," Marco said. "To facilitate that, we're interviewing everyone who was at the cottage this past weekend."

Melissa picked up a swatch of upholstery and began to smooth the edges. Her fingernails, I noticed, looked as though she'd been biting them. "Do you think one of Pryce's guests did it?"

"I wouldn't make any guesses at this point," Marco said. "Shall we get down to business?"

Melissa checked the time, as though wishing she could shoo us out now. "Ask away."

"Did you and Pryce end your engagement last Sunday?" Marco asked.

Melissa's hand went to her throat, as though he had caught her off guard. "We"—she drew in a breath and let it out—"decided to hold off on our plans."

She was putting on a brave front, but I knew she was hurting inside. "Was it a mutual decision?" I asked.

She hesitated for just a second, long enough to give herself away, then said firmly, "Yes."

"Would you give us a rundown of your movements

from Sunday morning until we met you on the deck today?" Marco asked.

"Sunday morning," she said slowly. Then, as though reciting a memorized story, she said, "I woke up, had breakfast, and then when Pryce decided to go for a run, I took a walk in the woods. Afterward, I went back to the cottage, packed my bag, and drove home. I thought it would be beneficial to get away, so I took a road trip up the east side of Lake Michigan to Mackinac Island, stayed two days, got my head together, and came home. I felt bad about leaving Pryce without any explanation, so as soon as I could, I returned to the cottage. That's when I met you."

"Did you let anyone know where you were going?" Marco asked.

"My brother."

"Before you left?"

"No, once I got there."

"Where did you stay?" I asked.

"At the Grand Hotel." She put up her hand. "I know what you're thinking. It's impossible to get a room on short notice, which is what Jillian was on me about, but this is the truth. I had to wait a few hours until they had a cancellation, and then they found a room for me." She shrugged, as though it was no big deal.

"Have you ever stayed there before?" I asked.

Melissa shook her head. "I'd heard how beautiful it was, though."

"Is there anyone at the hotel who can verify your stay?" Marco asked.

"I don't know," she said.

"Did you charge your credit card?" Marco asked.

"No. I prefer to use cash. I keep my credit cards for business."

"Did you have to sign in?" I asked.

She paused, looking perplexed. "You know what? I

don't remember, but I'm sure I did. That would only make sense, right? I was under a *lot* of stress. I mean, my whole life had turned upside down. It was horrible."

Tell me about it.

"Did you tell Jake that you and Pryce had called off your engagement?" Marco asked.

Melissa seemed surprised that we knew. "Yes, I did. Jake's easy to talk to."

"Did you know that your behavior with Jake looked flirtatious to some people?" I asked.

Melissa scoffed. "That's ridiculous. If Orabell or Jillian told you that, consider the source." As though realizing she'd just disparaged my cousin, she said sheepishly, "I didn't mean to dis Jillian. I love her. Really."

Right. "Did you share your suspicions with Jake about why Pryce called it off?" I asked.

Melissa looked startled. "Suspicions? I'm not sure what you mean."

"An ulterior motive," I said. "Something Pryce might have said when he called off the engagement?"

"We decided jointly that we weren't ready yet," she said, running her hand through her hair. "I didn't—don't—have any suspicions about him."

"Any plans to go forward with the engagement now?" I asked.

She smiled, as though she had a secret. "We're talking."

Another summit meeting? "Would you call Pryce a romantic man?" I felt Marco dart me a questioning look, but I ignored it.

Melissa leaned toward me, as though sharing a confidence with me alone, and said with a smirk, "You would know as well as I would that he's not."

"You're right," I said. "I would not call him romantic. I don't know about you, but I never received any flowers or love notes, which you'd expect from someone you were going to marry."

"That's Pryce," she said, raising one shoulder, as though it was not important. "There's not much anyone can do to change that, is there?"

Love note in Melissa's purse was not written to her, I wrote.

"How long have you known Lily?" Marco asked.

"We met a few months ago, when I started seeing Pryce. He took me to Beached on our first date."

That was a jerkish thing to do.

"How was your relationship with Lily?" Marco asked.

"Fine. We didn't have any problems getting along."

"Would you say you were on good terms with her last weekend?" Marco asked.

"Yes, I'd say that."

"Were you aware that Pryce and Lily dated during college?" I asked.

She nodded a bit too eagerly. "Pryce mentioned it right away."

"Any jealousy on your part?" I asked.

"Of Lily?" Melissa forced a carefree laugh. "No. Their relationship was over and done with."

Now, especially.

"How would you describe Jake and Lily's marriage?" Marco asked.

She ran her fingers over the little square of fabric. "Jake was crazy about Lily, but Lily never seemed into their marriage."

"Did you feel any strife between them?"

"Not really. She was critical of him and very cold, but Jake took whatever she dished out. In all honesty, I don't know why she married him. It was obvious she wasn't in love with him."

"Was Jake aware of her feelings when they got married?" Marco asked.

"Jake is Jake. He does things spontaneously."

"Did he express any anger about the way Lily treated him?" Marco asked.

"Not that I remember, but I wasn't around Jake much."

"Why do you think Lily married Jake?" Marco asked.

"Maybe she didn't want to be single anymore," Melissa said. "Loneliness is tough."

"Do you think Lily could have been in love with someone else?" I asked.

"I don't have a clue. We weren't close, just, you know"—she shrugged—"casual acquaintances."

"Did you and Pryce ever go out with Lily and Jake?" Marco asked.

"Never," Melissa said a little too quickly. "It was always in a group setting at the cottage."

"Think back to last weekend," Marco said. "Was anyone particularly angry with Lily?"

"Oh, Orabell, for sure," Melissa said.

"Why?" Marco asked.

"Because Orabell was certain Lily stole her expensive watch."

I noted that she called it a watch, not a timepiece. If Melissa did end up marrying Pryce, his parents would have to school her in Dune Haven etiquette.

"Do you know why Orabell believed that of Lily?" Marco asked.

"First of all, Halston and Lily flirted a lot, mostly behind Orabell's back, but sometimes openly."

"He's old enough to be her father," I said.

"He's also influential and very good-looking," Melissa pointed out. "It all depends on what you need in a husband."

"Was there an honest attraction between them?" I asked.

Melissa crossed one leg over the other and leaned back in her chair, obviously feeling more in control now. "Not mutual, no. From what I observed, Lily liked to toy with men's emotions."

"Including Pryce?" I couldn't resist asking.

Melissa shrugged one shoulder. "I truly believe Halston was in love with her. My second point is that Orabell is a nutcase," Melissa continued. "She accused *me* of flirting with Halston last Saturday evening. With Halston! My stockbroker! And all I did was ask him some tax questions. That poor man must be afraid to blink wrong for fear of sending her off on one of her tangents. I don't know how he puts up with her."

"He could divorce her," I said.

"I suggested that to him once," Melissa said. "But he wouldn't hear of it. He said taking care of Orabell was his duty, although I'd call it a penance. Personally, I keep hoping she'll fall off the pier and never be seen again."

Realizing what she'd said, Melissa's hand flew to her mouth. "I didn't mean that the way it sounded. I would never wish ill on anyone."

I had a hard time believing she was that magnanimous when Lily was alive.

Melissa pushed her sleeves up, sat forward, and put her elbows on her desk, very serious now. "If you ask me, I think you should be talking to Orabell about Lily's death."

"Why?" I asked.

"Because I'm almost positive she was aware of Lily's flirtation with Halston, and because I caught her snooping in Lily and Jake's room late Saturday evening—going through Lily's overnighter."

Melissa raised her eyebrows and sat back, clearly

waiting for our reaction, so I gave her one. "Really? She was snooping in Lily's bag?"

"Yes, she was. So perhaps Orabell found her missing watch in the bag and decided to take revenge on Lily by luring her out to the water."

"Wouldn't she most likely have called the cops about the watch?" Marco asked.

"This is Orabell we're talking about," Melissa said, "the woman who keeps poisonous plants in her kitchen."

"You know about her plants?" I asked.

"Oh, yes. I got to hear all about them when I was hired to redecorate. I got to hear about the plants *and* those crazy manikin parts she keeps in her closet." Melissa lifted her arms in a wide gesture and said with a wry smile, "I mean, seriously, can you trust a nutcase like Orabell?"

Could we trust Melissa? was the bigger question.

CHAPTER EIGHTEEN

"Why do you think Orabell believed that Lily stole her watch?" I asked Melissa, taking a sip of my now cold tea.

Melissa set the fabric swatch aside, clearly not needing it to calm her nerves anymore. "The simple answer is because it turned up missing after Lily catered an event there."

"Do you think it's possible Lily took it?" Marco asked.

"I've only been around Lily at weekends here, so I really can't answer that."

"Any theory on where the watch went if she didn't take it?" Marco asked.

Melissa shook her head. "Someone on the catering staff snatched it? Or maybe Orabell simply misplaced it. That wouldn't surprise me either. It's happened before."

"She's had other watches go missing?" Marco asked.

"Didn't anyone tell you about her Tiffany?" Melissa asked. "You'll have to ask Halston, because that happened before I started coming out here. Seems like a pair of diamond earrings went missing, too, also before August."

"How did you hear about these missing items?" Marco asked.

"Pryce told me."

"How did you happen to find Orabell snooping in Lily's bag?" Marco asked.

"Well," Melissa said, "we had all decided to sit on the Burches' deck, and the temperature was dropping, so I went back to the Osborne cottage to get my sweater. I passed the bedroom Lily and Jake were using and heard strange sounds inside, like someone muttering. I knew Jake and Lily were both at the Burches', so I peeked around the door and there was Orabell, bent over Lily's overnighter, pawing through her things and muttering to herself."

"Did you say anything?" I asked.

"Are you kidding? And suffer Orabell's temper? No way. I backed up and left. Then I had second thoughts, so I cleared my throat a few times so Orabell would know someone was nearby. When I came out of Pryce's room with my sweater, she was gone."

"Did you know she was gone because you looked inside their room?" I asked.

Melissa nodded.

"Tell us who was present at the Burches' when you returned with your sweater," Marco said.

Melissa contemplated for a moment. "Everyone but Lily was there. She had to go to work."

"Had Orabell returned?"

"Yes, but she was in her kitchen. She joined us a few minutes later with a platter of brownies."

"Did she seem upset? Angry? Nervous?" Marco asked.

Melissa's eyes darted to the clock on her wall. "I'd have to say she seemed pleased with herself, like the cat that caught the canary—and I really need to close up the shop now."

"Recap?" Marco asked, as we headed toward his Prius. He'd had to park in a public lot near Pisces because the one behind Franklin Street had been full.

I opened the notebook and tilted it so I could read by the streetlamps. "Number one. Melissa bites her fingernails. They were a mess. I made a note to ask Jillian if that's usual."

"Good observation."

"Thanks. Number two. Melissa had access to Lily's overnight bag after she shooed Orabell away. She could have gone through it, too. Number three. Halston's reaction to Lily's death was almost as great as Pryce's, which gives credence to Melissa's tale of flirtation between Lily and Halston.

"Number four. I'd be shocked if Melissa got a room at the Grand at this time of year without making reservations, even from a cancellation. Also, she used cash? She carries that much cash around? Those rooms aren't cheap."

"Ever stayed there?" Marco asked.

"No, but my brothers and their wives go once a year. Number five, she was a little too vociferous about claiming she had no jealousy of Lily's past with Pryce. It struck me as phony."

"Me, too. Is there a number six?"

"Yep. It felt like Melissa was pushing really hard to convince us that Orabell was crazy enough to kill Lily, even bringing up the plants in Orabell's kitchen. I have a hard time imagining Orabell taking revenge on Lily by drowning her."

"I thought so, too. Anything else?"

"Yes, number seven. Melissa had a love note from Pryce in her purse that I'm certain was taken from Lily's bag."

"That explains your question about flowers and love notes—and why I never saw the tea biscuits."

"Sorry. I saw an opportunity and grabbed it."

"Don't apologize, Sunshine. That was good sleuthing. Tell me how you reached the conclusion that the note wasn't for Melissa."

"It was on Pryce's stationery, in his handwriting, and said, 'I love you.' Remember her agreeing with me that Pryce isn't romantic? If he'd left her a love note, I promise you she would have bragged about it. Plus, if he'd written that to Melissa and then dumped her, she wouldn't keep it folded in a purse. She'd burn it."

"She'd actually burn it?"

"Or shred it or dump candle wax on it. That's what jilted women do, Marco."

"Is that what you did?"

"I didn't have anything to burn."

"Would it have helped?"

"For about five seconds."

Marco glanced at me, as though waiting for me to say more. When I didn't, he said, "Anything else about Melissa?"

"The question is, did she get that note from Lily's bag? I think she did a little snooping, too, and found the note."

"Why would she take it?" Marco posed.

"Maybe she had intentions of using it against Pryce — or against Lily. I just don't trust Melissa. If she lied about staying at the Grand Hotel, who knows what else she lied about? Maybe she never left Indiana. I'm putting her at the top of my suspect list."

"Do you think Melissa is strong enough to hold Lily underwater?"

"She could've taken her by surprise."

"She could also have had an accomplice."

"Oh, that's good, Marco. We know she was talking to Jake, and we saw her being chummy with Halston, so who knows? Maybe it's one of those two."

"If Halston was in love with Lily, it doesn't seem likely that he'd kill her."

"Are you kidding? Simplest explanation in the book of romance. Unrequited love. Maybe he wanted Lily to run away with him and Lily told him to get lost because, with Melissa out of the picture, she was going after Pryce. Maybe Halston snapped."

"So what kind of emotion was Halston displaying when Pryce announced that Lily had drowned? Was it shock or was he pretending to be shocked?"

"We need another interview with him."

"First let's find out whether Melissa lied about being at the Grand." Marco took his smart phone out of his pocket and held it out. "Want to make a call to the hotel?"

I loved Marco's new phone. While he drove to Bloomers, I pulled up the Internet, did a search on *Grand Hotel*, *Mackinac Island*, *Michigan*, and waited. Within seconds, a list appeared. I clicked on the first one and it took me to the Grand Hotel's home page. Then I searched prices and availability for the next weekend.

"Just as I guessed," I said. "There's nothing available, and if there were, the smallest, least expensive room is five hundred fifty-eight dollars per night. Melissa would've had to have over twelve hundred dollars on her, plus ferry fare, cab fare—since cars aren't allowed on the island—and incidentals. I don't believe for a minute that she went there, Marco."

"Call the reservations desk."

I clicked on the link for the phone number and waited while it rang. In a few seconds, a friendly woman came on the line. "Now what?" I whispered.

Marco took the phone, whispering back, "Watch and learn."

He explained that he was a PI working on a murder case and just needed to verify that a person had indeed been a guest. There was a loud click on the other end.

"So what exactly was my lesson?" I asked.

He held out the phone. "Call Reilly and ask him what he can do to help."

"Yeah, like he'll talk to me. Last time I asked him for a favor, he said I was trouble waiting to happen."

"Don't worry. He'll talk to you. Use your charm. And ask him if he'll get us Lily's autopsy results, too."

"You're the one with the charm," I said. "All I have are freckles and an Irish temper—and I believe Reilly was the one who pointed that out."

I scrolled through Marco's contacts until I came to the *R*s, which took about three seconds. Marco kept his phone number list short and to the point. Me, Bloomers, Down the Hatch, various Salvares, our favorite pizza place, and Reilly.

Sean Reilly and I went way back. Well, actually only a year, but he had trained as a rookie under my dad when he first joined the New Chapel PD, so it felt like we'd been friends forever. Anyway, he'd helped us out on several murder cases, always under the radar, of course. He'd lose his job otherwise.

I found Reilly's number, pressed it, and listened to the rings.

"You've got my voice mail," said a deep male voice. Then it beeped. Just like Reilly, it was to the point.

"Hey, Sarge, it's your fave florist," I said cheerfully. "Marco asked me to call you, so give him a call back. Bye."

I handed the phone to Marco. "There you go."

"And here you go," he said, pulling up in front of Bloomers.

"Thanks. Wish me luck for tomorrow. I don't have a clue as to what your mother is planning."

"Then just focus on having dinner with me tomorrow."

"Maybe we should just eat sandwiches on our way to the lake. It'll give us more time there."

"Sounds like a better plan. I'm going to head back to

the bar to help Rafe. Give me a call when you get home tonight. I want to know you're safe."

My phone rang, so I dug it out of my purse and checked the screen. And groaned.

"My mom, your mom, or Jillian?" Marco asked.

"The latter," I said, putting the phone to my ear. "If she has another baby name, I'm going to hang up." I assured Marco I'd call later, then got out of the car and started walking toward Bloomers' bright yellow door. "Hello, Jillian."

"I've got the perfect solution for your shower outfit dilemma. Since you won't accept the dress as a gift from your mom, I'll pay for the dress and you can reimburse me over the next year, ten dollars a week. How's that?"

"First of all, no," I said, stepping inside and turning off the burglar alarm. "Which means there doesn't need to be a second of all."

"Okay, then the dress can be an early birthday gift from me."

"Why are you pushing that dress so hard?"

"We want you to look—modern."

"You don't think I'm modern now?"

"Not if you wear that ugly brown print dress. Please, Abs, don't embarrass us. Wear this cute little green dress, okay?"

"It's not my style, Jillian."

"How do you know if you won't even try it on?"

"I've got to go. Talk to you soon."

"You are so consternable."

"That is not a word. Bye."

Thursday

I put in two hours at Bloomers, then went home and crashed—and was up again in seven hours, ready to get right back to it. Unfortunately, Francesca was also ready to get back to my paradise, and was waiting at the front door, equipped with pans of food, when we opened at nine.

"*Bella*," she said, coming through the purple curtain, "I did just what you asked and made less food."

That was less?

"See? Only lasagna bites and sweet creamy cannoli."

Huge amounts of them. So she'd interpreted *less* to mean fewer choices. I wondered what it would take to make her understand that I wanted to see no more food at all.

The day passed quickly as Lottie and I prepared one arrangement after the other in order to be ready for the evening viewing at the funeral home. I had to admit that having Francesca there was proving helpful. Not only did she give us the time we needed to do all the orders, but she kept customers coming into the shop, and both factors were great for business.

When Francesca left at two o'clock, Lottie returned to the cashier's desk, grumbling. Grace came in later with a glass of iced tea for me and a surprising announcement.

"As motivational speaker Brian Tracy says, 'There is never enough time to do everything, but there is always enough time to do the most important thing.'"

"And that means?"

"Lottie and I think it might be a good idea to hire Francesca part-time."

CHAPTER NINETEEN

"They actually want me to hire your mother, Marco," I complained between bites of a thinly sliced, marinated roast beef sandwich that Marco had supplied for our journey up to the lake.

"For Grace and Lottie to come to you with that request, Abby, I'm guessing they feel they need more help."

I held Marco's sandwich up to his mouth so he could take a bite. "But I can't afford another person on the payroll."

He swallowed the juicy mouthful, then took a swig of bottled water. "You just said you've had your best day yet."

"Are you taking their side?"

"Abby, look at me. Whose side am I on? How about yours? How about thinking about Grace's quote for a minute. Did you catch the words 'the most important thing'?"

"Lottie and Grace are feeling swamped."

"That's what they're trying to tell you, sweetheart. You're used to handling a bunch of things at once, but that doesn't mean they are. True, Lottie owned Bloomers before you did, but I'll bet she wasn't dealing with someone's mom selling crazy art projects, or someone needing to take time out to help someone's fiancé investigate murder cases."

"Your mom lives in Ohio, Marco. If we hired her, she'd have to move permanently to New Chapel."

"Believe it or not, I wouldn't mind that. I know your mom gets on your nerves with her art projects, but think about how it would be if she moved away, and you saw her and your dad only a few times a year."

"You're the one who sent Francesca back to Ohio the last time she came to town."

"And I'm not proud of it, Abby. New Chapel was her home at one time. She still has friends here. Maybe she's lonely in Ohio. And maybe, just maybe, Lottie and Grace sense that not only will my mom be a moneymaker at Bloomers, but she'll also free you up to help me out more, just like Rafe taking over some of my work at the bar will free me up."

Before I could reply, Marco held up his hand. "Before you start defending yourself, just think about how nice it would be to know Bloomers was making money and that you were free to come and go as you please. It's a place where most shop owners would love to be."

I took another bite of my sandwich. It wasn't that I disliked Marco's mom, or resented her bringing in more customers. It was that I didn't want her interfering in my career. I'd already dealt with one set of interfering almost-in-laws, and it wasn't something I was prepared to go through again.

Yet how could I hurt Marco's feelings? I loved him. I couldn't reject his mom. And how could I disappoint Lottie and Grace when they seemed to need Francesca's help?

"I'll think about it," was all I said.

Marco reached over to squeeze my shoulder and give me a smile. "That's all I ask."

I had just taken the last bite of my sandwich when my phone rang and Jillian's name popped up on the screen. "Here we go again," I said. "It's Jillian."

"What?" I said into the phone. I wasn't in the most pleasant of moods.

"Abs, you'll never guess where I am."

"At Neiman Marcus."

"Nope."

"Nordstrom."

"Nope."

"Windows on the Square."

"No, silly. I'm not shopping."

"Then I've got nothing."

"I'm at the Burches'."

"I would not have guessed that." I held the phone away and whispered to Marco, "She's at the Burches'."

Marco's turn to groan.

"Jake wanted to show off his new toy," Jillian said, "and as soon as Claymore heard what it was, we had to come. We're going to be leaving soon, but if you get a chance, you have to see this."

"Are you going to tell me what it is or not?"

"Of course I am, but first, guess how Jake arrived here."

"Drunk?"

"No."

"Jillian, I don't want to play a guessing game."

"You take the joy out of everything. Okay, fine. I'll just tell you. Jake showed up on a Goldwing. Surprise!"

"A Goldwing motorcycle?" I held my hand over the phone and whispered to Marco, "She's talking about Jake."

He nodded.

"It is one honking big Honda motorcycle, Abs. Black and silver and so tricked out, Claymore says it has to cost fifty grand, which everyone knows Jake doesn't have. Correction. Didn't have. And you'll never guess how he bought it."

"Jillian. Stop. No guessing games."

She sighed wearily. "No games now. No games at your shower. Face it, Abs, you are just antisocial."

Antisocial? "Hey! You got it right."

"I'm so glad you can finally admit it. That's the first step toward recovery. Anyway, Jake told Halston he bought it with—ta da—insurance money! Seriously. Claymore did a little checking around—he has connections in this town like you wouldn't believe—and found out that Jake took out insurance policies on himself and on Lily a few weeks ago. Now, what does that say to you?"

"That Jake wouldn't have received insurance money already."

"Of course he wouldn't, silly. He probably borrowed what he needed for a down payment. What I was going to say was that he must have known Lily was going to die. Why else would he have just taken out insurance on her?"

Frighteningly, that *was* what I was thinking.

Jillian whispered, "The other thing I wanted to tell you is that I have a new name for the you-know-what."

"Go ahead."

"Amethyst."

"That's very pretty, Jillian."

"Thank you. And we're going to have two middle names—the middle names of each of our mothers. So the whole name will be—wait for it—Amethyst Gayle Helene Osborne. Isn't it pretty?"

"If you use initials, it'll sound like someone choking."

"Using initials is so yesterday."

"Thank you. So how do you spell amethyst?"

"A-m-y-t-h-y-s-t."

"Nope."

"A-m-i-t-h-i-s-t."

"Wrong again."

There was dead silence for a moment; then Jillian hissed, "Buzz kill."

Click.

"Jake bought a loaded Goldwing," I told Marco as I put away my phone. "And Jillian found out that Jake bought insurance policies on both himself and Lily a few weeks ago."

"Sounds like a bad made-for-TV movie."

"Almost too coincidental, though, don't you think?"

"Anything that sounds the least bit off, we investigate."

"Got it. Speaking of investigations, did you get any new information on our suspects today?"

"Nothing that raised any suspicions. But I did hear back from Reilly. He confirmed that no one had registered at the Grand under Melissa's name."

"I knew she was making that up. So the question remains, where was Melissa?"

"Reilly also said that the coroner found finger marks around Lily's throat and back that indicated she'd been forcibly drowned."

"Just as Jillian said. And that would take someone with strength. Lily wasn't a tiny person."

"If she were drugged or drunk, that probably wouldn't matter, but the drug tests haven't come back yet, so I'll reserve judgment."

I settled back to enjoy the duneland scenery and before long, we were turning onto Elm Street. We parked in Pryce's driveway and walked through the wooded lot to the Burches' property, where I spotted a large black and silver motorcycle in front of their garage door. Marco headed straight for it, so I had to hurry to keep up with his long stride.

"What a gorgeous machine," he said, running his hand over the supple leather seat.

"Ever wanted to get one?" I asked.

"Oh, yeah. Still do."

"Hey, come to check out my new girlfriend?" Jake asked, swaggering around the side of the cottage, beer bottle in hand.

"Nice machine," Marco said, studying Jake's expression.

"Ever ride one?" Jake asked.

"You bet," Marco said.

"Want to take it out for a spin?" Jake asked, dangling a key ring.

"Maybe another time," Marco said. "Got a few minutes to talk to us?"

"If this is about Lily," Jake said, taking a wide-legged stance and folding his arms, "then no, thanks. I've already talked to the cops."

"Then you know they've ruled Lily's death a homicide," Marco said.

"Yeah, I know that," Jake said, thrusting his chin forward. "I also know you're talking to me now because you think I had something to do with it."

"Not necessarily," Marco said. "We're gathering as much information as possible so we can find out who's responsible."

"But, see, finding out who's responsible is what the cops are for." Jake threw one leg over the motorcycle seat and started the engine. "See you around."

Obviously, Jake felt he'd been cleared. He didn't understand how slowly detectives worked.

"What's your hurry?" Marco called.

"I'll tell you what my hurry is. You're here to get me to say things that make me look guilty, and I'm telling you, I didn't have nothing to do with Lily's death."

"Then who do you think killed her?" Marco asked.

"That's the other thing about having cops working on the case. I don't have to think about it. But if you want something to chew on, how about the Burches? Orabell's a wack job, and Halston has secrets. And here's something else—both of them are liars. There. Chew on that info for a while."

"What kind of secrets?" Marco asked over the engine noise.

"I've said all I'm going to."

Jake revved the engine, but before he could leave, I called, "I understand you took out insurance policies on both yourself and Lily just a few weeks ago."

"You're trying really hard to make me out as the bad guy, aren't you?" After giving me a spiteful glance, Jake took off with a roar, kicking up a cloud of sand.

Marco watched him ride away. "Interesting that he's trying to put us onto the Burches' trail, yet he doesn't seem to have any qualms about staying with them."

"He also doesn't act at all aggrieved about his wife's death," I said, "yet Jillian told me originally that Jake was devoted to Lily."

"It could be that Jake was simply devoted to Lily's money and how to hold on to it."

"Which he was managing to do until Pryce broke up with Melissa and rocked the boat," I said, continuing the thought. "Then it's possible Jake sensed that Lily might leave him for Pryce, so he killed her, cashed in on her life insurance, and is just waiting for the probate court to give him Lily's assets."

"It's a solid motive. It'd be helpful to know whose idea it was to take out those life insurance policies. I'll

do some digging into that and see what I can find out."
Marco put his arm around my shoulders. "Let's take a
walk out to the Osbornes' pier. I want to see what it
looks like at night."

We walked hand in hand from the Burches' house to
the beach and then proceeded west to reach the Osborne
pier. We stepped onto the wooden dock and walked to
the end, a distance of about thirty feet, where we saw
Pryce's motorboat moored. Turning around, we gazed up-
hill toward the Osborne cottage, where we could see lights
on inside.

"Lily could have been out here without anyone inside the cottage noticing her," Marco said. "Let's test it
by calling Pryce."

I took out my cell phone, scrolled to Pryce's name,
pushed *dial*, and handed the phone to Marco. "Here you
go. You talk to him." Because I surely didn't want to. The
sound of Pryce's voice still sent a chill up my spine.

"Pryce," Marco said moments later, "Marco here.
Look out at your pier and tell me what you see."

We watched as Pryce moved up to the sliding glass
doors and cupped his hands around his eyes. Then he
put his phone against his ear. "It looks like someone
might be standing on the pier."

"Wave at him," Marco said to me.

We both waved our arms over our heads. "What do
you see now, Pryce?"

"Movement. Two people. Hands in the air. Is that you?"

"Yes, Abby and me. I'm putting you on speakerphone
now. We wanted to find out how well you can see activity
on your dock after the sun goes down. Can you make
out our faces?"

"Not at all. Perhaps if the moon were out. At any rate,
I wouldn't have been standing at the door watching the
pier. And I was in bed well before midnight."

"How about Jake?" Marco asked.

"He was up late," Pryce replied. "When I went to my room, he was watching a movie on TV. I don't know what time he finally retired."

"That takes care of Jake's alibi," Marco said. "He was using you as his witness."

"There's no way I'll verify his whereabouts," Pryce said. "Do you need me to come outside?"

"Not at this time," Marco said. "Thanks for your help."

Next we turned our attention to the Burches' cottage, which stood a good distance off and way up on a sandy hill. Their pier was a distance of about the length of a football field from where we stood, and we could just make out their dinghy bobbing in the water up against the dock.

"Marco, it looks like someone's in their boat," I said quietly, pointing.

As we watched, a figure rose, tied a rope to one of the posts, and jumped up onto the dock.

"It looks like Halston," Marco said in a low voice. "Let's go see what he's up to."

We walked along the sandy shore until we were about fifty feet from the Burches' pier; then Marco called out, "Hello! Halston, is that you?"

The figure turned in our direction. "It's me. To whom do I have the pleasure of speaking?"

"Marco Salvare," my handsome prince said as we got closer, "and Abby Knight."

We could see Halston's inquisitive expression change into one of alarm. "What are you doing out here at this time of night? Has something else happened?"

"We're still investigating Lily's death," Marco answered. "How about you?"

He strolled up the pier toward us, wearing a fishing

hat with lures stuck in the band, a short-sleeved blue cambric button-down shirt, khakis, and brown canvas boat shoes. Behind him, I saw a shiny metal box the size of a fishing tackle box left on the dock. Halston had not placed it there when he'd climbed out of the boat.

"Just came in. Been out fishing. No luck catching anything worthwhile, however." He stepped off the end of the pier onto the sand. "Ended up tossing everything back." He smiled. "Anything I can do to help?"

"We wanted to see what the view was like from the Osbornes' pier," Marco said.

"Doubt you can see anything after dark without the moon up," Halston said. "From my windows, I can see my pier only if I use night binoculars."

"Did you hear anything unusual between eight and midnight Tuesday night?" Marco asked.

"'Fraid I wouldn't be of help with my hearing, and Orabell didn't mention hearing anything unusual."

"What time did you go to bed that night?" Marco asked.

"Ah! You're looking for alibis. Mine is simple. I went to bed at ten, as always when there isn't a party going on. Orabell's bedtime is identical to mine. We had to provide them to the detectives who came to call. Haven't seen the fellows since, so I assume we're in the clear."

With our police force, it was wise never to assume.

"Do you sleep in the same bedroom as your wife?" Marco asked.

"'Fraid I have a snoring problem that keeps my wife up, so no, we don't—and I see where you're going with this. We can't swear to each other's whereabouts if we're not in the same room. Detectives didn't have a problem with it, but if need be, Orabell can vouch that I was sound asleep all night because she gave me one of her sleeping pills."

"Do you take her pills regularly?" I asked.

"Not at all. Just too much on my mind right now."

"What kind of things?" I asked.

"Ah! I see where you're going with that, too. 'What's on his mind that keeps him awake at night?' you're saying. And I'll tell you it's what keeps most everybody up. Money concerns. Don't want that to get around, however. Wouldn't look good for a broker to be having money woes, would it? So let me assure you that my clients are in good hands. That's not an issue at all. Wouldn't do anything to jeopardize their investments."

I hated to interrupt his stream of consciousness, but Halston was wending away from the topic, which was alibis. "Did Orabell take a sleeping pill Tuesday night?" I asked.

"Said she did," Halston replied, then added, "Didn't mean that the way it sounded. No reason to doubt her. Of course she did."

"Does Orabell know about your money problems?" Marco asked.

"Good heavens, no. She wouldn't be able to take the stress. Fragile woman, you see. Believes I can pluck money from the proverbial money tree, too."

"Doesn't that cause more money problems?" Marco asked.

Halston smiled. "You've got a lot to learn about women, son. Don't see what this has to do with what you're working on, however, which is what happened to Lil."

"I never know what little piece of information will help me solve the case," Marco said.

"Is it true Lily catered eight parties for you this summer?" I asked.

Halston's smile froze in place. "That sounds about

right. Suppose Orabell gave you that information. She'd know better than I. She's my social director."

"That must have caused some of your money concerns," I said. "By Orabell's estimation, catering those parties would have set you back about sixty-four thousand dollars."

"What's your point?" Halston said, his polite veneer cracking just a little.

I was working on a theory, but didn't want him to know yet. "Besides your wife's Piaget, has anything else gone missing from her collection?"

"Seems like a few things." He scratched his ear. "A pair of earrings, from my recollection."

"I believe I also heard that her Tiffany watch—timepiece—was gone, as well," I said. "Did they turn up missing after a party, too?"

"I'd forgotten about the Tiff—ah! I see where . . . You think it's possible Lily has stolen before. As I told you a few days ago, Lily is—was—a professional, but now that you mention it, her being a thief would be sad if it were true."

"Do you think it's possible, then, that Lily took both watches and the earrings," I asked, "or is it possible Orabell misplaces her things?"

Halston stuffed his hands in his pants pockets and jingled coins. "I wish I could say one way or the other, but I don't even have dates that would pinpoint when the items went missing."

"Would Orabell know?" I asked.

"Best you don't bring it up. She tends to come undone when talking about missing possessions. Poor thing grew up as poor as a church mouse."

"How undone do you mean?" I asked. "Undone enough to behave irrationally?"

"Now look here," Halston said sternly. "I see where

you're going with this and I resent it. My wife has her quirks, but she is no murderer."

"I didn't mention anything about the murder," I said.

"You were heading that direction," Halston snapped, giving me a scowl. "I believe I've said enough. Good evening to you both."

He lifted his fishing hat, then strode up the sand to the stairs that led to his deck. When he was out of sight, I motioned for Marco to follow me, then walked to the metal box at the end of the pier.

"See this tackle box?" I said to Marco. "Wouldn't you think Halston would've had it with him if he were fishing?"

Marco crouched down to look at the box, then swung around to study the dinghy. "His fishing rod is in the boat. Maybe he decided he didn't need the entire tackle box."

"I don't know, Marco. My dad liked to fish, and when he went out onto the lake, he always had his tackle box with him. It's like carrying a first aid kit. There's something in it for every situation."

"Think about it, Sunshine. What would he have been doing out on the water that he couldn't tell us? If he just went for a boat ride, why not say so?"

"It's just a gut feeling that he's up to something. Maybe it's because Jake planted the idea in my head that Halston has secrets. And here's another thing I noticed, Marco. Not once did Halston ask us to speak up, and I purposely talked quieter than normal to test him. I'm beginning to think that there's nothing wrong with his hearing."

"What would it serve to pretend to be hard of hearing?"

"For one thing, he could pretend not to hear Ora-bell." Yikes. I'd almost put air quotes around *pretend*. I was hanging around Jillian too much.

"And for another thing?" Marco prompted.

"I had just the one. But here's something else I've been pondering. What if Halston is covering up for Orabell?"

"If he's covering for her, his protests are definitely on the weak side. I noticed before that he will seem to defend her, but he doesn't do a very good job of it."

"Okay, then, let's switch it around. What if his weak defense is intentional? What if he's actually the killer and he's trying to make his wife look crazy so the police will suspect her? If she's in prison for murder, she can't charge up their credit cards."

"It's plausible, but there's something about that theory that doesn't sit well with me. I think Jake is our strongest suspect right now."

"Then what's our next step?"

"Besides getting the insurance information, we're going to have to do some surveillance on him."

"After the bridal shower."

A movement behind Marco, way up high on the hill, caught my attention. I put my hands on his arms and said quietly, "Someone is watching us from Halston's deck."

Marco responded by pulling me into his arms for a long kiss.

"I'll have to remember that line," I said breathlessly afterward.

"Do you still see anyone?"

I shifted my gaze back up the hill. "No."

"Could you tell if it was Halston?"

"I just saw a figure in shadow."

Marco turned for a look but didn't see anyone either and didn't feel that whoever it was posed a threat. He took my hand and led me off the pier. "Let's go home. We got the information we came for, and I've had a long day."

"Tomorrow will be long, too. Don't forget, we have to

decorate the Fraternal Order of Police hall in the evening."

"The fun never stops."

Friday

The morning dawned bright and sunny, which was better than my mood after I got to the shop and saw that Francesca had set up the kitchen as her workstation. Instead of bringing in platters of appetizers, she was now making them in our tiny galley area, then carrying them through the workroom to get to the shop.

By noon, I was so full of Italian food, I couldn't eat the ham and cheese sandwich I'd brought with me. Instead, I poured out my frustrations to my diary.

> *Dear Euphorbia,*
>   *I'm stuffed so full I might not fit into my shower dress tomorrow. Every time Francesca brings a new plate of food out of the kitchen, she insists I sample it. Not that I want to turn it down. Who doesn't like crostini? Pizza Margherita? Cipolline? Almond biscotti?*
>   *How would it ever work to employ her? Grace, Lottie, and I would gain fifty pounds in the first month. And I won't even go into—*

Lottie stuck her head through the curtain. "Jillian is on the line. Want me to shoo her away?"

"You know what happens when you shoo away a fly? It just keeps coming back." I put my diary away and picked up the receiver. "What is it, Jillian?"

"I'm sitting here in my apartment with my mom and your mom, Abs. They're so distraught that they wanted me to call and beg you to wear the green dress and the

Jimmy Choo heels. They said they'll never ask another thing of you ever again if you do."

"Why does it sound like you're in a grocery store? Are you shopping?"

"Grocery store?" Jillian forced a laugh. "What would make you think that?"

In the background, I heard, "Cleanup in aisle four."

She *was* at the grocery store, and I had a feeling she was alone, too. "Let me talk to my mom."

"Um, your mom is kind of indisposed right now."

I heard a crash of metal, as though she'd run her shopping cart into someone else's cart.

"Watch where you're going," an unfamiliar voice cried.

"Give up, Jillian. You're not with our distraught moms, and I'm not wearing the dress or the shoes. And would you pick up some bottled water for me while you're there?"

She hung up on me.

Marco phoned just before I closed up shop for the day. "Hey, Sunshine, I'm not going to be able to help you decorate for a few hours. Our power went out an hour ago, we've got a bachelor party booked for the evening, Rafe isn't here yet, and I'm waiting for an electrician. Any chance we can decorate in the morning instead?"

"Sure. That'll work. I can start preparing the food instead."

"Great. Thanks, Abby. How did it go today with my mom, if I dare to ask?"

"For the customers, it was fine. They probably got the freshest, tastiest Italian food in town. For me, it wasn't too bad. Your mom worked up front or in the kitchen most of the day and she only brought up the shower twice. Then she left at three o'clock.

"I've just got to find a way to tell her not to bring in food, Marco. I feel like I've gained five pounds today, and I really don't want Bloomers to be known as a place to eat. We need to come up with a solution."

"I'm sorry, babe, about my mom and about this evening. I promise I'll make it up to you later."

"You know," I said in my sultriest voice, "that paybacks can be murder."

His voice was low and husky when he said, "I can handle anything you toss my way, Fireball."

"That brings all kinds of fun things to mind."

Lottie bustled through the curtain just then, so I changed my tone. "Speaking of things, have you heard anything more about Pryce's case?"

"I take it someone came into the room," Marco said.

"You know it."

"I talked to Mrs. Ambrose today, and she said the only two people she saw back in the house on Saturday were Melissa and Orabell. She didn't witness either of them in Lily's bedroom, because she was working in the kitchen."

"So we know of three suspects for sure who could have gone through Lily's bag sometime over the weekend—Jake, Melissa, and Orabell."

"Right. I also did some deeper sleuthing on Jake and learned that before he met Lily, he'd worked for an older woman."

"Doing what?"

"Whatever she needed—handyman, gardener, driver, personal fitness instructor . . . The woman took care of his housing and all of his expenses and was disappointed when he left to marry Lily."

"Sounds like Jake likes to find women who'll take care of him."

"I still haven't been able to find out whose idea it was to take out insurance policies, but I did learn that Lily had a will made before marrying Jake. Guess who she left Beached to? Are you ready? Pryce. Apparently, his money financed Beached to get it up and running."

"Wow. That can't help Pryce's case much. Does he know about it?"

"He's the one who contacted me. He found out this morning when he was called in for the reading of her will. According to Pryce, Jake was in shock after hearing it. He undoubtedly expected to inherit all of Lily's assets."

"An even stronger motive for murder. Marco, Jake is quickly rising to the top of my suspect list, too."

"Abby," Grace said, poking through the curtain, "I do apologize for interrupting, but we've got a customer up front who says she got food poisoning here today."

"Food poisoning?"

"Would you like to speak with the lady?"

"I'll be right up, Grace." To Marco I said, "Did you hear that?"

"I heard," Marco said with a heavy sigh.

"I think I just found a way to stop your mom from bringing in any more food."

CHAPTER TWENTY

When I went home after work that day, I was smiling. It didn't even bother me that it was an hour past closing, or that Marco was still tied up at Down the Hatch, because I'd eliminated a huge problem: no more appetizers. *That* would cut down on Francesca's visits to the store. Fortunately for us, the customer who thought she had food poisoning merely had indigestion from an overload of cheese and spices. Grace had accompanied the woman to the after-hours clinic and gotten a fairly prompt diagnosis.

Still smiling, I heated up a frozen dinner for my supper and worked on my shower menu. Simon was delighted to share my chicken and noodles entrée—the sauce was his favorite—but I had to put a stop to his jumping up on the counter while I prepared the dipping sauce for the bridal shower.

I pulled out the recipe I'd copied from a Food Network show and went over the ingredients. Peanut butter, ginger, chicken strips, cilantro, curry powder—yikes! Skewers! How had I missed skewers?

After six o'clock in the evening, the only place I knew that might carry authentic Chinese skewers was a store north of town called the International Shoppe, so I made the dipping sauce and put it in the fridge, then grabbed my purse, phone, and keys, dashed out the door, ran down the two flights of stairs, and hopped in the Vette. I turned on the ignition, then saw a note stuck under the windshield wiper on the driver's side.

I opened the door and snagged the note, then sat back in the car to read it.

It was on Pryce's stationery, in his handwriting: *Meet me on the pier at eight o'clock. We need to talk.*

I stared at the paper in surprise. Was there any reason Pryce would need to meet me privately? In the dark, no less? What would he need to talk about? Our disastrous relationship? His caddish behavior? And why would he write a note and stick it under my wiper?

Operating on the theory that the note wasn't written *to* me, I wondered why it was left *for* me. Did someone want me to know that Pryce had lied when he'd said he'd asked Lily to meet him only once? Or was there a more sinister purpose, such as to lure me down to the water alone?

That hardly made sense. The note-leaver wouldn't be foolish enough to think I'd take that risk. All our suspects knew Marco and I were a team. Whoever had slipped that note under my wiper blade had to figure we'd be together for any kind of meeting.

What if it was intended for both of us? Or what if, as I'd thought earlier, it was just to tip us off that Pryce had lied? Or what if it really was Pryce's request?

There was only one way to find out, and that was to be at the lake at eight o'clock, so I called Marco at the bar to tell him about it.

"Hey, Sunshine, you'll have to speak up," he practically yelled. "We've got a bachelor party going on here." In the background I heard noisemakers, horns, and male laughter.

"Marco, I just found a note on my windshield purportedly from Pryce saying he wants to meet on the dock at eight o'clock."

"I'm sorry. What was that again?"

Trying to condense my request, I said, "Pryce. Wants. To. Meet. At the cottage! Can you get away for a few hours?"

Shouting again, he said, "I caught something about meeting at the cottage. I can probably leave here in an hour or so. How's that?"

From the sound of things, Marco would be really lucky to get away in an hour, and with almost a half hour drive from the town square, we'd never make it by eight. "I may go on up there," I called. "If I do, I'll be careful."

"Did you say *careful*? About what?" Amid loud shouts and clapping, Marco yelled, "Abby, if there's any danger in what you're proposing . . ."

My voice was getting hoarse. "Just give me a call when you're done there."

I put away my phone and read the message again. If the note really was from Pryce, and I went to the cottage, what was the worst that could happen? That I was wrong about him wanting to apologize? What was the best that could happen? He'd apologize and I could watch him grovel.

If the note wasn't from Pryce, it was obviously from someone else in that group and possibly the killer. Did I really want to put myself in jeopardy when all I had to do was to call Pryce and ask him if he'd left me a note? But if he said no, then what? I still wouldn't know who left it or why.

Just go to the International Shoppe and forget about it, that nagging voice in my head whispered. *You don't need to know who put it there.*

Unfortunately, it was contrary to my gut feeling, which was telling me that I needed to do some surveillance work. If someone was hoping to make Pryce look guilty, I needed to know why.

I stuffed the note in my jeans pocket, fired up the Vette's engine, and headed north. On Route 49, I turned off at Indian Border Road, pulled into the store's parking lot, and dashed inside, casting a hurried peek at my watch. Half an hour until eight o'clock.

With the help of a friendly stock person, I found the skewers, paid at the cash register, and dashed back to the car. I turned on the ignition, then glanced at the pink and gold sky. Ten minutes until sunset. Fifteen minutes to get to the cottage from the International Shoppe, and I'd be there early enough to set up a surveillance before the last rays of daylight had faded.

The sun was almost down as I parked the car off the road on Elm Street a few hundred feet before Pryce's cottage. With a bright yellow Corvette, I didn't dare get any closer if I wanted to take whoever might be on the dock by surprise.

I sat there for a moment thinking what Marco would do to be invisible and stay safe. In my glove compartment, I found a black knit hat Marco had given me for stakeouts, so I put that on, tucking my red locks up inside. I also had a small flashlight and a tool to cut through seat belts and break windows in case of emergency, and a black Windbreaker in my trunk, also one of Marco's gifts. I tucked the tools in my purse, donned the jacket, then started up the road.

Let Marco know, a voice whispered. It sounded so real, I glanced behind me, but of course no one was there. Imaginary or not, however, it was sound advice.

@ Pryce's cottage to do surveillance. Come when U can, I texted, then dropped the phone in my purse and put the strap across my body, leaving my hands free.

As I came up to Pryce's front yard, I heard a woman some distance away warbling, "Halston?"

Through the trees I caught sight of Orabell standing on her front verandah, a loose turquoise blouse and long, gauzy white skirt billowing around her in the late summer breeze.

"Halston?" Orabell called again.

I hurried alongside Pryce's garage and snuck through the trees to reach the front of his house. Peering through a window, I saw the warm glow of lamplight coming from the back of the cottage, which could have meant that Pryce was home or that he had a lamp on a timer. I made my way over the sand and scrub near the house and around to the back, where I crouched alongside the deck to study the pier.

The sun hovered at the edge of the lake like a fried egg on a plate, illuminating the Osbornes' dock and a small motorboat moored there. I watched until the sun dropped out of sight, but saw no sign of anyone waiting for me.

"Halston?" came a voice not far behind me. "What are you doing out here?"

I turned to see Orabell step out of a thicket of pine trees, a martini glass in her hand. She peered at me curiously. "You're not Halston."

I removed my hat, feeling a bit foolish now that I'd been discovered.

"Oh, Aggie, it's you!" she exclaimed loudly, then hiccuped. "Why didn't you say so? Why are you wearing a black ski hat and jacket on such a warm evening? Are you spying on us? And where's Mark?"

"It's Marco, and he'll be along soon." I ignored her other questions as I slipped out of the jacket, rolled it, and tucked it in my purse.

"I can't find Halston. You didn't pass his car coming in, did you?"

"No, sorry. I haven't seen him." I glanced between the trees to the lake, where the sun had turned the water into liquid gold. Sunset would be in just a minute.

"Damn fool said he had some sort of meeting to go to this evening and took off." She sighed heavily.

A tiny alarm went off in my head. "Did Halston tell you who he was meeting, Orabell?"

"That's what's so puzzling. He'll usually say so if he's meeting with a client. I don't know what could be keeping him. It's past sunset and he hates to miss his sunset martini." She finished off her drink, then gazed around, a perturbed frown on her face. "I hope nothing happened to him."

"Has Halston ever done this before?"

"Never." She paused, a baffled look on her face. "I take that back. He did the same thing a few nights ago."

"What night was that?"

"I don't remember exactly. It might have been Tuesday . . . or Monday . . . or a day last week. Sometimes I get my days mixed up. Blame it on my age, I guess."

Or on the number of martinis consumed. "This past Tuesday was the night Lily drowned."

She flinched so subtly, if I hadn't been watching her closely, I would have missed it. "Oh, that's right. What was I thinking? Then it couldn't have been Tuesday evening. Halston and I played bridge with some friends until all hours of the morning."

"Are you sure? Because that's not what Halston remembers."

"Can't say I didn't warn you about my memory. Like Halston's always saying, 'Orabell, you'd lose your head if it wasn't attached.' I don't know. Maybe I should listen to him and see a shrink. Couldn't hurt, could it?"

Before she could rattle on further, I said, "Orabell, this is important. What did you do Tuesday night?"

She blinked rapidly, clearly taken aback, then said impatiently, "Whatever Halston said we did."

"I'd like to hear it from you."

She glanced back through the trees toward her cottage, as though she couldn't wait to escape. "I don't remember."

"It's really important, Orabell."

"What's so gol-danged important about it that you have to come out here and sneak around in a black hat and jacket?"

She put me on the spot and all I could do was stammer, "I—I'm trying to catch a killer."

"Halston? Is that who you're thinking the killer is? Is that why you keep asking about Tuesday evening? Well, let me tell you something, missy." She shook her index finger at me. "You're an amateur. You're focusing on the wrong person. Why don't you turn around and look at the house behind you? That's where your focus should be."

"What do you mean? That Pryce killed Lily?"

"Never mind what I mean," she said crossly. "Get your partner out here. He's the pro. He'll get it."

I knew Orabell was about to leave, but I wanted to keep her talking because it was obvious she knew a lot more than she was willing to say. "What will he get? I don't understand what I'm supposed to tell him."

"Just tell him what I told you. I'm going back to my house," she announced.

"Can we come over to talk to you when my partner gets here?"

"You're welcome to join us on the deck as long as you don't turn the evening into a question and answer session. Jillian and Claymore are there already, with more coming—Jake, Melissa, Pryce when he gets home from work, and Halston, eventually. If you come," she said drily, "it'll be a party."

With that group, it was always more like a circus, and was I really in the mood to play ringmaster? However, it *could* be an opportunity to find out who left the note on my car. First, however, I wanted to finish questioning Orabell without Halston to influence her.

"Before you go, would you do me one more favor so I can move forward with the investigation? Just think back to Tuesday night. It's really important."

She had turned to go, but now swung around to face me, clearly irritated. "If Halston said we weren't playing bridge, then we watched TV, Miss Nosybody, as we do every night. Then I took a sleeping pill and went to bed. Does that answer your question?"

"Did Halston take a sleeping pill, too?"

"The old fool doesn't need pills to sleep. Anything else you need to know, ask Halston. He's bound to be back soon. He left a full pitcher of his cocotinis in the refrigerator. He wouldn't make 'em and let 'em go stale, you know."

I watched her stagger toward her house, then turned to scope out the beach. The air was redolent with the smell of fish and wet sand, a scent that reminded me of childhood summers at the dunes with my family. Tonight, however, the beach was empty. The only sounds were of waves slapping softly against the sand and gulls crying far overhead as they swooped and dived as one body.

My stakeout was a bust. If someone had wanted to lure me out to the pier, I doubted he or she would try it now, but I gave it another five minutes anyway, then heard a muffled voice coming from Pryce's cottage, as though a TV set was on. Was he home from work? Could he have left the note for me after all?

The sun had gone to bed, making the area behind Pryce's house very dark now. I put on my black hat and jacket, circled around the deck to the steps, then crept up the stairs and proceeded cautiously to one side of the sliding glass door. I kept low to the ground, below the level of the windows, and, in a crouch, peered around the doorframe. To my surprise, Melissa stood at the kitchen counter in a pale blue silk bathrobe, filling a glass with wine. An empty wineglass sat beside hers.

I peered around again and saw Melissa lift the wineglass to take a drink, causing a circle of diamond-like crystals on the thin gold watch she wore to sparkle in the overhead lights. It was definitely not the rubber watch she'd had on when she talked to us at Pisces. But it was identical to the watch I'd seen in a photo just days earlier—Orabell's Piaget.

Was it possible Orabell and Melissa had the same watch? Or had Melissa, and *not* Lily, stolen Orabell's costly timepiece? According to what Marco had learned from Claymore, Melissa hadn't attended that party, but what if the watch had been missing *prior* to the party and Orabell hadn't yet realized it?

I could just hear Marco asking, *Does it have any bearing on the murder investigation? What would it prove if Melissa did have the Piaget? That she was a thief?*

I raised my head just as Melissa looked in my direction. Quickly, I ducked out of sight, praying I hadn't given myself away. Staying beneath the windows, I crawled to the far end of the deck so I'd be closer to the steps in case I needed a quick getaway. I waited a few beats and when no one came outside, I slowly lifted my head.

Melissa was standing in front of the sink on the far side of the kitchen, her back to me, washing dishes, talking to someone just outside of my range of vision. Because of the distance between us, I couldn't hear what she was saying, only that she sounded happy.

Go home, a voice whispered in my ear. *You're in danger.*

With a shiver, I glanced behind me, but no one was there. I scanned the deck and what I could see of the shoreline, but nothing moved.

Go home, the voice whispered again. *Now.*

I lifted my head again and saw Melissa rinse a glass and set it in the drainer. Movement on the far side of the kitchen caught my eye. A man's bare leg came into view. I clapped a hand over my eyes, afraid I was about to see Pryce walk into the room naked.

Hearing a voice that was definitely not Pryce's, I peered through my fingers and gasped. Jake!

He was dressed in a blue swim thong and a pair of flip-flops, reminding me that skimpy bathing suits simply weren't meant to be worn by any male, muscular body or not. But thank goodness the windows weren't open or my gasp would have given me away for sure.

Jake moved up behind Melissa and slipped his arms around her waist, pulling her against him. She laughed and leaned her head back against his bare chest, then turned toward him for a long kiss.

Were Melissa and Jake having an affair right under Pryce's nose? How brazen could two people be? How despicable? How sneaky? How potentially murderous?

Was that what Orabell had meant by turning my focus on Pryce's house?

A lively tune began to play, ending their steamy kiss. Melissa grabbed her cell phone from the counter, looked at the screen, and her eyes widened in alarm. She said something to Jake, and he grabbed his clothes lying over the back of a kitchen chair. Had Pryce texted that he was on his way?

By Jake's reaction, I knew I was right. He pulled on his jeans and T-shirt, grabbed a set of keys off the counter, and jogged toward the sliding glass door. Yikes.

I rolled up against the siding and lay still, my face

turned down toward the deck. Thankfully, no outside lights were on, and Jake wasn't expecting anyone to be there; otherwise, I wouldn't have been all that hard to spot.

I heard the glass slide back, then Jake say softly, "Call you tomorrow, Melly-belly."

Oh, ugh.

I turned my head just far enough to see Jake jog down the steps to the pool area. On my hands and knees, I scurried to the edge of the deck and watched as he disappeared among the trees, heading in the direction of the Burches' cottage; then I crawled back to the window and peered inside.

The kitchen was empty. Melissa had no doubt left to get dressed before Pryce showed up. However, her brown and white Coach purse was on the counter, the very same purse I'd found the folded love note in.

So what did I have? Two people with motives for murder: Jake didn't want to lose out on Lily's money, and Melissa didn't want to lose Pryce. Two people who might have banded together to get rid of the thorn in both of their sides—Lily.

And now Jake was gone, Melissa was upstairs, and Pryce was absent for, hopefully, the twenty minutes it took to get from his office to the cottage. I'd call that the perfect opportunity to do a little sleuthing.

CHAPTER TWENTY-ONE

I eased open the sliding glass door just enough to squeeze through, then paused to make sure no one was in the vicinity. I tiptoed into the kitchen, unzipped Melissa's Coach purse, and searched through the contents but found nothing that might tie her to Lily's murder, not even Pryce's note.

I stopped cold at the sound of a thumping, as though someone was coming down carpeted stairs. As high heels clicked against tiles, I slid the purse back into the corner and ducked down behind the island.

Footsteps came into the kitchen and stopped.

"Pryce?" Melissa called softly. "Are you home?"

Why did she think Pryce was here?

Duh! Because I'd left the sliding glass door open.

"I know someone is here," Melissa said. "I've got my cell phone and I'm dialing 911."

"No, wait!" I jumped up, causing Melissa to stagger backward with a shriek until she hit the refrigerator.

"You nearly frightened me to death," she cried, her hand over her heart.

"I'm sorry. I didn't mean to scare you. The door was unlocked, so I let myself in."

"You couldn't ring the front doorbell like a friggin'

normal person?" she asked, tossing her phone on the counter. "What are you doing here anyway?"

Think fast, Abby. "Actually," I said, drawing out the word so my brain had time to regroup, "Pryce asked me to meet him."

She narrowed her eyes as she came toward me, stopping inches away. "This evening?"

I backed up until I bumped against the granite-topped island. "That's the plan."

"What are you meeting about?"

"I don't know. His note just said he wanted to talk."

"Back up," she said.

As if I could.

"He wrote *you* a note?"

"Yes. I'll show you." I stepped to one side and pulled the note out of my purse.

She snatched it from my hand and read it. "Where did you get this?"

"It was under a wiper blade on the windshield of my car."

Her gaze cleared, as though she suddenly understood. She dangled it under my nose. "Pryce didn't write this note to you."

"How do you know that?"

"You told me yourself that he never wrote you notes, so why would he start now?"

A question for which I had no answer. In fact, she echoed my own doubts. Then for some reason Jillian's words jumped into my head: *Rumor has it that Pryce still carries a torch for you.*

Even if I were gullible enough to believe that, I knew Melissa wouldn't buy it. Instinct told me to go on the offensive. "What are *you* doing here?"

After a split second's hesitation, she lifted her chin. "Waiting for Pryce to get home."

"With your car keys in your hand?"

She glanced down at her hand, opening her palm as though she was surprised to see them there. Instantly, her fingers tightened around the key ring. "I was going out to my car to get something."

"I didn't see your car out front."

"It's in the garage. Pryce gave me the code for the door, if it's any concern of yours."

"In case you've forgotten, I'm still helping with a murder investigation."

"So," she said slyly, "are you here to meet with Pryce or is that a ruse so you can spy on me?"

I quickly countered her question with, "Both."

Melissa studied me for a moment, as though deciding whether I was serious; then she walked over to her purse and slipped the strap over her shoulder. "Well, good luck with that."

"And good luck explaining to Pryce what you were doing here," I said, as she headed for the sliding door.

Melissa stopped short, her back toward me. After a moment, she turned and sauntered toward me, her sly smile back. "I have every right to be here. Pryce and I are going to be married. In fact, we'll be announcing our reengagement tomorrow."

My turn to be stopped short. Despite everything that had happened between them, Pryce was still going to marry her? How could he have made that decision so soon after Lily's death? Didn't he have any heart at all?

So I was right to doubt Jillian's gossip . . . not that I'd ever trusted it. And yet I couldn't help wondering what would've happened if Pryce *had* left that note for me. What if he'd wanted to test the waters before he committed to an engagement with Melissa?

Ridiculous, Abby. Pryce couldn't be delusional enough to believe he had a chance against Marco. I mean, seriously, Pryce versus Marco? Comparing the two was basically comparing money with love. I already knew what it meant to marry into the Osborne family and I wasn't about to head down that path again. Maybe Jillian was happy living the life of a pampered wife, but I wouldn't be.

"Well, then, good for you," I said to Melissa. "But how do you think Jake will feel when he hears the news?"

Melissa's lips flattened into thin, hard lines and when she spoke, her voice was brittle. "Jake has nothing to do with this."

"That's not what it appeared to me just a few minutes ago. When I looked through the window, I saw some steamy passion between the two of you."

She shrugged. "So? Jake is fun. He's been a great diversion. But Pryce?" She tossed her keys into the air and caught them. "He's my future."

"You haven't told Jake about your upcoming re-engagement, have you?"

Her gaze grew guarded. "That is also none of your concern."

I circled around her, watching her expression closely, trying to make her uneasy. "Are you in love with Pryce?"

She shrugged again. "Doesn't matter."

"Why? Because he doesn't love you?"

"He loves me," she said in a defensive tone.

"Pryce loved Lily. You've known that for a long time. And if you weren't sure of it before, you were when you found his love notes to her."

Alarm flared in Melissa's eyes but she quickly doused it, putting on an air of indifference. "I don't know what you're talking about."

"I'm talking about the notes Lily had hidden in her overnight bag. You had one of them in your purse. I saw it when we were at your office."

"How dare you snoop through my purse!"

"How dare you snoop through Lily's bag."

"I did *not* snoop through Lily's bag. That was Orabell. I found a note tucked away in a bureau drawer in the bedroom upstairs. I didn't want anyone else to see it, so I tossed it in my purse."

"Or how about this? You waited until Orabell left Lily's bedroom, then took one of Pryce's love notes from her overnighter so you could confront Pryce with it. Were you hoping to shame him into marrying you?"

She folded her arms tightly across her shirt. "That is so ludicrous I'm not even going to defend myself."

"Sometime after you found those love notes, Pryce broke off your engagement, and you knew it was because of Lily, didn't you?"

Tears filled Melissa's green eyes. One spilled onto her cheek and she brushed it away with the back of her hand. "That's not true."

"Oh, boy, is it true. And it was the last straw, wasn't it? That was when you knew you had to take action so that Lily couldn't come between you and Pryce ever again."

She laughed through her tears. "Oh, my God! You really think I killed Lily. Are you out of your mind?"

She was trembling all over now, as though she were freezing. With a little more pressure, I felt I could get her to crack. "Seeing proof that Pryce loved Lily must have devastated you, Melissa. But it also became clear that as long as Lily was around, you'd never have a chance of marrying Pryce. And if you did, you would never be sure of his loyalty. So the only way to get Pryce back was to eliminate Lily."

Melissa's mouth was agape, so I pressed on. "All those dreams of living a pampered life, of being the beautiful wife that everyone admired, of attending all those social functions, of never having to worry about your business failing? *Pffft*. Up in smoke."

I saw the intense pain in her eyes as she stared at me. It was easy to see that everything I'd said had hit home. She was ready to confess.

To my amazement, Melissa swiped the tears away with the backs of her hands, then merely shrugged and started toward the door. "You know what? You can stay here and spout your silly theories all you want. I'm going to the Burches' to have a drink." She removed the Piaget and tucked it into her purse. "If you get thirsty, come on over."

I wasn't about to let her walk out that door without confessing, but how could I stop her? What would Marco do?

"I know how you murdered Lily," I blurted.

As though she hadn't heard me, she reached for the door handle, and I felt my heart sink.

But then, as though my words had sunk in, she stopped. She was definitely hearing me now. "What did you say?"

"I said, I know how you murdered Lily. You used Pryce's note to lure her out to the water. Then you pushed her into the lake and held her underwater until she drowned."

She swung to face me, her eyes narrowed in anger. "You are out of your mind. I was up in Michigan the night Lily drowned."

"No, you weren't. A cop friend of mine verified that with the hotel manager."

Melissa opened her mouth to reply, then pressed her lips together, clearly deciding it was better to keep quiet.

"You were right here in town when Lily drowned."

She blinked rapidly, as though trying to figure out a defense, so I reached into my purse and took out my cell phone. "Time for me to call the detectives to come out here for a little chat."

"No!" she cried. "Wait. Please, don't call."

I closed my phone calmly, not wanting her to see how excited I was. "Because?"

"Because," she hesitated, "I can prove where I was the night Lily drowned."

"Sure you can."

"I have a receipt from the motel where I stayed. If you don't believe me, follow me to Pisces and I'll show it to you."

"Why don't you save me time and tell me the name of the motel?"

"It's the Sandman Motel. You know the old place on Route Twenty, don't you? You passed it on the way here. Call them up. Give them my name. Then you'll see."

Could she be telling the truth? I did a quick calculation and came up with the answer. "Sorry, Melissa. If that's your alibi, it still doesn't work. The Sandman Motel is within five miles of here. You could have driven there and back in twenty minutes."

Melissa closed the door, as though afraid someone might overhear us, and said in a hushed voice, "I swear to you I never left my motel room that night."

"The only way that's going to work as your alibi is if you had someone who could swear under oath that you were at the Sandman at the time of Lily's death, which was between eight p.m. and midnight." I paused to let that sink in. "Got anyone in mind?"

She nibbled her lower lip, clearly nervous. If she wasn't ready to confess, I would give up sleuthing forever.

"Okay," she said with a sigh. "I have someone who will swear to it."

So much for my sleuthing plans. "Who?"

"You know, I think I'll save that for those cops you're going to call, because I really need a drink before I meet up with Pryce this evening. Oh, wait. I forgot about your little meeting. You did say you were meeting him this evening, right? So I guess you can both come over to the Burches' for a drink."

Using one of Marco's favorite tricks, I said, "Are you sure you want to save your alibi story for later? If you hold back now, the detectives will think you have something to hide. If you give me the witness's name, though, I'll let the cops know you're willing to cooperate, and that will make things go easier on you."

"Right. As if you could do that."

Right. As if I couldn't. I opened my phone and pulled up my contact list. Holding the screen out so she could see it, I said, "What name do you see there?"

She glanced at it with great reluctance, reading aloud, "Reilly." She sighed, added in a bored voice, "Sean," then, as if the next word suddenly leaped off the screen, said, "Sergeant."

"Now you know I have friends in high places who I can ask to help you. So what will it be, Melissa? Let the cops take you away in handcuffs or tell me the name?"

Her eyebrows drew together as her gaze searched mine, as though she was trying to determine how much pull I had. Then, after a long hesitation, she said, "You're right. What do I have to lose if I tell you now? It's Jake."

Wait. What? Jake! "Okay, now it's your turn to back up. Are you saying *Jake* was at the motel with you?"

"Like I said, Jake's a diversion."

And there went my brand-new theory, which meant I hadn't solved the case at all.

Hold on, Abby. Think about it. Jake was with Melissa. That doesn't mean they didn't commit murder together.

"See you later," she said.

"Hold on, Melissa. Just because Jake can verify you were at the motel doesn't mean you or Jake is innocent. All that means is that you can verify Jake's alibi and he can verify yours. The cops wouldn't buy that for a minute, especially since Jake lied about being here all night. In fact, they'd accuse you of being in on the murder together."

Melissa opened her mouth, but nothing came out.

And I'd just come up with the best theory yet. "Now I understand why you're being so cavalier about your affair with Jake. You needed someone to do your dirty work, and there sat poor, lonely, gullible Jake, all worried about Lily leaving him for Pryce."

Melissa tossed her hair back. "You think having an affair with Jake makes me guilty of murder?"

"No, but it can make you coconspirators in murder. All you had to do was convince Jake that Lily was ready to leave him"—at once the rest of the theory fell into place—"and that's why you took that note! You showed it to Jake when you had breakfast with him Sunday morning so you could manipulate him into helping you."

She laughed harshly. "You are so wrong."

"Making him your ally was easy, wasn't it? You only had to scare him into thinking he was about to lose his wife and meal ticket, assure him that you'd be there for him, then convince him that he needed Lily out of the way so the two of you could be together. That was a brilliant play, Melissa. You were solving both problems, his and yours."

"You really are crazy, aren't you? It's no wonder Pryce dumped you."

"I may be crazy, but you're the one who has Orabell's watch. Who do you think the cops will believe?"

"The watch you saw isn't Orabell's," she said.

"Then let's take it over to the Burches and show her," I said. "Or maybe I should call the cops after all."

Melissa stared at me but said nothing until I pressed 911 and held the phone to my ear. "All right," she cried. "It *did* belong to Orabell, but I didn't steal it. I got it as a gift."

"Was that before or after you and Jake drowned Lily?"

"We didn't murder Lily," she said. "Stop saying that."

"Prove it."

She dug through her purse and found her cell phone. "I think it's time to call my lawyer."

Great. If she lawyered up now, I'd never solve the case.

As she scrolled through her phone book, I said, "I don't think Pryce is going to be making any kind of engagement announcement tomorrow if there's a conspiracy-to-commit-murder charge hanging over your head, Melissa."

She paused.

"Maybe you can prove your whereabouts with a receipt, but once I tell the cops about Jake being at the motel, too, don't doubt for a moment that you and Jake won't be their prime suspects. It already looks suspicious that you've got a stolen watch in your possession."

"You've got everything wrong," Melissa sneered. "Do you want to know the absolute truth about the watch? Here it is. I got it as a gift from Halston. Now chew on that!"

CHAPTER TWENTY-TWO

"*H*alston gave you his wife's Piaget?"

"He needed to pay me for my decorating services."

"Do you expect the detectives to believe that Halston allowed his *wife*, as well as everyone else who was here last weekend, to believe that Lily took the watch, when actually he gave it to you as payment for decorating his house, when you didn't even get the chance to decorate it?"

"I did decorate! I redid all three bedrooms and baths, which no one ever mentions. Orabell wouldn't let me touch her family room, that's all. Ask Halston if you don't believe me. I couldn't say anything because he begged me to be quiet about it."

"Why?"

"Halston has been doing everything possible to pay off Orabell's bills, while she spends like nobody's business. The poor guy pawned his expensive watches, cuff links, and even his wedding band to keep them out of debt. He's already taken out a second mortgage on his properties, sold his BMW, and bought a used SUV. All they have left of any value is Orabell's jewelry, and now he's having to sneak that out, too."

My second theory was starting to wobble. "Why should I believe you?"

"Go check their property records at the courthouse. You have connections on the police force, right? Have your sergeant buddy sneak a look at Halston's bank records. Then you'll see that I'm telling the truth."

The wobble was getting bigger.

"Look, Abby, I know you don't think much of me, but Halston has been a very good financial adviser. He knows how I've struggled to build up my business, and I'd hate to see him suffer just because he paid my bill with a watch, so please don't say anything about Orabell's Piaget, because I promise you, if Orabell finds out what Halston has been doing, she'll make life even more miserable for him than she has already—if that's possible."

"Halston told you about his financial problems?"

"It sure wouldn't have been Orabell. She wouldn't tell me what day it is, and that's not because of my decorating. Oh, yes, I know what's being said about my talent. The truth is that Orabell doesn't like me because she thinks I want her husband. She watches me like a hawk to make sure I don't flirt with Halston.

"Frankly," Melissa continued, "I'm worried about Halston. With all that debt hanging over his head, I don't know what he'll do to extricate himself, short of taking away Orabell's credit cards and selling off the rest of her jewelry. He puts on a good front, but I know how worried he is. I'm just hoping he doesn't do something stupid."

"Like?"

"Like maybe kill himself for the insurance money."

"Halston is a stockbroker, Melissa. He would know there's no payout for suicide."

"Well, then I hope they have friends who will take them in, because he's just about out of options."

Or—maybe not.

A new theory was forming.

"I'm going next door for a drink," Melissa said.

"Okay, but before you go, I have to warn you that I will be telling Pryce what I saw here tonight."

She paused at the sliding glass door, then slowly smiled. "No, you won't. You were going to marry him for the same reason I am, and you don't want me to tell him that."

"What are you talking about?"

She folded her arms across her shirt. "I'm talking about you marrying him for his money."

"That's wrong! I thought I loved Pryce."

"Right." She gave me a wink, as though we shared a secret, then slipped through the sliding glass door and shut it behind her.

I turned away from the door. Melissa was so wrong. I remembered how the girls in my law classes were always talking about what a catch Pryce would make for some lucky woman, what a life of ease she'd have. Living in the lap of luxury, someone had called it. A fairy tale come true. A trophy wife, another had said. But that wasn't me then. I'd never wanted to be a trophy.

A snippet of conversation came back to me: *Were you in love with Pryce back then?* Marco had asked.

No.

That was a quick response.

I've had a lot of time to think about it. It took me a few months, but I realized finally that I was in love with the idea of marriage to Pryce.

The sound of a door slamming jolted me back to the present. Pryce was home, and I was in his house. Did I really want to have to tell him about Melissa and Jake, or the note on my windshield? Did I really want to be alone with him?

No to all of the above. I closed the sliding glass door behind me, then hurried down the stairs to the pool area and took off across the sand to get to the Burches'.

"Well, look who finally showed up," Jillian said, as I climbed the steps. "Where's Marco?"

"He should be here anytime now," I said.

My cousin and Claymore, Melissa, Jake, and Orabell were gathered on the deck. Claymore had a chair next to Jillian; Melissa and Jake sat on opposite sides of the deck, facing each other, while Orabell stood near the door.

Jillian patted the empty spot on the padded bench where she sat. "I saved you a seat."

"Have some appetizers," Orabell called, a martini glass in one hand. Clearly forgetting we'd parted on less-than-friendly terms, she gestured toward the table, where she'd set out nuts, chips, crackers, and wedges of cheese. "They're just begging to be eaten."

"Halston isn't here yet?" I asked, dropping my purse beside the bench.

"We're still waiting," Jake said, taking a pull of his beer. He looked across the deck at Melissa and gave her a smile. Despite what she'd said about not loving him, I could see by the slight softening of her expression that she had a thing for Jake.

"Have you seen Pryce?" Melissa asked me, that sly smile still tugging at the corners of her mouth. "He texted that he'd be here shortly."

"No, I haven't seen Pryce, Melissa."

Putting on an expression of concern, she rose. "That's odd. He sent the message a while ago and said he'd be right here. I hope he's all right. Maybe I should check on him . . . unless you want to, Abby."

I gave her the barest hint of a scowl. "No, that's okay. You go."

"Claymore can go," Jillian offered.

"I'm already up," Melissa said, as she hurried away. "Be back in a while."

"I'm hungry, Claymore," Jillian said with a pout. "Would you be a darling and bring me some nibblies?"

Claymore jumped up from his chair and scurried to do her bidding.

"Anyone in the mood for one of Halston's stupid coco-tinis?" Orabell asked, weaving slightly as she stood. "He left a pitcher in the fridge. We might as well use it up. You'll have one, won't you, Annie?"

"I'll stick with ginger ale," Jillian said.

Claymore presented her with a plate filled with good-ies. "Here you are, my love. Eat up."

Jillian took one bite of cheese, chewed for a few mo-ments; then her eyes widened. Jumping up from the bench, spilling the plate in the process, she covered her mouth and dashed inside the Burches' cottage.

"Well," Orabell said with a shrug, "that's what hap-pens when you're expecting."

Wait a minute! Orabell knew about Jillian?

"Yeah, I remember one of my girlfriends puking when she got knocked up," Jake said, then burped.

Jake knew, too?

"My poor Jillian," Claymore said, picking up the re-mains of her food. "She just can't seem to get it through her gorgeous head that her morning sickness can last all day."

"Is everyone in on the secret?" I asked.

"That Jillian's preggers?" Orabell asked. "Well, of course we are."

I was stunned. "How did you find out? She made me swear not to tell."

"She did that with everyone," Claymore said with a sigh. "My therapist said hormones were to blame. But please don't let on that you know. Dr. Eggers said it's better for her right now if she thinks she's in control." He got up and started toward the door. "I'd better say good night now and take my beloved home to rest."

"And I'll go get those martinis I promised," Orabell said, making her way carefully across the deck.

"I'm sticking with beer, Orabell," Jake said. "So what are you doing here, Abby?"

"Actually," I said, "I'm working on my theory about who killed Lily."

Jake's arm froze, the bottle halfway to his mouth, while Orabell paused at the door to glance back at me. "You still want that 'tini, then?" she asked.

"Abby's not working yet, so bring her one," Jake said, then lifted the bottle toward me, as though toasting me. "We all need some downtime, right?"

"I'll bring one for Mark, too," Orabell said, then stepped inside and shut the door.

It was just Jake and me on the deck now, the perfect time to do a little questioning. "So," I said to Jake, "remind me again of where you were the night Lily drowned."

Jake's smile dissolved, and in an annoyed voice, he said, "What happened to your downtime?"

"I'm always working. So where were you?"

"I was asleep at Pryce's cottage."

"What if I told you that I know where you really were?"

"So go ahead. Tell me. Make my day."

"You were at the Sandman Motel."

He glanced at me out of the corner of his eye as he took another sip of beer. "With a friend," I added.

Now I had his full attention. Jake put down his beer. "What if I told you that you were out of your freaking mind?"

I said quietly, "What if I told you Melissa said she was with you at the motel?"

"I don't know what she's talking about, lady. I was sitting right here on the deck having a drink with Halston, and then I went back to Pryce's for the night. Ask Halston if you don't believe me."

"I would if I knew where he was, but he's conveniently missing."

"Don't look at me," Jake said, hoisting the bottle once again. "Ask his wife where he went."

"Orabell doesn't know either. She was out looking for him when I got here, which was during your little tryst with Melissa at Pryce's cottage."

"That's it. I'm outta here." He set his bottle down hard on the table beside his chair and stalked off the deck and down the steps, disappearing among the elms.

At that moment, Orabell came outside with a pitcher and three martini glasses on a tray.

"Where did Jake go?" She hiccuped loudly.

She was obviously on her way to sloshdom, *and thank you, Jillian, for putting that word into my vocabulary*. "Jake's a little annoyed with me," I said. "I was questioning him about Tuesday night and he didn't seem to like it."

"That's Jake. Selfish, childish—*hic*—and immature. So what can you do? Shoot him? Anyway, I'm glad you decided to join us, Annie." She made her way over to the portable bar and placed the tray on the counter. "I've got a drink here for Mark when he comes. You did say he was coming soon, right?"

"Right. Anytime now." I didn't even bother to correct her about the name. She wouldn't remember it anyway.

She filled one of the glasses and carried it over to me. "For the life of me, I can't imagine where Halston is."

"Thanks," I said, taking the ice-cold drink. "Did you check the pier to see if your boat's there?"

"That's the first place I looked, because Halston's silly fishing hat is gone." She took the other glass, then lowered herself into a chair. "I don't know what to make of his disappearance. I'm not sure whether to be angry or worried."

I took a drink and tasted chocolate along with another flavor. Was it coconut? Whatever it was, I was thirsty enough to keep sipping.

"I guess I shouldn't be too concerned," Orabell said, adjusting her long skirt to cover her calves. "Halston's always going over to clients' houses in the evenings. Problem I have with that is, he's a good-looking man, and there are a lot of money-hungry women out there who'd love to get their hands on him." She took a swallow of martini. "And that includes Melissa. You saw how she flirted with Hals the other evening. She's a gold digger, just like that Lily was."

Except that Halston didn't have any money, and Melissa knew it.

"Who do you think killed Lily?" Orabell asked.

Her question surprised me. "I'm not at liberty to say."

"It's not Halston, I hope."

"I really can't talk about it."

Orabell studied me for a while, her eyes narrowed, as though she was working through a puzzle. Then she slapped her knee. "I know who you're thinking. I heard you questioning him while I was inside. You're a smart woman, Abby. That's who I picked, too."

She finally got my name right!

"Yes, ma'am," she said, "guilty as sin. Doesn't wait a week for his wife to be declared dead before he's going after another woman. Shameful situation, just shameful. Doesn't seem to care a fig what it looks like to others.

"Of course, the same could be said about Lily. She was as shameful as he is, married to one man, shacking up with another, and trying to get her hooks in Halston. I know why she stole my Piaget. It's because I raked her over the coals for flirting with my husband. Oh, yes, I caught her in the kitchen with Halston, the hussy. She didn't like what I had to say, I can tell you that. And then my beautiful timepiece disappeared. Her revenge for being thwarted.

"So I told Lily, 'Two can play at that game,' and then I did all I could to embarrass her in front of the others. Did she give me back the Piaget? Not on your life. She already had Halston on her side, so she didn't need to. Oh, he wouldn't admit it, but did I have a bone to pick with him the next day. 'Want to play the old fool?' I asked him. 'Tell Lily you're leaving me for her and watch how fast she runs.' Ha! Would he do it? No, the coward."

Orabell rose and reached for the pitcher. "You're in need of more cocotini. Have to say, Halston may have his faults, but he knows how to make a fine martini."

While she refilled my glass, I turned to look out at the water to see if I could spot a motorboat, but because of the thick cloud cover, all I could see was inky blackness. My vision blurred slightly, so I shook my head to clear it and felt dizzy. I turned back toward Orabell and saw her start toward the house, weaving a little more than before.

"I need some crackers," she said, her words slurring. "My stomach's empty. Want some, too, Ag . . . gie? Boy, oh, boy, Halston made these 'tinis s-s-strong."

Instead of continuing toward the house, Orabell staggered toward one of the deck chairs and nearly fell into it. "All of a sudden, I'm not feeling well."

I tried to bring her into focus, but her image blurred before my eyes. There was a bad taste in my mouth, too, and my head was beginning to pound, as though I had a really bad hangover. "Orabell," I said, my throat tightening, "I don't feel well either. I think something's wrong with these drinks."

"Ow," Orabell moaned. "My stomach is twisting like a snake."

Mine was definitely feeling queasy. I set the glass aside. "When did Halston make the martinis?"

"I don't know. He left me a note about them." She rose. "Would you—*hic*—excuse me, Aggie." She lurched across the deck, propelling herself from one chair to the next until she reached the door. Then she pushed it open and fairly fell inside.

I could barely keep my eyes open now. My head ached, perspiration dampened my face, and fear swirled about me. Was it possible Halston had poisoned the drink mix? Or could it have been Jake . . . or Melissa, both of whom had found a reason to leave before the drinks were served?

No one here is trustworthy, my foggy brain whispered.

I glanced around for help, but I was alone. I rubbed my temples, trying to think. Where was Halston? Why had Jake conveniently stormed off? Why hadn't I heard his motorcycle start up? Why had Melissa made a quick exit? Why was I alone on the deck? Was there a plot to kill me? Had they all conspired?

I sounded paranoid even to myself, but my thoughts were spinning so rapidly, I couldn't keep them in check.

No crazy thinking, Abby, I told myself. *Focus!*

But I couldn't focus. My entire body felt hot and my limbs weighted down. At the same time, something inside me warned that if I stayed where I was, I would not be alive to tell Marco what had happened. But where could I go and be safe? To Pryce's? Could I trust him? What if it was Pryce who lured me here? What if he was in on the plot? Did I dare attempt to reach my car in my condition? And then how could I drive?

Get out of there, I heard a voice whisper, or maybe it was saying, *Get to the pier.*

I knew I had to trust that voice. It had helped me before, and if I'd listened earlier, it would have kept me out of the danger I now found myself in. Using the arms of the chair to push to my feet, I managed to drag myself up to the railing, then staggered along it until I reached the stairs. It was all I could do to keep the ground in focus as I made my way down that long flight of steps.

By sheer will, I forced my unwilling legs to carry me toward the shore. Fearing Halston, or whoever had poisoned the drink, was following me, I kept glancing over my shoulder, which caused me to stumble twice before falling to my knees and heaving the contents of my stomach onto the sand. I gasped for breath and looked around. Where could I go?

I had to phone for help.

Dread gripped me. I'd left my purse on the Burches' deck.

I heard a rustling of dead leaves and looked around, startled to see a dark figure moving toward me through the trees. I wiped my mouth on the back of my hand and staggered toward the water, my heart pounding in apprehension. With great effort, I dragged myself to the wooden dock, then collapsed on the sand to vomit again. When I straightened, I saw a young woman in a red coat standing on the pier, and she seemed to be motioning for me to hurry.

"I can't make it," I cried. "My legs are paralyzed." My vision blurred and I blinked hard to bring her back into focus. But there was no girl in a red coat. There was no one but me. I'd imagined her.

I heard footsteps pounding on the sand and turned with a gasp to see someone running toward the pier.

What were my options? Scream for help, or stay

where I was and hope whoever was coming toward me wasn't the killer?

I screamed.

Jump into the lake! a voice whispered. *Hurry! You'll be safe.*

Gathering my strength, I ran out onto the pier and plunged straight into the chilly lake, sinking like a stone beneath the inky water, until I thought my lungs would explode. I hit bottom and used what was left of my strength to push off, rising to the surface and gasping for air.

A blurred figure ran onto the dock, hands gripping something long and thin. A knife?

Swim away from the dock. Hurry!

I remembered a buoy tethered some distance away from the shoreline and swam toward it, hoping my direction was right. I wasn't a strong swimmer and my muscles were still heavy and lethargic, but fear sent adrenaline coursing through my body.

I kept going until I couldn't go another stroke. Treading water, I looked back at the dock but saw no one on it. I was a good distance away, but still had a long way to go to reach the buoy. How long could I keep swimming?

Then I heard what sounded like oars slicing through water. I blinked to clear my eyes and saw what appeared to be a dinghy bobbing toward me.

Was it Halston? Was the killer coming to finish me off?

With a new rush of adrenaline, I began to swim toward the shoreline, hoping I could make it onto the sand. What then, I had no idea. I was exhausted.

"Give me your hand," I heard.

Out of breath and strength, terrified, I dog-paddled as the boat came alongside me.

"Give me your hand."

I looked up and saw a figure in a red coat reaching

out to help me. "You're not real," I said, then took in a gulp of water and coughed.

"Of course I'm real." A red-sleeved arm reached out. "Abigail, for God's sake, take my hand."

"Pryce?"

Chapter Twenty-three

"Yes, it's me," Pryce said. "Would you please take my hand?"

My vision cleared enough to let me see that he was wearing a gray and red sweatshirt. I sank back under the water, nearly swallowing another mouthful of murky liquid. I was getting weaker. I knew I couldn't dog-paddle for long. But could I trust him? "How did you know I was in the water?"

"I stepped outside onto the deck to start up the charcoal grill and heard you cry out. I grabbed my binoculars and saw you jump in the water. For God's sake, take my hand before I have to dive in to get you."

Almost at once, I felt a warmth spread through my chest, filling me with enough strength to reach out and take the hand Pryce offered. He hoisted me into the small boat, where I huddled, shivering, on a seat, water puddling around me. He put a heavy plaid lap blanket over my shoulders, then picked up the oars again and began to row.

"Pryce, we can't go back to the pier," I managed through chattering teeth. "It's too dangerous."

He put his hand on my forehead. "You're burning up. I've got to get you back."

"No, Pryce. Listen to me. Someone at the Burches' tried to poison me, and just now, when I was trying to get away, I was chased across the sand. That's why I jumped in the water. Someone was chasing me with a knife."

"Abigail, you're delirious. I didn't see a single soul on the beach or on either of the piers, and certainly nobody with a knife."

Had I imagined it? Had the poison made me delusional? "You have to believe that someone tried to poison me, Pryce, because I got very ill after drinking Halston's martini mix. I think I threw up enough of it to save myself. Orabell drank it, too, and also got sick. I don't know what condition she's in."

I could see by Pryce's skeptical look that he didn't believe me. "Why would Halston want to poison either of you?"

I rubbed my temples, trying to ease the pounding. "I don't know. I've tried to make sense of it, but the only thing I come up with is that he killed Lily and was afraid Marco and I were onto him."

"How does Marco fit into this scenario?"

"One of the martinis was for Marco."

"How do you know that?"

"Orabell told me. She was passing them out to whoever wanted one, but Jake declined and Melissa had already taken off for your cottage."

"Abigail, trust me, Halston wouldn't harm a fly."

"Where is he, then? He's been missing all evening and wouldn't tell Orabell where he was going."

"Halston is probably meeting with clients, and Orabell no doubt forgot that he told her. It's happened before."

"Then the killer must be Jake or Melissa, because *someone* came running out of the trees to chase me."

"Melissa is at my cottage, and Jake took off on his

motorcycle about twenty minutes ago. I heard him leave. As soon as we get back, I'm going to call for an ambulance. You need to be checked out."

I gave up and huddled farther beneath the blanket, grateful that the outside temperature was warm. I couldn't seem to make Pryce understand the danger we were in because my thoughts were as cloudy as my vision. Was that the work of the poison? What if I'd imagined someone chasing me with a knife?

Pryce patted his pants pocket, then muttered, "Damn it! I left my phone on the kitchen counter."

"Pryce, please listen to me. Maybe the poison has affected my thinking, but for my sake, can't we just wait out here until Marco arrives?"

"Abigail, I can see my dock from here, and no one's on it. I'll stay a good distance from the Burches' pier, if that makes you feel better. Why isn't Marco with you?"

"He was busy at the bar, and I didn't want to wait on him because I wanted to find out who put one of your handwritten notes on my windshield asking for a meeting tonight."

He stopped rowing. "I didn't leave you any note."

"I know that now. I wanted to find out who did. The note said to meet you on the pier at eight o'clock, but no one showed up."

"What you're describing—someone arranging a meeting using one of my notes, poisoning the drinks, chasing you with a knife—sounds like the workings of a crazy person, and I'm telling you, it's not Halston. Orabell, perhaps."

"If I hadn't seen Orabell get sick, I'd agree with you."

"Perhaps she was only pretending to be sick."

"Do you understand why I'm afraid to go back? I don't know who to trust. We just need to stay out here until Marco arrives. He'll see my car and know I'm around somewhere."

"I hope Marco realizes he may be in danger, too."

"So do I."

"Good man, that Marco. You're lucky to have found him. Just goes to prove that mistakes of the past don't have to affect the future."

Just what was Pryce insinuating? "Are you talking about *my* mistakes?"

"Let's just say I hope you treat Marco's family better than you treated mine."

"Are you kidding me? Your parents are the reason you broke our engagement. They couldn't stand the thought of a daughter-in-law being a failure."

"Abigail, you pushed my parents away. They were completely sympathetic with what happened. You were so humiliated that you lashed out at everyone around you. Ask Nikki. She witnessed it."

"My roommate, Nikki?" That was a laugh. She and I'd had some great conversations about what a heel Pryce and his parents had been.

"You couldn't stand it that you'd have to be dependent on me," Pryce said. "You hated that I had money."

"Again, wrong. I didn't hate that you had money. I hated that your parents didn't think I was worthy of being an Osborne because I'd flunked out of law school."

"They actually liked you, Abigail, until you made us all feel like our money was a handicap. My psychologist said that was your insecurity talking."

"You saw a psychologist because of me?"

"I wanted to understand what I'd done wrong. Why you turned away from me."

"Pryce, you turned away from me! You made me feel insignificant, and then you asked for the ring back. You broke up with me, not the other way around."

"I had no choice but to ask for the ring back."

"Because your parents dictated it."

"Because your actions dictated it."

Boy, did we see things from opposite ends of the spectrum. "So all this time, you thought the breakup was my fault."

"Of course it was your fault. I wasn't the one who flunked out of New Chapel School of Law. That's what started it all." Pryce used one oar to turn the boat. "It's a pity really. We could have had a lucrative union."

Lucrative. The romantic word every woman wanted to hear. I ignored his comment, tilting my head to let water drain from my right ear.

"We still could," he added.

"What?"

"We could have a lucrative union." He held up his hand just as I was about to protest. "Before you get bent out of shape, think about it. Your flower shop is successful, so you wouldn't need my money, which is what you rebelled against before. You're independent in your own right, and because of my wealth and connections, you'd have all the resources available to an Osborne. Think what a relief it would be never to have any financial worries ever again. No need to struggle to keep your flower shop running if you grew tired of it. What a great life you could have, Abigail."

I could have? He sounded like a time-share salesman. An arrogant one, at that. "What about you, Pryce? Would you want to be married to a woman who's in love with another man? Would you have a great life being married to a middle-class, freckled, impetuous, hot-headed florist who didn't give a fig about country clubs or political functions?"

"You could learn."

I didn't answer him. There was no way I'd marry Pryce. Sure, it would feel great to never worry about money or my shop failing. Sure, I'd have the chicest clothing in town. Sure, all I'd have to do would be to show up to functions, dress well, look good, and shut up. And, yes, sure, it was tempting. I wouldn't have been human if it wasn't.

Yet I couldn't help but think back to how miserable I'd been while I was dating Pryce. How lonely I'd felt even in his company. How low-class. How unimportant. I compared that with how it felt to be with Marco, and there was no question what my heart wanted.

When I said nothing, he picked up both oars and started rowing. "I'm going to head back. I've waited long enough."

Had he waited long enough for my answer or for a safe harbor? This time I didn't protest. I'd had my fill of Pryce for one day, and Marco had to be there by now.

Neither one of us spoke until we approached his dock.

"Stay where you are," Pryce said. "I'm going to come up alongside. I'll make sure it's okay before you get out."

While he looped the rope around a post, then stepped up onto the pier, I scanned the beach, which was eerily silent, the only sounds water lapping against the pillars and an occasional gull calling overhead. Thick black clouds blanketed the sky, and the three-quarter moon was but a faded disk. The only illumination came from the torchlights on his deck.

Pryce walked the length of the pier and came back. "I don't see anyone around here, Abigail."

I shivered as it started to rain. "I don't have a good feeling about this, Pryce. It's too quiet."

"It's always quiet out here. Let's get up to my cottage and call for help." He leaned over and reached out a hand to help me up.

Suddenly, footsteps pounded on the wooden boards and a dark figure loomed up behind Pryce. I saw arms rise up high and a knife glint. "Pryce!" I shouted. "Look out!"

He had turned on one heel just as the knife sliced downward, missing his back but cutting deep into his arm. With a cry of pain, Pryce grabbed his arm and tried to get out of the way, but the arms rose again, ready to strike. A thin face peered out of a hooded black coat, its eyes wild, its lips drawn back to bare its teeth.

"Orabell!" I screamed, causing her to jerk around at the last minute.

I grabbed Pryce's hand and forced him to leap into the boat. As I yanked the rope free, I heard a furious cry as the knife's metal blade hit the wooden planks. My heart sped as I pushed against the post, propelling us away from the dock.

Pryce sat groaning in the bottom of the boat, his right hand clasping his left upper arm. I grabbed the oar handles and began to stroke as fast as I could, while Orabell stood on the pier screaming, "I'll kill you if you come back here. Do you hear me? I'll kill you!"

Pryce lifted his gaze from the blood seeping between his fingers to Orabell. "Dear God. She's crazy."

Orabell began to run along the shoreline, following along with us, so I had no choice but to row farther out, until the black mist that had settled over the surface swallowed us up.

"Abigail, I need medical help."

"I know that. Can I stand in this dinghy?" I asked, dropping the oars.

He nodded, so I rose carefully, cupped my hands around my mouth, and yelled, "Can anyone hear me? This is Abby. I'm in a boat on the lake and need medical assistance."

"That won't help. The cottages are set too far back for anyone to hear you."

Feeling the small boat sway precariously, I sat back down, damp, bedraggled, and frustrated. How was I going to get Pryce help?

"Where are you going?" Pryce asked through gritted teeth as I resumed rowing.

"I'm going to move parallel with the shoreline until I find someone to help."

"You'll row forever looking for people outside in the rain after dark."

Pryce was just one big bundle of optimism.

I noticed that the blood had spread down his sleeve to his wrist and I knew he was losing strength fast. "You need a tourniquet. Are you wearing a T-shirt under your sweatshirt?"

He shook his head, then closed his eyes. "I think I'm going to pass out."

I dropped the oars and knelt down beside him. He was grimacing, gritting his teeth, his forehead dotted with beads of perspiration, his complexion waxy even in the dim light of the moon. I looked around for something to stem the flow of blood and spotted a fishing tackle box tucked beneath a bench. Inside, I found a Swiss Army knife, so I flipped out the scissors and laboriously cut a strip from the blanket he'd placed around my shoulders, then tied it as high up on his arm as I could.

"I could die out here," he said in a weak voice.

"You'll be okay," I said, even though I knew he could still bleed out. I couldn't tell how bad the wound was, but by the amount of blood he'd already lost, I knew the knife had sliced deep.

The rain stopped as suddenly as it had started. We drifted for a while, neither of us talking; then I leaned forward to look at his arm. "It looks like the blood has stopped spreading, so the tourniquet must be working."

"My fingers are numb."

I knew I had to remove the tourniquet soon so he didn't lose feeling in his right arm, but I feared that if I did, he'd continue to bleed. We were far away from Pryce's boat dock now and enveloped in fog, undoubtedly invisible to anyone on the beach. How would Marco find us? How would I find my way back? I dared not row toward the shore for fear that Orabell was still stalking us. What could I do?

I folded my hands and said a prayer.

We drifted for what seemed an eternity, with Pryce coming in and out of consciousness. I licked my lips, wishing for a long drink of water. Would we be out here all night? Would Marco think to look for me on the water? Would he find us in the fog?

Sometime later, I heard a distant motor. I tried to wake Pryce up, but he was out cold.

The prow of a motorboat appeared, and then I heard that wonderful, husky male voice call out, "Abby!"

Tears sprang to my eyes and my throat closed so tightly, I could barely get out the words. "Marco! Over here."

The entire boat became visible—a police boat with a blue flashing light on top—with Marco sitting at the prow, his eyes searching through the mist and finding me at last. When the boat came alongside, Marco climbed in and caught me up in his arms. "Thank God you're okay. I was so worried we wouldn't find you."

I clung tightly to the man I loved with all my heart. "You did find me, Marco. You found me. That's all that matters now."

"I love you, Abby Knight," he murmured in my ear, then kissed me with such great passion and emotion that its magnitude nearly bowled me over.

Two officers moved Pryce into the boat. Then, once

Marco and I had climbed aboard, we made our way back to his dock, with Pryce's dinghy on a tow rope behind. On the way, I told them what Orabell had done to Pryce, and they filled me in on her capture.

Marco had arrived at the Osborne cottage just as Melissa was getting ready to search for Pryce, who'd gone out to grill fish and hadn't returned. They went to the Burches' and found Halston in his bedroom, drugged with sleeping pills. They roused him long enough to learn that Orabell was behind it, and then they called the police.

A search of the beach had finally located Orabell hiding under a neighbor's deck, crouched in the corner like a wild animal, raving about conspirators trying to steal her jewelry, and Halston in on a plot with Abby and Marco to do away with her.

An ambulance had taken Orabell to a mental facility, and another was called to take Pryce to the hospital. Marco insisted I go, as well, just in case the poison was still in my system. Then, in the wee hours of the morning, he drove me home and put me to bed, promising I'd feel much better after a restful sleep.

I didn't wake until noon the next day, with an upset stomach and a headache.

"Hey, sleepyhead," Marco said, bringing me a cup of soothing chamomile tea, "how are you?"

"I feel like I went on a drinking binge last night."

"That's because Orabell used sap from the nightshade vine in those martini mixes. Luckily, she didn't use a lethal dose, and you emptied your stomach of it right away, or we wouldn't be sitting here discussing it."

"That's a comforting thought."

"Here's another one. Guess what day it is."

"Friday?"

"Saturday."

"Oh, no, Marco! Our shower is this afternoon! And I haven't even decorated the hall yet—or prepared all of the food." I started to cry. "This was supposed to be the best shower New Chapel has ever seen and instead it'll be a disaster. What can I do? It's too late to call everyone and cancel."

Marco gathered me in his arms. "Sweetheart, do you really think your friends and family would let you or your guests down?"

"What do you mean?"

"All I know is that we're supposed to show up at the FOP hall at two o'clock, so go do whatever you need to do and I'll drive you there."

"Us, Marco. Remember?"

"I'll drive *us* there. Now go shower. You smell like the lake."

So that's what I did. I showered, dried my hair, glossed my lips, bronzed my cheeks to diminish the freckles, put on my brown and white sundress, which was too tight and, as Jillian had said, way too out of fashion, and dug out my one pair of black heels.

"I can't go like this," I said to Marco, standing before a long mirror. "I look frumpy. What was I thinking?"

"Abby, you'll be fine. You're just going to have to forget about what you're wearing and go to have fun. Besides, I think you look gorgeous."

"Thank you, Marco, but I don't feel anywhere close to gorgeous. I can't believe I'm saying this, but I should have listened to Jillian."

Marco put his hands on either side of my face and tilted my head up. "Look into my eyes, Sunshine. What do you see? Do you see a man who loves you? Do you see a man who would love you even if you had on rags? Does it matter what the rest of the world thinks?"

I gazed up at him, and my heart swelled with love. "Thank you, Marco."

There was no way to tell him that, yes, I did care what the rest of the world thought. That was what being female was all about. But I put my hand through the crook of his arm and walked to the car anyway.

CHAPTER TWENTY-FOUR

"Marco, I shouldn't have gone to Pryce's cottage alone."

Marco turned onto Washington Street and headed south to Indiana Avenue. "Do you really want to talk about that now?"

"It's better than worrying about what awaits us at the FOP hall. I sure didn't see Orabell as a killer. I knew both Melissa and Jake were worried that Pryce would take up with Lily again, and the fact that they were staying at the Sandman Motel together made me think they could've been partners in crime, especially when Jake didn't seem particularly upset about Lily's death. Then when Halston was mysteriously absent, and left behind that pitcher of poisoned martinis, I thought he had killed Lily."

"Halston told us this morning that he knew Orabell was off her rocker, as he put it," Marco said, "but he never guessed she was responsible for Lily's demise. He did know that Orabell had researched the nightshade vine, but he believed her when she said she was learning how to make a medicinal tea from the leaves, because she'd used other plants to make teas before, like rose hip tea."

"So Orabell really used the leaves from the night-shade plant to poison the martinis?"

"That's what she finally admitted. Fortunately for you, she hadn't tested it out on anyone, because in the preparation, she didn't use enough to kill. She had a clean batch for herself and the others to drink and basically mimicked your symptoms to make you believe she was ill, too."

"So I was the only one she gave the poison to?"

"Only because I was late. She made up a special pitcher for you and me. It's part of police evidence now. She told the detectives that we were conspiring with Halston to have her locked away for life so Halston would be free to pursue other women. And she was sure you had your eye on her jewelry."

"She really is crazy, then."

"Psychotic, according to what Reilly learned, with episodes of paranoia and delusions."

"Halston was right to want to take her to a psychiatrist. Amazing how Orabell could come across as just a little loony."

Marco glanced at me. "Are you ready to think about the shower instead?"

"I don't know which is worse, Marco, coming that close to death or facing public humiliation."

"Here we are," he said, pulling into the police hall's parking lot. "I guess you'll find out soon enough."

Marco opened the door for me and I stepped inside, prepared for a disaster. We had to walk up ten cement steps to get to the large hall, and there I stopped to gape. Groups of women—friends, my relatives, and Marco's—were standing along the walls or sitting at round tables, with plates in their hands, laughing, chatting, and apparently enjoying themselves. In a far corner, Lottie's sons performed their juggling act to rounds of applause. On a big roll-down screen at the front of the hall, clips of photos from Marco's and my childhoods were playing, to the great delight of my guests.

A buffet table near the door was loaded with pans of meaty lasagna, risotto with mushrooms, and chicken linguine in pesto sauce, big bowls of golden potato salad and colorful bean salad, and plates of crusty Italian bread. Another table held platters of panna cotta with strawberries, tiramisu, zabaglione, and a towering cake made to look like a Roman cathedral.

The whole room, in fact, looked Italian, with large posters of Rome, Venice, Capri, Livorno, Pisa, and Milan hanging from the walls, along with the streamers I'd purchased. Yellow paper tablecloths covered the round tables, with pots of brightly colored gerbera daisies in the middle. And as favors—Mom's sleep masks and the pinwheels I'd ordered, which some of the women were waving around, having a great time.

"Oh, my God, Abs," Jillian cried, rushing toward me. Before I could hide behind Marco, she had grabbed my hand and was leading me toward the women's restroom. "I thought you'd never arrive. We've got to get you fixed up."

"Marco?" I called back.

He gave me a wink. "Didn't I say you'd be fine?" And then he walked toward the buffet table, leaving me in Jillian's hands.

My mom met us in the restroom carrying a dress bag and a shopping bag. While Mom unzipped my old sundress and slid it down, Jillian slipped the green dress over my head—the same one she'd brought to show me at Pryce's cottage. Mom had me step into the same expensive Jimmy Choo shoes that Jillian had brought to Bloomers, while Jillian arranged my hair in a loose updo using the tortoiseshell clip she'd tried to use unsuccessfully on me before.

"I found the best baby name of all," she whispered in my ear. "I'll tell you after the shower."

I couldn't wait.

When they were done, they turned me to look in the mirror.

"Well, Abigail, what do you think?" Mom asked, beaming behind me.

"Isn't it perfect?" Jillian asked, pressing her hands together in excitement.

I gazed at my reflection in shock. There stood a chicly dressed and coiffed redhead who merely resembled me. And she had on kickin' shoes, too. I couldn't wait to show Marco.

"So?" Jillian asked, as I wobbled toward the door on heels that felt like toothpicks.

I went back and gave both her and Mom hugs. "I feel like a princess."

"Your prince is waiting," Mom said, then hugged me again. "I'm so happy for you, honey. You really have found your Prince Charming."

"If you only knew how wonderful he is, Mom."

"If you're talking about what happened at the Osbornes' cottage," Mom said, starting to tear up, "Marco filled us in, but you can give us the full story after the shower. If I talk now about what almost happened to you, I'll cry."

Jillian sniffled, too, then ran to clutch me against her. "My wittle cuz," she sobbed, then sniffled again, and hurried out of the washroom with a wail.

Mom shook her head. "Pregnancy hormones."

"You know about the baby, too?"

"Who doesn't? Jillian has been going around telling everyone, then making them promise not to say a word."

Mom sighed. "I can't even begin to imagine what kind of mother Jillian will be, can you?"

"No," I said, and laughed, because we both knew what kind of mother she'd be—a fashion-conscious obsessive hovercraft of a mother.

"I'm so relieved you're safe," Mom said, pausing just before the hall entrance. "You're my baby, Abigail. You always will be. If something happened to you, I don't know what I'd do." She smiled through her tears. "That's why I'm so happy you've found Marco. If anyone can keep you safe, it's him. And if anyone can make that terrific man happy, it's you."

We walked into the hall, arm in arm. I'd never felt closer to my mom than I did at that moment.

Just inside, we were met by Marco and his mom, who looked gorgeous, as usual.

Marco gave me a slow once-over, his deep love for me shining in his eyes. "You look amazing, Sunshine."

"*Bella!*" Francesca said, holding me at arm's length to admire me. "*Magnifica!* Marco, your bride-to-be puts you to shame. You should have dressed up!"

"Abigail," Mom said, "Francesca made most of the food here today."

"Thank you, Francesca," I said. "The food looks delicious."

"I'm sorry you didn't have your festival theme," Francesca said. "Your mother, your father, Lottie, Grace, Jillian, Claymore, and I did the best we could to decorate at the last minute."

"The hall looks wonderful," I said. "I feel like I'm on vacation in Italy."

"Just so you know," Francesca said with a wry smile, "everything has been prepared with love and sanitation."

"And all that Chinese food you bought," Mom said,

putting her arm around me, "is in the chest freezer in our garage."

"It's a good thing you like Chinese," Jillian said snarkily. "You'll be eating it for the next six months."

"Can't wait," Marco said.

I turned to gaze through the wide doorway at all the guests enjoying themselves, then said to Marco, "Our wedding shower is a success after all."

"And you didn't have to do it all yourself," Grace said, gliding up to stand in our circle.

"Try *any* of it," someone added.

I turned to find Nikki standing behind me, her arms open, ready to hug me. "I came back from my conference early," she said. "I wouldn't have missed your bridal shower for the world."

"As George Bernard Shaw wrote in *Pygmalion*," Grace said, "'We are all dependent on one another, every soul of us on earth.'"

"We did the flower centerpieces for you this morning," Lottie said, squeezing in beside Grace.

I gazed at all their loving faces and my heart overflowed with happiness. "I don't think anything could top this. Do you, Marco?"

He moved in next to me and put his arm around my back. "I don't either. Thank you all for pulling the shower together at the last moment."

"It's the best gift anyone could have given us," I said, eyeing a mound of wrapped presents on a nearby table.

"Ah, but that's not your big gift," Francesca said. "Maureen, would you like to do the honors?"

Uh-oh. Mom had made something.

"Abigail," Mom said, "and Marco." She took my hand and Marco's hand in hers. "I wish your father could be here to see your faces, but I couldn't budge him away from the baseball game on TV. He was adamant that a bridal shower was for women only."

Marco gave me a look that said, *I told you so.*

"Here's your surprise," Mom said. "We—Francesca, your father, and I—got together and decided to give you—are you ready? A destination wedding in beautiful Cozumel, Mexico!"

"We're going to cruise there on one of those big fancy ships," Francesca said, pressing her hands together in excitement.

"You know, those megaships with an entire shopping mall inside?" Jillian asked, wedging herself into the circle. "Can you imagine what fun all your guests will have?"

I gave Marco a panicked glance.

"The return trip will be your honeymoon," Mom added. "It's a package deal. Your dad found it online."

"I've never been to Cozumel," Francesca said.

"It's beautiful," Mom said. "Jeffrey and I went there a few years ago."

"I've always wanted to go," Lottie said, rubbing her hands together. "Herman and my boys are really gonna enjoy it."

At which point everyone began talking at once.

I took Marco's hand and pulled him out of the circle. "Marco, this is awful!" I whispered. "Can you imagine what it would be like to have our families with us on a cruise ship for days on end? On our honeymoon?"

"I'm trying hard not to imagine it."

"It'll be a disaster. You know they won't leave us alone. And here I was hoping we could go down to Key West for the honeymoon." I sighed sadly. "That's out of the question now."

"Is it?"

"Of course it is. This is a huge gift for our parents to give us. We can't reject it and hurt their feelings."

Marco eyed the group of chattering women. "Sounds to me like they'd be going on this cruise whether we would or not, Sunshine."

"What are you saying?"

Marco pulled me into his arms and gazed at me, a tiny grin playing at one corner of his mouth. "Think about it, Abby. What do you really want to do for your wedding and honeymoon?"

"What do I want to do or what should I do?"

"You know what I mean."

"What you mean is, this is our wedding. Our honeymoon. Our decision."

"You bet it is. So what do we do? Pile on board a huge luxury liner with our families and whatever guests want to attend? Or . . . ?"

We gazed at each other for a long moment, needing no words, and then I smiled.

When we kissed to seal the deal, I knew everything was going to work out perfectly, because my gut was never wrong. Almost.

Abby and Marco's wedding is fast approaching when her mother becomes the number one suspect in a murder case.

Turn the page for a sneak peek of the Flower Shop Mystery

Seed No Evil

Available now from Obsidian in paperback and as an e-book.

Monday mornings are the bane of most people's existence. I, however, view them as curtains going up on a brand-new play. So when I opened the yellow frame door with its charming beveled-glass center and stepped inside my personal theater—that being Bloomers Flower Shop, located in the heart of New Chapel, Indiana's cozy town square—I couldn't wait to find out what the opening scene was going to be.

I entered Bloomers stage right and feasted my eyes on the scenery—a plethora of flowers in various arrangements, a veritable artist's palette of tones, tints, shades, and hues that covered the color spectrum. And then there were the sounds—telephone ringing, bell over the door jingling, and my assistants, Lottie and Grace, coming to greet me with their cheery voices.

"Abby, sweetie," Lottie said, her head of short, brassy curls shaking a warning, "we've got a bad situation. Nine orders came in for funeral arrangements, and there's not a single lily in the cooler. I don't know what happened. I thought I ordered them on Thursday, but apparently I forgot. I put in a call to our main supplier, but the truck won't be here until later today."

"Abby, dear," Grace said in her lovely English cadence, "I'm sorry to add to your woes but disaster has struck the coffee and tea parlor. The espresso machine gave up the ghost, and the clotted cream has curdled well beyond the pale. Also, the chap is here to install the security door in the rear of the shop but says the hinges are so rusty on the old one, it'll take him twice as long and require that the door stand open for a length of time. He charges hourly, by the way."

Not exactly the cheerful sounds I'd expected.

"Your cousin Jillian called," Lottie said, reading from a pink memo. "She said to tell you she'll be here tomorrow afternoon to something or other."

"What does that mean?"

"It means she mumbled so I wouldn't be able to understand her. I asked her to spell it and she said—and I quote—*I. T.* And then she snickered and hung up."

"And your mum is in the back," Grace added. "I believe at the moment she's supervising the door installation."

Cue the curtain guy and dim the lights. I want a refund on my ticket.

As every good thespian knows, the show must go on, and so must the floral business, for many reasons, the most important of which is to pay the bills. Besides, what could be so awful that it would take away from the joy of my upcoming marriage to the man of my dreams? Another of my mom's horrific art projects that she expected me to sell at Bloomers? More of Jillian's harping about my ad hoc wedding plans? Not a chance. Nothing could mar my complete and utter happiness.

"Why is Mom here so early?" I asked.

"We'll let her go into it, shall we?" Grace suggested, getting a nod of agreement from Lottie.

Grace, a diminutive sixty-something-year-old, was wearing a pale gray skirt and a baby blue sweater set with silver earrings and a pearl necklace, all of which set off her short, stylish gray hair. Lottie, in contrast, a big-boned, forty-something Kentuckian, had on her traditional white stretch jeans with a bright pink T-shirt and deep pink Keds. Her choice of color, she claimed, ensured she was always "in the pink," which, as the mother of teenaged quadruplet sons, wasn't an easy feat.

"Did Mom bring another art project?" I asked, hoping to mentally prepare myself.

"That's why she's here," Lottie said. "Go talk to her. She's upset."

I walked through the shop, stepped through the purple curtain into my workroom, and breathed in my nirvana. Although the space was windowless, the colorful blossoms and heady fragrances made the area a veritable tropical garden. Vases of all sizes and containers of dried flowers filled shelves above the counters along two walls. A large, slate-covered worktable occupied the middle of the room; two big walk-in coolers took up one side, and a desk holding my computer equipment and telephone filled the other side. Beneath the table were sacks of potting soil, green foam, and a lined plastic trash can.

Beyond the work room was a tiny galley kitchen and an even tinier bathroom. At the very back was the exit onto the alley, guarded by a big, rusty iron door that had needed to be replaced since probably sometime around 1970. That was where I found my mother, watching a man from the door store struggling with the hinge pins.

"Abigail!" Mom called, brightening. She stepped around the installer and came toward me, putting her arms around me in a motherly hug, the kind she ends by leaning back to inspect me. "Did you have breakfast today? You look pale."

By pale, she meant my freckles were showing more than usual. Along with being a mere five feet two inches tall and having fiery red hair, I was also blessed—or cursed, depending upon my mood—with freckles, part of my Irish heritage. Erin Go Braugh.

"Lottie makes breakfast for us on Mondays, so I haven't eaten yet," I said. "Why aren't you in school? What's up?"

"I skipped the In-Service meeting this morning. Can we sit down?"

Uh oh. That was a bad sign.

My mother, Maureen "Mad Mo" Knight, had been a kindergarten teacher for almost twenty years and always said that after working with five-year-olds for that long, nothing could ruffle her feathers. Her caramel brown hair was always in a neat chin-length bob, her big brown eyes were a sea of cocoa calm, and her peaches-and-cream complexion glowed with good health. The worry lines in her forehead, however, were new.

I led her back into the work room and pulled out two wooden stools just as Grace bustled in with cups of coffee and a plate of blueberry scones.

"Here you go, loveys. Lottie will be making breakfast in a bit, Abby, and I'll be off to pick up a new espresso machine. I should be back before nine, but just in case, be sure to keep your eye on the clock."

"Thanks, Grace." I took a sip of coffee and sighed with pleasure. "Delicious, as always. Do I taste a hint of cinnamon?"

She gave me a coy smile and glided out of the room. Grace never divulged her gourmet coffee recipes.

"Okay, Mom, tell me what's going on."

"I'm frozen, Abigail. I have artist's block and that has never happened to me before. You know I'm usually brimming with ideas for a new project, but this time I haven't been able to come up with a single one that's worth anything. Not one! I sat in front of my pottery wheel for two hours on Saturday and stared at a lump of wet clay. The only idea that came to me was to make a clock in the shape of a giant tick, with tick hands."

"I'm not getting the reference."

"You know. A tick 'n clock? As in a ticking clock? The stumbling block was that I couldn't think of anything to associate with tock. I'm telling you, Abigail, artist's block is terrible."

Not as terrible as actually making a tick 'n clock.

Mom prided herself on her creativity. The kind of art she made was subject to change weekly, because she was continually moving from one medium to the next, first trying clay, then plaster, followed by vinyl, feathers, beads, mirrored tiles, knitting yarn, felt, and finally back to clay. Mom completed a new piece each weekend, then brought it to my shop on Monday after school so we could put it out with our other gift items . . . if we dared. And because she truly believed she was helping us draw in customers, I never had the heart to discourage her.

"What can I do to help?" I asked, sipping my coffee.

"I was hoping you'd ask. I'd like you to find out what's going on in our local chapter of PAR. There's a rumor spreading among the members that the board of directors is considering changing the policy of their animal shelter from no-kill to kill."

"That's horrible, Mom. They're supposed to protect animal rights."

"Tell me about it," Mom said. "I can't stand the thought of homeless animals being put down. This could ruin PAR's reputation, not to mention all the good work our organization has done for this community."

PAR, which stood for Protecting Animal Rights, was a statewide organization with a large chapter that drew members from New Chapel and the surrounding towns. A few months back, I had helped PAR lead a protest

against a proposed dairy factory. The megacompany behind it had a reputation for pumping its herds with bo-
vine hormones so the cows would produce more milk.
Unfortunately, that caused the men who drank the milk
to grow breasts. With my help, PAR stopped the dairy
factory in its tracks.

Because my mom grew up on a farm and loved animals, she'd been happy to step into my role at PAR when
I got too busy helping Marco, my hunky husband-to-be,
with his private investigation business. She'd led a few
protest movements and had seemed delighted to be working with a charitable organization that could make such
a difference in animal rights.

"Have you heard why the board would want to change
the policy?" I asked.

"No, and I don't even know for certain whether the
rumor is true. But if so, your father says it has to be
about money. I know it's more expensive to run a no-kill
shelter, but if this change happens, I can guarantee that
our members will be outraged and our chapter may fold.
Who'll raise funds to support the animal shelter then?
It's in enough financial trouble as it is. Who'll protect the
rights of all the innocent creatures that live within our
boundaries? What if another megafarm wants to plant
roots in New Chapel?

"Abigail, this situation is distracting me to such a degree that I can't create. And when I can't create, I get
harried. And when I get harried, your father gets cranky,
and we argue all the time. And that distracts me even
more. Do you understand why I need you to investigate?"

"I'm not sure how to go about investigating a non-
profit organization, Mom. Marco is the private eye."

"I was hoping he'd help, too. The reason I wanted to
come by Bloomers on this particular morning is that the

monthly PAR meeting is tonight. The meeting starts at seven o'clock and lasts about an hour . . . or longer if they're arguing, which they seem to be doing a lot of these days.

"There's a social gathering afterward, which would be the perfect opportunity for you to talk with the board members, especially our chairwoman, Dayton Blaine, as well as Bev Powers, our executive director. Wait. What am I saying? You know who they are. I don't need to explain them to you."

Everyone in New Chapel knew who Dayton Blaine was. Her family owned Blaine Industries, a company started by her great-grandfather, which gave her a lot of clout in town. Bev Powers was the town councilwoman, in the newspapers constantly because she was always suing someone.

"Please say you'll help, honey. I need to know the animals will be safely taken care of so I can get back my creative edge."

How could I refuse when she looked at me with those large, imploring eyes? "Will that take away the worry line between your eyebrows?"

"I'm afraid that's going to be a fixture until I see you and Marco happily married."

Seeing us married wasn't something Marco and I had planned to have happen. Dealing with my mom and Marco's mom, not to mention my high-maintenance fashion plate cousin Jillian, all of whom had decided how our wedding should proceed, had pushed Marco and me to the point of planning an elopement. This was especially true after our parents had gotten together and chosen a wedding destination cruise to Cozumel for the entire bridal party and guests, with our tickets as their wedding gift. Our honeymoon, as they saw it, would take place on the return trip. Imagine a honeymoon with an entire family present—make that our *crazy* families present. I was still having nightmares.

Fortunately, I had talked to my father in time to stage an intervention and the cruise tickets were never purchased. Whew. We had compromised by planning an intimate wedding for immediate family only, followed by a private honeymoon, followed by a gigantic reception for all the relatives and friends who would be left out of the wedding ceremony.

"Mom, you don't need to worry about the wedding. My dress is ordered, invitations sent out, flowers chosen, and reservations made for the wedding dinner. That's the beauty of having such a small affair. Two bridesmaids, two groomsmen, and thirty people are super easy to plan for."

"I hope you won't regret having such a small ceremony, honey, but I am abundantly happy that you aren't eloping. It would have broken my heart if I couldn't see you and Marco exchange vows. You might be an adult, but you'll always be my little girl."

The fear of breaking hearts was the main reason we'd changed our minds about eloping. Our moms and my dad would have been crushed, and we just couldn't do that to them.

Back to the subject at hand. "I'll talk to Marco during my lunch hour and see if he's free to go with me to the meeting. Do you want me to pick you up?"

"Thanks for asking, but on Mondays at five o'clock I volunteer at the animal shelter, and sometimes I'm there two hours, so I'll just meet you instead."

"It sounds like a plan, Mom."

"I'll feel so much better with you and Marco looking into this," Mom said, giving me a hug.

"We'll do our best to find out what's going on."

On the minus side, what we would do with that

knowledge was beyond me. Every case Marco and I had worked on since we'd teamed up a year ago had centered on a murder investigation. But being creative was important to my mom and she was important to me, so we'd figure it out.

On the plus side, with my wedding coming up soon it was a *huge* relief to be working on an investigation that had absolutely nothing—nada, zero, zip—to do with murder.

Also availabe from

Kate Collins

In the national bestselling
Flower Shop mystery series

Abby Knight is the proud owner of her
hometown flower shop. She has a gift for
arranging flowers—and for solving crimes.

"A sharp an
—Ma

Available where
per

facebook.com/